For Austin

God &
California

"Life is Contradiction."

Chris Millis

Chris Millis
y'all '16

The Vermont Press
Stowe, Vermont

Praise for Chris Millis's GOD & CALIFORNIA

"You write good, kid. You're funny."   —Billy Crystal

"Chris Millis is my favorite kind of writer. He creates lunatics that you find yourself relating to—and then can't help rooting for them!"   —Rob Schneider

"Chris Millis has a gift for making idiots likable. He has the amazing ability to create eccentric characters and place them in outlandish situations leading the reader on an emotional and unexpected adventure. Chris's books are witty and intelligent. He's a fast thinker—and smart, too. I look forward to reading everything he writes. Love him!"
—Jonas Akerlund, Grammy Award-winning film and music video director

"This provocative, wickedly subversive novel is populated by lowlifes and dreamers on the road to contrition; it's suspenseful, surprising at every turn, laugh-out-loud funny, and beautifully realized. Chris Millis is a true visionary and one of a kind."
—Neil Landau, bestselling author, screenwriter, "Don't Tell Mom the Babysitter's Dead"

"The premise is irresistible. Chris Millis's highly accomplished comic novel stands alone. A truly original variation on the road trip template."
—Richard Panek, *The 4 Percent Universe: Dark Matter, Dark Energy, and the Race to Discover the Rest of Reality*

"As one who witnessed 9/11 at 16-years-young, was sent to fight a war at nineteen in a region where religious war has endured as long as civilization itself—and who has thus longed to speak with God—I can react in only one way to Chris Millis's protagonist, Norbert Sherbert: I worship him. If only all veterans could be so brave."   —Ryan Smithson,
Ghosts of War: The True Story of a 19-year-old GI

"Chris Millis is one of America's most original, hip young writers. His clever and hilarious sense of humor and wonderful eye for subtle details are exquisite and engaging. Simply put, he sees the world in a quirky, satirical way that leaves readers surprised with new insights. With *God & California*, Millis takes his creativity and wild fiction to the next level."

—M. L. Liebler, Detroit poet,
Wide Awake in Someone Else's Dream

"Bravura storytelling. Chris Millis's complex, ever-evolving novel is a high wire act. It stirs the heart with all-too-human pain, then suddenly makes you laugh out loud. A perceptive, lyrical, moving, brilliantly funny book. A superb piece of writing."

—Mark Piznarski,
film and television director, "Veronica Mars"

Praise for SMALL APARTMENTS

"*Small Apartments* was written in three days and won the 3-Day Novel Contest. People take three years to write something this well thought out. The reason for me to do the movie was the story and the character." —Billy Crystal

"The book is really well written. *Small Apartments* is a metaphor for thinking and living your life. A really funny comedy with really strong characters. On top of that, it has this very serious undertone. There's so many life-changing moments. I can't see any reason why *Small Apartments* could be a studio movie— and what could possibly be better?" —Jonas Akerlund

"It's dark and warm at the same time, which is quite rare. It's a murder mystery and I think in some ways it's a bit of a love story." —Matt Lucas

"Something very unique. Absurd and irreverent. Sometimes we have too much time to think. Just go into the madness and play." —James Marsden

"It's this incredible combination of a lot of different emotions. It made me go on a roller coaster with my feelings, and I love that. All the characters are so alive and so interesting. Everyone has their own story that you could happily watch a movie about just them. I think the movie is going to really make a stamp."

—Juno Temple

"I'm sure it's going to become a cult movie. It's just nice to be involved in something that is a little bit different than the big studio paint-by-numbers. These are the movies you want to do that gives you soul."

—Peter Stormare

"I think (the film is) going to be kickass. And if it's not, then I'm a monkey's uncle."

—Rosie Perez

"If an Oscar were awarded every year for the most unique film, the most eccentric film, and the most unlikely-to-suc-ceed-from-a-creative-perspective film, then ... *Small Apartments* would be a shoe-in for all three ... one simply cannot help but to gaze in wonderment at what unfolds in the film ... It's a film that really must be seen to be believed; it requires a wide-open mind and a little bit of faith that it will get better, but improve it does and without losing the rare combination of repulsion and charm that make *Small Apartments* arguably the most unique movie of 2013 ... It's a wonderful cast in a won-derful movie that should be at the top of every open-minded cinephile's must-see list."

—Martin Liebman, Blu-ray.com

"*Small Apartments* is animated by a palpable and redeeming affection for its characters, no matter how deluded, ridiculous, or scuzzy they might be ... a weird, oddly likeable, and strange-ly engaging little comedy about the imperfections of humanity and our inveterate need for connection."

—Nathan Rabin, *The Onion AV Club*

"There's a definite Coen—brothers influence ... Quirky is an easy word to describe *Small Apartments*, but the peculiar na-ture doesn't undervalue the odd impact of this black comedy with occasional serious and poignant undertones."

—Dan Bullock, *The Hollywood News*

Chris Millis
God & California

Chris Millis is a prize-winning, bestselling writer. He adapted his debut novel, *Small Apartments*, into the acclaimed cult film directed by Jonas Akerlund and starring Billy Crystal (in his first independent film), Matt Lucas, James Caan, Johnny Knoxville, James Marsden, Rebel Wilson, Amanda Plummer, Juno Temple, Peter Stormare, Rosie Perez, David Koechner, Dolph Lundgren, Saffron Burrows, DJ Qualls, David Warshofsky, Scott Sheldon, and many more. It made its world premier at the South By Southwest Film Festival in 2012 and was released worldwide the following year by Sony Pictures. He writes for film, television, and magazines and is a frequent celebrity collaborator for books and screenplays. He holds an art degree from Buffalo State College and an M.F.A. in Creative Writing from Goddard College, Vermont. Chris lives in upstate New York and Los Angeles with his wife and identical twin sons.

www.chrismillis.com

Chris Millis gives kick-ass presentations and workshops around the country for colleges, organizations, and companies on how great storytelling will literally make you a better human being. For information regarding his availability, contact him at chrismillis@me.com

Printed in the United States of America

Library of Congress Cataloguing-in-Publication Data
Millis, Christopher Harry, 1972—
        God & California : a novel / Chris Millis – 1st ed.
        ISBN 978-0-9840434-2-2
        First Edition Paperback Original
        Thirteen Books Publishing
        The Vermont Press is a curated collective of independent publishers
        Fiction. I. Title

Nancy McCurry, lead editor
Shawn Kerivan, Lloyd Noonan, editors
Greg Melvin, copy editor
Hillary Hersh, designer and cover art

www.thevermontpress.com
www.thirteenbooks.com
www.chrismillis.com
Twitter: @ChrisMillis
www.facebook.com/chrismillispage

For contrarians, everywhere.

Foreword

Dear Reader,

You didn't buy this book to read about me. And if you did, you've bought the wrong book. Besides, there's too much to do. I've got emails to reply to, chocolate to eat, soccer results to fret about and, time permitting, reality television to watch. And that's before I've even trawled the net looking for footage of men with muscles having sex with other men with muscles. But, hey, that's just me.

No, you bought this book because you want to read a good story. And contained within this volume lurks a very good story indeed. I say that because one of the last books the author wrote was *Small Apartments*, which got turned into a movie and I got to play the lead. Imagine that. A lead in a movie, albeit a very low-budget one, shot on HD, with Billy Crystal, who was nice, and James Caan, who was a bit grumpy.

So I sort of feel duty-bound to write the foreword to this one. Because if enough of you buy this book, maybe it'll get turned into a movie, too. Then I can use the same sort of emotional blackmail that the author used on me to get me to write this foreword to get him to give me a part in the movie adaptation of this book, thus increasing my personal standing in Hollywood and leading me to get potentially larger roles in the sort of big-budget movies (with actual royalties) that the author of this one could only dream of writing, poor man.

Hence, what you are reading now. It's a cynical, passion-less exercise in networking, basically. I do know one thing about the book, though, because I was having lunch with Chris Millis himself (excuse me while I pick that name up) and the waiter came to take our order, and I made sure, as I always do, to request that no cheese appear anywhere.

Chris's ears pricked up. Well, I say "ears." He only has one, actually. Oh no, hang on, no, he does have two. Sorry, I was thinking of Van Gogh. Anyway, his ears pricked up and rather than say, "Oh you don't like cheese? I love cheese. Couldn't live without it. Cheese, cheese, cheese, cheese, cheese . . . "

Actually, he said, "Oh, thank God for that. Another cheese hater."

We immediately bonded. He then told me that one of the characters in this book virtually defines himself by his hatred of cheese. Good. Because, folks, it's time to get the message out there. We were born with taste buds and the power of scent to save us from danger. Hence . . . "Oh, what's that smell? It's a burning curtain." = Run from house fire. "Oh, I just bit into some chicken and blood gushed out." = Decline undercooked poultry. But then— even though we consider ourselves no longer primitive beings—unfathomably: "Oh, lovely, some rancid, moldy, yellow, hardened fatty milk that smells of week-old socks and tastes of murder."* = Eat lots of it, as if nice.

Seriously, cheese is the most disgusting thing on earth, bar none. It is, in some ways, even more offensive than religion.

I hate cheese. The taste, the smell, the texture. And don't try none of that, "Oh, but this is goat's cheese" shit on me, either. It's cheese, okay? It's fucking cheese. When I sit opposite you in an Italian restaurant and the man comes round with the block of Parmesan and the grater, a part of me dies inside. Hell, you could probably eat me and I wouldn't even feel it. I'm that gone. In fact, cheese upsets me even more than when you read in *USA Today* about a spinster getting bludgeoned to death by a crack-addled teenager and it turns out she had only twelve cents in her purse. Even the use of the word "cheese" out loud provokes me. When I become president, I'm banning it.

And none of this "three strikes" liberal nonsense. Anyone who says it out loud is going down for life. Don't say I didn't warn you.

I could go on, but I won't. Partly because Mr. Millis will, I'm sure, invest himself far more eloquently than I in the horrors of Satan's curdled milk. But mainly because that Internet porn won't watch itself. Do excuse me.

M. Lucas
London

*Stilton

God &
California

"As I understand it, and my understanding is vague at best, another smaller group of people stole some air- planes and crashed them into buildings and we're told that they were zealots fueled by religious fervor. Religious fervor. And if you live to be a thousand years old, will that make any sense to you? Will that make any goddamn sense?"

—David Letterman
in his first broadcast after 9/11

GOD

"Better sin the whole sin, sure that God observes."
—Robert Browning, "Before"

1

It was on a cold, gray, slushy Sunday morning in Ticonderoga, New York when Norbert Sherbert Jr. first got the notion to break all Ten Commandments in a week. The notion formed in his brainpan while he was seated on a hard metal folding chair inside the long defunct Orange Julius, inside the Route 9N strip mall, now known as the Church of Abundant Waters and the Splendiferous Blood of Christ. It was Norbert's first time inside that house of worship.

Once seated, Norbert studied the church's modest décor as he listened to the electric guitar interlude. He could not help but think that in the beginning it was probably man that created God in his own image and not the other way around. God: with His long white beard, flowing robes and beefy pectorals—think Sistine Chapel. God: the literary character. God: that overbearing fellow those TV preachers jump up and down, bark, whoop, howl and sob about, whipping their megaflocks into frothy frenzies. The jealous, vengeful, anthropomorphic Bible God who micromanages the daily affairs of each soul on the planet. As I understand that God, thought Norbert, He is easily perturbed. In many ways, He's just a grander version of myself. Even Caucasian, just like me.

No, thought Norbert, no. That God probably doesn't exist. More likely, that God is the preeminent example of the poverty of the human imagination.

But just because you don't *believe* in a thing, thought Norbert, that doesn't necessarily mean that thing don't exist. Conversely, just because you *do* believe in a thing, that doesn't mean it *does* exist. Like unicorns, and traditional nuclear families, and pots o' gold hidden deep in forests at the terminus of rainbows, and the Apollo moon landing. Such was the relationship between Norbert and the Christian version of God that Sunday morning.

Norbert's existential reverie sent him sliding into day-dream. In his dream, a football tumbles end-over-end at Norbert's head. He watches it through the tubular grid of his helmet's facemask, head arched upwards. Norbert's arms form a basket that absorbs the impact of the somer-saulting oblong spheroid. He takes off running, nothing but green turf unrolling beneath his feet. The whole length of the field is before him and he is running. Pumping his fists into the air, the ball buried deep in his armpit. In his knees, Norbert feels each collision with the turf. He huffs and stretches and dashes toward the opposite end line. He is happy, so happy and, without effort, he watches himself from outside his body, running in pure joy as his coaches and teammates leap and holler and cheer along the side-line. Norbert recognizes where he is: the State High School Football Championship game inside the Carrier Dome in Syracuse. Norbert has received the game's final punt on his own end line and he is racing the length of the field. Time is expired. He is almost there. A touchdown wins the game. He thrusts his right foot forward in a final, victorious stride—but is stopped. Grabbed from behind. Someone has caught up to him, seizing his left leg. Norbert lunges forward, extending each tendon from his toes up through his fingertips to the limits of their elasticity. He crashes to the turf—brought down inside the final yard, of the final play, of his final game. Norbert has fallen short. He has lost: the touchdown, the game, that seductive sensation of power, of certainty, of joy. The opposing team pours onto the field in a churning wave of bliss. Norbert sits up, removes his helmet. Elbows on kneecaps, he cradles his head in his hands.

Norbert emerged from his reverie with a spasm, seesaw-ing his numb buttocks atop the hard metal seat inside the

Church of Abundant Waters and the Splendiferous Blood of Christ. He looked at Arlene. She knew he was looking at her, but she didn't look back. How much she's changed, thought Norbert. *What am I doing here?*

Church, he thought. An Orange Julius, he thought.

What a guy does for love.

Norbert and Arlene had been an item since high school. They had remained exclusive while Arlene went away to a private college and Norbert attended a two-year commuter school near home. Then they stuck it out while Norbert was stationed overseas. Back in high school, Arlene had never been one for churchgoing. She was not a religious person. Sometimes, if it was a sunny day, she would call it a "blessing." If someone sneezed, and she knew him, she would invoke the deity. Things of that nature. But Norbert never regarded such remarks as veiled testimonials of some deeper faith that lurked below.

Arlene was Catholic, though she had scarcely attended Mass outside of friends' weddings since wearing curls and ribbons. She was baptized and took her first Communion in a church named for St. Paul the Hermit who, according to Catholic myth, had fled to the desert to live in a cave until he was 113. In Afghanistan and Iraq, Norbert had met plenty of people who lived in caves: not as romantically monastic as St. Paul must have wished for it to appear.

Arlene's parents considered themselves *pragmatic Catholics*. Her mother had introduced Norbert to that term over rump roast. During high school, her parents vehemently disapproved of Arlene's positions on contraception (she enthusiastically ingested it), and abortion (which, to their displeasure, Arlene called "choice"). They told her there was no place for her at the right hand of the Father unless she changed her style of thinking. They even pooh-poohed her fashionable low-rider, hip-hugger jeans and tight tank tops, which Norbert had no objection to. Indeed, Arlene's fashion sense had remained little changed over the span of their years together, a testament to its timelessness. If statistical data were available for such things as Most Oft-Made Comment My Girlfriend Makes Regarding Her Parents, Norbert was certain Arlene's would be, "Those people drive me f'n crazy!"

To be fair, Norbert was also discontented with the DNA dough from which he had risen. But imbedded somewhere in that colorfully mysterious twisted ladder his parents had at least passed to him the gene for keen observation. Norbert had observed, keenly, how Arlene desperately, frantically craved her parents' approval. The more Arlene protested her parents' values, the more transparent was her need to validate her life choices—particularly her choice to stick it out so long with Norbert. The silent voice of her parents influenced dozens of Arlene's daily decisions, though she would drink hot motor oil before she'd admit it. That's even why she and Norbert now lived together in Ticonderoga, so far from good restaurants and robust cell phone signals. Her folks had moved there from Syracuse to escape "The Big City."

Norbert stole another hard look at Arlene. He pictured her in those jeans. *Delicious.*

But Arlene's attitude toward her faith did a 180 after Norbert's injury. She started thumping the Good Book pretty steady then. It became her rock of certainty. Her latest faith-based obsession, after devouring several books her mom had given her for Christmas, was the Rapture—an approaching event in which the faithful will be carried away to a blessed afterlife, while sinners (such as Norbert, Arlene explained) would remain to face the music, or whatever. To Norbert's taste, this God talk around the apartment had become oppressive. Everything was, "Pastor Zack said this," and "Pastor Zack thinks that." This one-sided discourse was the source of much recent disharmony.

Norbert decided it was about time for him to wake up early on a Sunday and get a firsthand look at this Pastor Zack character.

Norbert grabbed the tattered paperback hymnal from beneath the forward folding chair and absently leafed through it. He was a compulsive reader, reading most of the daily minutiae people pay no mind to—the backs of toothpaste tubes and shampoo bottles, remote control operator's manuals, movie credits. Norbert always pictured the author behind these blocks of text, selecting his words with great care, crippled with the same fear of rejection, as were the great novelists. The demon on the shoulder! Some writer, somewhere, thought Norbert, struggled over the wording of: "For optimum results, wet hair, lather, rinse and repeat." Or, felt a sense of duty to his fellow man when he penned: "Apply toothpaste onto a soft bristle toothbrush. Brush thoroughly after meals or at least twice a day or as directed by a dentist or physician." So much information out there, thought Norbert. Is it possible to know it all? Is it even worth trying? And besides, it's always the people who never read anything that ascend to positions of authority (perhaps because they waste no time in reflective thought). At least that was his experience in the military.

As an extension of his love for the printed word, Norbert had kept a notebook since he was sixteen. He called it his notebook even though other folks—mostly females and men involved in community theater—might call it their journal, or worse, *diary*. While he was deployed in the desert, his ass-crack filled with hot sand, Norbert scribbled in his notebook more than ever before. He never intended for the things inside it to be seen by other people—not even Arlene. It was personal, private stuff. A periodic purge of his gray matter. After his third tour, in the in-between, he continued to write in it, or draw, or just lie there staring at blank pages, wondering what might fill them. The notebook had a soft brown leather cover, scuffed and dark and fragrant as a catcher's mitt, with a couple of long strings that could be tied into a bow—which Norbert always double-knotted. It was thick (about 300 pages), and still, after all these years, only about two-thirds filled with Norbert's musings. The notebook was nothing the teenaged Norbert would have ever purchased for himself. It was a gift from his father's father, Grandpa Sherbert. It had not been Norbert's birthday or Christmas or any other gift-giving holiday scenario. Norbert's grandfather had simply tossed it onto Norbert's stomach one summer afternoon without explanation as Norbert lounged on the musty sofa inside his grandparents' camp on Lake George. As Norbert asked his grandfather what it was for, the screen door slammed. Grandpa Sherbert was already down the steps headed toward the lake, pipe in mouth, fishing rod on shoulder. This was not an unusual style for conferring gifts in Norbert's family. Indeed, it was the Sherbert way. Norbert opened the book to reveal an inscription on the inside cover written in his grandfather's hand. It read: *A man's life, if he's living it right, has many beginnings.*

Having received very little from his grandfather, outside the occasional sarcasm about his clothing or haircut, Norbert resolved in that moment to treasure the notebook, making it his constant companion.

Pastor Zack, head holy man and musical director of the Church of Abundant Waters and the Splendiferous Blood of Christ, wrapped up his electric guitar solo—a sleepy, deliberate version of "Stairway to Heaven" he had been fingering on his Fender knock-off for the better part of ten minutes. He was seated on an identical metal folding chair, beside a lone amplifier, facing his congregation inside the former hot dog joint and purveyor of 16 distinctive juice blend recipes.

Pastor Zack set aside his guitar and stood to address his flock. There was no pulpit. Only the anticipatory air of discovery separated them.

"Who's digging on a prayer?" asked Pastor Zack.

A murmur of approval swept through the congregation like an August breeze.

"Well then, 'Get on up! Get on up! Get on up!'" chanted Pastor Zack, in mimicry of the Godfather of Soul.

In response, all souls and their worldly containers rose to their feet.

"Let's start with the name of the Father, and of the Son, and of the Holy Spirit," said Pastor Zack.

Everybody drew a cross in the air in front of themselves and said, "Amen."

"The Lord be with you," said Pastor Zack.

"And also with you," answered his flock. Norbert started to sit down, but there was much more.

"Dear friends," said Pastor Zack, producing a name-brand athletic plastic squeeze bottle, "this water will be used to remind us of our baptism. Let us ask God to bless it, and to keep us faithful to the spirit He has given us. God our Father, your gift of water totally brings life and freshness to the Earth; it washes away our sins and brings us eternal life. We ask you now to bless this water, and to give us your protection on this day, which you have made your own. Renew the splendiferous living spring of your life within us and protect us in spirit and body, that we may be free from sin and come into your presence to receive your gift of salvation. We ask this through Christ our Lord."

The flock responded with an Amen. Norbert fidgeted with the hymnal, turning it over in his hands. Arlene's irritation was palpable.

Pastor Zack squeezed the bottle. Clear tracers of thrice-purified water arced above the parishioners' heads, cascading down upon their heaven-bent faces and upturned palms. The bottle empty, Pastor Zack again snatched up his guitar and played the introductory riff to the refrain of "Take Me to the River." On the proper note, to Norbert's dissatisfaction, everyone struck up in song. Even Arlene.

Norbert read the hymnal's cover: *Jesus Rocks! Contemporary Songs for Modern Worship.*

"Washing me down," sang Arlene with a wriggle. "Washing me down."

Pastor Zack let the electric guitar dangle around his neck from a strap embroidered in some vaguely Native American motif. He said, "May almighty God cleanse us of our sins and through the Eucharist we celebrate make us worthy to sit at His table in His heavenly kingdom."

"Amen," responded the motley congregants of the Church of Abundant Waters and the Splendiferous Blood of Christ.

"You may be seated," said Pastor Zack.

Norbert thought of his mother. She still attended regular church services with the Episcopalians. Once Norbert had outgrown Sunday school (physically much later than mentally, for the record), he was no longer forced to accompany her. "Let the kid play outside," said Norbert's father. "Why the hell should he be cooped up in a church? He should be hitting a ball, not holding a candle."

It was for the best.

From his earliest days, Norbert was quizzical. But his relentless, probing questions had mushroomed into a great source of irritation for Mrs. Greenleaf, the Sunday school instructor.

"Why do we blindly believe all these crazy Bible stories then laugh at the stories the Greeks and Romans believed?" Norbert would ask. "Aren't they all equally ridiculous?" Or, "Why did Cain need a mark on his head when he was banished from Eden to wander in the Land of Nod? After he murdered Abel, weren't his parents, Adam and Eve, the only other two people alive on Earth?"

Mrs. Greenleaf was eventually compelled to pull Norbert's mother aside during coffee hour to inform her that Norbert was becoming a disruption and that he was wasting class time.

So religiously, Norbert was indifferent. But that did not mean he was unaffiliated. As far as the United States government was concerned, Norbert was a Baptist. That's because, on the first day of boot camp at Fort Benning, Georgia, Norbert's large, black drill sergeant not so much asked as demanded that Norbert scream his religion at the top of his voice. This was so some P.F.C. in some hidden office could stamp it, along with Norbert's blood type and other particulars, into his dog tags just in case he got shot or blown up or run over or otherwise dispatched in the desert by the enemy—or one of his comrades.

Friendly fire, the army called it. *Fratricide.*

"I DON'T GO TO CHURCH, DRILL SERGEANT!" hollered Norbert.

Norbert's reply only exacerbated his drill sergeant's already profoundly dyspeptic disposition.

He said to recruit Norbert A. Sherbert Jr., "CHOOSE A RELIGION NOW, SHIT STAIN!"

As an incentive to choose quickly, the drill sergeant offered to snatch up Norbert by his tiny pecker and swing him in tight circles above his head until Norbert made his selection. Norbert asked the drill sergeant which Lord he worshipped, and he answered the Baptist one. Norbert had no immediate objection, quickly resolving that crisis of faith. And so, Norbert officially became Baptist. In sorting out that episode, Norbert experienced what some imperiled souls later recount as a Moment of Grace. It was an important lesson in young Norbert's education to the advantages and expediency of dispassionately regarding the religious beliefs of another.

Pastor Zack's sermon, or "fellowship" as he called it, focused on the Bible stories of God's conversations with Moses and Noah. Actual conversations! These chats of His invariably centered on something we humans did to piss God off. According to Pastor Zack, God always wants to be clear that there are severe consequences for not obeying His laws: the Ten Commandments. God instructed these men to convince each mortal in earshot that if they did not follow His laws, He would flood the earth, or smite them individually (according to His caprice), or command boils to form on their private regions, or encourage their fellow congregants to stone them to death, et cetera.

Norbert was surprised to find himself intrigued by Pastor Zack's sermon. Hmm, he thought, let's say this Bible God really *does* exist—after all, *a lot* more people believe He does than believe He doesn't. I'd sure like to speak with Him, thought Norbert. I'll wager He'd like to speak with me, too. I would hope He thinks I've earned that much, given the sacrifices I've made. What makes me so different from those guys in the Bible? They were nobody special before God chose to speak to them. Moses? Noah? Just the regular schmoes of their time.

The first thing Norbert would be sure to ask God is why He allowed a Saudi grad student to blow apart his best friend, P.F.C. Timothy Sullivan, with a body bomb, turning Sully's fit, young, radiant body into a mound of red hamburger on an unpaved road in Tikrit. When Sully was killed, he was standing exactly where Norbert should have been. Should have been, but was not.

But God's conversations with the earthbound have tapered off quite a bit in recent memory. Hmm, thought

Norbert, hmm. What would a regular guy like me have to do in today's world to warrant God's undivided attention? What could I do that's so outrageous it would perturb Him enough to earn me a face-to-face with the man Himself?

What if I didn't just break one commandment, thought Norbert, or a few commandments, but all Ten Commandments? And what if I broke them all in a single week?

No, thought Norbert, no. That would be wrong. Or would it? How about this? What if I broke each commandment in such a fashion that it was undeniably the morally correct thing to do in each instance? Breaking His top ten laws as a result of always choosing to do the right thing. That might piss a guy off. That, thought Norbert, has potential.

"Brothers and sisters," said Pastor Zack, "Please rise so we may prepare ourselves to celebrate the sacred mysteries. Let us call to mind our sins."

Plenty of them, thought Norbert. A long silence fell upon the parishioners inside the defunct Orange Julius. Norbert presumed this was an opportunity in the program for private prayer and/or personal reflection. Suddenly, the room began to speak in one voice, "I confess to almighty God, and to you, my brothers and sisters, that I have sinned through my own fault, in my own thoughts and in my words, in what I have done, and in what I have failed to do; and I ask blessed Mary, ever virgin, all the angels and the saints, and you my brothers and sisters, to pray for me to the Lord, our God."

"May almighty God have mercy on us," said Pastor Zack, "forgive us our sins, and bring us to everlasting life."

"Amen," everyone agreed.

"A-frickin'-men," said Pastor Zack. "Let us pray."

"What did everyone just finish doing?" whispered Norbert to Arlene. She ignored him.

Silence again, then, the flock erupted in a final "Amen." After that, everybody was allowed to sit back down.

What are the Ten Commandments anyway, thought Norbert? He searched the floor for a Bible. It occurred to him that he would not even know on what page to look for them. Does the Bible have an index? Thou shalt not kill, steal, commit adultery. Coveting was one. Thou shalt not covet. You weren't supposed to work on Sundays. The list got foggy after that. Norbert's mind wandered. He did not consider himself to be one of the world's great thinkers but he did enjoy losing himself in thick books that didn't get made into movies—unlike the Bible.

Norbert loved a good argument. Controversy! Differences of opinion! Sometimes out of a clear blue sky, just to get a rise out of Arlene, Norbert would express his thoughts on some hot-button issue. He loved watching that half-inch between Arlene's eyebrows disappear as she knit a crooked unibrow of consternation. Arlene would sit up straight, scoot to the edge of their denim couch, and load both barrels. That's when Norbert knew he had her.

Arlene was not a listener. She was someone who thought of what to say next while others were speaking. This, in Norbert's view, is what made her a below-average debater. He believed her great weakness was her tendency to generalize, especially when conversation turned to the nation's social ills—Republicans, social media, pundits and so forth. Arlene was feisty, but Norbert felt she ignored the finer points. He would always tell her, "If you want to win an argument, focus on the details." When she got rolling, she *loved* taking Norbert to task. She was a taskmaster. And lucky for Norbert, she was just as progressive in the sack as she was with her social agenda. That was, of course, back when they used to have sex.

"J.C.," said Pastor Zack, "you said to your apostles: I leave you peace, my peace I give you. Look not on our sins, but on the faith of your church, and grant us the peace and unity of your kingdom where you live for ever and ever."

"Amen."

"The peace of the Lord be with you always."

"And also with you."

"Splendiferous," said Pastor Zack. "Let us offer each other a sign of peace."

Everybody started shaking hands and hugging. Pastor Zack strummed a medley that began with The Beatles' "Hello, Goodbye," and transitioned seamlessly into John Lennon's "Give Peace a Chance."

Norbert turned to Arlene, but she was engaged in a hug, disappearing within the pillowy parts of a fleshy young woman wearing ill-fitted corduroy kulats and rubber clogs. A young man in a pilled green knit sweater, standing directly behind Norbert, extended his hand. The young man's facial hair was arranged in either a goatee or a Vandyke, Norbert never bothered to learn the difference. He also sported a tiny barbell pierced in the nook below his lower lip, just above his chin. Norbert knew from his reading that this adornment was called a labret. He also knew that it was once reserved for the male members of the higher castes of the ancient Aztecs and Mayans, but was now solely the irksome aesthetic practice of hipsters.

"Hey, brother," said the young man. "I don't think we've met."

"That's correct," answered Norbert, shaking his hand.

Norbert moved on to the next hand and gave that a shake. He received a few puzzled smiles, but everyone seemed friendly. They offered Norbert peace and Norbert said, "Back atcha."

Norbert ate the Communion wafer: home-baked, organic with a hint of olive oil. It was his first time having the pleasure. He had only read about the procedure and seen it in the movies and on television. Arlene did not speak while they waited in line, her face as inanimate as a bus schedule. When they reached the front, Norbert watched what Arlene did, then copied her when it was his turn. She drank the wine, but Norbert chose not to. It was flu season and, throughout the Mass, dozens of hacking coughs ricocheted off the four bare walls of the former Orange Julius. The coughs were particularly endemic of the very old and very young in attendance.

I suppose I should be impressed by the commitment of sick old people electing to attend church services, thought Norbert, but I would just as soon prefer they stay home. I'm not about to share the same cup with any of them— let alone *all* of them. When it comes to airborne illness, thought Norbert, the elderly and children are like pigeons.

The drive home from the strip mall was a chilly one. Arlene was upset about what Norbert had placed in the collection plate.

"The only cash on me was a single and a five," said Norbert. "And the Ford needs gas."

"You should have put the five in the plate. If you need gas so badly, you can borrow money from me."

"I don't need gas, Arlene, the pickup does. I can go for days without gasoline. I'm like a camel."

Norbert asked her how much cash she had on her. She replied that she had none. He knew that would be her answer. Arlene never had any cash on her. She had credit cards, but those were only for things like fair trade coffee, organic produce, and shoes. Important things. Norbert did not belabor the point. He'd fought this battle many times and always arrived nowhere. He also elected not to mention that he could not borrow money she did not have. And he did not mention that it was she, not he, who had left the Ford's tank empty.

Norbert concentrated for a moment on rubbing some-thing out of his right eye. It turned out to be a dead lash.

He held it out to Arlene.

"Make a wish."

She crossed her arms. She didn't want to play.

"C'mon," said Norbert. "You can wish for me to put a fiver in the collection plate next time."

"Next time?" said Arlene, in a voice equal parts shock and annoyance.

"Sure," said Norbert. "Why not?"

Norbert held his finger aloft until Arlene blew the lash off his fingertip with a reluctant puff from the corner of her mouth.

"What'd you wish for?" asked Norbert.

"You don't want to know."

They pulled into the service station. Norbert pumped. He enjoyed the smell of gasoline. He kept his window rolled down so he could talk with Arlene.

"It's cold," she said. "I'm rolling up your window."

"Leave it down," said Norbert. "I want to look at you."

"The gas smell is giving me an f'n headache."

Norbert inhaled deeply through his nostrils. "Ahhhhh-hhhhh." He squeezed the last few pennies so the number was on the nose and slid the handle back into the pump.

Arlene shook her head, "Five dollars of gas. Unbelievable. You're a child."

"I've been saving my nickels for something special," said Norbert. He paid inside, climbed back into the Ford and pulled away from the station. "Let me ask you a question pertaining to your new fascination with all things holy."

"Norbert, please. My head is pounding now from the gas."

"What's your take on those stories your pal Pastor Zack was talking about in his sermon? Do you really think there have been times when your God has had actual face-to-face conversations with regular people, or do you think it's all more allegory and such?"

"*My* God?" said Arlene. "That's clever, Norbert. Very deep. What do you care, anyway? In case you haven't noticed, which I'm sure you haven't, I've already given up on your taking an interest in anything to do with my renewed commitment to my faith."

"I'm just making *God*-versation."

"You're so vulgar. And just so you know, you were not supposed to take Communion. You're not Catholic. You're not anything."

"I'm Baptist."

"I'm not talking about your stupid army story," said Arlene.

"National Guard."

"Whatever. I'm talking about you being baptized. Taking First Communion."

"I don't want to alarm you Arlene, but that was not a Catholic church back there. It was an Orange Julius."

"It may have been non-traditional, but it was modeled after the high Mass. I found Pastor Zack's service uplifting."

"I could still smell remnants of Mango Passion."

"It was a place of worship. Period."

"Who elected you pope?" laughed Norbert. "Pope Arlene the First."

"Anyway. It doesn't matter. I'm just telling you how it works. There are rules."

"Well, this is enlightening," said Norbert. "Tell me about the rules. Tell me about the Lamb of God. What did the melodious Pastor Zack mean by that? He said I've sinned through my own fault and then asked God and the angels to have mercy on me, forgive me my sins and bring me everlasting life. Like with the water bottle. When he splashed me in the eye with that water he said it was to forgive my sins and save me from being sick and to protect me from evil."

"That's right. Absolution. To forgive you your sins for the past week."

"So according to the Church of the Abundant Water and Splendid such and such, which you contend is based in Catholic doctrine, I'm currently sin-free?"

"In the eyes of the church," said Arlene.

Norbert stood on the brake. The Ford skidded to a complete stop in the middle of Route 9N. Arlene locked her arms as she and Norbert were thrown toward the dash, then backward into their seats.

"What are you doing!" screeched Arlene.

"Did you see that?"

"See what, Norbert! See what! Are you insane!"

"I damn near just hit a snowshoe bunny rabbit. It's that bugger's lucky day."

He started the truck forward again, at a crawl, then back up to speed. Without missing a beat he said, "But what if I, say, broke one of the Ten Commandments last week?"

"What?" said Arlene, trying to reclaim her composure. She retrieved her purse that had slid onto the floor in front of her, spilling its contents. "What are you saying? Which commandment?"

"It's a hypothetical. Why? Does it make a difference?"

"I guess not," said Arlene, distracted. "Technically, if you are truly sorry for the sins you committed, you're forgiven."

"No shit?" Norbert was silent for a long moment. He started to speak, then thought better of it. Finally, he figured *What the hell?* "What if I broke all ten?"

"You are infuriating."

"Seriously."

"That's just stupid, Norbert. Why would anybody break all Ten Commandments in a week? You would have to commit murder, adultery . . . I can't do this now. My head is pounding. Please don't speak to me."

They drove along in silence, past snow-covered rolls of feeding hay wrapped in white plastic. Past a caved-in pole barn, a billboard advertising an upstate Indian casino, browning Christmas trees dragged to the road. Past a dead, frozen possum.

"You know what your problem is, Norbert?"

Arlene had woken Norbert from another daydream, having fallen under the seductive trance of the dancing mud flaps on the truck ahead. Norbert didn't bother to answer. Arlene always answered her questions for him.

"You're incapable of fun."

"Fun?"

"That's right. You're in a funk, and you've been in it for too long now. You're depressed. You only talk and think about one thing and I'm sick of it. I'm sorry, it's not Christian and it's not sensitive to your situation, but there it is. I've been with you through all of it, Norbert. Right at your side. Believe me, it hurts me to say it but I'm tired of hearing about it. Get over it. *Move on.*"

A surge of adrenaline howled through Norbert's corpuscles. *Get over it?* I should slap her mouth, he thought. *Move on?* Instead he smiled, leaned deeper into the seat cushion, and propped one hand atop the steering wheel.

"Arlene, have you ever fired at screaming ragheads with a .50-caliber machine gun from inside a Blackhawk helicopter?"

"What?"

"Have you?"

"Norbert, please."

"Have you?"

"Of course not." Arlene folded her arms and turned toward the window.

"I'm just sayin', until you've done that, you don't know what fun *is.*"

"You're so vulgar. I see that now. I guess I didn't want to see it before."

"Vulgar? Is that your new word? That must be you taking your liberal arts degree out for a spin. Excuse me, Arlene. I didn't go away to a big college, so I talk how regular people talk. Let me clue you in on something: not everybody gets shit handed to them. Some people are born, even though they don't ask to be. They go to community college, or work, even though they don't want to. Thoughts of such things tend to make them bitter. As a result, they fall into the practice of sprinkling their conversations with vulgarities because their lives are fucking miserable. And that's if you're lucky. Sometimes . . . Sometimes . . . "

Here comes the shit storm, she thought.

"Sometimes people get blown up at nineteen because some *raghead* in a white Nissan truck hides a body bomb under his *raghead* jacket. If the *raghead* is close enough, they get turned into instant hamburger in a flash of fire. If they aren't, they die screaming, crying for momma. Full of sin."

Norbert cranked up the heat full blast just to occupy his trembling hand.

"Or they don't die," he said. "And sometimes, that's worse."

"All you can do is live by the Golden Rule," said Arlene quietly.

"Do unto others? Bullshit."

"Obey the commandments," she said. "And have faith."

"You've changed, Arlene. A lot."

"I have changed, Norbert. I have worked hard to change. Every day, I change my thinking more and more about all sorts of things. Important things. Those books my mom gave me . . . "

"About the Rapture?"

"I'm not going to apologize because the spirit of Christ is alive inside me. You need to prepare your own soul, Norbert. You have a lot of work to do. I could help you. But you shut me out at every turn."

Norbert knocked gently on Arlene's skull.

"Hello? Hello? Has anyone seen Arlene? Is she in there? She's about 5'8", dark hair, used to give me blowjobs in the back seat of my Turismo during study halls."

Arlene pulled away. Norbert sighed.

No words were exchanged for two miles. They passed a floral roadside memorial fixed to a speed limit sign. Above the arrangement was a white card wrapped in clear cellophane with black, hand-drawn letters that read: "You are with the angels now." Norbert grimaced. They passed several orange signs warning: Slow! Road Work. Fines Doubled. But it was Sunday, and the road crew was observing the fourth commandment.

Arlene broke the silence.

"Norbert. Listen, Norbert . . . I've met someone."

Norbert slammed the brakes, pulled the Ford onto the shoulder. "You're banging another guy?"

"No."

"You just said—"

"I said I met someone, Norbert. Someone gentle, who honors me. He's God-fearing and devout. He knows humility."

"But you're not fucking him."

"Just let's go home."

"I don't understand," said Norbert.

"I don't expect you to understand. Right now, you're incapable of understanding anything about my life. Just . . . just accept it as God's will. Just let's go home."

Norbert threw the Ford back into gear and spun the tires. They lurched back onto Route 9N and sped along in silence for about a mile. Inside, Norbert was devastated but remained cool-cucumber.

"You must have known this was coming," said Arlene. "I've been pulling away for months. Just listen to us this morning. We can't even be civil."

"I thought this tension was on account of all your new

God stuff. I thought that as I got better, you'd eventually snap out of it."

"Snap out of it? Snap out of God? That doesn't even make sense. That's your problem, Norbert. You only see what you want to see."

Norbert reached up under the dash and pulled down his cigarettes from their hiding place. This got a mild rise from Arlene, but only mild. He didn't make a show of it, and she responded by pretending she didn't care. Norbert cracked the window and lit up. The only sounds were the Ford's tires dipping into gouges in the asphalt and the ricochet of road salt inside the wheel wells.

"Who is he?" asked Norbert without moving his eyes from the road. "Where'd you meet him? How long?"

"I'm exhausted, Norbert. My head is pounding. Just let's go home."

Norbert blew a white rope of smoke into the whistling gap in his window. He looked at Arlene. This time he waited until her wet green eyes met his. "This is all because of—"

"No," she said coldly. "It has nothing to do with that. Christ almighty, Norbert, how do you expect me to live with you when you can't even live with yourself?"

2

Doughy, ruddy-faced, Wilberforce Wendell checked himself into the Robin Hood Motor Court off Route 9N in Ticonderoga. The Word-a-Day calendar on the counter reminded him it was Sunday. His internal clock was off. How odd, thought Wilberforce, that I didn't *feel* it was Sunday. For so many years the Sabbath had been the focus of his week. Not anymore. Now everything had changed and Wilberforce was in the process of deciding what to think about those changes—indeed, what to *do* about those changes. The word on the calendar was:

om·pha·lo·skep·sis *n* Contemplation of one's navel.

An omen, perhaps? Wilberforce had his antennae up for signs.

Wilberforce opened the door to Room 3 with his key—the Robin Hood still used actual, metal keys—and took quick stock of his quarters. It was small and boring—not unlike my former flock, he thought. He tuned the cheap clock/radio to a country-western station. Modern country music—country rock, they called it—was not to his taste, but it would have to do. For now, everything will just have to do, he thought. He preferred a more uneven melody, less production polish, with gravelly vocals on topics ranging from heartache to heartbreak. Maybe it was just the mood he was in: "Gloomy Gus," Margaret would call it. He had been a Gloomy Gus for some time now, and every time it seemed the sun might peek through he'd rush to do something dumb, something to ensure his life was all storm clouds.

He'd really done it this time. But there was a big part of him that believed he deserved every bad thing that ever happened to him, and worse. He had a lot to sort out.

That's why he was on the move again. He'd always had

the itch for travel and adventure—but with a purpose, usually the highest purpose. This was the first time he felt adrift, physically and metaphysically. Perhaps strangely, he was not unhappy. Just uncertain.

Wilberforce heaved his leather bag onto the twin bed nearest the door. From an outer zipper-pouch he removed his King James Bible. He knew that this moment in his life was designed by his Creator as an opportunity to reflect on the Holy Scriptures. In fact, that is precisely what he would suggest if, instead of it being himself skulking into the Robin Hood Motor Court, it were some parishioner wandering into his former office. He knew he would urge that parishioner to open his own King James to search for comfort, even answers. Hm, thought Wilberforce. Add hypocrisy to the list of my failures and indiscretions. But never mind that. I'm not in the mood for those kinds of answers anyway. That's the ancient purple prose of faith, and I have never felt more a part of the modern world than I do right now. I feel heavy.

He flopped onto the other bed. Absently, he caressed the embossed leather of the cover of his King James Bible, ran his finger along the smooth gilded edges of its pages. The Bible was a gift from his father, a great, good man who was not really his father. Wilberforce had been adopted and because of that had devoted much of his work to children's missions. Off the top of his head, he could think of at least a dozen places he might turn inside his King James Bible to offer guidance to that wayward soul who had hypothetically wandered into his office. He might then turn to his concordance. If he looked long enough, he could probably locate relevant passages referencing the Robin Hood Motor Court itself, allegorically of course.

Wilberforce stared up at the brown water stains in the asbestos ceiling tiles. In that moment he could feel his mind and body entirely within Room 3 of the Robin Hood

Motor Court off Route 9N in Ticonderoga. The dual spheres of his being were not suspended between birth and death, heaven and hell, reason and faith, or curiosity and certainty. No, none of that. He sensed no weightlessness to his soul. He was just . . . there. He felt so . . . so . . . *corporeal*.

He needed a sign: a divine jolt. So many mistakes, thought Wilberforce. He rolled onto his belly, slid open the top drawer of the nightstand and was surprised to find it empty—no Gideon's Bible. Someone must have needed it, he hoped. He deposited his King James and slid the drawer closed.

He resolved to take a shower. Will the water pressure be satisfactory? Will the temperature remain hot for as long as I choose to stand beneath the pulsating flow of steaming liquid? Will there be adequate flat spaces upon which to place my various miniature travel-sized toiletries? These were the earthly mysteries Wilberforce Wendell was keen to investigate on this Sunday morning in February.

Later, dried and dressed, Wilberforce sat in his fleece jacket at the edge of his bed slowly turning a long tribal knife in his hands, training one eye on the clock/radio. The moment the numbers changed he stood, tucked the knife deep inside his bag, and exited the room, locking the door. As he walked toward the office, the noon fire whistle sounded—more of a sustained, wailing siren, really, that rose steadily into a crescendo then trailed off. Wilberforce asked the clerk where he could go nearby for a cold draft beer and decent corned beef sandwich. The clerk directed him to a family-owned establishment called Tessy's.

Wilberforce straddled his Vespa and strapped on his helmet. Embellishing its dome was a full-color airbrushed rendition of the *Creation of Adam* from the ceiling of the Sistine Chapel. Below the art, across the back of the helmet, the word "Redemption" was displayed in a bold, biblical font. He fired up the 150 cc single-cylinder 4-stroke air-cooled engine and headed off in the direction of lunch.

3

When Norbert and Arlene arrived back at their apartment on Elk Road, a moving van—its rear door open, its trailer three-quarters full—was parked out front. Upstairs, the apartment was nearly bare, save for a few boxes. Norbert was still too stunned to be angry. He had been sucker punched in a fashion far more injurious than brass knuckles or a fistful of dimes—he had been cold-cocked by a woman's prerogative. Norbert was convinced he recognized one of the burly movers from the 10th Mountain Division out of Fort Drum.

"Hey fella," said Norbert, "you in Fallujah?"

"Huh?"

"Tikrit? Kabul?"

"Look," said the mover, "this entertainment center is kinda heavy." The movers had confiscated all things Arlene: denim couch, television, bookshelves, kitchenware—it was all hers, all but Norbert's notebook, his clothes, his paperbacks and harmonica. Arlene had grown to despise Norbert's soulful musings in the key of C. He knew this because she told him so, out front, just as they exited the Ford.

Both oak dressers were hers. Norbert watched the movers overturn each of his drawers into a pile in the corner of the bedroom.

Arlene, who initially wanted to minimize conflict by waiting outside, squeezed past one of the movers into the apartment. She went straight to the princess wall phone in the kitchen and started working to unhook it.

"What are you doing?" asked Norbert. Up till that moment he had been seated on an overturned milk crate in a disbelieving fog, desperately fighting the urge to tackle one of the movers through a window.

"This is my phone," said Arlene.

"No it isn't. We bought that phone together. Remember?"

"I don't remember anything of the sort." Her fingers probed the edges of the plastic device, searching for the secret to dislodging it from the wall.

"In fact," said Norbert, rising, "that's the first thing we purchased together for this apartment."

Arlene stopped her busy fingers. She placed them on the counter. She did remember.

"I wanted a cordless phone. Digital," said Norbert. "But you said this one was 'cute.' It reminded you of the one in your bedroom growing up. The one you used to talk to me on until the sun peeked under your window blinds."

"Fine," said Arlene. "We bought it together."

"We bought it together," said Norbert. "With my money."

"What's the deal, Norbert? You want to keep this phone? Fine, keep the stupid phone. I don't need it where I'm going anyway."

Onto the counter, Arlene emptied the wicker basket containing all the unpaid bills.

"This is my basket," she said. "I bought it with a gift card."

The movers waited down in the truck. Arlene scanned the apartment with a final, critical eye for omission, but it had been successfully vacated of all her possessions.

At the door she paused. For an instant, Norbert thought she might get wistful—but no. She steeled herself. She was a tough nut, Arlene, when she had set her mind to something.

"Well," she said. "I guess this is goodbye."

"You'll be back. You've loved me for too long."

"Everything is changing around you, Norbert, and you're staying the same. You're stuck, and that makes me sad."

"Things can't end like this for us. You'll be back. We've been through too much together."

"No, Norbert. It's over. We're over. I've made my peace with this decision. I've prayed long and hard over it. Prayed for you. With a full Christian heart I've tried to save you. But in the end, Norbert, you can only save yourself."

"Thanks for the heads-up."

"Hilarious, Norbert. You're quite the wit. But it's not my job to laugh anymore at your quips. Are you going to say goodbye to me or not?"

"You'll be back."

"Fine, Norbert. Have it your way. You have to spoil everything."

"Spoil what? You're leaving me for another man."

"I feel really sad for you, Norbert. I do."

"I'm fine."

"You know what I mean."

Norbert crossed to the door. He held the knob in his left hand and with his right made a grand sweeping motion like a Park Avenue doorman.

"Maybe this makes me a foolish girl," said Arlene, leaving, "but I'd like to stay friends. It's the Christian thing to do."

"Sure," said Norbert. "Let's do that."

"Good friends."

"Sure."

Norbert followed her outside into the chilly afternoon. When she reached the bottom of the porch steps he said, "Arlene."

She turned. "What, Norbert?"

"Do me one favor?"

She hesitated. "It depends a lot on what that favor is."

"It's easy," said Norbert. "You might even enjoy it."

"Okay."

"When you're with this new guy, the one who's God-fearing and devout."

"Yes?"

"When you're fucking him, think of your 'good friend' Norbert."

Arlene shook her head. She sighed.

"You're a child."

Norbert watched her climb into the truck, wedging herself between the two, thick-necked movers. The engine roared to life. Blinker flashing, they moved into the road heading east. From his porch, hands in pockets, collar up, Norbert followed the truck's progress, away from their apartment on Elk Road where they had built their little universe together, such as it was.

Fifty yards.

One hundred yards.

One hundred and fifty yards.

The truck's tires made an abrupt chirping sound. The left turn signal flashed. The truck swerved gently to the side of the road and parked. The strapping movers spilled out of the cab, walked to the rear of the truck, threw open the metal door and extended the serrated ramp.

Norbert, mouth agape, whispered, "What. The. *Fuck?*"

Then, onto the porch not two hundred yards from where Norbert stood, appeared Pastor Zack. He opened his arms to Arlene, who eagerly bounded into them.

Motherfucking preacher man.

Norbert ambled down his steps and marched, mumbling and cursing, straight at the nesting lovebirds.

Halfway there, Norbert watched Pastor Zack step in front of Arlene, shielding her. When Norbert was upon them, Pastor Zack held out his open palms like some stigmata, or elementary school crossing guard.

"Ho! Slow down there, friend," said Pastor Zack. "Take a breath."

Norbert pulled up short. "Did you just tell me to take a breath?"

"Yes," said Pastor Zack, smiling. "I did."

"Don't tell me to take a breath. If you tell me again to take a breath, it will be your last."

"All right, Norbert," smiled Pastor Zack.

"Copy that?" said Norbert.

"I'm sorry? I don't understand what you just said."

"Are we clear?"

"Yes." Pastor Zack's voice upshifted into a new, proselytizing gear—his cadence suddenly a parabola of intonation. "Norbert, I know this comes as a tremendous shock to you—and believe me, I counseled Arlene to handle this much differently—but here we are, left with only one recourse."

"And what recourse is that? Me yanking your pecker off through your asshole? Then beating you with it?"

"Um, no," said Pastor Zack. "I was suggesting we sit down and talk."

"See what I mean?" said Arlene to Pastor Zack. "He's so vulgar."

Norbert locked eyes with Arlene. "You've been talking with this clown? About our personal affairs?"

"Talking is what I do, Norbert," said Pastor Zack. "It's my gift from J.C. I have offered Arlene two good ears and a shoulder in her time of need. In fact, I want you to feel free to come to me yourself, anytime, to rap about your challenges."

"Challenges?"

"Yes," said Pastor Zack. "Stemming from your time in Iraq and Afghanistan."

Norbert stepped aside so one of the movers could pass, his face obscured behind a large cardboard box.

"Arlene has told me quite a lot about your struggles."

"My struggles?" Norbert shook his head. He knew he was going to eventually have to drive his fist deep into Pastor Zack's nasal cavity. His self-control was on overdrive to delay that foregone conclusion.

"Your challenges, your struggles. Your crisis of faith," said Pastor Zack. With each word his speech grew slower, more deliberate. Pastor Zack felt very much at ease in this dynamic, like he was reclining into his soft office chair inside the converted dry storage pantry of the former Orange Julius. "I am speaking specifically about the after-effects of your war-related trauma."

A mover passed carrying a driftwood lamp and a pair of surround-sound speakers.

"That's mighty magnanimous, coming from a thief," said Norbert. "What about God's law? You've clearly broken one of His Ten Commandments."

"I don't understand what you are saying," said Pastor Zack. "What is he saying?" Pastor Zack asked Arlene. Arlene shrugged.

"You stole my girlfriend," said Norbert. "Thou shalt not steal."

"No," said Pastor Zack, chuckling and a bit relieved he had evaded judgment. "She came to me willingly. I would never break a commandment."

"It's adultery," said Norbert.

"No again," said Pastor Zack. "Neither I, nor you, nor Arlene is married. There is no adultery involved here."

"I already told you Norbert," said Arlene. "We haven't had sex yet."

"You haven't blown him?" said Norbert.

Pastor Zack and Arlene studied the cracks in the sidewalk.

"What about coveting, then?" said Norbert. "That's one, too. Isn't it? I'm literally your neighbor. You coveted my girlfriend, you phony sonofabitch. How do you get around that one?"

"Look," croaked Pastor Zack, "as previously stated, Arlene came to me first. In her time of need. I've done nothing wrong here. I'm a facilitator of, uh . . . I'm part of God's . . . "

"Oh be quiet, Zack," said Arlene. "Quit while you're ahead."

"What a crock," said Norbert. He balled his fist. What will it feel like, he thought, Pastor Zack's cartilage collapsing beneath my knuckles?

"This is absurd," said Pastor Zack (a word he pronounced as *ab-zerd*.) "Patently absurd. My actions don't warrant this scrutiny. Mine is not the life that should be slid beneath a microscope. I'm a good person, God-fearing and devout. I know humility. I live each day by the commandments. When the blessed day comes, I will stand in judgment for my actions at the foot of my Maker, not before any man."

"The commandments," said Norbert. "The commandments. You pious bozos with your oh-so-convenient interpretations of morality. You cherry pick your precious scriptures, twist the truth, revise it, tinker with it to suit your actions. You prefer your principles a la carte. For you, there probably is no *truth*. Everything is relative, subject to *your* interpretation. What do you know about the world? What do you two know about right and wrong? You don't know shit! You haven't seen what I've seen. You want to know what I think of God's law? I'll show you."

Pastor Zack and Arlene readied themselves. They were frightened of what Norbert might do next.

One of the movers approached Norbert with an armload of Arlene's clothing, the satin hangers still threaded through their sleeveless holes. Norbert seized the pile of garments from the mover's grasp. He pushed past Arlene and Pastor Zack, up the steps into Pastor Zack's house.

Arlene and Pastor Zack looked at one another. They looked at the mover. A moment later, Norbert reemerged. He stalked past them, down the sidewalk, up the ramp and into the truck. He reappeared holding a stack of pillows and Arlene's down comforter. Again, he brushed past the dumbstruck bystanders.

"What on earth are you doing?" asked Arlene.

Norbert did not respond as he disappeared back inside the house.

Out again, down the stoop, Norbert hustled toward the moving truck.

"Norbert!" shouted Arlene. "What. Are. You. Doing?!"

Norbert stopped, turned. "Working," he said.

"Working?"

"On Sunday," said Norbert. He marched up the ramp and reemerged with a box of dishware.

"Patently absurd," marveled Pastor Zack.

"You're insane!" said Arlene. She turned to Pastor Zack. "He's insane! You see? You see what I've been dealing with? I told you, he's got the Gulf War disease."

"I don't believe that is an accurate diagnosis," said Pastor Zack. "As I understand it, that particular affliction is exclusive to our veterans who served in the first Middle East conflict, under President Bush the Elder. But yes, I see what you are saying." Pastor Zack shook his head grimly at the sight of Norbert ambling past him, like a surgeon looking down at a terminal mass of cells. "Clearly these actions are absurd."

"Oh, just you wait," said Norbert, striding past them, hefting the box for a firmer grip. "This is just the beginning."

"The beginning of what?" asked Arlene.

"Never you mind," said Norbert. "Just go on about your business."

Norbert made three more trips back and forth over Arlene's protestations before she and Pastor Zack, exasperated, climbed into Pastor Zack's bio-diesel sport coupé and zipped off to Quizno's.

"Don't even think about him," said Pastor Zack, turning toward Arlene as he shifted and sped away from the conflict on Elk Road. "Put him out of your mind entirely. Focus on our trip to GODCON. We'll leave all this madness behind to fellowship and renew our faith and souls."

"Yeah," said Arlene, folding her arms, glancing back in Norbert's direction, though he was now obscured from view. "I guess."

Arlene wriggled her nose, sniffing the vehicle's interior. "Jesus Christ, Zack, this car smells like french fries. It's driving me f'n crazy!"

Back at Pastor Zack's house, Norbert stayed and finished the job with the movers. It was just past 11:30 a.m. when he shook their meaty paws and thanked them for allowing him to slow their progress for the sake of sin.

4

In Topeka, Kansas, Elton Berryhill was updating his website. He had just finished uploading brand new images of two of the meanies. The first was a recent digital photo sent as an email attachment by a loyal subscriber. Elton, using software he purchased via the Internet for $50, compared the photo to a driver's license in the state of Maine's D.M.V. database. The photo was a match, so Elton was happy to post it. I see you, thought Elton. I see you. There is no place you can hide.

The second image was from a series of recent photos Elton had taken himself using his Canon digital telephoto from the driver's seat of his burnt sienna Oldsmobile Cutlass Supreme. Elton was in a position to take these photos thanks to a tip from an alert loyal subscriber who was a waitress in a downtown diner in Cedar Rapids, Iowa. The round-trip from Elton's house was nearly 800 miles and took Elton just over twelve hours with bathroom breaks and a stop for a proper sit-down supper at Cracker Barrel, a folksy Interstate eatery Elton approved of because it did not serve alcohol. But Elton believed the crusade to Cedar Rapids was worth every sore neck muscle the moment he focused his lens on that meanie's red, blotchy face. Elton filled half a memory stick (not an easy task) with pictures of the meanie buying three newspapers, reading in the park, eating at the diner where the righteous waitress worked and finally climbing the stone steps with his pale, flabby legs and disappearing inside his shabby apartment. Each time he laid eyes on one of the meanies, Elton felt the same churn and swirl of joy and anger strangling his every tendon and synapse.

Being a waitress must be hard work, thought Elton, because you're on your feet all day and you depend on tips to make ends meet. The alert loyal subscriber employed at the diner in Cedar Rapids said as much to Elton in the body of her email. She also wrote to Elton, "If you get close enough to that fucker, kneecap him." Adding this postscript: "Godspeed. May God bless you and keep you in His loving care."

Surely, thought Elton, there will be a place at the right hand of the Father on the day this brave, industrious Christian goes to meet her Maker.

Elton's computer began to emit a sound not unlike a large gospel choir rising to a glorious crescendo. This sound alerted him that he had just received another email from a loyal subscriber. Praise Jesus! The email informed Elton of the location of another meanie, this time much closer, only an hour east in Kansas City, Missouri. A day trip! So many blessings on this day!

Elton bolted straight up from his chair. The chair, with its clever wheels, rolled backward until it came to rest against the table opposite Elton's computer. Elton began to pace his office, which was really a corner of his mother's basement where he had arranged three folding banquet tables into a horseshoe, piling them high with his electronics, research materials and inspirational literature. This was Elton's cockpit. He called it The Halo.

The wheels on Elton's chair were clever because Elton had installed them himself, replacing the original wheels that came standard. The new wheels spun free and easy like rollerblades allowing Elton to zip back and forth inside The Halo across the concrete floor with great speed for maximum efficiency. Elton liked to zip around. After pacing twelve times, for the apostles, Elton returned to his chair and zipped around.

He stopped abruptly in front of his workstation to glare

at the digital photo forwarded by the alert loyal subscriber in Kansas City, Missouri. I see you, thought Elton, I see you. There is no place you can hide.

Upstairs, the doorbell rang. Elton reflexively hollered for his mother to answer it but remembered that she was still at the first of her two jobs. In the morning she worked as a chambermaid at the Holiday Inn making beds, emptying trash cans, extending thin paper ribbons over sanitized toilet bowls, folding the ends of bathroom tissue into triangular points, and sponging blood and jism stains from the bedspreads, walls and carpets. In the afternoons, she worked second shift at the Home Depot. Elton's mother insisted on calling herself a "checkout girl" despite the fact that Elton corrected her each time, saying she was a "cashier," and a low-paid one at that.

Annoyed, Elton rose from his chair, performed the sign of the cross in reverence to the 3-by-5 portrait of the Blessed Mother taped to the side of his monitor, and climbed the stairs into the house. He peeled back the lace curtain to see who was ringing the doorbell in the middle of the morning.

It was his next-door neighbor.

To Elton's delight, his neighbor held in her hands a package from the FedEx man. Elton knew precisely what was contained within the FedEx box because all week he had faithfully monitored his package's shipping progress by going to the FedEx website and pasting in his tracking number.

Then yesterday, to his horror, Elton was forced to leave the house to pick up his mother at the emergency room after she decided to have another of her "spells" during her afternoon shift at the Home Depot. Having experienced shortness of breath in Plumbing Fixtures, corporate policy dictated that she be transported to the hospital via ambulance—a totally unnecessary and wasteful indulgence, in

Elton's opinion. His mother had simply, as always, neglected to take her pill. At a great cost of time (for Elton) and money (for the Home Depot), Elton's mother was finally administered her pill by a plump, distracted nurse who draped her torso in what Elton believed to be an outrageously tacky floral-themed garment of low quality. Finally, after much aggravation, they were allowed to exit the hospital. All this theater occurred during the exact window of time when the FedEx man's route brought him past the Berryhill house in Topeka. As a result, Elton returned home to find a FedEx sticky note on the front door window informing him he had missed the delivery but, since he had signed for the package electronically, it had been left next door— rather than placed, exposed, at the top of his porch steps, because of its value. And, of course, Elton's neighbor was not home when he went knocking. The Lord doth test me, he thought, as he returned to his house empty-handed. Each day he tests me in a thousand small ways.

Elton yanked open the front door with such gusto that his unsuspecting neighbor leapt backward, throwing up her arms in a defensive position as if she had just caught a peripheral glance of a Frisbee spinning toward her head. When the next-door neighbor recognized Elton, she relaxed. *Slightly.*

Elton's laptop computer with wireless broadband Internet access had finally arrived. Praise Jesus! At last, Elton could update his website from the road, keeping it up-to-the-minute, providing his loyal subscribers with a professional-quality online experience. He could now upload his digital photos and video and post his crucial information instantaneously, rather than hurrying home to Topeka at speeds often well above those posted by the various state departments of transportation.

Elton hefted the weight of his new laptop in his hands. He was so happy he could sob. The device was so much more than its weight in circuitry, aluminum, and plastic, it was an instrument of God. Elton understood in that moment that he bore the heavy burden of righteousness in his hands, and it was good. So many blessings on this day! Elton fell to his knees and thanked his Intelligent Designer for granting him such bounty. He also prayed that He would continue to grant Elton strength and that He would continue to protect Elton's treasure so that he may smite the meanies in His glory. The neighbor waited politely for a few moments, watching Elton busily move his lips to a silent litany. Eventually, wordlessly, she drifted back to her residence.

His prayer complete, Elton did not linger in the doorway. He raced downstairs to The Halo to tear open and fondle his new hardware and to blog as he had never blogged before.

5

As Norbert climbed the steps back into his now bare apartment on Elk Road, he stopped at his box to retrieve the previous day's mail. Mingled with the various bills (each with Norbert's name peeking through its cellophane window) was a colorful postcard. On the front, a photo taken from the summit of Big Sur—the crooked brown coastline, the purple sky at sunset. The image warmed Norbert's cockles in the February wind, reminding him of nothing he had seen before. Norbert flipped the card. It began:

"Sugar Bear, Where you at?"

It was from Norbert's buddy Pete, a fellow former member of his Guard unit. According to the postcard, Pete had been trying to reach Norbert for days, leaving messages on voicemail and with Arlene. Pete had a big favor to ask of Norbert—something "fun"—and he wanted Norbert to get in touch with him, pronto.

"That is," wrote Pete, "if you're still alive."

Norbert was pissed. Clearly, Arlene was not giving him Pete's messages. She hated Pete. Since high school, she had considered him rude and crude—which, he was. She called him "Man Whore." And yet, here was Pete with the offer of something "fun"—a state of being Arlene had earlier proscribed Norbert as being incapable of. We shall see about that, thought Norbert.

Standing in his kitchen, Norbert punched Pete's number in Monterey, California into the princess wall phone.

"Sugar Bear," answered Pete. "You're alive."

The favor was this: Pete had an uncle in the used automotive and salvage business. He was located in upstate New York just a short drive west of Norbert. Soon after returning from service, Pete charged his uncle with the task of hunting down a very specific, classic automobile—*a Cadillac*—commensurate with his new California lifestyle. His uncle had recently located and purchased said vehicle at a police auction in Miami-Dade and had driven it up to his lot where it now awaited transfer. Pete wanted Norbert to pick up the vehicle from his uncle and drive it cross-country. In return, Pete would reimburse all his travel receipts and Norbert could stay for as long as he liked in Pete's spare bedroom and "swim in the ocean, get drunk, get laid, get funky."

Pete told Norbert, "Look here, Sugar Bear: whenever you feel like going home, go home. I'll buy you a one-way ticket back to Albany. Or, if you would prefer to make this trip without joy or anticipation, you can bring along Arlene. I'll pay to fly her cranky ass home, too. Whachoo say?"

Perhaps Arlene knew Norbert better than he knew himself. "Nah," said Norbert. "Can't do it."

"What's the obstacle, brother? Up-front cash? I can wire you a grand tomorrow morning. I'm making sick money out here building websites for these expense account douche bags."

"I just don't feel up to it," said Norbert.

"What's going on, Sugar Bear? You sound like you just drew shit patrol."

"Arlene left this morning. She thinks she's in love with her pastor."

"Damn," said Pete. "Her pastor?"

"Pastor Zack."

"She'll be back. Give her time."

"That's what I told her," said Norbert, "but I'm not sure I believe it."

"She hates my ass," said Pete. "I'd offer advice, but I'm biased."

"I know."

"If I was inclined, I would say something to the effect of, 'Let the bitch stay with her pastor.' That is, if I were inclined to offer my opinion."

"Copy that," said Norbert. "Thing is, she's had a full-blown come-to-Jesus."

"Shit. You got to get outta that cracker-assed town. Come eat some pussy in the sunshine. Ain't no problem God invented that a fresh set of titties can't solve." Pete caused his lips to reverberate wetly, a sound intended to simulate his face buried betwixt yielding bosoms.

"You lookin' at my postcard? The one I sent you?"

"Yes," said Norbert.

"You see that motherfucking ocean?"

"Yes," said Norbert. "I see it."

"When's the last time you stuck your toe in the Pacific Ocean?"

"Never."

"Never. That's some sad, sorry shit. You gotta bust out, son. I'm offering you a gift, Sugar Bear. It's imperative that you drive my sweet-ass new ride cross-country. If you stay where you're at, you're gonna start drinking and then maybe smoke some dope, and then before you know it you're gonna disappear up your own asshole. Don't think about it. Just drive my Caddy out here. It'll take you a week, tops."

"A week?" said Norbert, intrigued.

"Yeah. Six days, a week, tops."

"A guy could accomplish quite a bit on the road in the course of a week. Constantly moving, no one certain of his whereabouts." Norbert fell silent for a long moment.

"You still there?" said Pete.

"Okay, I'll do it."

"Hooah, motherfucker."

"Hooah," Norbert agreed.

Pete gave Norbert all the information he needed to pick up the vehicle, directions to the auto yard, and his home address in Monterey. Norbert carefully transcribed everything into his leather notebook. Pete was pleased—then, suddenly, as they were about to hang up, he was terror-stricken by a second thought.

"You got to promise to be super careful with this vehicle, Sugar Bear. It's a classic."

"I will."

"It took my uncle a year and a half to find just the one I was looking for. It's a one-of-a-kind." Now it was Pete's turn for his end of the line to fall silent.

"You there?" said Norbert.

"I love you, baby, but you gotta promise to be super careful with this ride."

"I will."

"You promise? I watched you drive a Humvee into a latrine pit. You promise to be super careful?"

"Sure. I promise."

"Swear to God?"

"Jesus Christ, Pete! You contacted me. You want me to drive this fucking thing out there or don't you?"

"Just swear to God. It'll make me feel better."

"I swear to God."

"Okay," said Pete.

"Feel better?"

"Yes," said Pete.

"Good," said Norbert. "I'll see you in a week."

Norbert hung up and wandered into his bedroom. He sifted through his clothes piled in the corner and located his harmonica. He cleared it, played a short blues riff, and stuffed it into the inside pocket of his leather jacket. He located his Folger's cash can and removed the small, dark velvet-covered box hidden inside. He lifted the spring lid to admire the diamond engagement ring with the white gold band that he had invested the better part of three months of government checks into. He had planned to offer it to Arlene in six days, on Valentine's Day, at that new family-style Italian restaurant off Route 9N, the one with the big-breasted hostess with straight, white teeth.

Tucked into the box's lid, folded into a hard square, was the receipt for the ring. Norbert unfolded it, studied it. He stuffed the ring and receipt into his leather jacket. Norbert descended the porch steps, climbed into the Ford, and pulled onto Elk Road. He was headed into town to see Mr. Klein, the jeweler. Then it was on to Tessy's to get stone drunk.

Driving along Route 9N, a few dozen feet from the turn into Tessy's, Norbert fiddled with the radio. One would be inclined to believe that this country-western unpleasantness is programmed on every goddamn station, thought Norbert.

Distressed and distracted by the warblings of some millionaire in a cowboy hat, Norbert glanced up just in time to see a man on a Vespa, approaching from the opposite direction, lose control of his scooter on a patch of black ice. The man skidded beneath the front fender of Norbert's Ford in a cascade of sparks, a sickening scrape, and the groan of metal meeting metal. Norbert watched the event—which lasted, maybe, three seconds—unfold as though frame-by-frame, wondering wordlessly out of the purest curiosity how the whole thing would turn out. It was a sensation he had numbed through combat.

Norbert killed his engine and leapt down from his truck. "You okay?"

The man stood. He counted his appendages.

"Yes," he said. "I think so. I wasn't going very fast."

"What's your name, fella?" asked Norbert.

"Wilberforce Wendell."

"You just making that up? You don't have to lie to me."

"No. That's my name."

"You drunk, Wilberforce?"

"Not yet."

"I'm sorry you went down like that," said Norbert. "But you seem to be okay."

"So it seems," said Wilberforce.

"You going to Tessy's?"

"That was my intent."

"Why don't I buy you a drink," said Norbert.

"That seems reasonable," said Wilberforce, "since after all, this incident is your fault."

"Whaddya mean?"

"You were clearly over the double line."

"You slid on the ice. I was engaging in evasive maneuvers."

Wilberforce stared at Norbert. Norbert stared back.

Conversational cul-de-sac.

In the dark, wood-paneled confines of Tessy's bar and restaurant, Norbert and Wilberforce sat facing each other in a booth against the wall. They ordered whiskeys with beer chasers and asked for menus.

The men waded cautiously into conversation: Norbert waiting to see if this Vespa enthusiast harbored a litigious take on how their traffic incident had just transpired. He watched closely for a spontaneous case of whiplash and/ or back spasms to develop. For his part, Wilberforce gauged whether the Ford's driver thought he was getting a new pickup truck out of the deal.

"So what's your story, Wil—?"

"Wilberforce. Wilberforce Wendell."

"You look pretty put-together, Wilberforce. Khaki pants, loafers with little tassels, pullover fleece. What's that, Polo?"

"Lands End."

"You look like you should be at a charity golf tournament. What brings you barreling ass over tea kettle into Tessy's on a Sunday afternoon?"

Wilberforce was silent for a long moment. So long, that Norbert thought he either hadn't heard, or was choosing to ignore, the question. Then finally—

"Lost love," said Wilberforce.

"Oh. Huh. Sorry to hear that." Norbert wasn't sure where to go from there, so he offered, "What was her name?"

"The Catholic Church."

"What do you mean?" laughed Norbert. "Wait a minute . . . You were a priest?"

Wilberforce raised his eyebrows.

"You're shitting me." Norbert tossed back his whiskey. "What happened?"

"I fell in love. Shattered my vows. Left in disgrace. Yada, yada. My autobiography might be titled: *How to Ruin Your Life in Three Easy Steps* by Wilberforce Wendell."

Norbert leaned back against the booth's shiny red cushion. He sipped his beer, letting Wilberforce ponder his fall from grace. Wilberforce read instantly what Norbert was thinking.

"It was a woman," said Wilberforce. "I ran off with my church secretary, Margaret. She was *all* woman. It was scandalous, but not *that* scandalous."

"I'm relieved to hear that."

"I figured you would be."

The waitress returned. Norbert ordered what he always ate at restaurants: chicken fingers and fries. "That's on the kiddie's menu," Arlene would say, "between tater tots and peanut butter and jelly sandwiches."

"What do you care?" Norbert would respond. "All you ever order are yard clippings slathered in fat-free vinaigrette. Mind your own plate."

"You're a child."

Wilberforce ordered a Rueben once the waitress assured him that the corned beef would be sliced paper-thin and would not arrive in thick slabs that he could not tear with his teeth, thus appearing foolish. He asked for his Russian dressing on the side so he could dip his sandwich. He also ordered a Bloody Mary.

"A most blasphemous name for a beverage that has become an innocuous part of the national vernacular," said Wilberforce.

"Indeed," Norbert agreed. "That will total three drinks in front of you."

Wilberforce slurped down the whiskey; pounded the beer; smiled.

Norbert filled another protracted silence by closely scrutinizing the recurring patterns in the faux wood grain of the wall paneling. Wilberforce was not at all uncomfortable with the absence of conversation.

"So where is your lady friend this afternoon?" said Norbert.

"She left me."

"Why?"

"I cheated on her."

Wilberforce's Bloody Mary arrived with a tall leafy vegetable protruding from it, which he quickly discarded. He offered Norbert the tip of his straw.

"You want a sip?"

"No thanks," said Norbert. "I don't drink through straws. I decided long ago that no beverage is improved by being delivered though a plastic tube."

Wilberforce craned awkwardly to get a better view of the young waitress's undulating black stretch pants as she returned to the kitchen.

"When did this happen?"

"What's that now?" said Wilberforce.

"When did your lady friend leave you?"

"Margaret. A week ago Saturday. Oh, it was a trifle. It was meaningless. She was a waitress at Ruby Tuesday's. I arrived for happy hour and stayed till after hours. She was a grad student in comparative religion. She found me fascinating and I found her . . . well, needless to say, the electricity was instant. We went to her small, second-floor apartment and made foggy love on her Ikea couch. It was uncomfortably exhilarating. After, as a memento, I took one of the buttons from her uniform suspenders. It was foolish but I am an aging fool. It was the button that did me in. Margaret found it, and though I could have explained it away easily enough, the last twenty years have been a lie so I told her the truth. She slapped me and took my car. I presume I'm still responsible for the payments. I'm fortunate I still had the Vespa—a summertime indulgence."

"Have you tried to contact her?"

"I know where she is, she's with her mother in Denver. The truth is I don't care to contact her. From here on out I will move forward, not back. Margaret was the key that freed my lock, so to speak. The morning dewdrop that spread open my flowering concupiscence, if you'll allow me to wax poetic."

"You're allowed," said Norbert.

"She was a moment and that moment has passed. My awakened libido has come as quite a shock. I can't seem to get enough. My appetite now is, well . . . it's impossible to satisfy. This is all quite new to me, and I'm very much in the process of discovering how to harness it. It's actually more depressing than you might expect. To complicate matters, it appears I have a certain—at the risk of sounding conceited—primal magnetism."

Wilberforce noticed the waitress returning with their lunches. He winked at Norbert and whispered, "Observe . . . "

"Hello," said Wilberforce.

"Hi," said the waitress.

"That's a lovely tattoo on the inside of your wrist."

"It's Tibetan. From Tibet."

"I believe it means strong flower," said Wilberforce. "Is that correct?"

"I don't really know."

"Are you from Tibet?" asked Wilberforce.

The waitress giggled. "No. I just thought it looked cool in the tattoo parlor."

"Well, I think it's gorgeous," said Wilberforce, boldly seizing her wrist, tracing the graphic with his thumb. "I think that anyone who wears this must have a wise and ancient soul."

"My parents hate it."

"You don't live their lives, kitten. It's only fair they don't presume to live yours."

The waitress smiled and twisted a strand of her brown hair around an index finger. She bounced her right heel. "You guys need another round?"

"Hm," said Wilberforce, feigning indecision. "Tempting."

"On the house," said the waitress.

"Delightful!"

The waitress wandered halfway back to the kitchen then stopped abruptly and turned toward the bar.

"That's amazing," said Norbert. "She just forgot where she was going."

Wilberforce put his head in his hands, "Oh! The flesh is weak. I don't know what possesses me. Surely dark forces are in league against me. But I deserve bad things."

"Bad things? That girl could be your daughter. She's hot."

"Waitresses are my temptation, Norbert. There have been so many."

"So many?"

"There are so many restaurants. Everywhere you turn: Applebee's, Bennigan's, Friendly's, Pizzeria Uno, Outback Steakhouse, TGI Friday's, Cracker Barrel—that sober, corporate approximation of hillbillyness—and, of course, Ruby Tuesday's. The list goes on. Every new town thick with an identical grove of formulaic eateries, each laden with the heavy fruit of young, voluptuous, bright-faced waitstaff eager to be plucked. Forgive me, Lord."

Wilberforce took a moment to compose himself. With a paper napkin from the dispenser on the table he dabbed a bit of moisture from his forehead. He swabbed some snot from his nose.

Norbert leaned in toward the center of the table, in a whisper he said, "Are you telling me that you've been traveling around, via Vespa, banging waitresses?"

"Dozens of them. From destinations large and small. Wives and schoolgirls and everything in between. I have coveted. I have made a graven image of the Girl in the Apron. The saucy server with her pad and pen and sensible footwear. Oh! I am Lucifer himself! A fallen angel! *The Road to Ruin* by Wilberforce Wendell."

"Here are your whiskeys," said the waitress. "Can I clear away any of this stuff?"

"What is your name, sweet seraph?" said Wilberforce, quickly composing himself.

"Mindi."

"Mindi, you have a face that would make the monks climb down from Shangri-la."

"Thanks."

"Yes, Mindi," said Wilberforce, "you may clear away these empty glasses."

Wilberforce took an ambitious bite of his corned beef sandwich. "Bless your heart," he said as he chewed. "This corned beef *is* sliced thin."

Mindi smiled and exited with an armload of glassware as Wilberforce wiped his mouth with another paper napkin. "But enough about me, Norbert. Tell me something about yourself. Something sui generis."

"What's that mean?"

"Unique. Something original. In Latin it translates to *of its own kind*."

"Hm, okay," said Norbert. "Well, I once left a trucker's dump in one of Saddam's solid-gold shitters."

Wilberforce liked that. He burst out with a big belly laugh that made his cheeks turn red and caused the thin veins in his nose to darken.

"Why were you over there? Can I presume you were serving the nation? You don't strike me as an embedded reporter. Or a contractor, for that matter."

"I was in the Guard. Three tours."

Wilberforce nodded solemnly. "How long have you been home?"

"A year and a month. Officially."

"Miss shooting at things?"

"I do," Norbert smiled. "Very much. And blowing shit up, of course."

"Where were you?"

"Afghanistan. Iraq. All around in Iraq."

"Did you jump from airplanes, Norbert?"

"Not in combat, but it was part of my training. I highly recommend it."

"Yes. Isn't it thrilling?"

"Were you in service, too?"

"No."

Wilberforce told Norbert that after he graduated seminary from the University of Notre Dame, he worked in many parishes and in orphanages and had also spent three missionary years spreading the gospel and tending to the sick and hungry in The Federated States of Micronesia, mostly in the state of Yap. He told Norbert stories about exploring ancient passageways in ocean kayaks, base jumping, and scurrying up mangrove trees with bare feet. He was also a certified diver and said that he had swum with manta rays in the Gufnuw Channel and in Tamil Harbor.

Norbert brooded as he listened, sipping his whiskey. This did not go unnoticed by Wilberforce, who gradually became self-conscious of the sound of his own voice.

"I'm rambling again," said Wilberforce, "monopolizing the conversation. Right about now, Margaret would spear her bony elbow under my rib cage and tell me to shut up."

"I'm sorry," said Norbert. "My mind is somewhere else."

"Anything you want to talk about? I did used to listen for a living."

Norbert put a cigarette in his mouth then remembered it was against the law to light it. "My girl left me this morning."

"Oh, I'm sorry. Did she take your dog and best shotgun with her?"

"Huh?"

"Just a joke. Not a good one, either. I listen to a lot of country-western music."

"Oh," said Norbert. "That's too bad."

. "Please do go on."

"Well, there ain't much else to it. She found Jesus, then she fell for a guy who works for him. The hell of it is, I was going to propose to her in a week. On Valentine's Day."

"Were you together long?"

"Since high school."

"I'm sorry, Norbert."

"Aren't you going to tell me it's all part of God's grand plan for each of us? Something like that? Isn't that what they train you to say?"

"I don't talk like that."

Norbert and Wilberforce drank sixteen glasses of beer between them before the young waitress ushered them out the door, slipping a scrap of paper into Wilberforce's palm. Wilberforce invited Norbert to stay and chat some more in his room at the Robin Hood Motor Court off Route 9N.

"I've got a bottle of Dewar's," he said. "Unopened."

"I'd invite you to my place," said Norbert, "but she took all my chairs."

Norbert and Wilberforce paused to look at the mangled Vespa in the bed of the pickup.

They fell over laughing.

As soon as they entered Room 3, Wilberforce clicked on the clock/radio, engaging immediately with the country-western song wafting from its rattling speaker, improvising his own lyrics for the refrain. He told Norbert he liked music that "told a story," then went into the bathroom to take a leak.

Norbert took stock of the room. He had driven past the Robin Hood Motor Court dozens, maybe hundreds, of times but had never experienced the pleasure of standing inside one of its rooms. And a pleasure it was. Probably once an ambitious commercial enterprise undertaken by a plucky husband-wife entrepreneurial team in the late '50s or early '60s, thought Norbert. But no one had given it much love since then. It had become another of the nation's outposts of the ill, the depressed, the angry, the criminal, the federally subsidized, and the transient. No lovers communed here during clandestine lunch hours. No newlyweds waylaid here en route to livelier locales. What else can be said? It was an American motor court.

There was a soft, leather overnight bag on the bed nearest the door. One suit coat and two pair of pressed slacks hung in the closet draped over hangers the guests could not steal. There were a few magazines and that day's newspaper, a Milky Way wrapper, and two potato chip bags. On the bed, near the too-flat pillows, Norbert studied a stack of manuscript pages held together with a latticework of rubber bands. The papers were worn around their edges, wrinkled and dog-eared with innumerable yellow sticky notes protruding in all directions, creating an intricate layering effect strangely pleasing to the eye. Norbert read the cover page: *Spinozan Determinism: An Apology for the Pragmatism of Mechanistic Monism in the 21st Century. Wilberforce Wendell, Ph.D. Candidate.*

Norbert could summon not a single specific thought or opinion regarding this discovery. He called into the bathroom, "How long will you stay here, Padre?"

"Just tonight was the plan," said Wilberforce, running the water in the sink. "But now, *sans Vespa* . . . Never in one spot for too long. *Umquam porro.* Ever forward. New places, new adventures." Wilberforce came out of the bathroom rubbing his face with a hand towel. He chuckled, shook his head. "To be perfectly frank, Norbert, I'm in a bit of a rut. I'm waiting for . . . I'm seeking . . . Well, this may sound silly to you, but in my own way I am waiting for divine guidance. I'm looking for a sign."

"From God?" asked Norbert.

"Sure. If He's up for it. I've screwed up again. I'm stuck. I just need Him to give me a nudge."

Norbert poured the Dewar's into a pair of clear plastic cups. He said, "Can I ask you a question relevant to your prior vocation?"

"Ask away."

"What's your take on those stories in the Bible where God speaks face-to-face with regular people?"

"You mean like Job?"

"I don't know that one. Who was Job?"

"Job was a pawn in a bet between God and Satan in a test of true faith," said Wilberforce. "He was a good man who suffered terribly. He wanted to pour out his heart to God, but he was afraid to complain about his circumstances. He wished for death but longed to first bring his case before God. Job was a man who became increasingly exasperated with his friends because, though they wanted the best for him, they kept offering him lousy advice. Job thought he wanted God to answer him, to explain."

"Did he?" asked Norbert. "Did God explain?"

"Sort of."

"God spoke to Job directly?"

"From a whirlwind," said Wilberforce. "He said, 'Who is this that darkeneth counsel by words without knowledge? Gird up now thy loins like a man; for I will demand of thee and answer thou thee.' Something . . . something . . . 'Or who shut up the sea with doors, when it brake forth.' You get the idea."

"God sounds pissed."

"You should read what he said to Job's friends."

"Do you think there's any truth to that?" asked Norbert. "Or is a story like that from the Bible just a metaphor or a parable or whatever?"

"I think it happened. But consider the source. I was a priest."

"Do you think there's anything someone could do today that's big enough to piss God off like that? Annoy Him to such a biblical degree? To, I don't know, goad Him into a direct conversation? Make Him show Himself?"

"A lot has transpired over the past two millennia, and yet, He has remained hidden from us. And though much base evil abounds in the world today, God remains a mystery that takes no earthly form. Then again, in the story Job answers the Lord. 'I have heard of thee by the hearing of the ear: but now mine eyes seeth thee.' So, as far as that goes, under certain circumstances, God does seem willing to reveal himself to man if properly enticed. Who knows? I guess my answer to your question is: *Maybe*."

"What would your pal Spinoza say about it?"

"Huh? Oh, yes. *The Beast*," said Wilberforce in reference to his perpetually incomplete, and ever-growing, doctoral dissertation staring up at him from the bed. "Well, he might have quite a lot to say, actually. But he essentially thought it foolish to believe in a god that interacts with us through something as unimaginative as normal human conversation. No, he believed that all was God. God, or Nature is how he phrased it."

"What's that mean?"

"The concept is rather complicated in its simplicity. He thought it absurd to believe in a God that played a hand in our human affairs, a God that could reciprocate our love for Him. He felt the best way, the *only* way, to connect with the divine was through the ultimate attainment of an intellectual love of God. A sort of melding of conscious-nesses between our individuality and the eternal oneness of all things. Spinoza said that the mind's highest good is the knowledge of God, and the mind's highest virtue is to know God. He said blessedness comes from a certain kind of knowledge, the knowledge of the union that the mind has with the whole of nature."

Norbert took a big gulp of scotch. "Huh."

"Yeah."

"Is that the gist of what you say in that stack of papers over there?"

"That, along with a multitude of other rambling non sequiturs. I may regret knowing the answer, but why are you interested in pissing off God to, as you say, a biblical degree?"

"I'd like to speak with Him," said Norbert. "Face-to-face. *Supposedly* He's done it before. My thinking is: Why not again? Why not me?"

"Well," said Wilberforce, "when you ask: Could a man today do *something big enough*, what exactly do you have in mind?"

"Breaking all Ten Commandments in a week."

"That could do it. I'm not aware of any such precedents."

"I'm off to a running start, too. I already worked today on the whadyacallit?"

"Sabbath."

"Right. Only nine more to go and the week has barely begun. Plus, I've just agreed to drive a buddy's car cross-country where there will be ample opportunities to break the commandments along the way."

"I fear I'm stating the obvious to you," said Wilberforce, "but there are some pretty sketchy commandments. Serious stuff. Working on the Sabbath is an easy one to break. Everybody does it. I assume you know the list gets more difficult."

"Don't assume anything, Padre. I have yet to familiarize myself with the list in its entirety."

Wilberforce retrieved his Bible from the nightstand and opened to Exodus, chapter 20. He parted the book by eye, needing to flip forward only two pages.

"Stealing, adultery, thou shalt not kill," said Wilberforce. "Those are the big three. The trifecta of sin, so to speak. An immoral hat trick."

"Piece of cake."

"Are you married?"

"No."

"Forgive me for asking: Were you called upon to kill in the military?"

Norbert refilled his plastic cup, topped off Wilberforce's. "Why? Does that count?"

"It wouldn't count toward your compression of the mission into one week. Actually, the commandment's proper translation is thou shalt not murder. So, in final judgment, I suppose it boils down to intent."

"I'll leave that to the philosophers," said Norbert. "Like your Italian friend over there."

"Spinoza was Dutch. Portuguese, actually."

"All I know is, when you're over there it's kill or be killed. You kill Hadjis for survival, you kill them to protect your buddies, to protect the guy next to you. You do your job with the tools, assets, and resources you have and you don't question it. You find, engage, and eliminate, then you get the fuck outta Dodge. Sometimes you kill for revenge because the day before they got a few of your guys with a roadside IED. Is that murder? Or is that eliminating a threat?"

"Out of the heart proceed evil thoughts," said Wilberforce, "Murders, adulteries, fornications, thefts, false witness, blasphemies. Book of Matthew. Adultery, murder—those are steep hills to climb in one week when you're unmarried and, presumably, not a psychopath."

"Where there's a will there's a way."

Wilberforce handed the Bible to Norbert along with a pad of Robin Hood Motor Court stationery and the pen from his front pants pocket.

"What kind of pen is this?" asked Norbert.

"A Fisher Space Pen AG-7."

Norbert shook the pen.

"Not necessary. It has a nitrogen compressed-ink cartridge."

"Oh, the upside-down astronaut pen?"

Wilberforce tapped his finger on the writing tablet. "Number one through ten. Show me how you would set out to break each of them?"

Norbert went straight to work, laboring over each commandment while Wilberforce sipped his scotch and listened to the country-western music emanating from the motel's clock/radio. When Norbert was finished, Wilberforce reviewed the list.

"What about number six?" said Wilberforce. "Murder. You left it blank."

"Yeah, you make a good point about that one. I'm not really a psychopath, to my knowledge. No question, that one's a thinker. I figure I'll just leave it open-ended for now."

"Allow providence to play its part."

"Something like that."

"Why would you endeavor to do this, Norbert? Why would you choose to sin so completely? Whatever your misgivings with God, there is certainly a better outlet for your energies. Nietzsche wrote that 'he who has a *why* to live for can bear almost any *how*.' So, my only real question for you is: Why?"

Norbert took a drink. "Are you familiar with the term Angel Flight?"

"No."

"When I was at Walter Reed, whenever a soldier lost his fight, the entire hospital staff would line up as they moved his body to the roof to be choppered away. It was quite a thing. The good part was, it didn't happen often. If a soldier was going to die it was most likely going to happen in a theater field hospital. If he made it out of there, he had a good shot. Of course, some guys never even made it to the field hospital. Some guys, in an instant, were just turned into a mound of red hamburger, caked in sand. Nothing left to put back together. Guys like my pal, Sully.

"When I first started seeing them line up for those Angel Flights I thought, that's nice. That's a nice tribute. But after a while, I started to think about that name: Angel Flight. *Angel*. It really started to irk me. I thought, where was this guy's fucking angel when he could've really used one? Or were they implying that he's flying off to become an angel himself? Regardless, I thought it strange to equate either situation—him getting wounded by some chanting raghead, or him getting choppered off the hospital's roof to be laid into a box—with some cartoon Christmas tree ornament with feathered wings and a golden circle suspended over its head. The two images could not be more disconnected in my mind. And as time went on, I started to get more and more pissed off about it until finally I said something to one of the nurses who passed it along to one of the doctors who immediately prescribed something to help me sleep.

"So, you ask me why I want to break the Ten Commandments? My first answer is because I don't think it matters. I don't think God exists, and it would be an interesting diversion on a long road trip. And now that I have fully reacquaint myself with his big list of laws, I'm even more convinced that God and his big list are creations of man—very much products of their day. I mean, look at these. These are the words of an omniscient, omnipotent deity unfettered by space and time? Given His one, big opportunity to roll out His rules for all mankind to live a good and decent life, this is what He delivers? Take number ten here for instance: 'Thou shalt not covet thy neighbor's house, thou shalt not covet thy neighbor's wife, nor his manservant, nor his maidservant, nor his ox, nor his ass, nor anything that is thy neighbor's.' *Covet thy maidservant?* God thinks we should keep slaves? Or does that just refer to paid help? He sets out from the get-go to define certain people as inherently inferior to others? There's a hierarchy of human worth established by the apparent force that created all humanity in His own image? Does that mean that, since abolishing slavery in America, we've blasphemously evolved past what is morally correct? An a priori caste system ordained by God Himself? God, who supposedly knows all and sees forever into the past and future, thinks it's important to lay down the basic etiquette concerning my jealousy over my neighbor's cattle and livestock? How many neighbors have you had in your life that owned a donkey? I live in upstate New York, not ancient Judea. The entire concept of *New York* didn't even exist when this was written. But then, of course, that's exactly the point, isn't it? This language and this list don't exactly evince the timeless wisdom one would expect from the being that created all the heavens and the Earth. How come there's nothing on this list about the Internet, or dark matter and dark energy, or nuclear holocaust or oil or, I don't know, Wal-Mart?

"But my second answer is: Hey, maybe I'm wrong. Maybe I'm the idiot. Wouldn't be the first time. Maybe there *is* an actual Cloud Man who sits on His big Cloud Throne scratching at His thick, snowy beard watching everything and everyone all the time, listening to our prayers and curses and electing where and when to meddle in our affairs, commando style. So, on the outside chance that the Cloud Man exists, the benevolent God of this Bible, I'm perfectly willing to risk his wrath in an all-out effort to provoke his attention."

"There is ample precedent for upsetting God to the point of exposing himself to us," said Wilberforce. "I'm reminded of the second Psalm, 'Then shall He speak unto them in his wrath, and vex them in his sore displeasure.' But again, Norbert: *Why?* What's so important about getting His attention? Even, as you admit, you're so skeptical that He exists in the first place?"

"Because if I'm wrong, and a God that converses with humans can and does exist, then I have a question for Him."

"Which is?" asked Wilberforce.

"That's a private matter. I reserve it for that unique encounter, should it occur."

"Fair enough. But let me understand, essentially you don't believe in God, but you want to speak with Him face-to-face?"

"Correct," said Norbert. "And that's not just the Dewar's talking. Because, see, follow my thinking here, just because I'm dubious of God, that doesn't mean he doesn't exist. I'm not the final authority on the matter. It's not necessarily what *is*, it's only what I *believe*."

"Well," said Wilberforce, "you might have a problem there. By my estimation that's a glitch in your plan. God is about faith. At least that's what I've been taught. Faith equals God. No faith, no God. 'Blessed are those who have *not* seen and have believed.' John 20:39. Although, on the other side of the argument, the paleontologist de Chardin once said that "matter is spirit moving slowly enough to be seen.' So perhaps God could manifest and have a chat, if He so chose. In this world, there is much known but much more that remains unknown. Such is my willing allure toward the mysteries of faith."

Norbert's wheels turned. Wilberforce sipped his scotch. After a protracted silence, Norbert said, "Come along."

"Huh?"

"Come with me. Consider yourself my spiritual adviser. My intermediary with the Big Man Himself. Free trip to California. You said it yourself: Uptown porthole."

"Umquam porro."

"Right. Ever forward. New places, new adventures. California is a great place for second-story men like you and me. And let's not forget, there are a lot of chain restaurants along the road. A lot of waitresses."

"Indeed there are," said Wilberforce, intrigued.

"You believe in God. I mean, *really* believe. If you were to ride shotgun with me in something so taboo to your faith, wouldn't He have to take double notice? Maybe then you'd get that nudge from Him you've been hoping for."

"I'm tempted," said Wilberforce, "I'm always up for a new adventure, but not one that could potentially conclude in a state penitentiary. I have a preternatural aversion to our culture of corrections."

"We'll have a rule: stay along for the ride for as long as you feel comfortable. You're free to walk away whenever you like. I'll even pay to have your Vespa repaired. We'll throw it in the trunk."

"That seems like overkill. The Vespa is fully insured. Though Margaret no doubt confiscated the paperwork . . . "

Wilberforce's thought trailed off. Again, he studied Norbert's list. "These aren't so terrible," he said.

"Highly doable."

"Hm. Break all Ten Commandments."

"Yep."

"In a week."

"One week."

"To provoke God's attention and force him into a conversation, just like the men in the Bible did."

"Correct."

"So that you, a young veteran, might ask Him a personal question. And that I, His former servant, might trouble Him for a gentle push along the proper path."

"That's the plan," said Norbert. "What do you think?"

"'The thing about smart people is that they seem like crazy people to dumb people.' That's a quote from one of my favorite wits: Anonymous. If it's God's attention that's sought, I think of the Third Psalm which reads: 'I cried unto the Lord with my voice and he heard me out of his holy will.'" Wilberforce polished off his scotch. "Here's what I think. I'll agree to accompany you on one condition. After you have broken the commandments, you must seek absolution from the Church."

"I just learned about that. Isn't that something to do with the Lamb of God?"

"You must feel truly sorry for what you have done and ask forgiveness for the sins you've committed. You must recognize the horror of your sins and confess it with a truly repentant heart. When you do, the blood of Jesus washes you clean and saves you from condemnation."

"That's it?"

"What do you mean *that's it?*"

"All I need to do is ask and I'm forgiven—regardless of the sins I've committed?"

"Technically that's how it works, said Wilberforce, "But

you must feel true remorse in your heart. If you would agree to seek absolution at the end of the week, I could justify my decision to travel with you. 'For by your words you will be justified, and by your words you will be condemned.' Matthew. Yes, my heart tells me I could live with that."

Norbert extended his hand. "Padre, that's a deal."

Wilberforce grasped Norbert's hand and shook it. "There's a bargain made."

The two men refilled their cups with scotch, stood to toast.

"To a new adventure," said Norbert.

"A hadj!" said Wilberforce.

"What's that?"

"An adventure."

"To the unknown," said Norbert.

"To the known that we have yet to discover," said Wilberforce. "Jacta alea est, said Caesar as he crossed the Rubicon in 49 B.C. *The die is cast*."

Wilberforce went over to his bag and removed his long, tribal ritual knife.

"But first, we shall become blood brothers."

"Really?" said Norbert, coughing on his scotch.

"No. I'm just drunk. This was a gift I shipped home from Micronesia. Does a real number on bamboo. 'In this world goodness is destined to be defeated. But a man must go down fighting! That is the victory. To do anything less is to be less of a man.'"

"That the Book of Matthew again?" asked Norbert.

"Walker Percy. *The Moviegoer*. What kind of vehicle are you delivering?"

"A Cadillac."

"Oh, very nice."

"I'll pick you up here tomorrow morning at nine. 'Let us indulge our own lunacy.' That's Chagall. The painter."

"Yeah, I know who Chagall is," said Norbert. "You sure bandy a lot of quotes."

"I don't work to memorize them, either. They just cling to my brain like wet toilet paper."

"Does it concern you that, after a while, it grows quite tiresome?"

"No. That does not concern me."

Norbert whistled. "Goddamn that's a big knife." Norbert tore out Exodus, Chapter 20 from the Bible Wilberforce had handed him.

Wilberforce shrieked!

"What's wrong?" said Norbert. "It's just a motel Bible."

"No," said Wilberforce, "it's not. That's my personal Bible. An ordination gift from my father."

The thin paper crinkled as Norbert continued to fold it, sheepishly.

"Also, before you leave," said Wilberforce, "just one more thing."

"What's that?"

"May I please have my astronaut pen back?"

6

Back in The Halo, Elton signed in as the administrator of his website's message board. What's this, thought Elton? As he read the new post, he could feel the heat creeping up his neck like the devil's walking fingers. It read:

> I think this website is essentially a good thing, but you always take everything too far. Where do you get these pictures, anyway? Are you following these guys? I find your stalker-like approach and your extreme dogma to be at best, boring, and at worst, creepy. It comes off as *holier than thou*. You God-nuts, you think you're right about everything. Well here's a flash: you don't have to be an inflexible asshole to be a moral person. Whoever hosts this website is a kook. Are you ever wrong about anything?

Elton was hot.

He cracked his knuckles, zipped three times around The Halo (for the Holy Trinity), and settled himself in front of the keyboard. His slender fingers pumped like pistons atop the clacking keys. It was as though his digits were unconscious conduits for the divine:

> What a strange question. What a strange, pagan question. I am right—*all the time*—because I have accepted Jesus Christ, who died for our sins at Calvary, as my Lord and Savior. What a strange, silly question, posed by an obvious fornicator and lover of meanies.

From where I sit at the right hand of the Father, you strike me as someone who worships false idols. "Do not turn to idols, nor make for yourself molded gods: I am the Lord your God." (Leviticus 19:4) "Woe unto him that calls evil good and good evil," (Isaiah 5:20). I am right because I live by the One True Law, God's law: the Ten Commandments. "Those who disobey God's laws hate him and those who hate God love death." (Proverbs 8:36) Just as Jesus said in John 7:19, "Did not Moses give you the law, yet none of you keeps the law." Maybe you believe *you* are right because you direct your faith into the puny contrivances of man, things like the Constitution and science. But in First John 2:15, God said, "Do not love the world, or the things in the world. If anyone loves the world, the love of the Father is not in him."

I could spend all night highlighting the tragic errors in your secular thinking, setting you on the One True Path to righteousness. But my mother has my supper waiting and it would be a sin to let it get cold.

Elton powered off his computer, rose from his chair, and drew a crucifix before him in the air. He exited The Halo to the other side of the basement where a long, red, leather, Everlast heavy-training bag hung from a floor joist by a thick steel chain and swivel.

Elton stood before the bag for a long moment, motionless and silent. He snapped up the wooden baseball bat leaning against the cinderblock wall, twisting his hands methodically into the smooth handle. Elton swung the bat with all his strength against the side of the bag. With excellent form, Elton stepped into each swing, always remembering to shift his weight from his back foot to his front. Pop! Pop! Pop! The bat's barrel reported against the stiff leather. Elton swung and swung and swung until his shoulders burned and his hair was soaked with sweat. When he was finished, he dropped the bat. It echoed through the basement as it bounced atop the concrete floor.

Elton bent forward, resting his palms just above his kneecaps. He took forty deep, heavy, satisfying breaths for Moses, who, in Exodus 34:28, "Was there with the Lord forty days and forty nights; he did neither eat bread, nor drink water. And he wrote upon the tables the words of the covenant, the Ten Commandments."

AND....

"And time is not kind to those who wait."
—M.L. Liebler
Wide Awake In Someone Else's Dream

7

Wilberforce was still asleep Monday morning when Norbert knocked on the door of Room 3 at the Robin Hood Motor Court. And he was not alone.

Norbert had to bang several times with escalating vigor to rouse him. When the door finally swung open Norbert was greeted by Mindi, the young waitress from Tessy's, so fond of Tibet. She answered the door, her hair matted and tangled, wearing one of Wilberforce's pullover golf shirts with a tiny equestrian embroidered over the left nipple—and nothing else. There was a pizza box on the chair by the door with three cold, stiff slices left inside. Norbert consumed one while watching Mindi circle the room gathering her clothes. She spent several minutes in the bathroom with Wilberforce, giggling, before disembarking in her Japanese hybrid compact.

Wilberforce insisted on showering, devouring another unscheduled block of time. He was under the water so long that at one point Norbert hollered, "I hope the Robin Hood has a hundred-gallon water heater!" But Wilberforce did not hear him over the force of the pulsating showerhead and the cowboy ballad he was belting out with zestful sincerity. After drying, he applied a liberal coating of talcum and musk—far too liberal, in Norbert's opinion, for the close quarters of the Ford. And he spent an uncomfortable amount of time fussing with his hair.

"Do you think I should brush in color, Norbert?"

"I think we should hit the road."

"Margaret told me I look distinguished."

"I think all chicks feel obligated to say that to their man at some point, concerning graying hair, baldness and such."

"'Vanity of vanities. All is vanity! Saith the preacher. Oh, I am wicked. A glutton and a winebibber, a friend to tax collectors and sinners.' Luke."

Outside, Norbert threw Wilberforce's leather bag alongside his own nylon bag inside the open bed of the pickup, bungeed tight against the back of the cab. Also tucked behind the elastic cords was a Styrofoam cooler packed with beer and Coke and salami sandwiches. Mangled and on its side lay Wilberforce's Vespa scooter.

Wilberforce did not want to rumple his pressed slacks and sport coats by rolling or folding them, so Norbert hung them from the back of the bench seat inside the cab. This was not so easily done since Wilberforce could not bring along the hangers bolted into the Robin Hood's closet. Norbert fashioned an impromptu clothes hanger by threading some stiff wire through a length of rubber tubing he found at the bottom of his toolbox. It was a rather nifty solution to a deceptively complex hurdle, he thought. It reminded Norbert once again of how well he might fare if ever cast away on a remote island. All this nonsense took far longer than Norbert had allotted, and they did not get on the road until the noon fire whistle was threatening to sound.

Wilberforce required that his dissertation, The Beast, remain close to his side, so it sat between them on the bench seat. Norbert had purchased the latest Rand McNally road atlas. It was also on the seat when they climbed into the Ford. Wilberforce immediately thumbed through it with his meaty fingers, suggesting adjustments to Norbert's planned route, indicating known restaurant locations along the way in black pencil. When the men reached the top of the long driveway leading out of the Robin Hood Motor Court, Wilberforce pointed, advising Norbert which way to turn. Norbert cringed. This unsolicited navigational gesture did not bode well.

"Listen, Padre." Norbert had settled on calling him Padre. Wilberforce did not roll off the tongue. Also, during their beery Sunday at Tessy's, he had insisted Norbert not call him Wilber, after the inquisitive pig. "You could drop me into the Gobi Desert at midnight and I'd find the nearest Dairy Queen. Without a GPS, I might add. Tuck that map away. I'll holler when—or *if*—I need it."

Norbert handed a photo to Wilberforce.

"What's this?"

"That's me on Saddam's gold shitter."

"Mary and Joseph," said Wilberforce, "that's spectacular."

"One of my rack mates took that picture," said Norbert. "A fella named Philip Philo Phipps. Red-haired Jewish kid from Yuma, Arizona. Built sorta like a scarecrow. He could swallow his dog tag chain and then pull it out through his nose. An Aqua Velva man. I remember he'd wake up with his asadachi and—"

"His what?"

"Morning erection. We had a Japanese-born communications specialist who taught us that. Once we got a hold of that one we wouldn't let it go. Literally. Phipps called his asadachi 'Bird.' He'd say, 'Mornin' Bird.' Then he'd rub one out onto a magazine or postcard or whatever was handy. 'A Bird in the hand is worth two in the bush,' he'd say."

"Sounds like a nice person," said Wilberforce.

"Great guy, Phipps. Hebrew Phipps. He thinks I saved his life. He's out of service now, too. Got a good gig at the Hoover Dam as an agent for the Bureau of Reclamation. Real hot setup. I'm figuring we might link up with him while we're on the road."

"Why do you say Philip Philo Phipps *thinks* you saved his life? Did you or didn't you?"

"Well," said Norbert, "over there things aren't so cut and dried. Maybe I'll tell that story when we're better acquainted. Suffice it to say, most war stories ain't so heroic once you scratch the surface of them. I don't know if you've known many soldiers, but the fact is most of our stories aren't about war at all. Not what people think war is, anyway. One thing about coming back to the civilian world, especially after some time has passed, you wind up rehashing and cursing or blessing those little minutes that take or save lives. It can start to eat away at you if you let it."

Annoyed, Norbert accelerated past a car that was puttering along ahead of them. As they zoomed by, they looked over to discover that the vehicle appeared to be piloted by a nest of gray hair and eight wrinkled knuckles.

"We used to have piles of disposable cameras stacked up from those Any Soldier care packages. There's more pictures in the glove box if you care to see them."

Wilberforce pulled out the envelope and flipped through the photographs. The sky outside the truck was overcast, cold drizzle falling. Much of the slush had frozen overnight into a brittle crust. Wilberforce lingered over a picture of a green-eyed Iraqi girl in a burqa. She was about 16, Norbert guessed.

Wilberforce ran his finger along the outline of her face. "On the morning of 9/11 I was preparing my sermon," he said. "At that time I had a parish in Northern Virginia. I wasn't watching the television, so I had no idea what was happening. My telephone rang. It was one of the trustees of the church, a woman in her eighties who never missed a Mass and tithed 15 percent of her fixed income every year. 'You see what them sand niggers are doing to us, Father?' she hollered into the telephone. 'Animals! Lunatics! Truman would never stand for this shit. We should make a parking lot out of that whole Middle East. The whole goddamn kit and caboodle!'"

About two hours later, they wobbled onto the plowed-up gravel lot of Duncan Hines's Fine Used Cars and Auto Salvage Emporium of Utica, New York. A string of red, white, and blue triangular nylon pennants dangled from a thin line flapping in the wind over a row of available used vehicles priced to move. A tall black man, gray at the temples, stepped through the front door of the small office and motioned for Norbert to pull around to the side and park in front of the garage.

Norbert and Wilberforce thumped closed their doors, stretched. The black man exited through the garage, crunching across the lot to greet them.

"You Pete's boy?" asked the man.

"I am," said Norbert.

"You over there with him?"

"I was."

"All right," said the man. He turned and walked toward the rear salvage yard. Dozens of vehicles in various states of disassembly were arranged in a grid that stretched back a few hundred yards. Norbert and Wilberforce followed close behind.

"Who's the other guy?" asked the man without stopping or looking over his shoulder.

"My spiritual adviser," said Norbert.

"He over there, too?"

"No," answered Wilberforce. "I was not"

"All right," said the man.

The man disappeared behind the garage. When Norbert and Wilberforce rounded the corner, he turned to look at them.

"There she is," he said. "1975 Cadillac Eldorado convertible. Four-wheel disc brakes, 500 cubic inches under the hood, 190 horsepower. 24,300 miles. All original."

"It's pink," said Norbert.

"Turbo Hydra-matic, front-wheel drive, power steering."

"It's pink."

"Automatic level control, power windows, power top, AM/FM, 8-track stereo."

"This car," said Norbert, "is pink."

"Pete didn't say it was pink?"

"No."

"All right."

Norbert looked at Wilberforce. Wilberforce shrugged.

The man handed Norbert the keys. "The tank's on 'E.' You're gonna need to fill it up."

"You're Pete's uncle?" asked Norbert.

"Yessir," said the man.

"Your name is Duncan Hines?"

"Since the day my momma named me."

"Well Duncan—"

"Folks call me Cakey."

"Cakey," said Norbert. "Pete never said anything about the car being pink. And that car is . . . *vaginally* pink. That car makes pink look like red. That is a ferociously *pink* car."

"Yessir it is."

"I–*we*–can't drive this thing cross-country."

"Why not?" said Cakey. "I just drove it up from Miami last week. Ain't nothing wrong with it."

"It's pink."

"It's a classic," said Cakey. "Look at that grill. Magnificent."

Norbert looked at Wilberforce again. "You're my spiritual adviser. Advise me."

Wilberforce smiled, "You have to admit, it'd be tough for Him to ignore us in this car. It's a real showstopper."

Norbert and Wilberforce transferred their bags to the trunk of the Caddy. Cakey gave Norbert the Caddy's title and other paperwork inside a stiff, yellow envelope. Norbert handed Cakey the keys to the Ford and Vespa along with $200 of Wilberforce's money as a down payment for the work that needed to be done (coaxed forth by a promise from Norbert of swift reimbursement through his buddy Pete). Cakey asked if they wanted a few beers for the road. After thoughtful consideration they declined, reasoning that the beers might make them sleepy.

En route to the New York State Thruway, Wilberforce reached around his neck and unclasped a long necklace with a pendant dangling from it. He looped it around the rearview mirror where it swung a few times, tapping the windshield, before coming to rest.

"This is my St. Christopher medallion," he said. "Good luck for our trip. Do you mind if I say a prayer?"

"Make it a mission statement, Padre."

"Grant us, O Lord, steady hands and watchful eyes, that no one shall hurt as we pass by. Thou gavest life, we pray no act of ours may take away or mar that gift of Thine. Shelter those, dear Lord, who bear us company, from the evils of fire and all calamity. Teach us to use this convertible Cadillac Eldorado automobile with its turbo hydra-matic for others' needs; nor miss through love of undue speed the beauty of the world; that thus we may with joy and courtesy go on our way. St. Christopher, holy patron of travelers, protect us and lead us safely to our destiny in the golden state of California as we endeavor to break your holy laws in your mercy. Amen."

"Well done," said Norbert.

"Where to first?"

"Syracuse. To break the fifth commandment."

Wilberforce nodded.

They drove along in silence for a while, each man enjoying the playground of his private thoughts.

"Can I ask you a question?" said Wilberforce.

"Shoot."

"Why does Philip Philo Phipps think you saved his life?"

8

In a confessional booth inside St. Peter's Catholic Church in Topeka, Kansas, Elton Berryhill knelt before his confessor, rosary in hand.

The tension between Elton and his priest was apparent. The priest reminded Elton, clearly not for the first time, that it was wholly unnecessary for him to confess every day—once per week would suffice. Elton responded by questioning the priest's credentials and admonishing him for affecting such a cavalier attitude toward the sacraments of penance. Elton also questioned his priest's total devotion to his faith. The priest rolled his eyes. This was well-trodden ground.

"Are you rolling your eyes?" said Elton.

"No," the priest answered.

"I thought I heard you rolling your eyes."

On the sidewalk downtown, Elton encountered a father in his forties standing behind his infant son in a stroller. The man was alternately licking his index finger and swirling it inside a small, silvery bag of nuts. Elton was pleased. He told the man how important it was for fathers to be involved in raising their children, unlike "certain elements" of the population. He praised the man for his commitment to family values. Then the man's gay partner emerged from the boutique they were standing in front of, kissing both his lover and their adopted child on the lips.

Elton stiffened, swallowing a bit of vomit. He reminded them that the Bible is clear: Men shall not lay with men.

"Your deviant lifestyles sicken me," said Elton. "'Adulterers, fornicators and homosexuals have no inheritance in the Kingdom of God.' One Corinthians, chapter six, verse nine. Surely, you and your bastard child will burn howling for mercy in hell, your eyes pecked out indifferently by large ravens."

He bid them good day.

Outside the First National Bank of Topeka, at the center of town, Elton encountered a motley, loosely organized group of students and veterans protesting U.S. military involvement in the Middle East.

"Your hand-scrawled placards are laughable," said Elton, "Like a child's craft project at a summer camp for the retarded."

Elton singled out one of the protestors, a rangy young man with wolfish chin whiskers and a nose hoop. "You, with that foul-smelling hair nest," said Elton. "There are four *r*'s in terrororism." He explained to them that the war on terror is "our generation's crusade, pitting Christianity against the armies of darkness." When one of the protesters, a community college student, told Elton that she doesn't even believe in God, he assured her that her secular humanism would be rewarded with "weeping boils, eternal damnation, and a pox on her children and her children's children."

"That is," said Elton, "if you don't murder them first in your womb after fornicating premaritally and smoking drugs."

Another protestor chimed in. "I'm against the war and I'm pro-choice and I'm a Catholic, just like you."

Elton said, "No you're not."

He bid them good day.

Inside the vault of the First National Bank of Topeka, a husky female bank employee, her hair wound into a painful bun, slid a safe deposit box from the wall. She walked across the vault, the sound of her low, orthopedic heels reverberating loudly off the walls, and laid the box atop a wooden table. She offered a chair to Elton. He seated himself in front of the box. The woman walked away, heels echoing like droplets falling into a pool of water from the ceiling of a cave.

Elton pressed his hands together, closed his eyes tight, and bowed his head, "Our Father, who art in heaven . . ." The prayer complete, Elton opened the box.

Inside were dozens of stacks of $1,000 bills wrapped in bands of brown paper. Elton buried his head inside the safe deposit box, inhaling deeply through his nose.

"Praise Jesus!"

He removed three bills and slid them into his leather wallet, embroidered with the word "Rejoice!" He then slid his wallet into the left front pocket of his crisp, wrinkle-free Haggar slacks and closed the box.

He informed the woman he was finished. She returned to the table, retrieved the box, and replaced it in the wall. She and Elton stood side by side as they each turned their key, securing the box in the wall. Elton put the key into his right front pocket and exited the vault into the lobby to exchange the bills for smaller denominations.

Two hours later, 60 miles east in Kansas City, Missouri, from the driver's seat of his Cutlass Supreme, Elton snapped digital photos of a man purchasing a chicken salad sandwich, a coffee, and a newspaper at a corner deli. Elton photographed the man through a window, seated in a booth, reading the newspaper. Elton photographed the man climbing the steps to his apartment.

9

Norbert had not seen his parents since the weekend he came home from service. The local VFW post had thrown him a community barbecue with hamburgers, coils of boiled pork sausage and good, skinless beef franks. There was a long paper banner hanging inside the pavilion that someone had printed out from a computer and taped together in three sections. It said: "Welcome Home, Cpl. Norbert Sherbert!!!!!" There were also red, white, and blue balloons, three taped to the mailbox by the road, along with a paper plate upon which someone had written, "Party Here!!" with an arrow pointing into the post's newly paved parking lot.

Norbert's aunts and uncles, his one living grandmother, and his cousins who still lived nearby were all in attendance. Some family friends and neighbors came, too. Mrs. Quackenbush, who lived next door to the Sherbert's for many years, was in her eighties and had just lost her husband of more than 60 years. Herb Quackenbush had not been a soldier in the Second World War but rather worked in a factory in Buffalo.

"He was 4-F on account of his eyesight and fallen arches," Mrs. Quackenbush had felt obligated to say on many prior occasions, this being no exception. She saw Norbert's "Welcome Home" party as an excellent occasion to reargue Herb's case. She cornered Norbert once while he tried to sidle up unnoticed to the condiment table to get a bottle of A.1. Steak Sauce for his hamburger.

"It's a terrible thing what's going on over there in the Middle East," said Mrs. Quackenbush. "They've got children blowing themselves up, all in the name of *whatzizface*."

"Muhammad," said Norbert.

"Muhammad."

"Or Allah."

"Mohammed! Allah!" snorted Mrs. Quackenbush. "Can you imagine a little girl blowing herself up for Jesus?"

Mrs. Quackenbush felt Norbert's arm muscles and was pleased. She remarked on the deep creases in his sun-scorched face and said that it was a shame what happened to such a handsome young man as himself. She called him a hero and said that she was proud of him. Norbert noticed that when she said that, his family within earshot refused to look at him. Norbert was used to it. Since returning to the real world, he quickly learned that it was a phenomenon he must grow accustomed to as a soldier or, he supposed, as a cop or fireman—anybody who puts his life on the line for the sake of others. Only strangers call you hero.

"Hero is a strong word for a guy who just wanted to earn money for college," said Norbert. "I didn't sign up to shoot Muslims."

Mrs. Quackenbush didn't seem to notice his remark. She began to explain that her husband had never wanted to remain stateside during the war, it was on account of his poor eyesight and fallen arches. Norbert excused himself by saying someone was waiting on the A.1. sauce.

"Herb Quackenbush was a coward," said Norbert's father when Norbert told him whom he'd been speaking with. Norbert's father was holding court with several friends and relatives while maneuvering around the VFW's propane Char-Grill like an after-hours short-order cook. "Just the thought of Hitler made Herb brown his trousers and run to momma. His mother's brother made a phone call to the draft board and got him that job in Buffalo. Herb worked there till V-J Day and not one day longer. Your grandfather told me all about Herb Quackenbush. There was nothing wrong with his eyesight; he worked a metal press three years for Chrissake. Still had all his fingers."

Norbert's father had enlisted in the Coast Guard during the conflict in Vietnam. He saw no combat, the Vietcong never forming an offensive as far west as the coast of Maine. His father never called the citizens of the nation of Vietnam *Vietnamese*. He called them slopes, gooks, zipperheads, or zips. Norbert's father graduated high school in 1969, and having received a fatal draft number, saw the writing on the wall. "Anything but the infantry" is what Norbert's grandfather told him at the time. Norbert's Grandpa Sherbert had been a nineteen-year-old member of the Band of Brothers—those lean, smooth-faced boys who dropped from airplanes on D-Day and fought all the way to Hitler's house.

There were two things Norbert knew about his grandfather's time in service. When Norbert was twelve years old, his grandfather took him fishing predawn in a boat on Lake George. A frosty fog hovered all around them. As the frigid dawn yawned into warm sunlight, the fog rose, pausing along the tips of the Adirondack pines until the afternoon heat burned it away; "bear's breath" is what Norbert's grandfather called it. The bitter cold cloud upon the lake made Norbert's scrawny frame convulse in involuntary spasms.

"It's cold out here, Grandpa," said Norbert.

"It ain't Bastogne," he answered then cast his line above the glassy water, turning his reel until it clicked.

The other thing Norbert knew about his grandfather's time in service was secondhand knowledge from a reliable source: his grandmother. She told him that Grandpa Sherbert would sometimes wake from nightmares of exploding trees. She confided that to Norbert in a hushed voice several years after her husband's passing.

At his welcome-home barbecue, Norbert's father, Norbert Sherbert Sr., wore an apron draped over his neck that tied in a bow around his paunch. It was orange and sported the Syracuse University logo on a pocket stitched to the chest. As a young handsome veteran, Norbert's father, fresh from service, had audited a couple of painting classes there at night when he and Norbert's mother were first dating. He snapped hundreds of black and white photos of working-class people (that he developed himself in a hall closet he had converted into a darkroom), sketched carelessly with vines of charcoal on large pads of news-print paper, smoked and brooded. He wanted to be an artist. Then Norbert's mother got knocked up with Norbert, so his father took a steady roofing job. For six months he noted everything his boss did wrong then borrowed some money from a relative for tools and a used truck and started his own roofing and siding business. He worked hard and made good money. In the winter he fixed a plow to the front of his truck, loaded a snow blower into the bed, and cleared driveways and sidewalks. Over the years he added new trucks, dependable employees, and eventually built a thriving business. Then, when Norbert was a junior in high school, his father blew out his back and was ordered to bed-rest for three months. It turned out his employees weren't so dependable when the boss was not around. Without him working long hours at the center of each project, his business disintegrated. In four months the Sherbert's were living off their meager savings. By fall of Norbert's senior year they were broke. They sold their two-story ranch and moved into a trailer.

Norbert's father owned Syracuse University hats, casual wear, pennants and, when there used to be money, season football tickets. He cheered for the Orange with a great passion from the threadbare reclining chair at the center of their mobile home. He cheered with the desperate enthusiasm a man exerts on a vicarious life being lived in some parallel universe—a universe he had been barred from entering. A portal missed.

As Norbert's welcome-home barbecue wound to a close that summer day, Norbert's mother pulled up a lawn chair beside him as he sat under the hot sun beside the shade of the freshly painted VFW pavilion.

"We all have a lot to be grateful for, Norbert."

"Yep."

"All things happen for a reason."

"Yep."

"God has a grand plan for each of us."

She placed her hand on Norbert's thigh, gave it a squeeze. It lingered there for a moment until she folded it back into her lap.

"Beans are good," said Norbert.

"I put bacon in them. Your favorite."

Norbert and his mother sat in silence watching parents try to gather their children as they ran around the yard like maniacs just sprung from the booby hatch. They ran circles around the adults and folding card tables and screamed and hollered and threw juice boxes at each other and burped and burst into sobbing fits and peals of laughter and knocked over a garbage can (leaving the mess for someone else to clean up) and generally created a noisy, uneasy atmosphere of chaos that made Norbert tremendously nervous and irritable, those precious cherubs.

Norbert turned down the radio as he steered slowly into the mobile home park. The Sherbert trailer was set back from a frozen patch of pea gravel that constituted a driveway. The aluminum exterior was shrouded in a beige skin of thick gauge, low-maintenance vinyl siding with the positive locking mechanism and unique weep hole to prevent water retention. Both were holdovers from Norbert Sr.'s former self-employed appreciation for craftsmanship and top-quality materials. Extending from the corner of the trailer like some futuristic cow-lick was a dish receiver designed to capture satellite television signals.

Norbert killed the Caddy's engine and turned to Wilberforce. He asked him to get out the list so they could review it before entering.

"Okay," said Wilberforce, "this is the fifth commandment: 'Honor thy father and thy mother that thy days may be long upon the land the LORD thy God giveth thee.' You wrote on your list that you want to tell them they ruined your life. How?"

"They never supported my dream to go away to a big college," said Norbert. "I had the grades, but they never offered me one iota of help. Whenever I mentioned the "c" word it was like I'd just released anthrax into the room. I'm not even talking about financial help—they haven't had a pot to piss in since dad lost his business. I'm saying that not once did they offer advice or so much as a word of encouragement—it was a non-issue. And because of that, I wound up joining the National Guard to earn money for school. That's how I ended up in Iraq. That's why I got wounded. That's why my life is fucked up today. This isn't how things were supposed to be."

"What's your plan?"

"I don't know," said Norbert. "I guess I'm just going to go in there and let 'em have it. Both barrels. That's how I dishonor them, right?"

"The eye that mocks his father, and scorns obedience to his mother, the ravens of the valley will pick it out, and the young eagles will eat it."

"Goddamn, Padre." said Norbert.

"Proverbs."

"How do you remember that shit?"

Wilberforce shrugged. "I forget more quotations than most people will ever memorize."

The Sherberts were not a *shoes off* family; neverthe-less, Wilberforce slipped off his loafers upon entering the main door into the living room. In plain view from the door, Norbert's mother stood at the sink watching her daytime stories on a flickering nine-inch black and white television she had been given as a hand-me-down from her sister shortly after Norbert was born. She was adjusting the aluminum foil-wrapped antennae.

"Norbert!"

"Hi, Mom."

"I don't know what to say. It's been so long, Norbert."

"I know."

"Too long."

Norbert's mother walked toward him, wiping her hands on her slacks. "Let me look at you." She grasped both his forearms.

Wilberforce could not determine if she was pleased or furious. He had a feeling Norbert knew the answer.

"I was just going to fix your father a Harry Burger," she said. "Are you hungry?"

"We are kinda hungry," said Norbert. "Mom, this is my friend Wilberforce."

"Bilver—?"

"Wilberforce. Very pleased to make your acquaintance."

"Were you and Norbert in service together?"

"No," said Wilberforce. "I was in a different service entirely."

Norbert's mother still had firm hold of Norbert's forearms. She looked him in the eyes.

"It's been a very long time."

"Not too long."

"Ten months."

"Not ten months."

"Don't tell me 'not ten months.' I'm your mother. How are you feeling?"

"Good," said Norbert. "Fine. Never better."

"How is Arlene?"

"She's good. You can fire up those burgers. We're not going to stay long."

"If I may ask, what is a Harry Burger?" asked Wilberforce.

"It's named for my Uncle Harry," said Norbert's mother. "He liked his with bacon, lettuce, tomato, onion, and peanut butter on a grilled hard roll, sliced into wedges, like a pizza. Do you take peanut butter on your hamburger, Filbert?"

"I don't see why not."

The toilet flushed. Norbert's father emerged from a small bathroom at the front of the trailer. Norbert Sr. had the television tuned loudly to a station broadcasting black and white documentary footage of a wild-eyed Hitler addressing a frenzied mob in Munich. The television was located at the epicenter of the trailer—its footprint so enormous, Norbert's father had to squeeze past Norbert and Wilberforce to reach his chair.

"Dad, this is Wilberforce."

"Pleasure," said Wilberforce.

Norbert's father looked through the window at the car they had arrived in. He looked at Norbert and Wilberforce then again through the window. He situated himself deep within his easy chair, simultaneously curling his fingers around the universal remote. He did not lower the volume of the television.

"Nice car," he said. "You girls grand marshaling a homosexual pride parade?"

Norbert and Wilberforce lowered themselves onto the floral-patterned couch purchased by Norbert's father at a yard sale as a gift for their twenty-fifth wedding anniversary.

"So," said Norbert Sr., "you need money?"

"No," answered Norbert. "Wilberforce and I are driving out west, to California. I'm going to hook up with Pete from my Guard unit. You remember Pete from school."

"The spook."

The cold meat hissed as Norbert's mother slapped the patties on the frying pan.

"Is there a job out there?" asked Norbert Sr.

"No."

"What's with the pink car?"

"That's Pete's. I'm driving it to him as a favor."

"I guess that makes sense. What's your story, Wilberfart?"

"Wilberforce," said Norbert. "He's coming along as my spiritual adviser."

Norbert's father looked Wilberforce up and down.

"I guess that makes sense, too. Did he come with the car?"

"What does everybody want to drink?" Norbert's mother called from the kitchen, six feet away.

"Scotch," answered Norbert and Wilberforce in tandem.

Norbert's mother searched through a high kitchen cupboard. She came into the living room holding an unopened bottle with a red Christmas bow tied around the neck.

"I don't know scotch. Is this good?"

"That's too good," said Norbert Sr. "Give them the White Label from the shelf over the dryer."

"I don't know who drinks scotch with Harry Burgers," she mumbled.

Norbert's father stared intently into the television as Hitler raged. Amidst the sizzle and warm fragrance of frying beef, the three men sat transfixed by the flickering images of the charismatic, but doomed, National Socialist.

Norbert's mother entered with the hamburgers, White Label and glasses balanced on a wooden tray. There was no coffee table, so Norbert unfolded TV trays from behind the couch. His mother served the food as Norbert poured the drinks. Wilberforce picked up one of the tri-angular-shaped hamburger quarters and studied it.

"Delightful." He popped it in his mouth, smiling as he chewed.

"Have a seat, Mom," said Norbert. "I want to say something to you both."

"Let me just straighten up in the kitchen first. I need to find Mr. Creepers so he can say hello."

Norbert's mother disappeared around the corner of the kitchen cabinetry into the rear of the trailer. Mr. Creepers was the Sherbert's longtime family cat of indeterminate age. He was an ever-present fixture in the Sherbert house, then trailer—always lurking under some piece of furniture, snoozing in a chair or centered in a stripe of midafternoon sunlight cast across the indoor-outdoor carpeting. Norbert's mother often wondered aloud, "Where's Mr. Creepers" or would interpret Mr. Creepers's featureless stares into the middle distance as insights such as, "I don't think Mr. Creepers likes that," or, "I think Mr. Creepers is hungry." When Mr. Creepers randomly deposited steaming lumps of yellow vomit throughout the trailer, she would suggest, "Mr. Creepers must be upset with his dry food," even though it was the only brand he'd been fed each morning and evening of his feline life. Mr. Creepers had come to live with the Sherbert's after being tossed onto their yard through the passenger window of a speeding car while Norbert was out front twisting and untwisting in a tire swing.

Wilberforce gobbled down the last triangular quarter of his Harry Burger. With his index finger, he scooped peanut butter residuals from behind his upper molars. He could not help but notice a plaque prominently displayed on a shelf filled with trophies. It read: New York State High School Football Champions, 1969. Behind the trophies rested a shadowbox containing military medals pinned to a field of deep blue velvet.

Norbert's father, his documentary having ended, scanned the channels for fresh stimuli.

Norbert's mother returned to the living room empty

handed, Mr. Creepers eluding her once again. She sat on a metal folding chair beside Norbert's father.

"All right, Norbert," she said. "What are we talking about? Where's Arlene? Why isn't she with you?"

So far, this visit was not progressing as hoped. Norbert had imagined himself taking immediate command of the conversation, setting the tone. He considered changing tack, not responding, saying nothing at all until he was good and ready. How might that go over? Simply standing up and—what? *Walking out? Driving away? Beginning his trip to California?* In films, such actions were profound, mysterious. But Wilberforce would certainly spoil this mystifying egress. Bewildered, he would no doubt remain seated on the floral couch, perhaps thinking Norbert had gone to retrieve something from the car. He would not, could not, follow Norbert's lead without some verbal prompting. They simply had not known each other long enough to form spontaneous wordless confederacies.

Norbert Sr. couldn't restrain from verbalizing the similarities between Norbert's love life and his other failures, such as the high school state championship football game in the Carrier Dome where Norbert had nearly scored on the game-ending punt, but was tackled an inch from the end zone. His father told Norbert he still, after all these years, couldn't get a tank of gas or buy a six-pack of beer in town without some asshole reminding him that it was his son who lost them that game.

"I guess now I'd do an even lousier job returning that punt, wouldn't I?" said Norbert to his father.

His father looked at him. "Not by much."

Norbert had had enough. He was ready to break the fifth commandment. He stood, crossed to the bookshelf, moved aside his father's trophies and took down his medals. He turned to face his parents.

But the words would not come.

Norbert stared at his father, who looked at the television. He couldn't do it. The words simply would not come. After a long moment, his lurking posture grew more conspicuous to his parents.

"What is it, Norbert?" asked his mother. "Is there something you want to say? Where on earth is Arlene?"

It was at this precise moment that Mr. Creepers staggered into the center of the family room and died. He made several unsettling gurgling noises (similar to the sucking sound when the toilet water has disappeared at the end of a flush), shuffled sideways a few feet, flopped over like a fat book and expired. The room was quiet for a long moment—no one knew quite what to make of it. Norbert's mother went to Mr. Creepers.

"Mr. Creepers?" she sang. She turned to Norbert Sr. "Could he be sleeping?"

"He's sleeping all right," announced Norbert Sr. as he returned to flipping through the channels on his gargantuan television.

Mrs. Sherbert wrapped the cat in a table linen from the cedar chest while Norbert dug a hole in the backyard with a shiny new spade he found hanging in the small, corrugated tin shed. Norbert enjoyed stabbing a spade down into real New York soil instead of sand that keeps caving in on all sides. He had said many times under the boiling sun that digging a foxhole in the desert is like bailing out the Titanic with a fucking coffee cup. The snow was slushy and it was difficult getting the spade down through the top layer of frozen earth, but Norbert managed and didn't ask for anyone's help.

After they tucked Mr. Creepers down into the hole, everyone stood blankly for a few minutes wondering if the moment required more, as the daytime talk show panels refer to it, *closure*. Norbert didn't think it was right to simply start turning dirt onto the little guy, and he could tell by his mother's darting eyes that she felt the same. He encouraged Wilberforce to say a few words. Wilberforce very kindly offered a nice prayer that seemed to lift everyone's spirits. In the extemporaneous blessing, Wilberforce said that, although he did not know Mr. Creepers personally, he had cohabitated with cats in the past (because no one really *owns* a cat) and was familiar with their independent natures and regal dispositions. He suggested that the Kingdom of Heaven would be the ideal place for a fat old feline, stuck in his ways, to while away those infinite rays of midafternoon sunshine provided in the Ever After. That would have been a nice visual to end on, Norbert thought, but true to form, his father chose to conclude the ceremony by saying: "Someone threw that cat on our front yard, we fed him and picked his turds out of a box of sand for twenty years, then buried him in the backyard."

With that, he stalked back into the house to find his chair. This particularly upset Norbert's mother. After Norbert's father disappeared through the sliding glass door, she turned to Wilberforce and said, "Not once has that man picked a turd out of anything."

And that was it. Norbert and Wilberforce left. Back on the road. Norbert had failed to strike the fifth commandment off his list. Maybe breaking all Ten Commandments in a week, thought Norbert as he motored back toward the New York State Thruway, isn't going to be so easy after all.

Norbert and Wilberforce didn't have much to say to one another once they resumed heading west on the thruway. Norbert's shadowbox of medals lay on the seat between them, atop The Beast. Norbert tried to remember some good times he had enjoyed with Mr. Creepers but couldn't recall any. He was just a cat, a marginal pet at best, and had lived far too long in the first place. The car radio was clicked off. It was dead quiet inside the sumptuous interior of the Caddy till just about Buffalo. Norbert, driving, cracked his window, lit up and blew a thin rope of smoke. It vanished at 80 mph.

"You know it's not good to smoke," said Wilberforce.

"Not convinced. I'm waiting to see more research."

"Why does Philip Philo Phipps think you saved his life?"

"Further down the road," said Norbert. "I'm not ready yet to tell that story."

"Why do you smoke if you know it's bad for you?"

"I've also set out to break the Ten Commandments. That's bad for me, too, isn't it?"

"Oh, you're still doing that? I wasn't sure," said Wilberforce. "Was I in the bathroom back at Casa de Sherbert when you got around to dishonoring your parents?"

After a silence, Norbert said, "I guess I was afraid."

"Which commandment is next? Or are you giving up?"

"That was just a hiccup back there. I'll get back on track."

"I'll understand if you give up. Breaking all Ten Commandments in a week, trying to provoke God into a conversation, that's hard. Don't be embarrassed if you want to quit."

"I'm not quitting."

"Okay."

"I'm not."

"Just putting it out there."

"Well, put it back in there."

Norbert and Wilberforce swayed silently up and down with the vehicle for a mile or two like a boat at sea. "Front struts are shot," said Norbert.

Several more miles passed in silence.

"I smoke because it goes against the grain," said Norbert. "These days, everybody just wants to know that what they do in their lives is okay by everybody else. No one wants to admit that they're different. They think they do, but in the end, they are terrified of standing out. They're all Fencepost Fuckers. All of them. The world is filled with Fencepost Fuckers."

"Fencepost Fuckers?"

"I have a Theory of Fencepost Fuckers. It states that everything you can dream up already exists. You can't invent something any stranger than what people already do, or have done, no matter how fucked up it may be or you think it is. If I can think it, it's already out there. Ergo, there must be folks who steal away in the dead of night and make love—sweet, sweet love— to fenceposts.

Granted, there's probably a degree of shame and/or guilt on the part of the individual engaging in this unique act. But to prove my point, I contend that they would like nothing more than for someone, anyone, to come along and tell them there's nothing wrong with getting off on fenceposts. So, before long, they seek out a community. They get on the Internet and, lo!—there are people out there just like them. They have websites and message boards and mailing lists. There's even a magazine and a catalog for all your fencepost fucking needs. Then Oprah, or some similar cultural clearinghouse, is alerted through one of her minions out trolling for weird shit to make us stop, think, and act upon. She says, 'Did y'all know folks are out there fuckin' fenceposts? Girl, it ain't for me, but I ain't saying it's wrong.' Then she gets some straight-talkin' psychotherapist to come on her network and say there's nothing wrong with fencepost fucking, that it's perfectly normal. Because see, *normal* is all anybody wants to believe they are. Americans are in the normal business and business is good. Then Madison Avenue and the pub-lishing houses kick into overdrive. Hucksters crawl out into the sun from beneath their rocks with books dashed off in a weekend that are about as clinical as an episode of *Quincy*. The books are gobbled up like kettle corn and shoot up to number one on the best-seller list and then lo again!—the first celebrity reveals his or her lifelong struggle with fencepost fucking. Their book comes out. They promote it on all the daytime talk shows. Create a Fencepost Fucking app. The cable talking-head pundit programs squawk about it for a couple news cycles. The late night talk show hosts make it a punch line in their monologues. Some popular sitcom makes it a storyline. Suddenly, like some unstoppable pop culture tsunami, Fencepost Fuckers aren't just out in the open, they're celebrated. People start to wonder why they aren't fucking fencepost themselves. It's not weird—it's a healthy, alternative lifestyle! Then it takes its inevitable turn. A made-for-television movie, with thick sanctimonious gravitas, shows us the darker side of fencepost fucking. The talk shows and 'news' programs follow suit. Then, finally, the horrendously unfunny *Saturday Night Live* cast does an unwatchable fencepost-fucking skit with no beginning middle or end. Or jokes. Then you know the heat is off. That program is the kiss of death for anything topical or interesting. The Grim Reaper of trends."

"Your theory is very Spinozan. He believed that all possible things exist."

"See that," said Norbert. "I'm a philosopher and I didn't even know it. So when are you going to finish that book of yours? It looks done to me."

Wilberforce groaned. *The Beast*. "It still needs tweaking. To his benefit, my dissertation adviser concurs. But he is a careful man, much more careful than myself. For instance, he writes out all his emails in longhand as a first draft. But alas, as Spinoza himself wrote in concluding his *Ethics*: All excellent things are as difficult as they are rare."

"Well, if you want my opinion on it, when a book weighs more than the table it's on, it's finished."

"There's merit to that stance," said Wilberforce. "Nevertheless, it still needs tweaking."

Norbert and Wilberforce looked to their right as the Caddy passed a pickup truck wherein the driver was smoking through a hole in his neck.

"That reminds me," said Norbert as he accelerated past the truck and swerved back into the right lane, "when I was at Walter Reed, a Marine in my ward got word that his father had set fire to his face because he was smoking with his oxygen tube still in."

Wilberforce slackened the seat belt around his belly. He stared down at his paunch in a state of omphaloskepsis. "Do you suppose, perhaps subconsciously, that your Theory of Fencepost Fucking is just a clever way of condemning homosexuality? By calling it something else?"

"Homosexuality?" laughed Norbert. "You miss the point entirely, Padre. It isn't about sex. People can pound whatever hole they please. I take no interest in that. No, I'm talking about *everybody*. Me and you and Oprah and everybody. People just want to feel secure that what they're doing, how they're living, is *normal*; that it's acceptable; that it's A-OK. As far as I'm concerned, that's why people file into church on Sunday, full of sin, close their eyes tight, eat a button of bread, and let some contrived sense of forgiveness wash over them.

"Take for instance a guy who commits the same sin I do, say, taking the Lord's name in vain. He goes to church Sunday and I don't. He receives mercy and forgiveness from his preacher and his God, and I don't. Does that mean that what he did is okay and what I did is wrong? We committed identical sins, the only difference is that he asked forgiveness from his invisible friend who lives in the sky and I didn't. He feels assured when he leaves his house of worship that what he did is now okay. That how he lives is okay. That's all people care about: feeling secure that what they think, what they do, how they choose to live, is okay. But it's all bullshit. All bullshit. Because if sins can simply be forgiven, how can they be sins in the first place?"

"It's about belief," said Wilberforce, fiddling with the car radio. "It's about faith. It's about the mystery of Christ. Augustine said, 'I should not be a Christian but for the miracles.' Dr. Johnson said, 'We cease to wonder at what we understand.' 'Humankind cannot bear very much reality.'"

"Who's that?"

"What do you mean?"

"I mean I can never tell when you're speaking or when some dead guy is using your mouth. Was that last one yours, the one about bearing reality?"

"T.S. Eliot. Life is contradiction, Norbert. Not everything is logical."

"Yeah, well, just because something is *illogical*, that don't make it poetry. 'If we do not create our own myth, we will be enslaved by someone else's.' That's William Blake. And that's my way of saying you're not the only one in this car who reads books."

"Bravo," said Wilberforce. "Maybe I'm wrong. Perhaps you're the true genius."

"A tortured genius."

"Is there another kind? Louis Aragon said that 'the nature of genius is to provide idiots with ideas twenty years later.' But that's fine. All as it should be, I suppose. As I age, I come to appreciate Spinoza's determinism more and more. Think about it, when you liberate yourself from the oppression of free will, you can begin to live your life, comfortable in the knowledge that all things happen according to plan."

"You really don't believe in free will?"

"Spinoza gave the example of watching a rock tossed into the air. If that rock were to suddenly achieve consciousness, it would believe it had free will. But of course from our perspective the concept of the rock's free will is quaint. The rock is headed in one, inevitable direction."

When Wilberforce couldn't locate any country-western music on the dial, he settled on the next worst thing: smooth jazz. After several miles of the John Tesh Radio Program, Wilberforce broke the thick, groggy silence.

"Why does Philip Philo Phipps think you saved his life?"

Norbert let the question hang there, as though snagged in transit, caught swinging between them from the Caddy's dome light.

"'Too many words are exhausting,'" said Norbert. "'Hold fast to the center.' Lao Tzu. *Tao Te Ching*."

Wilberforce smiled and turned toward the window, quietly satisfied.

Nothing but smooth jazz till Erie, Pennsylvania.

10

In Cleveland, the Caddy pulled up to a Days Inn. It was one of those two-story brick box affairs with a railed walkway running along the upper floor. At the check-in desk, Wilberforce threw Norbert for a loop when he requested separate rooms. Separate rooms! He also asked that they be located on the ground floor, facing the parking lot. All this he did without explanation, to Norbert or the bleary-eyed clerk. Norbert stared at Wilberforce sarcastically for a long moment, hoping that either the heat of his gaze or the telepathic darts he was throwing would cause him to turn and look, but he did not. Like Arlene, thought Norbert, Wilberforce understood that golden comedy moments can be easily quashed simply by not providing an audience. Wilberforce paid cash and Norbert ran it through on his embattled Visa.

While Wilberforce showered in his room next door, Norbert lay on his bed counting the tiny holes in each ceiling tile. He retrieved his notebook from his bag and opened to the first blank page. He wrote:

> Most of the commandments lack real zazz. I wonder if some of them have the necessary pop to actually get God's undivided attention. Some commandments are outdated, commonplace. Outside the big ones: murder, adultery, to a much lesser extent, stealing—outside of those, it seems that breaking God's laws doesn't exactly pack the existential wallop I was hoping for. Counting on. This is just like me, though, rushing headlong into something without thinking it through. Now I have a Spinozan ex-priest lothario hitched to my wagon. Well, anyway, I need to finish what I started. Complete the mission. That's what matters.

Norbert studied the torn pages of Exodus 20, the onion-skin paper nearly brushing his nose. He curled his bare toes, extending them several times as he read, in an effort to get the blood flowing in his tired accelerator foot.

"Thou shalt have no other gods before Me." That one's broken without me even trying, right? There are all sorts of gods. There are innumerable versions of God. Isn't God slightly different for each person inside each religion? Isn't belief ultimately personal and private? Just like a character in a novel, each reader's imagery of the words on the page is different. I think of Jay Gatsby. My image of that character is different from everyone else's—drawn strictly from black marks on a white page. Some people only see the movie actor Robert Redford. They can no longer conjure that original image drawn purely from their own imagination. That is, they knew what they believed, they saw it instinctually, until a more polished version arrived, telling them what they *really* saw, what they *ought* to believe. That's probably why so many Christians see God as a wizened, kindly, Caucasian grandpa. And Jesus as a muscular folk musician. Because their imagery has been ready-made, and provided in abundance.

When I picture God it's almost impossible to not see him without his long, snowy beard on his big throne in the clouds. This is just one, rather silly, image of God, but I can't shake it. But more important than what He looks like—which is important because it reveals so much about the lies we agree to believe in order to simplify the unfath-omably complex mysteries of our daily lives just so we can get on with our everyday shit—more important is the *relationship* each person has with the God they choose to believe in. If they choose to believe at all. Which, I think, is another sort of believing. So, to say, "Thou shalt have no other gods before Me" deserves the rejoinder: *Which Me? Which God?* Just this god here in Exodus 20? Just the God in this one book? Because I received my first library card at the age of four and I know there are a lot of other books.

I wonder why I chickened out in front of my parents? Would I have really said all that I intended to say to them if Mr. Creepers hadn't trundled in and died? The thing is, the opposite of honoring your parents need not be a venomous outpouring of anger and regrets aimed at breaking their spirits. All I really needed to say to them was that they had not, in my opinion, done enough; that they had failed me as my parents. I think that the honor a parent hopes to earn from his or her child can only be bestowed by that child. The child must, in his own voice or actions, say, "Good work, folks. Job well done. Sure, you're not perfect, but you did your best with what you had to work with. I love you for your efforts, your sacrifices, and I honor you with my appreciation. Thank you." For a child to withhold that appreciation—or, worse—to make it known he believes the opposite—that is what it means to dishonor. It wounds deeply. Parents need to believe that their decisions were for the best, that their actions and love is appreciated. It's what sustains them. They crave understanding through compliance. Willfully withholding appreciation from your parents, scorning their efforts—that is dishonoring them. It's cruel enough just to tell your parents that their best was not good enough. For everything else I thought I needed to say to them, that would have been enough.

Wilberforce banged on Norbert's door. Norbert rolled across the bed and stuffed his notebook into the nightstand drawer, atop the Gideons Bible and Book of Mormon. He let Wilberforce in to wait while he disappeared into the bathroom to put on a clean button-up shirt, dark blue jeans, and shiny three-quarter black boots that zippered up the instep. He achieved this shine in the traditional military fashion: spit-polish heated with a lighted match to a mirror finish. Norbert tugged on his leather mechanic's jacket and was ready to go.

Norbert and Wilberforce walked across the road to a Bennigan's. The air was cold and smelled of lake ice, but there was no snow to speak of. Wilberforce wore a long-sleeved yellow golf shirt with a tiny green horse on it, tan, pleated, cotton slacks with a hard crease down the center of each leg, and a pair of rubber duck-back boots. He completed the ensemble by zipping into a soft, dark-green L.L. Bean fleece pullover.

The Cleveland Bennigan's was typically unremarkable. There were plenty of mass-produced doodads and bric-a-brac (manufactured to give the illusion of antiques and rare yard sale finds) zip-screwed to the walls. The menu was a glossy megaphone of outrageous fun and value that had been relentlessly polished through wave upon wave of family focus groups. It was no Tessy's, with its flimsy brown paneling, brooding patrons and absence of natural light. Given a choice, Norbert would always take a Tessy's—with its flat, two-dollar drafts—over triple Oreo fudge-splosion sundaes. But rarely do such unambiguous choices present themselves on the road.

The hostess had a round, bright face with dark eyes like a Labrador puppy's. She could not have stood much over five feet but had the breasts of an eight-foot Amazonian. Wilberforce took immediate note of this. He shot Norbert a fast look, but Norbert decided to return his earlier slight at the reception desk by denying him an audience. They followed her to a booth below an assortment of Elvis Presley memorabilia. Wilberforce made an easy joke. The diminutive hostess giggled and smiled and told them to enjoy their meals. Wilberforce warmly assured her they would. It was immediately apparent that she was as help-less as an iron filing in the field of Wilberforce's sexual magnetism. Before leaving them, she shot Wilberforce a distinctly feline gaze that suggested he "save room for des-sert." Wilberforce studied her undulating buttocks beneath her shiny black pants, so common in the service industry, as she returned to her post in the catching area. The little tag on her uniform shirt introduced her as "Brandi."

Their waitress was tall and slender, her fair tresses pulled back and wound into what Arlene called a scrunchie. Norbert's first reaction to seeing her was swift and unan-ticipated, like feeling a junebug flutter below his belt. He was instantly gripped with the desire to lie alongside her, gazing into the butterfly constellation of freckles spread across her nose. It was his first carnal stirring in a week since sneaking up behind Arlene as she blow-dried her hair in front of the bathroom mirror. Arlene, still wet from her shower, was wearing only a pair of shimmering purple panties. Norbert had wrapped his arms across her warm breasts and buried his nose into her damp hair. She pulled away, telling him she was late for an appointment and admonished him for again failing to drag the garbage cans to the road for their early morning pickup. These garbage cans were an ongoing source of friction.

Her name was Lula, the waitress. Norbert asked if that was short for anything and she assured him it was not. Norbert ordered one of those tall beers that come served in a glass bowling pin. Wilberforce asked for a double Dewar's with two ice cubes. When Lula left, Wilberforce spent several minutes rearranging his pocket things and studying the King of Rock 'n' Roll's knickknacks on the wall beside them. Wilberforce also studied each young waitress as they breezed past with steaming trays of food, but kept zeroing back in on Brandi, the short, wide-eyed hostess at the door.

One thing he failed to do was open his menu. As time passed, Norbert became increasingly concerned that Lula would return with their drinks before Wilberforce had considered his order. This inattention to a simple courtesy was a source of great annoyance to Norbert. It again reminded him of Arlene. She was well practiced in this specific art of procrastination. When dining out, which was not often, she and Norbert would be seated, would place their drink orders, and then Arlene would immediately lose herself in some protracted monologue about the trials of her day. When the server returned with the drinks, she would invariably be unprepared to order, demanding "a few more minutes" in a barely concealed tone of irritation at the insolence of the waitress's attempt to bully along such a delicate process. Arlene would then resume the day's play-by-play and, when the waitress returned for a third time, would snap open the menu in great distress and, flustered, select the most expensive item therein. She might then, as the waitress departed, comment on her inappropriate choice of slacks for a "girl her size" or her "ridiculous eye shadow."

Three hours after their empty plates had been cleared, Norbert and Wilberforce sat stone drunk at the bar. Wilberforce sang the Notre Dame fight song, forgetting a few words in the second verse, but coming in strong on the refrain. The bartender didn't seem to mind the racket, probably because Norbert had switched to top shelf scotch and Wilberforce was fanning twenties on the bar. Brandi seated herself at the far corner to complete some paperwork. The bartender poured her a Coke.

"Hell with soda pop," slurred Wilberforce. "Send her a shot of tequila."

Brandi smiled. She quickly made eye contact with the bartender so he would know not to pour. She was having second thoughts about this vociferous drunk with the rubiginous ears and jowls.

"That's too bad," said Wilberforce, removing a thick fold of bills from his wallet—the first Norbert had seen of it! "Now where will I go tonight to blow my inheritance? But worse, much worse, with whom shall I blow it?"

This piqued Brandi's interest. She adjusted her bra straps and, after Wilberforce reluctantly downgraded the tequila shot to a cosmopolitan she, with some mild trepidation, seated herself beside him. Brandi said that she was her friend's ride home, and with that took a large gulp of her fruity drink masquerading as a martini.

Norbert wished upon a dead eyelash that Brandi's friend would be Lula the waitress. It was.

During Norbert's dinner order, Lula had smirked and asked him if he wanted a booster chair to eat his chicken fingers and fries. He answered no, not since he started using the big-boy potty.

Norbert liked that Lula looked straight at him while delivering her playful affront, no doubt testing how he might respond to a woman's sharp tongue. He was annoyed when Arlene would not look at him while bandying insults. She would pretend to read something or begin searching fruitlessly for some phantom item inside her purse or a drawer, say. When Lula reached the bar, to break the ice, Norbert playfully remarked on their saccharine exchange. She smiled then noticed, with dismay, that her friend Brandi was engaged with Norbert's companion, a large older man with wispy ear hair. Lula slid onto the stool beside Norbert and ordered a bottle of Heineken.

"Take that out of here," said Norbert, motioning toward Wilberforce's cash on the bar.

"You don't have to do that," said Lula.

"I know."

The bartender removed the correct amount from the cash pile.

"No, I mean, my drinks are free." Lula fidgeted with several items inside her purse. She let down her ponytail.

Norbert shuddered in a cold spasm as he watched the very end of her white-blonde hair brush the top of her right shoulder.

"Cheers," she said with a half-tilt of her bottle. She took a long swallow of the bitter Dutch hops.

"Do you think people can fall in love at a Bennigan's?" asked Norbert.

Lula looked over at Brandi and Wilberforce. She shrugged. "I guess they can fall in *like*."

"I suppose that's just as well, since most people don't know the difference."

"I suppose."

"Are you from here originally?" asked Norbert.

"Alas."

"Where can we go after here? To drink?"

"We?" Lula arched an eyebrow.

"Me and my friend." Norbert looked away as the words left his lips, knowing he'd squandered an opening. He was rusty.

"Oh. There's The Flats. But it's a drive."

"I think my friend is making time with your friend," said Norbert.

They looked over at them. Wilberforce was reading Brandi's palm, shaking his head gravely.

"No one ever talks about interesting things," said Lula. "They just recite lines from television shows and movies. Or yammer on about their social networking dramas. People are boring."

"So let's start a revolution in conversation tonight. You and me at this Cleveland Bennigan's. Pioneers of the New Small Talk! They'll write folk songs about us."

"No one writes folk songs anymore."

"If I challenge your intellect, Lula, will you stay and have another drink with me?"

"Give me a sampling."

"Okay. Do you believe in God?"

"I'll take a vodka with two ice cubes."

The bartender overheard, dropping two cubes into a glass.

"Are you seeing anyone?" asked Norbert.

"What's that?" snapped Lula.

"What's what?"

"That. The same tired old drivel, that's what that is." Lula laid her slender hand over the ice-filled cocktail glass as the bartender tilted the vodka bottle. He jerked his wrist to avoid splashing her. "I thought we were starting straight off with the third rail of polite banter. Breaking new ground. Two strangers diving headlong into the conversational minefield of religion. But no. You're blowing it, mister."

Norbert gently lifted her fingers from the mouth of her cocktail glass.

"We will of course discuss God and all the heavens in due course, but I like to know if a lady has someone waiting for her at home. Particularly before engaging in deep discussions with the potential of lasting into the wee hours of the morning."

Lula smiled and nodded to the bartender. He filled her glass and took more money from the pile on the bar.

"So?" said Norbert.

Lula sighed. "You're just passing through. Tomorrow you'll be who-knows-where." She combed her fingers through her hair and swallowed a gulp of vodka. Not through the skinny red straw, Norbert noticed.

"Maybe so," said Norbert, "but right now, I'm right here."

"There's this guy. He's cute. We're kind of hanging out.

Just coffee and two movies so far. His name is Andy. He's twenty-four, some kind of dot-com millionaire—so he says. Supposedly he designed some security encryption software for banks and credit card companies then cashed out early. Now he's like a consultant or whatever. Mostly he just talks about OTB and his sports book, but I digress." Lula looked up. She was caught off guard by Norbert's blue eyes. She looked back into her drink. "He's got a stutter when he's nervous," she said. "But the best part is today . . . today . . ." Lula took a sip of her vodka. She laughed a little and spit back into the glass.

"Today?" coaxed Norbert.

"This package from him is waiting for me here at the bar. Inside is a pair of shoes."

"Shoes?"

"Boots, actually. Red dominatrix boots. How weird is that? That's weird, right?"

"Were they your correct size?"

"Exactly my size."

"What did you do with them?"

"They're behind the bar."

"Andy with the Red Boots," said Norbert.

"Andy with the Red Boots," said Lula. "I thought this was a normal guy. Clean cut. Polo shirts. It just goes to show, you never know."

Norbert pictured Wilberforce's shirt with its tiny green horse over the left nipple. It never occurred to him to regard it as an emblem of sanity. Norbert thought that the padre would enjoy knowing his wardrobe was considered the uniform of normality.

"Lula, you intrigue me."

Suddenly, a meaty mitt clamped down roughly upon Norbert's shoulder, massaging it fraternally.

"It appears we are headed to the next venue," said Wilberforce. "Brandi is driving."

Brandi giggled. This was news to her. She playfully slapped Wilberforce in the chest and pinched the soft flesh of his upper arm.

"I don't even know your friend's name," Lula said to Wilberforce.

"Tell the lady your name, boyo," said Wilberforce.

"Norbert."

Wilberforce drained his scotch, crunching down on an ice cube. "Where are we going Brandi-wine?" Wilberforce and Brandi stumbled toward the door in a snarl. Norbert could swear he heard Brandi mention dancing. Lula finished her vodka. She dabbed her upper lip with a tissue she produced from a fold in her shirt cuff.

"There goes my ride," said Lula. "I guess I'm tagging along."

Lula slid down from her stool and smoothed her black skirt with her palms. She flipped her hair away from her shirt collar and grabbed her purse from the bar.

"Lula?"

"Yes, Norbert?"

"I don't know where we're going, but I think you should wear those boots."

11

Back in The Halo in Topeka, Kansas, Elton powered off his computer for the night. He stood, drew a crucifix in the air in front of him, and climbed the stairs into the kitchen.

Elton emerged from behind the basement door, once a crisp eggshell, now yellowed from decades of cigarette smoke. He grimaced at the hum of the microwave's rotating tray. He washed his blistered hands clean in the sink and dried them with a dark dishtowel.

"What is it?" asked Elton.

"Meatloaf."

"And?"

"String beans."

"And?"

"Mashed potatoes."

"Red potatoes?" asked Elton.

"Of course, my love."

"I've insisted you not call me that anymore. Didn't I insist? It's obscene. Did you leave the skins on?"

"Yes luv—Yes."

"Is there bread?" Elton sat in his chair nearest the refrigerator, the one with the special pillow tied to the spindles for lumbar support. "You didn't put the bread in with the plate, did you? It gets rubbery in the microwave."

"Your bread is warming in the oven, Elton." Elton's mother poured him a tall, cold milk in a clear glass with an illustration of the McDonald's Hamburglar on it.

"I hate this glass," said Elton. "It glorifies the criminal element. And besides, it's chipped."

Elton's mother softly whistled the tune to *Chattanooga Choo-Choo*. She stared intensely into the dimly lit microwave, as though her mortality was inextricably linked to its contents. The tray slowly turned: 28, 27, 26 . . .

"No whistling. If you want to whistle, go down to the docks and whistle with the lusty seamen."

"There are no docks, dear. This is Kansas."

"You know what I mean." Elton slipped his butter knife between his fingers. He drummed it on the table like a nervous test-taker. "What's taking so long?"

Elton's mother placed the warm bread on the oven to cool.

"Couple seconds now."

"*Meatloaf*," Elton snorted.

It was an old microwave, with a dial that turned. It made a sound like the bell of an egg timer when time expired. Elton's mother placed the hot plate in front of him and turned to slice the bread.

"Where's the egg? There's no hardboiled egg in it. How could you forget the hardboiled egg?" he wailed.

"I must have given you a slice without the egg in it. I'm sorry my luv—There's plenty for seconds."

"How could you miss the egg? How did you cut it? It's nearly impossible to cut it and *not* get part of the egg. This is unacceptable. The Lord doth test me daily in a thousand small ways. But I endure. I endure."

Elton folded his hands together and squeezed his eyes so tightly closed that someone happening into the room might suppose he was attempting to pass a painful bowel obstruction. Elton prayed, "Dear Lord, bless us this day, this food to our use. Make us ever mindful of the needs of others. In Jesus's name we pray. Amen." Elton's mother prayed half-turned and standing, Elton having not waited for her to be seated.

Elton forked a bite. "Did you use ketchup or barbecue sauce?"

"I made it how you like."

"Mm," said Elton, not implying that it was delicious, just acknowledging that he had heard her.

With her fork, Elton's mother cut her meatloaf into progressively smaller portions until it was a mound of loose hamburger.

"Why must you do that?" said Elton. "It's childish."

"I like to mix it with my potatoes."

Elton shook his head. "Give me strength," he muttered.

Elton and his mother ate wordlessly for several minutes. The buzz of the kitchen wall clock established a bass line beneath the cacophony of clacking, scraping flatware across the plates. Elton enjoyed a bit of potato, a bit of string beans, and a bit of meatloaf in every forkful. He used his index finger when necessary to ensure this taste medley occurred in each bite. He held his fork as a child holds a plastic shovel at the beach.

Elton's mother was not particularly interested in her meal. She ate only a few bites, her heart not fully in it. She continuously rearranged her plate, making tiny, incremental adjustments until she was satisfied it was at the exact center of her place mat. She sat heavily in her chair, heaving a succession of sighs. Finally, Elton looked up from his supper.

"What's the drama?"

"Nothing."

"Good." He resumed eating.

"It's just . . . this cable bill, Elton. It's so expensive."

"I need high-speed broadband. We've discussed this. Are you still unclear as to what I do for a living? Do I really need to explain this to you *yet again*?"

"You don't really do it for a living, dear. No one is paying you for your Internet thingy."

"It's my calling. My *mission*."

"I just don't understand why I should pay for it. I have all the bills, Elton—and the mortgage. It's getting harder and harder to make the ends meet. The heat bill is a scandal and we've needed a new furnace since before your father passed. I don't see why you can't just pay this one bill, at the very least. I have no use for the Internet. I can't even turn a computer on. I don't think it's asking too much for you to contribute to this house. And since you have all that money, I just can't see why—"

"Zip. Zip it. That topic is not up for discussion."

"But it's *so* much money, Elton. I don't think it's fair that—"

Elton balled his fist and struck the table with great force. The plates and forks and glasses leapt an inch, landing with a clatter. He rose. "You listen and listen good, woman. That money happened to me. You hear? It happened to me. And that's the end of it. This house can fall down around us and you'll never see a dime of it. That. Money. Happened. To *me.*"

Elton lowered himself back into his chair, adjusting his posture to maximize the effect of the lumbar pillow. He scraped the last of his mashed potatoes onto his fork, spearing the final few green beans and the remaining hunk of meatloaf. Once again, he had portioned it perfectly. Eyes closed tight, he tilted back his head and chewed reverently, swallowing the baked hamburger like it was the body of Christ.

"I went to Kansas City this afternoon," he said.

"Oh?" his mother said, absently. She rubbed the back of her neck, not looking at him. "Another one of your crusades?"

"Don't patronize me," said Elton, chewing. "You have an annoying habit of forgetting that you're not my mother. And by the way, do us both a favor tonight and TAKE YOUR PILL."

Upstairs in his bedroom, Elton knelt in his jammies beside his bed. He laced his fingers and squeezing closed his eyes so very tight, he whispered:

Matthew, Mark, Luke, and John,
Bless this bed that I lay on,
Before I lay me down to sleep,
I give my soul to Christ to keep.

Four corners to my bed,
Four angels 'round my head,
One to watch, one to pray,
And two to bear my soul away.

I go by sea, I go by land,
The Lord made me with His right hand,
If any danger come to me,
Sweet Jesus Christ, deliver me.

For He's the branch and I'm the flower,
Pray God send me a happy hour,
And if I die before I wake,
I pray the Lord my soul to take.

Christ visit the meanies in their sleep,
For what they sowed, they will reap,
Burn their souls and make them scream,
As I repose in righteous dreams.

Amen.

12

After a night of merriment in the clubs, Norbert, Lula, Wilberforce, and Brandi arrived back at the Cleveland Days Inn carrying plastic bags filled with burritos and a bottle of Irish whiskey. Wilberforce and Brandi, in a drunken tangle, made deliberate strides toward Wilberforce's room. Norbert motioned toward a few forlorn picnic tables below the second-floor concrete walkway.

"You wanna smoke?" asked Norbert.

"Okay," said Lula.

Norbert tapped the bottom of the pack. He offered her the cigarette protruding highest from the opening. She took it delicately, her eyes fixed on Norbert's. She brought the cigarette slow to her mouth. He lit it.

"Kinda cold," she said.

"We should go inside. You're in a skirt."

"Gotta get used to the cold," said Lula. "If you want to stay a smoker, I mean."

They crossed the parking lot to an area below the upper walkway, the tall heels of Lula's red boots clicking, scraping across the macadam. Norbert let the whiskey bottle, still wrapped in its brown bag, dangle loose and casual from his fingertips.

At the table, Lula sat on top with her feet propped on the bench seat. She leaned forward hugging her knees for warmth. Norbert sat at the edge of the bench.

"You want a drink?"

"Okay."

"Might warm us up," said Norbert, cracking the seal. He twisted off the cap, offering the bottle to Lula first, as a gentleman should, he thought. She tossed back her head, the hot booze rushing down her throat. It was a good-sized guzzle, Norbert noted. He followed it with a snoot of his own.

"You've got some moves," said Norbert. "You can dance."

"Must be the boots. You're more of a hip-swayer, yourself. Conservative."

"Cautious. So, besides dancing, what are some of your other talents?"

Lula took a drag of her cigarette. "I have a natural gift for alphabetization. For example, I can pick up any dictionary and open to the page of whatever word you call out."

"How did you stumble upon your awareness of this gift?"

"I just love to read. I love words, the smell and feel of books. I can't even count the hours I've spent wandering through bookstores—especially used bookstores. It's a shame they're all disappearing."

"Gotta make room for more Dunkin' Donuts."

"Thing is, I don't think you choose a book," said Lula, "I think it chooses you. I don't know, maybe in a way God chooses you through each book. You know, like the God Consciousness? The point is, I've learned to listen to the little voices in my life. I can't count how many times I've pulled down a random book, opened to a random page, and read precisely the words I needed to read at that exact moment. I'm sorry, but that's no accident. That's a rule of the universe. I think that if our minds weren't so noisy, so stuffed with trivial bullshit, so conditioned to ignore authentic moments, writing them off as coincidences, then we would see those moments for what they really are— God's whispers. Glimpses at the order of all things."

Norbert took a swig from the whiskey bottle. "So you're pretty religious, huh?"

"No. Not at all."

"You keep talking about God."

"Sure, God—whatever. I don't really know what else to call it. Everybody in this country wants to stick you in their neat little box so they know which version of their bullshit to throw at you. It's all so slick and polished."

"Are you an atheist?"

Lula thought for a moment. "I guess the definition of an atheist is someone who believes in nothing, and that's not me at all. I believe in everything. All possibilities. I think I'm very spiritual. I sorta feel like I'm above religion, y'know? I mean, I know that sounds conceited. But I feel like, at my most basic level, I'm willing—eager, even—to say 'I don't know' why something is the way it is. Besides, what does that whole concept of atheism even mean? Where else in life are you made to define yourself as someone who does not believe in something? That's stupid."

"Like people who carry umbrellas when it's snowing," said Norbert.

"Huh?"

"That's another thing that's stupid."

"The way I envision it," said Lula, "is like we're each this single thread in a really intricately woven tapestry. If you pull out just one thread—*your thread*—the whole thing unravels. During my last summer in college I went with a friend to South America to visit her family. We traveled all around: Guyana, Venezuela, Colombia, Ecuador, Peru. Everywhere we went, people were the same: same hopes, same dreams, same fears. Strip away the color, the politics, the religions, and we all want the same things: to enjoy our time while we're alive and to leave a better world for our children."

"Why have you stayed in Cleveland?"

"My mom, she had breast cancer. My parents are divorced. I stayed to take care of her. When she passed, I guess I just forgot to leave."

"I'm sorry."

Lula shrugged. "I'll leave someday. I'm waiting, I guess. For what, I have no idea."

"Where would you go if you could?"

"Oh, I don't know. Probably California."

Norbert laughed. Incredible, he thought. "Why California?"

This time Lula laughed, she was embarrassed. "Why am I telling you this?"

"You've barely told me anything yet," said Norbert.

"I write," said Lula, blushing. "I'm a writer, I guess. I've finished three screenplays and I'm working on number four."

"What are they about?"

"Romantic comedies, I guess—for lack of a better definition. Very talky. The jump-off always involves the heroine doing something impulsive. I'd go to California just to, I don't know, see if I'm any good. I write because I think the only way to combat everybody's incessant chatter is to just completely throw yourself into something and become excellent at it. I think that, to achieve total awareness of your true self, of your unique value, is the one sure way to become impervious to bullshit. You want your burrito?"

"Sure," said Norbert.

Lula fished inside the plastic bag. "But having a writer in your family is a blessing and a curse, I think," she said. "A blessing because there's someone in the world who may tell your story. A curse because they may tell the truth."

"There," said Norbert, pointing inside the bag. "The one that says 'No Cheese.'"

Lula shook her head, handing Norbert his burrito. "I've never known anybody that doesn't eat cheese. Are you allergic?"

"I just don't like it. Smells funky. Tastes bad."

"Do you eat pizza?"

Norbert chewed his burrito. It was tiresome, this lifelong ritual of explaining to the uninformed The Great Conspiracy. But Lula was so pretty and kind. And Norbert believed he was very close to exploring beneath her panties.

"I do eat pizza."

"I don't understand. If you eat pizza—"

Norbert sighed to himself. "I *have* to eat pizza. I have no choice. I couldn't very well get through life without eating pizza. It's the number one communal meal. It's the only time I eat cheese. Let's talk about you."

"What about nacho-flavored chips?"

"Nope."

"Because that's not really cheese."

"I don't eat them."

"Cottage cheese?"

"Well, that's not *really* cheese, either. I have eaten it. I can live without it."

"What about cheesecake?"

"I sometimes eat cheesecake, depending on the social situation. But that's different, too."

"There doesn't appear to be any logic to your system, Norbert. No rules governing your disdain for cheese. It seems to teeter on a case-by-case basis." Lula took a long drag on her cigarette. She balanced it on the edge of the table and lifted her burrito.

"I guess I'm just a complex man, Lula. My life is riddled with contradictions."

"Like Swiss cheese," she smirked.

Norbert had little tolerance for puns, even if they were tongue-in-cheek. He took another long swallow of whiskey.

"What about calzones?" she continued. "That's basically a rolled pizza."

"How about we talk about something else?"

Lula smiled. "What else do you want to know?" She took an ambitious bite of her cheese-filled burrito. "I've already shared my philosophy about the universe. While wearing red hooker boots, no less."

"For starters, I'd like to know why you make people feel shame over hating cheese? Does it give you an inflated sense of power?"

Lula laughed—an involuntary, snorting laugh—like a violent hiccup—at the same moment she was attempting to swallow. In an instant, Norbert recognized that the burrito bite had lodged in her windpipe. She brought her hands to her throat, convulsing backward and forward in a fit of fear and embarrassment. She was choking.

Norbert helped her down off the picnic table, wrapped his arms around her, and Heimliched a spicy chunk of beef and tortilla from her air passage. It worked just as he was taught it would during his first aid course in basic. He kept his arms wrapped loosely round her waist as she bent forward, catching her breath.

"You all right?" Norbert gently patted her back and ran his fingers softly over her vertebrae.

"Yes," gasped Lula. She stood straight. "I'm mortified. That's never happened to me before." She spit.

"Now do you see what happens when you eat cheese? It's just a matter of time."

Lula laughed, turned to face Norbert. He pulled her close. He slid his hands beneath her coat, kneading his fingertips into her lower back like bread dough. Norbert ran his thumbs up and down her thin waistline. No extra meat on her, he thought. He hoped she would not call attention to these advances. He easily became self-conscious about his choice of intimate maneuvers. Her hair smelled like strawberry bubble gum and cigarettes. In the dark of the early morning, under the concrete walkway of the Cleveland Days Inn, Norbert and Lula stared into the black flecks in each other's eyes.

"I have cheesy-burrito puke-breath," said Lula.

Norbert inhaled through his nose; he nodded in agreement. They kissed. Their tongues probing like accusing fingers. Norbert cupped Lula's buttocks with both hands; squeezed. She moaned in a small voice—an excellent sign, he thought. He slid his right hand beneath her shirt. En route to her left breast, he brushed her bare belly. Lula jerked away.

"Your hand is *freezing*." She shivered. "Let's go inside."

Norbert grabbed the whiskey, left the burritos.

Inside Norbert's room, struggling to remain attached at the lips, they wasted no time tearing off their coats. They shed their shirts, Norbert peeling his away from his chest in a great flourish like a passionate Spaniard. Lula stepped back, unzipped and kicked off her boots, stepped out of her skirt and unhooked her bra. Slowly she wriggled free of her shoulder straps, stepping forward into Norbert's embrace. She seized his belt with both hands and began to unbuckle it.

Norbert placed his hands gently over hers, stopping her. He kissed her neck and shoulders and breasts. Lula closed her eyes, heaving warm breaths, her mouth open wide. Again, her hands went to his buckle.

"I want these off," she whispered.

"I want *these* off," Norbert whispered back, snapping the elastic of Lula's panties.

"You have a condom?"

Norbert knew he did not. Arlene had been on the pill. A fuzzy image of a vending machine in the motel men's room flashed behind his eyes. But he would need to get dressed again. Was there loose change in the truck? They would lose all this momentum. They would never re-establish this same heat after a five-minute rubber run. It would be awkward when he returned. They would talk. Shit! thought Norbert. Shit! Shit! Shit!

"No," said Norbert, "I don't have one."

Lula kissed his ear. "Well . . . Maybe I can do something else." She kissed his neck. His chest. She raked her nails down from his shoulders, leaving thin white tracks in her wake. She knelt. She kissed his soft belly. She wrapped her fingers around his belt buckle.

Norbert stepped away.

"There's a condom machine in the lobby, I think. I'm pretty sure." He pulled on his shirt.

"Uh, okay," said Lula, confused.

"Be back in two minutes. Five, tops."

Norbert walked briskly, almost hopping with each stride, through the darkness beneath the concrete walkway. Two new, fluorescent condoms wrapped in clear plastic crinkled inside his jeans pocket. He was sure he remembered this exact scene from a movie. The actor, Norbert could not recall his name but saw his face, forgot the girl's room number on his way back from some silly errand. Concentrating hard to place the actor, his name dancing drunkenly at the end of his tongue, Norbert looked up to see a young man standing directly in his path. The man, shorter than Norbert, wore an expensive puffy ski parka and an Indians ball cap, the brim pulled low over his eyes. It was clear his intention was to halt Norbert's progress. Norbert stopped. Up close, the man looked strong in that way stocky guys do, sporting a bulbous double chin so common in those who lift a lot of free weights but pay no mind to their diet.

"Where you headed?" asked the man.

Norbert thought perhaps the man was some sort of undercover motel security dick, unlikely as that seemed. He could not think of any response this particular goofball was entitled to.

"I said where you headed?"

"What's this about? Who are you?"

"Where you headed, asshole?"

"None of your fucking business," said Norbert. He felt the heat flush into his face, neck muscles tense, eyes narrow into his *You lookin' for trouble you just found it* stare. He gave a quick look toward the parking lot to see if there was more trouble closing in. Nope.

"If you've got Lu-Lula in that room," said the guy in the puffy jacket, "I'll make it my f-f-fucking business."

Norbert laughed. "O-O-Okay, tough guy. Just s-s-simmer down."

As a boy, Norbert learned from his Grandfather Sherbert that at the first sign of trouble, the first instant you sense you are in any physical peril, you should hit whoever or whatever threatens you as hard as you possibly can, preferably in the nose or throat. But this guy did not feel threatening to Norbert at all. His presence, his appearance—his word choices, even—registered as comical. His squared-off sideburns, his clean-shaven face, his (Norbert now noticed) expensive cross-training sneaker boots, all made Norbert want to break into a wide grin, throw his arm around the guy, and ask him who was putting him up to such nonsense.

Then the guy pushed Norbert hard in the middle of his chest. Norbert staggered backward, flailing wildly for his balance, landing sharply on his ass. The guy stepped forward and pointed down at Norbert. As he spoke—screamed, really—a shower of tiny spittles rained from his mouth on each hard consonant.

"You keep your hands off Lu-Lula. You hear me, asshole?! Keep your dirty, f-f-fucking hands off her!"

Norbert scrambled to regain his feet. He was a few yards beyond the row of picnic tables and had nothing to grab hold of to hoist himself up.

Lula, who had been listening closely for Norbert's return footsteps, heard her name being screamed outside the door. She dressed quickly and dashed out in her stocking feet to see Norbert on the ground with a dark, puffy figure looming over him.

She called out, "Norbert?!" stepping quickly, fearlessly, toward the action.

The man turned to face her.

"Andy?" said Lula, slowing her gait as she approached. "Andy . . . I don't understand. What are you doing here? What's going on?"

"Andy with the Red Boots?" said Norbert.

"Lula," said Andy. "I was just protecting you from this, this s-scumbag loser."

With terrific effort, Norbert seated himself upright, his right leg bent, his left extended. Andy heard the scrape of Norbert's boot behind him. He flinched, turning back to protect himself. Andy looked down at Norbert, his left pant leg bunched up to just below the knee.

"What the fuck?!" said Andy with the Red Boots, his stutter gone, his voice thick with incredulity and no small measure of delight. "This guy's a fucking cripple? You're cheating on me with a fucking retard?"

Lula looked down at where Norbert's left leg should have been. Should have been but was not. Instead, a thick metal cylinder extended from the line of Norbert's rumpled jeans, disappearing into his black, zippered boot.

"Norbert," said Lula, "Are you okay?"

"Norbert?" said Andy. "What kind of hayseed name is that?"

Lula went to Norbert, helping him to his feet. With his weight fully resting—depending—on her, Norbert tried to step toward Andy. He winced at the abrupt pain, nearly crumbling to the pavement, saved by Lula's arm fast around his waist.

Andy laughed. Moments ago, as he sat drinking single malt in his vehicle, screwing up his courage, contemplating the coolest, movie-inspired method to approach this man with *his* Lula on his arm—this man who had disappeared into a seedy, highway motel room with *his* Lula—this man that Andy had followed home from the club and the late-night burrito truck with *his* Lula. How they had mocked him on the dance floor at Billy's, Andy thought. Dancing in the red boots he had bought her and left for her as a gift at her work after she made it clear, with her eyes, that she was ready to take their relationship to the next level. Andy had been frightened (frightened!) when he realized how tall and lean this strange man with Lula was (so much taller than he at first thought when he saw him alone, set apart from the swarm of people moving in and out of the clubs along Front Street in The Flats). He had almost avoided this confrontation. To think! As Andy with the Red Boots sat fretting, lubricating, in his sport utility vehicle watching Norbert return from the lobby, he had doubted his ability to best him in a physical altercation, should it come to that. But now, now that he saw Norbert was a gimp, Andy laughed because he was not afraid. He had already pushed him down once, with ease. And now, *look at him*. He needed a girl to hold him up. And what was that name Lula yelled? Norbert? *Norbert!* What sort of hick name was that?! Yes, Andy was quite comfortable now. He had complete command of the situation.

"I hope you see how pathetic this is," said Andy to Lula.

Lula, disgusted, slowly walked back toward the room, Norbert's arm draped heavily over her shoulder. Andy with the Red Boots walked alongside them.

"I thought we had something very special, Lula," said Andy. "Instant c-chemistry. You could be my one, true love, if you would just w-wake up to realize it."

"You're crazy as a shityard rat," said Lula. "Go home, Andy. And lose my number."

"Crazy?! Who's crazy? Me, for wanting to show you what real love is? Or, or, you for wanting to throw it all away for a one night stand with some, some f-fucking cripple."

"Wait," said Norbert, wincing. "Wait. I need to rest."

Lula stopped, helping Norbert lean backward against one of the brick columns supporting the walkway above.

"F-fucking cripple!" Andy threw a punch at Norbert's head. Norbert ducked. Andy's right fist crunched into the red brick. He howled. Norbert came back with a quick jab to Andy's nose, breaking it. Andy shrieked in anguish, blood spurting from his crooked nostrils.

"Get me back to the room," said Norbert.

He threw his arm around Lula again. Andy with the Red Boots spun in dazed circles, hands clasped to his crimson face, wailing and yowling.

Wilberforce emerged from his room. He met Norbert at the door. "What's happening? Are you all right?"

"Get your shit," said Norbert.

"Why? Are we—"

"Just get it!"

Wilberforce hustled Brandi back into his room. Norbert and Lula fell through the door into Norbert's room. He closed and locked it.

"Norbert," said Lula. She was breaking down. "I can't explain any of this! I barely know him! He's just some crazy, spoiled rich guy. Obviously he's not right!"

"Sit down," said Norbert.

"I can't!"

"Sit down now."

Lula sat at the edge of the bed. Norbert peeled back the curtain to check the parking lot. Andy had opened his puffy jacket and was using his Polo shirt to sop up the blood cascading from his busted nose. Lights were on. Several doors along the outdoor corridor were open a crack, projecting triangular bars of light across the black pavement. There was a knock at the door: Wilberforce.

Norbert let him in. Brandi followed close behind. She went to Lula's side on the bed. Norbert closed the door.

"I don't think he's armed," said Norbert. "But you never know."

"Who is he?" asked Wilberforce.

"You got your shit?"

Wilberforce lifted his bag.

"We're leaving."

"Norbert!" said Lula. She began to cry. "I'm sorry. I can't explain any of this. I had no idea—"

"It's okay," said Norbert. With difficulty, he crossed to her from the door. Wilberforce took up Norbert's post at the window. He peered behind the curtain. Norbert swept his fingers through Lula's soft hair. He held her warm cheek in his palm, bent forward and kissed her tenderly on the lips. He rubbed a mascara-filled tear with his thumb then turned to Wilberforce.

"What's he doing?"

"Leaving. Could be going to his car. I can't see behind the column."

"Let's go."

"Norbert," said Lula. "Why can't we just—"

"I'm sorry Lula, but I've got to go." Norbert limped back to the door. He rolled up his left pant leg, above the knee and adjusted the harness on the prosthetic. He was clearly in pain.

This was Wilberforce's first look at the thick steel tube extending down from Norbert's knee socket. Norbert met his stare. Wilberforce turned back to scout through the window. Satisfied, Norbert rolled down his pant leg. He lifted his grip from the chair by the window. Wilberforce took it from him.

Norbert looked at Brandi. "Lock this door behind us, with the bar. Stay with her. Call the police. Leave us out of it, if you can."

Brandi went to the door. Norbert and Wilberforce slipped into the night. She closed the door swiftly, latched the bar.

In the parking lot there was no sign of the puffy, blood-faced Andy with the Red Boots. Wilberforce helped

Norbert into the passenger side then tossed the bags into the backseat. Wilberforce settled in behind the steering wheel. He made a series of tiny adjustments, checking his mirrors, scooting forward to wield maximum pressure on the accelerator. Rooms were returning to blackness. There was no movement they could see around the vehicles. Wilberforce started the engine, threw the car in reverse and backed away from the motel. Behind them, an SUV roared to life. It sprang forward, clipping the chrome corner of the Caddy's trunk, sending forth a spray of red plastic. The Caddy fishtailed counterclockwise. Wilberforce cranked the wheel all the way to the right and hit the gas. In their wake, the spinning tires left a cloud of fear and anger as the Caddy barreled into the cold Ohio darkness, west toward the onramp for Interstate 80. Andy made chase. Turning out of the parking lot he lost control, jumped the curb, and smashed into a metal light pole.

Lula and Brandi watched from the room. The police were on the way. When the one, good taillight on the Caddy had faded into the distance, Lula grabbed the red boots from the floor, unbolted the door and flung them into the parking lot. She slammed shut the door, turned to Brandi and cried. Brandi wrapped her arms around Lula as she stroked her back.

"Shh," she said. "Here, sit down, sweetheart." She lowered Lula into the chair by the window. "You know what you need, honey?"

Lula knew the answer: that bottle of whiskey.

"You need the word. That will give you strength. There has never been a better moment than right now for the word." Brandi went to the nightstand and slid open the drawer. "Hm," she said, removing Norbert's notebook. "That's strange. What in God's name is this?"

For a long stretch of highway there were no other tail-lights or headlights on Interstate 80. Norbert smoked and brooded in the passenger seat with the window cracked.

No radio, no speaking until they started seeing signs for Toledo. A sense of grave anticipation hung in the space between the two men. Wilberforce wrestled silently with how to broach the matter of Norbert's missing limb while Norbert turned over in his mind how he would choose to explain it, if at all, once Wilberforce finally gathered the nerve to ask. The tension lessened a bit as they drove through an uncertain patch of intersections and off-ramps. Wilberforce was able to break the silence with simple directional questions.

"Do we stay straight on Route 80 or follow 90 west?" asked Wilberforce.

"Yes," said Norbert, looking at the map.

"Does one break off? Which do I follow?"

"They're both the same road," said Norbert. "Just keep straight."

"You'll let me know if I need to turn?"

"Just keep straight," said Norbert. "No turns."

For miles the Caddy was the lone set of headlights streaking along the dark pavement. Wilberforce drummed his fingertips atop the steering wheel. He curled his upper lip, exposing his teeth, studying them in the rearview mirror. He scratched between two of his front teeth then licked the spot he had scratched. He adjusted his seatbelt to allow more slack at the belly.

"That was some brouhaha back there, huh?" offered Wilberforce.

Norbert didn't answer.

"Do you think you broke that guy's nose? I think you broke it. What do you think?"

"I guess," said Norbert.

"What happened? Who was he? How did it start?"

"I don't want to talk about it."

"I think we should talk about it," said Wilberforce.

"Too much talk today. I'm tired."

"Still," said Wilberforce, "I think we should talk."

"About what?"

"About your leg. I think we should talk about your leg."

"What about it? It's gone."

"This is not a recipe for successful communication."

"Good," said Norbert. "

"Good?"

"I'm tired and I don't feel like talking—about back at the motel, about my leg, about nothing."

Norbert leaned deeper into the seat cushion and closed his eyes.

"Why does Philip Philo Phipps think you saved his life?"

"Let's just be quiet for a while."

Wilberforce took his foot off the accelerator. The Caddy coasted to a stop.

"Are you nuts?" said Norbert. "You can't stop on a highway."

"Why does Philip Philo Phipps think you saved his life?"

"Quit clowning around. Hit the gas. Let's go!"

"Answer my question. Questions."

"It's complicated."

"How did you lose your leg?" said Wilberforce, "I doubt that's complicated."

"No," said Norbert. "Unfortunately, it's not."

The Caddy stood idling in the westbound lane. Steamy clouds billowed from the rear exhaust, disappearing into the Midwestern blackness. A pair of tractor-trailer headlights appeared behind the Caddy. In the mirrors, they both watched the vehicle closing the gap between them.

"Go!" said Norbert.

"I want us to establish some genuine discourse on this trip. Why does Philip Philo Phipps think you saved his life?"

The tractor-trailer barreled closer.

"Go!"

Wilberforce crept the Caddy forward at a few miles per hour. He steered the vehicle over the center line.

"How did you lose your leg?"

The headlights of the tractor-trailer bore down on the Caddy. The trucker blared his diesel horn.

"Go, you crazy fucker!" screamed Norbert.

Wilberforce gazed at him blankly. "I sense desperation in your voice."

The tractor-trailer was upon them. Wilberforce slowly cranked the wheel to the right. He stood on the gas and the Caddy leapt forward as the tractor-trailer howled past, horn blasting.

"I still don't hear you talking."

"Talk, talk, talk," said Norbert. "People these days talk and talk and talk too goddamn much. It's an illness. Everybody feels bullied into an opinion, running off at the mouth about every single thing. Sometimes you just don't give a shit. That's the truth, Padre. People can't accept that." Norbert turned to Wilberforce, "Fine, I'll tell you about my leg."

Wilberforce turned the Caddy back onto the road and brought it up to speed.

"I know what you want. You want me to tell you a story about my case of hard luck. Spin a good yarn. Tell a war story. You want me to talk about my feelings, my fears and disappointments. Well, I'm not gonna do that.

"You sense a desperation in me? Let me tell you, desperate is the moment you realize your half-assed decision to earn money for a big college by being a soldier every other weekend has transplanted your ass into the fucking desert.

"Desperate is sand in your weapon and your eyes and ears and between your toes and down your neck and up your ass crack. Hot sand in pores and cracks and crevices you can't get a bar of soap into. Not that you get bars of soap.

"Desperate is no beer and no pussy for sixteen months. Thinking you're getting deactivated after eleven, like every other grunt in the history of the Guard, then getting jerked around so many times you don't know which way is up. Desperate is learning your hitch is extended by another mandatory year by presidential executive order. Desperate is overnight fire watch. Desperate is a first sergeant with a hard-on for crisp uniforms in the middle of a war in a goddamn sandbox.

"You go through a door over there and you have no clue what's on the other side. Could be a guy with an AK, could be a lady feeding a baby.

"Desperate is crowd patrol in open air markets when it's 130 degrees on an average day, when any second one of those dirty towel heads can take a pot shot from some shadow in your six o'clock. It's the Wild West over there. I still don't like crowds. Since I've been back, in busy rooms, I stand with my back against the wall, watching the door.

"Desperate is twilight checkpoints. Nissan trucks with no tags. Desperate is smiling and nodding your head at some hare-lipped Saudi grad student with dead eyes just before he clutches his belly and unmakes your best friend with a body bomb—taking along your left leg, just below the knee. You scream and cry and howl and drag yourself over to your buddy. There ain't nothing left of him, but you grab what's there and you squeeze it tight in the red mess and the sand, that fucking sand, that soaks into your fatigues and you holler some more. You see orange heat through your eyelids. Then colors swirl and it goes dark and you float above the action and understand on some detached level of consciousness that you will live and he will die and that's the end of it. He will get nineteen years—*nineteen years*—and you will get a trip to Walter

Reed for 10 months of surgeries, skin grafts, physical therapy, awkward visits, and white-hot pain.

"You can't sleep. And when you do sleep, the dreams come—dreams of firefights, rockets, and rounds chipping stone just above your head. Dreams of jumping on a trampoline when you were nine years old and climbing rock trails in Lake Placid, dreams of high-stepping through rubber tires on the obstacle course at Fort Benning, of running with the football tucked deep beneath your shoulder, returning a punt in the state championship game. And even dancing, dreams of dancing—even though you never cared to dance. It's always there in your dreams, your leg, but then you wake and the only thing there is the pain and the guilt and the sadness. The pain of that red stump, the sadness of a lost buddy, the guilt of knowing it was you ordered to stand in that spot at that moment. And it would have been you, *it should have*, if you weren't late because you were off fucking around. If you weren't always such a goddamn comedian.

"And when it's all over, when it's finally time for you to go home, they send you to your 'Don't Beat Your Wife' briefing, you check a box that says you're not depressed or considering suicide and—boom! You're back in the civilian world, just like that.

"Since I've been back, I've seen people desperate for bigger tits or whiter teeth, desperate for a midnight blue Lexus SUV or Italian granite with just the right vein of copper running through it for their new half-acre of countertop. Desperate for a cell phone so small and thin it looks like you're talking into a potato chip. I guess there are just different degrees of desperate, Padre. But I've come to accept that disparity. It's my problem, mine alone. People tell me I need to 'buck up,' 'dust myself off,' 'get over it.' People fascinate me. It all fascinates me. Now more than ever.

"So, I'm going to California. I am going to the place where they buried the hamburger that was once my friend Sully. I am going to tell him I am sorry that he only got nineteen years. Even though I don't believe he's there, not really, it's the only spot on this earth where it makes sense to converse with him. And even though I feel an ache of pathetic emptiness in these words as I speak them, I am going there anyway. Because for me, that's the end of this road.

"I'll leave my hardware with him: this Purple Heart and Bronze Star for valor that the army sent me home with for disobeying orders, clowning around, and getting him blown to pieces. Medals are teardrops pinned to a soldier's chest. For me, they are tears of shame and guilt. I will leave them there with him. Then I will go to Sully's parents and I will tell them the truth about his death: that it was my fault. Then, maybe I'll talk with God, face-to-face. Or face-to-whatever."

And then, thought Norbert, I think I might just wade into that blue Pacific Ocean and never wade out.

"Well, if you do speak with God, I'm curious to know what his voice sounds like," said Wilberforce, trying to lighten the moment. "Record it for me. I'm only half-joking you understand. At bare minimum, you have to take notes."

"Shit!" hollered Norbert. "Fuck!"

"What?"

"My notebook! I left it at the motel. Holy fuck! How could I be so stupid?"

Four hours later, at around 9 a.m., they arrived in South Bend, Indiana. Wilberforce stopped for gas and coffee at a Phillips 66. When Norbert went in to pay, he could not help but notice that the attendant was dressed head to toe in attire celebrating the Michigan Wolverines football program.

"Must be a tough town to live in when you're from Michigan," said Norbert, handing the attendant his credit card.

"Not from Michigan."

Norbert looked the man up and down. The maize and gold. The snarling wood creature screen-printed across his chest. "Where you from?"

"Vegas."

"Huh," said Norbert. "I'm headed out that way myself. Got any recommendations?"

"For what?" The attendant ran Norbert's card through a small device beside the register, tapped some numbers into the keypad.

"Hot spots. Local knowledge."

"Nope," said the attendant, handing Norbert back his card.

"I've always wondered," said Norbert. "What do they call people from Las Vegas?"

"My name is Scott," said the attendant. "People call me that."

Norbert signed his receipt. He said, "What're the Irish playing Michigan in basketball or something this week?"

"North Carolina," said Scott.

As an afterthought, Norbert paid cash for a quart of 10W-30 and asked Scott if there was a phone he could use. He was directed to the side of the building.

About ten minutes later Norbert walked toward Wilberforce as he swabbed the windshield with the complimentary squeegee dipped in blue fluid. Norbert popped the cap off the motor oil and, while using a key to pierce the thin membrane of metallic film glued over the container's spout, slipped and punctured the tip of his left index finger.

"Fuck. Goddamn it."

"What happened?" said Wilberforce. "You hurt yourself?"

Norbert pinched his fingertip, presenting Wilberforce the bright red bubble at the tip.

"No blood for oil," said Norbert, sucking at his finger as they climbed back into the Caddy. "Normally, I don't go for puns, but that was too good to resist."

"Well, it's a good policy," said Wilberforce as he fired up the 500-cubic-inch engine and pulled into traffic. "Well?"

"Well, what?" said Norbert.

"What about your diary?"

"It's not a *diary*," said Norbert. "It's a notebook."

"Did you reach the motel?"

"Yes."

"And?"

"And nothing. They don't have it."

"You had them check the drawer?"

"I had them check all the drawers. Had them ask the cleaning staff. It's gone. Vanished. I don't want to talk about it."

"It'll turn up," said Wilberforce.

"Nothing ever turns up. It's gone."

"Why would anyone want to steal a stranger's di—notebook, Norbert? It's just been misplaced. It'll turn up. Did you give them any contact information?"

"I told them if anyone returns it, call Pete Hines in Monterey, California. The number and the address are written inside. I offered a reward."

"How much?"

"I didn't say."

"Good thinking," said Wilberforce. "It'll turn up."

"No it won't. It's gone. But that's fine. In fact, that's just perfect. I need to start letting go."

"Sometimes you have to give yourself over to providence, Norbert. 'I returned and saw under the sun, that the race is not to the swift, nor the battle to the strong, neither yet riches to men of understanding, nor yet favor to men of skill; but time and chance happeneth to them all.' Ecclesiastes."

"I don't want to talk about it anymore," said Norbert. He shut his eyes and tried to sleep. Tried, but did not.

As they approached the campus, Norbert sat up, taking sharp notice of the glinting golden dome atop the main building. A flush of resentment reddened his face when he considered what it would have been like to attend a big college—and not just *any* college. He allowed himself to daydream what it might have been like to attend the University of Notre Dame. These students cannot possibly appreciate it the way I would have, he thought. I would have swallowed every moment like moist, ripe fruit; licked each day on campus like thick, sweet syrup from my greedy fingers. My life would be so different, he thought. So much better.

Norbert felt a dull throbbing commence behind his right eye. He rubbed his lid lightly with his fingertip, looking over at Wilberforce, wondering if he could somehow divine the source of his physical discomfort. Wilberforce was picking his teeth with the corner of a matchbook.

Norbert pictured the Sherbert trailer in Fonda, his drunken father—smooth, ghostly shins exposed—convalescing before his oscillating fan. Of the student body of Notre Dame, his father would say: "Rich pricks, all of them. Born on third base convinced they hit a triple. Handed everything their whole lives. First job will probably be with their daddy's bank or corporation. They're all there to major in 'Screw the little guy.' Notre Dame? That college is the worst of the lot! They're in cahoots with the pope. Vatican West."

Norbert Sr.'s only real exposure to such places as Notre Dame was through televised football. You either loved or hated the Irish, and Norbert's father hated them. For him, there was only Syracuse. Also a very expensive private university—a fact that did not deter Norbert Sr.

Syracuse. A basketball school that most fans needed constant reminding still had a football squad. He said he hated it, but Norbert suspected his father secretly loved to watch his team lose. Following a team of losers was one of the pure pleasures in sport. There was nothing so satisfying as an encyclopedic devotion to a losing team.

You could love a loser boldly because the power was in the hands of the person offering his love. To love a winner was to be a front-runner, the worst sort of sports enthusiast.

But Notre Dame was a winner. Eleven national championships. Seven Heisman Trophy winners. All while maintaining, over the objections of many alumni, rigorous admissions and academic standards. To Norbert, it was a kingdom, a temple. They parked the Caddy and walked the main quad. They sat inside the Basilica of the Sacred Heart, lit candles in the Our Lady of Lourdes Grotto. Such money spent, such beauty devoted to an unembarrassed belief in stories, thought Norbert.

In the Hammes Bookstore, Norbert purchased a navy blue watch cap with the classic "ND" emblazoned on the front in gold stitching. On the back, an embroidered shamrock.

They walked through the bitter wind to the stadium, lingered. Norbert pulled the cap low over his ears, his eyes watering from the stinging cold. Below his red nose, clouds formed and vanished. Norbert and Wilberforce stood before the stadium's rear gate, hands plunged deep into their coat pockets.

"What d'ya think?" asked Wilberforce.

"Not bad," said Norbert. "Not too fucking bad."

"Can't leave without seeing Touchdown Jesus."

In the shadow of the Hesburgh Library, the two men gazed up at the 134-foot-high, 68-foot-wide Word of Life Mural: *Touchdown Jesus*.

"Now this is America," said Norbert. "Right here in this single image."

"What do you mean?"

"Synergy."

"I don't follow," said Wilberforce.

"Big time sports. Big time Jesus."

13

Leaving South Bend, Wilberforce suggested they visit St. Agnes's Children's Mission. St. Agnes's was an orphanage Wilberforce had volunteered in while a student of divinity. He had returned to visit on several occasions.

"It's been a while since my last appearance," said Wilberforce. "I wonder if Sister Kate's tennis elbow has cleared up."

Norbert thought St. Agnes's would be a church, but when they parked the Caddy along the curb out front and killed the engine what he saw looked more like a red-brick YMCA in bad decline.

"Wait till you meet Sister Kate," said Wilberforce. "She's a sweet dish of syrup. What a life force! Sister Kate could light the Christmas tree in Rockefeller Center by just holding the plug in her hand. And salty humor? I tell you, Norbert, if she had not donned the habit, she'd be wearing the watch cap and petty coat of a merchant sailor. She's just what these kids need."

Wilberforce's reference caused Norbert to picture a nun in a crow's nest on watch for icebergs in the angry North Atlantic.

Immediately inside the thick oak double doors, Wilberforce caught sight of Sister Kate's backside. He removed his shoes and bolted into a silent sprint down the glassy linoleum corridor. Several feet from the unsuspecting nun, Wilberforce shifted into a power slide in his stocking feet and delivered a full, open-handed swat to her blessed behind. Whap!

"Peace be with you!" he bellowed.

The nun screamed—an unnerving, unhappy, gurgling scream—as a stack of loose papers exploded into the air, cascading downward. Wilberforce soon realized that the nun was not Sister Kate at all. Indeed, he had assaulted the buttocks of a nun he had never met, bringing her within one half-heartbeat of an infarction.

Outside the door of the mother superior's office, Wilberforce and Norbert sat together on a hard wooden bench. Behind the door there echoed a breathless tirade of indignant outrage. The words were not all distinguishable, but the sentiment behind them was clear. The animated silhouette of the accosted nun could be seen through the door's frosted glass. A few feet in front of their penal bench, the office secretary clacked away on her computer keyboard, pausing now and again to frown over her glasses at the guilty parties.

The door of the mother superior's office jerked open. A hot-faced Sister Anne stalked out and wheeled on the balls of her feet to face Wilberforce. Her brain boiled with thoughts but she could not form any into words, or even syllables for that matter.

Wilberforce smiled and winked. "I am sorry Sister. But in all fairness, Jesus did say, 'If someone strikes you on the right cheek turn to him the other also.' Ergo, I still owe you one."

Sister Anne made a growling noise originating deep within her intestinal tract.

"Sister Anne," said Mother Superior, "remember your Ephesians. 'Instead be kind to each other, tenderhearted, forgiving one another, just as God, through Christ, has forgiven you.'"

Sister Anne could see she was outnumbered, that her lack of humor for the act so callously perpetrated upon her sacred bottom was now a handicap. She could not stomach the thought of remaining another instant so they could all titter at her humiliation. What an impetuous child, this oafish ex-priest, thought Sister Anne. If only he *were* a child, she would bring her measuring stick down with great force upon his chubby digits. Sister Anne pointed a trembling finger at Wilberforce, held it suspended for a long beat, then stalked away.

"Father Wendell," said Mother Superior, "care to step into my office, or are there more introductions you wish to make?"

Wilberforce and Norbert followed the woolen nun into her dully-lit office. Before they could find a seat, she said, "I have difficult news to deliver, Father. Sister Kate, is dead. Vespa accident."

"Sweet Jesus," stammered Wilberforce.

Clearly, thought Norbert, Vespas are a menace in the hands of clergy.

"It happened only a week ago," said Mother Superior. "Everyone here is still quite in shock."

"We had so much in common," said Wilberforce, shaking his head. "She was a beautiful soul." Wilberforce asked no questions as Mother Superior described the details of the accident. Sister Kate had been on her way home from yoga. It was dark. There was a blind corner. Black ice. No drunks or teenagers were involved. It was, alas, God's will.

Though he had counseled hundreds of grieving parishioners through the years, Wilberforce's own grief was a separate matter. He considered Sister Kate to be one of those cheerful souls who would always be in his life—a phone call away, a thrilling surprise pop-in visit—always picking up where they had left off, whether it be a month or five years. Wilberforce seemed distant after digesting the news. Mother Superior asked him if he wanted a glass of water; he asked for something stronger. Mother Superior went to her file cabinet and from the bottom drawer, hidden beneath bulging manila folders, she removed a long wooden box. Inside the box was a half-filled bottle of Midleton Very Rare Irish whiskey.

"How did that get in there?" asked Wilberforce.

Mother Superior winked, "Leprechauns." She poured a snoot into three coffee mugs. They raised a toast to Sister Kate: "Slainte."

There came a muffled, apologetic knock on the door.

"Enter," said Mother Superior, deftly stowing the wooden box inside a low desk drawer in a fluid motion.

"I'm sorry to interrupt," said Sister Isabelle, "but you wanted me to update you on Sasha's progress after today's geography lesson."

"Yes, Sister Isabelle," said Mother Superior. "This is Father Wendell—"

"The *former*," said Wilberforce.

"Yes. The former," said Mother Superior. "And his companion—"

"Norbert."

"Oh," said Sister Isabelle, the usual fear and awkwardness she felt when summoned to Mother Superior's office now compounded by the presence of these strange men. "I should come back."

"No, please," said Wilberforce, rising. "Have a seat."

Norbert stood also. He smiled a goofy smile at Sister Isabelle. He couldn't shake the notion that he had stumbled into some Bing Crosby picture, surrounded by all these real-life nuns. Having no Catholic upbringing, he associated not an ounce of fear at the sight of them. Thus far, this children's mission was to Norbert like some grand pageant.

Sister Isabelle recoiled from the chairs offered to her, her discomfort acute. She could not decide what to do with her hands.

"How was Sasha's lesson, Sister?" Mother Superior was an old pro at keeping people focused on the task at hand.

"Oh. Not very good, I'm afraid. No, not very good. He is behind in his capitals and rivers. His mountain ranges are satisfactory. But most distressing, he is very confused about the Balkans."

"Who isn't?" laughed Wilberforce. His joke fell flat.

"I think he is distracted," offered Sister Isabelle. She watched Mother Superior closely to see if her observation was relevant.

"Certainly he is," said Mother Superior. "It is only natural. He has been made to believe he can be returned, like some power drill. He thinks he is unloved. But that isn't true, is it Sister?"

"No."

"Who loves him, Sister?" said Mother Superior.

"We love him," answered Sister Isabelle.

"*Jesus* loves him," said Mother Superior.

"Oh yes. Jesus does love him." For the first time, Sister Isabelle looked directly at Wilberforce and Norbert, standing behind their chairs. "Jesus loves us all."

"What did you assign him, Sister?"

"I gave him a list of his capitals to memorize. He must print each one ten times. Also, blank maps of Europe. He must color in the nations and identify them."

"All right," said Mother Superior. "Did he say anything to you?"

"Say anything?"

"Anything I should know about?"

"No, no," said Sister Isabelle. "He seemed upset, frustrated, about how slowly he's progressing. I just think he's sad. He's a sad little boy."

"Thank you, Sister," said Mother Superior. "I know you're needed in the kitchen."

"I'm preparing the dough for tomorrow."

"Yes, I know."

Sister Isabelle closed the door silently by turning the knob all the way to the right, then slowly allowing the spring action to feed the lock back into the jamb. Quiet as a church mouse pissing on cotton.

"This is Sasha's second go-round with us," said Mother

Superior. "He has not had it easy." Mother Superior explained how, the previous spring, a married couple in their early thirties had arrived at her office door. She was a Ph.D. in literature with short dark hair, kind, searching eyes and an easy smile that revealed very successful orthodontics. He was a building contractor, slowly assuming his father's business and reputation. They had come highly recommended through a broker with whom Mother Superior often collaborated.

Sasha had come from Russia. He was born in Provideniya, a small fishing village on the Bering Sea. His father had perished in those icy waters, having been swept over the side of a crab boat. Sasha was the youngest of seven. His mother, unable to care financially for the large brood, put the oldest (15 years old) to work at sea and disperse the youngest three to relatives. Sasha was the "lucky" one who went to live with an aunt, the father's sister, in Linkville, Indiana—traveling by sea, then train, then air with his nervous young uncle who felt obligated out of guilt over his brother's (Sasha's father's) death. Sasha's uncle had, in fact, attempted suicide over what he considered to be his part in the death of his brother at sea, but the selected knife was dull and not up to the task. Community sympathy in the wake of his failed effort was not as he had anticipated.

The aunt, once slender with a beauty mole that eventually grew into a cancerous growth requiring surgical removal, had matured into a fat, sleepy woman fond of Pabst Blue Ribbon and watching her afternoon stories while lounging on the divan in her purple housedress. She had made it to the states as a mail-order bride. Her husband, a diminutive, milquetoast attorney with a horseshoe of fine, auburn hair was "disappeared" one day. It was later revealed that he had gotten in deep with a group of gentlemen who enjoyed thoroughbred horse racing, and as an extension of their enthusiasm, took bets on the results. Sometimes, they would even attempt to manipulate those results to their satisfaction, such was the extent of their enthusiasm for the "sport of kings."

The fat aunt had enlisted the services of her missing husband's partner to get him declared dead so that she could be awarded the benefits of his life insurance policy, a substantial sum. She had been cleared of all suspicion of foul play, having no discernible contacts in the outside world and a limited range of movement. It was then just a matter of finding the attorney's purloined body.

Sasha arrived at the aunt's house, along with her youngest brother, the fisherman with the superficial scratches on his wrists. She was under the mistaken impression that there would be money included with the delivery of this nephew she had never laid eyes upon and that his stay with her would be brief. That he was, indeed, en route to some other terminal destination. Such confusions can arise when favors are asked over great distances via postcard. The postcard from Provideniya, which the aunt displayed on her refrigerator behind a magnet resembling a miniature potholder reading "Bless This House," had a picture of an Alaskan King Crab on it.

The uncle lasted one night on the divan before going out for smokes, never to return. Sasha lasted three weeks, mostly keeping the foam rubber koozie extending from his aunt's flabby right wrist filled with Pabst Blue Ribbon. Sasha was not enrolled in school and he was discouraged from venturing outside, lest the neighbors' curiosity be piqued. She would not allow anything to queer the insurance investigation into her disappeared husband.

Eventually, a man who smelled like coffee grinds, motor oil, and ammonia, who came by twice weekly with three cartons of Indian reservation cigarettes (and also to throw his thing into the cow on the divan), in one of his flaccid post-coital moments, agreed to take Sasha for a drive "upstate." The evening drive transported Sasha a short jog up Route 31 into South Bend where the man suddenly stopped, pulled the car to the curb, asked Sasha to step out to check the right rear tire's pressure (under the pretense that the car was, "Pulling to the right like a motherfucker") whereupon the man squealed away, leaving Sasha standing in front of a brick building that looked like a rundown YMCA with a sign in front that read: St. Agnes's Children's Mission. Sasha was seven years old. In fact, that is the first thing he said to Sister Kate when she opened the front door. He said it in Russian.

Three months and three days after Sasha's eighth birthday, he was adopted by that couple in their early thirties from Brownsburg, an Indianapolis suburb. Being established in their careers, and having accumulated, through world travel, many objects of great value that resided on low shelves where toddlers could easily molest them, they preferred to adopt an older (and by calculated assumption, more grateful) child that would assimilate into their schedules, rather than the inverse.

Sasha *was* grateful. He had worked very hard on his English, hoping and praying for this day to come (though he mostly prayed for the benefit of the nuns, having serious doubts about the existence of a benevolent God due to recent life events). In Brownsburg, Sasha was enrolled in private school. He played soccer and began violin lessons on a larger instrument called a *viola*—his slender fingers and Russian origin being the impetus for the selection, by his adoptive parents, of that instrument. Sasha was a world away from Provideniya and things were good. Things were very good.

It happened on a Tuesday morning. Sasha's adoptive mother, an adjunct Freshman Composition professor at Valparaiso University, was writing a biography of the

Hoosier popcorn magnate Orville Redenbacher. She was performing research into the Redenbacher Papers housed in the Indianapolis Public Library. Her husband had an appointment to look at commercial property nearby. They drove into the city together.

Witnesses said the pickup truck was ten, maybe fifteen feet off the ground, turning as it flew like shot from a rifle. It landed at an angle on the passenger side of their vehicle, killing her instantly. She never had a chance. Sasha's adoptive father said he never saw it coming. He said it to the police and to her parents and to dozens of others for weeks—anyone, really, who would listen. There was nothing he could do. They were stopped at a light, in the middle of traffic. He didn't have a scratch on him.

The driver of the pickup, who of course walked away from the tragedy unscathed, was high on pot, sipping from a flask of Kamchatka vodka he kept balanced between his knees. He was a carpenter speeding to a job site when he lost control of the vehicle, hit the rear end of another vehicle stopped at the red light on the opposite side of the intersection, and launched airborne. The drunk, pothead carpenter's next job would have been working on the commercial property Sasha's father was driving into Indianapolis to view that morning. That is, if the drunk pothead had not been sentenced to prison for five years in a plea agreement. Also of mild interest, the small fishing village where Sasha was born is located on the Kamchatka Penninsula, along the Bering Sea. Small world.

It took one day less than a month after he laid his wife in the ground before Sasha's adoptive father decided he simply could not raise Sasha as a single parent. You see, he explained to a stoic Sister Kate, it was always my wife who insisted we adopt. My grief, he explained, is all-consuming. It is not a healthy environment for Sasha to be raised in.

"Your grief will pass," said Sister Kate, "eventually. It will subside and you will go on. I know you can't fathom that now, but things will get better. You have Sasha to think about. Pour your love for your wife into him. He is *your* son now. Trust in your faith."

"My faith," he snorted, rearranging himself in his chair. He did not intend to sound so vicious. He said, "I simply can't do it."

"You *can't?*" said Sister Kate.

He looked at her for a long moment, setting his face with that same million-dollar, deal-closing stare his father had cultivated and taught to him. Then he said, "I won't."

Sasha came back to live at St. Agnes's on a Sunday morning after Mass. His adoptive father married a mortgage broker the following autumn, though Sasha would never know anything about it. There is a trend toward autumn weddings. The temperature is more pleasant in the church, the majority of which lack air conditioning. And the foliage is a big plus. It's beautiful. Then, of course, there is nature's whole poetic reminder of life, death, rebirth. The sense that nothing is ever permanent.

"Will you be staying for a meal?" Mother Superior asked Wilberforce and Norbert.

"No," said Norbert. "We gotta be getting back on the road."

"Would you like to have a look around before you go?" she asked Wilberforce. "I know how personal this place is to you."

"That would be delightful," said Wilberforce.

A light snow was falling. The nuns were allowing the children to run free about the grounds (under close supervision) rolling snowmen, running and diving atop sleds. Two boys kicked up snow into a group of girls—for which they were quickly admonished. Norbert, Wilberforce, and

Mother Superior stood inside the mission looking through the dark, wooden grid of a large picture window. Norbert could feel the cold air on his bare skin smuggling through the panes of glass. Weather stripping, he thought. Caulk.

"How are things here?" asked Wilberforce.

"Oh, you know very well how they are," said Mother Superior. "It's always a struggle. The diocese has suffered financially throughout the scandals. Attendance is down. Contributions are paltry. It's been a hard winter, and now it seems we can hold off no longer on a new roof. We make phone calls, we twist arms, we pray."

Wilberforce nodded.

"How is Margaret?"

"Are we to pretend you don't already know?" asked Wilberforce.

"I didn't want to be presumptuous."

"I have made mistakes."

"We are all sinners," said Mother Superior. "Some more than others. And your dissertation, what of that?"

"How do you know about that?"

Mother Superior simply stared back. *Was he kidding?* As if any detail could escape her notice.

"It needs tweaking," said Wilberforce.

"Spinoza is an excellent study for you. In his *vanitas* he describes the melancholy thoughts that follow when we at last achieve what we claim we always wanted."

Mother Superior was quite comfortable with the protracted silence that followed her remark before she was summoned away for a telephone call. As she exited, she reminded the men that they were welcome to stay for lunch. Norbert asked for the location of a rest room. She told him to follow her so she could direct him. Wilberforce remained at the window. A girl squealed. A clump of snow had become knotted in her dark, curly hair. A nun trudged double-time through the snow, snatching up a boy by the collar of his winter jacket.

Wilberforce walked the hall, peeking into vacant rooms. At the far end, yellow light from an open door washed the polished floor. Inside, dozens of single beds with hard, hospital corners lined both sides of a long room. At the back left corner, Wilberforce noticed the lone figure of a boy seated atop his bed, barely moving, papers, crayons, books, and a music player with headphones spread out before him. The boy did not look up. Even when Wilberforce, his heavy footfalls telegraphing his cautious approach, was upon him, the boy did not look up.

"What are you working on?" asked Wilberforce.

The boy did not respond. Wilberforce could see that the papers were Xeroxed, wordless maps of Europe.

"Are you working on the Balkans?"

The boy shrugged.

"Well," said Wilberforce, "I wouldn't worry too much. By the time you're done coloring they will all have changed anyway."

No response. It was not fear Wilberforce sensed, it was . . . sorrow. "Still," croaked Wilberforce, clearing his throat, "You should learn them just in case. I can help. Do you want me to help?"

The boy shrugged.

Wilberforce knelt and rested his elbows on the bunk. He sifted through the papers. "Let's start with the easy ones, huh? What's this big one in the middle?"

He shrugged again.

"C'mon now. I don't believe you for a second. You know this. I can tell by looking at you. Look at the capacity of that cranium. That noggin holds a ten-pound brain or my name isn't Wilberforce Wendell."

The boy giggled.

"It is! My name is Wilberforce Wendell. Is that a silly name? Now," Wilberforce pointed at the map, "what is this country right here?"

"Poland," said the boy.

"Exactly. I knew you couldn't hold it in. So much knowledge. It's not fair to the rest of us when you refuse to share it. So how will we remember, forever and ever, that this is Poland?"

Wilberforce opened the box of sixty-four Crayola crayons with the built-in sharpener. "We need a color that begins with 'P.' How about pink?" Wilberforce slid a crayon from the carton. "Hm. This looks pink, but they're calling it 'salmon.' No matter, here's another. '*Carnation* pink.' I don't know. Is this close enough? What do you think?"

"I don't like pink."

Wilberforce smiled. "I don't like pink either. Our car is pink. They say it's the new black, but don't believe them. I've worn black most of my adult life. Pink will never be an alternative to black. Okay, how about purple?"

The boy nodded.

Wilberforce slid another crayon from the carton. "Here we go again. It says 'blue violet.' Let's try another. Now this says 'violet,' but in parentheses it says 'purple.' Do you know what parentheses are?"

The boy shrugged.

"It's when they put little boomerangs on both sides of a word to make it look like you're whispering. You understand?"

The boy nodded.

"Good. You take this and make Poland purple."

The boy took the crayon and filled the luckless Slavic nation with hard, jagged strokes of purple.

"Do you know what the capital of Poland is?" asked Wilberforce.

"Warsaw."

"That's right. Very good."

"Many cities and towns in the United States are named after Warsaw," said the boy. "There are eight total in the states of New York, Illinois, Indiana, Kentucky, Missouri, North Carolina, Ohio, and Virginia. There are Troys in fourteen states. Do you wish to know them?"

"No, that's not necessary. That's quite impressive, though. Where did you learn that?"

From beneath the spread of books, the boy lifted a slim volume of Rand McNally's *Almanac of World Facts*. "It's from 1995, so there could be more by now. I can only relay the information I've been provided."

"Yes," Wilberforce agreed. "Of course."

"I miss the Internet," said the boy. "The family I used to live with had the Internet. The nuns don't think we should have the Internet."

"Why?"

"Because of porn."

"Oh."

"Predators."

"Yes. I guess that makes sense."

"Plus, I'm eight and I probably understand more about computers than any of them."

"Yes, they are at an unfair disadvantage, nuns."

"My name is Sasha."

"Hello, Sasha. I'm Wilberforce."

"I know. You already said."

"You are a very intelligent boy, Sasha."

"I'm sad."

"You are?"

"That's what the nuns say. I hear them talking in the halls."

"They worry about you. They pray for you. Don't worry. Your time will come."

"I'm not worried."

"Oh. Good."

"I just don't want to be here anymore. I want my own room again. I want cable television. I want the Internet."

"Your time will come."

Sasha nodded. He twisted the dull violet (purple) crayon into the built-in sharpener. "Yeah, I guess."

"I'm serious. I wouldn't hesitate to have a bright, handsome boy like yourself come live with me."

"Really? Then why don't you adopt me?"

"I can't."

"No?"

"No. I'm going to California."

California. Sasha liked the sound of that, so exotic. What a word! He rolled it around on the tip of his tongue CAL-I-FORRRRRR-NI-A. CALIFOOOOOOORNIA. He had read the word many times, but it occurred to him this was the first he had heard anyone say it aloud. He loved it. What an amazing word! Sasha found it difficult to believe that a word sounding so beautiful was also a place, a physical place in the world. *California*. Breathtaking.

"Why are you going there?" asked Sasha.

"Oh, well . . . we all say we are *going* somewhere," said Wilberforce. "It's out of habit. But to put it more precisely, we are really *leaving* somewhere. We leave what we know for the hope of what might be. Devouring the past with each new mile traveled. We can't really go anywhere, only leave. There is no such thing as a destination."

"I left Russia."

"Do you remember it?"

"A little. It was cold. There was the sea."

"Close your eyes," said Wilberforce. "Do you see the water? The boats rocking in the harbor? The saltwater frozen to the pier? Do you see your mother?"

"Yes. I see my father, too."

"That's the same as traveling. Going to California. Arriving. Leaving again. It's the same. Think about that during all those times when you would rather be someplace other than here in the Mission. Close your eyes and travel."

Sasha opened his eyes. "I guess. Still, I think I'd rather go someplace for real."

"I understand. It's just a game. A trick on the mind."

Norbert entered. "We outta here?"

"Yes," answered Wilberforce. "Just a moment."

Norbert retreated back into the hall. He had been listening at the door for a few minutes, picking his spot to interrupt. Children made him uncomfortable—especially the twice-orphaned variety.

"When I get to California," said Wilberforce, "I will call Mother Superior, and if you are still here, we will talk on the phone. How does that sound?"

"Okay."

"I will give her my phone number, and I will tell her you have my permission to call when you are feeling lonely, or whenever. Does that sound like a good arrangement?"

"Can you also tell Mother Superior to give us the Internet?"

Wilberforce laughed. "I will tell her, but I'm afraid I have about as much clout as you do on that score. We'll work on her, though. Okay?"

"Okay."

"You see, I'm leaving but you can close your eyes and still see my funny face and hear my silly name anytime you choose. California is only as far away as you make it in your mind."

"Okay," said Sasha. "Drive safely."

Wilberforce pictured the airborne vehicle turning in slow motion, its stoned, drunken operator behind the wheel. He watched it smash into Sasha's adoptive mother in a groan of metal, and glass, and heartbreak. "I will," said Wilberforce. He dug into his pocket and handed Sasha a fistful of candies. "Shh," he said, bringing his finger to his ruddy nose with a wink.

Since they refused to stay for lunch, Mother Superior insisted they follow her into the kitchen so Sister Isabelle could make them both sandwiches for the road, featuring an assortment of meats. Mother Superior, who supervised Sister Isabelle's sandwich artistry closely, refused to acknowledge Norbert's insistence that cheese be withheld from his sandwiches. "You can't have a sandwich without cheese," she said.

Norbert insisted.

"You've never tried *this* cheese," she said.

Norbert assured her it made no difference the style of cheese.

"If you don't like it, you can always take it off," she said.

Wilberforce wanted to say goodbye to Sasha, but he was nowhere to be found.

Mother Superior said, "It's nothing new. He hides."

"He hides?" said Wilberforce.

"Yes, since he's come back to us, he hides. Sometimes for hours. Eventually we find him."

Out of Norbert's view, Wilberforce pressed an envelope into Mother Superior's hand.

"It's not enough for a new roof," said Wilberforce, "but it's something."

"Where will you go next?"

Wilberforce leaned in, "Margaret is staying with her mother in Denver. I have it in my mind to pay her a visit."

"Why are we whispering?" said Mother Superior.

Wilberforce motioned toward Norbert. "We haven't discussed it yet. This isn't really my trip."

14

The bell atop the glass door jangled as Andy with the Red Boots—two black, swollen eyes, a splint down the center of his nose with surgical tape spread across it—entered a Phillips 66 station in South Bend, Indiana.

Andy asked the attendant, a grizzled, oily, middle-aged man, if he remembered seeing a tall, skinny guy with a limp yesterday, maybe traveling with another guy—stocky, medium height.

"Nope," said the man. "But I wasn't here yesterday. Scott was."

"Is Scott here today?" asked Andy.

"He's in there," pointed the man, "changing a tar."

Andy found Scott in the garage working a piece of bent iron between the rubber and rim of a truck tire. He asked him if on the previous morning he had seen a lanky peckerwood fitting Norbert's description traveling in a pink Cadillac.

"I did," said Scott, banging his thumb and then bringing that grimy digit to his mouth for sucking.

"Did you speak with him at all?"

"Twenty dollars," said Scott.

"What about twenty dollars?"

"I'll tell you what he said to me for twenty dollars."

"Are you serious?" said Andy. He wrinkled his face in disbelief, creating a sharp pain in his nose, which he touched gently. Scott shrugged and went back to work on the truck tire.

Andy handed him a twenty. "What did he say to you?"

"You look ridden hard and hung up wet, fella," said Scott. "Somebody knock you out?"

"What did the tall guy say?"

"He wanted to know who Notre Dame was playing in basketball. I told him it was the Tarheels."

"I see," said Andy. "Joke's on me, right? Very good. Well played, sir. What will you spend your new $20 on? I suggest an aggressive soap."

"He also mentioned he was headed to Vegas."

"Did he tell you when he'd get there?"

"I took him to mean he'd get there eventually."

Andy with the Red Boots returned to his car. An automatic pistol lay on the seat. He opened his laptop. The history of Norbert's credit card activity was on the screen. Andy had used his own security software to track Norbert down. He closed out of the program and opened a new window, booking a flight from Chicago to Las Vegas, Nevada.

15

Elton Berryhill powered off his computer, sign of the cross, and climbed the stairs into the kitchen. What's for dinner tonight, thought Elton, twice-warmed meatloaf?

Elton's mother was not in the kitchen.

Elton climbed the stairs to the second floor, calling for her. He was hungry. *Why does God test my patience so?* he thought. *Woman, what have I to do with thee?*

In the upstairs hall, Elton called her name.

He found her in the bathroom, dead on the tile floor. Elton opened the medicine cabinet, snatched her prescription and screamed, "Take your pill! Take your pill! Can't you get it through your thick skull?! God helps those who help themselves!"

He emptied the bottle onto her body.

In Ma Berryhill's bedroom, Elton dragged her through the door and tucked her into bed.

"You who are not my blood," said Elton, 'may you be washed in the blood of Christ.'"

In his own bedroom, clean, showered, and in his jammies, Elton knelt beside his bed and read aloud from Thessalonians:

> We do not want you to be unaware, brothers and sisters, about those who have fallen asleep, so that you may not grieve like the rest, who have no hope. For if we believe that Jesus died and rose, fallen asleep. Indeed, we tell you this, on the word of the Lord, that we who are alive, who are left until the coming of the Lord, will surely not precede those who have fallen asleep. For the Lord himself, with a word of command, will come down from heaven, and the dead in Christ will rise first. Then we who are left, will be caught up together with

them in the clouds to meet the Lord in the air. Thus we shall always be with the Lord. Therefore, console one another with these words.

The word of the Lord.

16

Two hours west of St. Agnes's Children's Mission, Norbert and Wilberforce approached the Indiana-Illinois border.

"So what about Lula?" asked Wilberforce.

"What about her?"

"You seemed smitten."

"She's beautiful," said Norbert. "Tall, thin, blonde. Smart, too. Sarcastic. I like that. She's a writer. She wants to move to California, maybe. Someday. There was something else about her, though. Something, I don't know. It sounds foolish to say."

"Say it anyway."

"Enduring," said Norbert. He cleared his throat then went to light his cigarette, which was already lit. "Something that lasts. Something that was there before we met."

Wilberforce nodded. He scratched something out of his left ear, studied it, discarded it with a flick. "Will you try to get back in touch with her? See her again?"

"How?"

"You can always go back to Cleveland."

"No," said Norbert. He pictured California: what Sully's grave might look like, standing face-to-face with Sully's parents, with, hopefully, God Himself. He pictured the Pacific Ocean on the cover of Pete's postcard, throwing itself against the jagged brown cliffs of Big Sur. The ocean, thought Norbert. *The ocean.*

"What about you and whatsername? Brandi."

"Another trifle."

Norbert reached into the backseat for his Charles Williams paperback. He noticed that the blue wool blanket, previously balled against the door behind the driver, now lay roundly above the foot wells. Norbert poked the blue mound. Beneath the fabric, his fingertips recognized the unmistakable sensation of human animation. He poked it again and the blue mound came to life.

"Jesus-fucking-Christ!" shouted Norbert.

Wilberforce swerved onto the shoulder. The tires rolled briefly over the rumble strips grooved into the pavement for the benefit of sleepy motorists. He jerked back onto the roadway.

"What is it?"

"There's someone in the backseat!"

Wilberforce screeched onto the shoulder and killed the engine. Both men leapt several feet from the vehicle. They composed themselves, then approached the rear doors warily. As Wilberforce neared the driver's side door, he craned his neck to look down between the front and rear seats.

A face appeared in the window.

Terror-stricken, Wilberforce shrieked girlishly, clutching at his chest.

It was Sasha.

Sasha: the savvy, sad Russian boy. He had hidden himself inside the Cadillac. Conspicuously, the only pink vehicle parked in front of St. Agnes's Children's Mission.

In Joliet, Illinois, Norbert, Wilberforce, and Sasha stopped for lunch to discuss this new situation. As they approached the front door to the restaurant, two window washers stood out front: one man busily engaged in his vocation, the other off to the side talking into his cellular phone. As Norbert passed the cell phone man, he overheard him emphatically declare, "No, no, no! When angels fall to earth they become mermaids!"

Just inside the door, Norbert came face-to-face with a young man sporting a beard. The young man gave

Norbert a familiar nod. This puzzled Norbert until he caught a glimpse of his own reflection. Several days of beard growth had accumulated on his pale, angular face. The young man's kindred acknowledgement was as if to say to Norbert, "We people with facial hair must stick together."

Seated at a round table in the center of the restaurant, Wilberforce stunned Norbert by arguing that Sasha should come along with them to California. "He should see America," said Wilberforce.

"He lives in Indiana," said Norbert.

"Indiana is not America. As your spiritual adviser, it benefits you to know that scripture teaches, 'to know children is to know God.' Jesus said in John 14:18, 'I will not leave you orphans.' You must admit, this will raise your profile another notch in the eyes of the man Himself. Unless, of course, you've abandoned your mission completely. It pains me to mention that you are still yet to break a *c* since we left Monday morning."

"I haven't abandoned anything," said Norbert. "I'm searching for inspiration. Much like yourself."

"I'm searching for *divine guidance*," said Wilberforce. "There is a distinct difference."

"What's a *c*?" asked Sasha.

"Never mind," said Wilberforce. "Do you want to review your list?"

"No," said Norbert. He fell silent, thinking. "If this kid stays with us, does that take care of stealing? Commandment number, what is it, six?"

"Eight," said Wilberforce. "Technically, you don't steal a person, you kidnap them—so no. Plus, bringing him along is really my idea. If Sasha does accompany us I would have to say, as your adviser, that you would still need to steal something."

"Is a *c* a commandment?" asked Sasha.

"If you really want him to come along so badly, you need to call the mission and clear it with the Head Mother in Charge," said Norbert. "The nuns are going to go nuts when they realize he's not just hiding—he's gonzo."

"Fine," said Wilberforce, "I'll call her right now."

"You're nuts," said Norbert. "There are fifty reasons she won't allow it to happen. She *can't* allow it to happen. There are laws."

"You're a funny one to invoke the sanctity of laws."

Norbert smirked, rattling the ice inside his empty glass.

"We'll see," said Wilberforce. "Let me use your cell phone."

"I don't have one," said Norbert. "Haven't you noticed?"

"How did you call the motel?"

"I used a pay phone at the gas station."

"A pay phone?" said Wilberforce. "They had a pay phone?"

"They did. Use your cell phone."

"It's gone. Margaret checked my call history, then smashed it."

"That's a conundrum," said Norbert.

Wilberforce scanned the room. His eyes stopped on the pretty hostess inside the front door. "I'll bet she has a cell phone," said Wilberforce, rising. "I'll be right back. I just may have some small influence over Mother Superior's decision-making."

"Whatever," said Norbert, leaning back in his chair, folding his arms. "Knock yourself out, Padre."

Sasha and Norbert sat uncomfortably for several excruciating minutes. Norbert kept looking over his shoulder in the direction of where Wilberforce had disappeared.

"How's your Coke?"

"Fine," said Sasha.

A long moment passed in silence.

"Fizzy?"

"Yes," said Sasha.

"Good," said Norbert. "Good."

Wilberforce chatted up the hostess. Her tag read: "Staci." He leaned in, whispering something into her ear that caused her green eyes to widen. She pushed him playfully on the shoulder. He did not place any phone call.

Back at the table, Wilberforce said, "He's coming with us."

"You're shitting me?" said Norbert.

"I am?" said Sasha. "To California?"

"Yes," said Wilberforce. "All the way to California."

"What did you say to the nun?" asked Norbert.

"She thought it was a splendid idea," said Wilberforce. "I'll fill you in later on the details."

The food arrived. Norbert cut a meatball in two with his fork, speared one half, popped it into his mouth and instantaneously spit it back onto his plate. Wilberforce looked up but said nothing. Sasha, head down, didn't notice.

"Sonofabitch," said Norbert. "You see? This is why I don't deviate. I don't deviate from fingers and fries."

The waitress, breezing past the table, paused. "Everything all right?" Her body leaned in the opposite direction with an almost magnetic pull.

"Smell this," said Norbert.

"Excuse me?"

"Give this a whiff." Norbert stabbed the fork into the other half of the meatball, the half he had not regurgitated, and held it aloft for the waitress's inspection. "What's this smell like to you?"

The waitress looked at Wilberforce. He shrugged. Norbert drew tight circles in the air with the red, congealed meat. "Smell it." For the moment, Norbert had her full attention, a difficult task with any waitress. She leaned forward and sniffed.

"What's that smell like to you?"

"Meat."

"What else?"

"Sauce?"

"What else?"

"I don't know. Oregano?"

"Cheese," said Norbert. "It smells like Parmesan cheese."

"Oh yeah," agreed the waitress. "Can I get you guys anything else? Does the little guy need another Coke?"

"Why do you suppose this smells like Parmesan cheese?" asked Norbert.

The waitress could not disguise her edginess. She was thinking three tables ahead. "I don't know, Mister. 'Cause it's got cheese in it."

Norbert brought his open palm down hard upon the table. Patrons turned to gawk.

"Pin a rose on you. Can you show me where on your printed menu you advertise cheese in your meatballs?"

"Look Mister Guy—" started the waitress.

"Trick question. Nowhere on your printed menu does it stipulate that these balls are made from anything but meat. It doesn't say 'cheesy meatballs,' it doesn't say 'meat and cheese balls,' it does not even include a parenthetical informing the customer that a component in this other-wise ball of meat, is cheese. Cheese, therefore, is a *covert* ingredient. Would you agree?"

The waitress jabbed her fist into her hip and shook her finger at Norbert.

"How about bread crumbs? You're not figuring on them. Everybody knows meatballs are made with bread crumbs, but they ain't on the menu neither."

"You've just argued in a circle," said Norbert. "Bread crumbs aren't included because, as you say, everybody knows they're critical to the integrity of the meatball. They're not included because they are assumed, whereas, Parmesan cheese is not. Parmesan cheese is an ingredient at the sole discretion of the chef. A *shadow ingredient*. Therefore, if it is to be used, the customer should be noti-fied in advance."

"What's with the hassle, Mister? You allergic or something?"

"I don't like cheese. It tastes bad. Is a life-threatening medical condition the only way you people in the food service industry can comprehend why an individual consumer such as myself would not want to shovel this putrid, vomitous cow piss into his mouth? I'd rather lick between the toes of an ultra-marathoner. I'd rather rim a seal's touch hole than eat Parmesan cheese. When I order a meatball, I expect meat in the form of a ball. Take this Italian ass fungus back into the kitchen and pass along this message to the chef: meat and bread crumbs. And tell him if he gets the idea to drop a goober or rub his johnson all over my meal, I'll know it before it gets here. Tell him I'll come back there and pull his large intestine out through his nose and strangle him with it."

Wilberforce emitted a low whistle and clicked his tongue. He polished off his diet cola, confident they would be making a fast exit.

"What's the problem?" said the manager, a tall man in his forties with puffy, dark-rimmed eyes and a great, black pompadour. He had drifted into the vortex of the disturbance from the lectern at the door with its white grease board diagram of the restaurant's floor plan pasted to its top. The commotion was at table 32.

"Mister Guy here is throwing a shit-and-fit because there's cheese in his meatballs," said the waitress.

"What do you want, guy?" said the manager. "There's cheese in everything. It's an Italian restaurant."

"It's an Olive Garden," said Wilberforce. "This place is Italian like Sammy Davis Jr. was Hebrew."

Sasha giggled. He didn't know who Sammy Davis Jr. was, but he liked the word *Hebrew*.

"That's it," said the manager with a wave of his hands. "You guys are done. You're disturbing the other diners.

Let's go. Don't make me call the cops. Some example you're setting for your kid."

"That's fine by me," said Norbert. "I'd rather eat from a paper cup standing in a bus station." He shifted his weight in his chair, reaching deep into his jeans pocket for his money clip. "Box up this spaghetti," he said. "I'll eat it on the road. And don't you worry about the example I'm setting for him," Norbert pointed at Sasha with a cash-filled fist. "He's a good egg. He knows what the score is. He knows it ain't right to deceive people with global cheese conspiracies."

Sasha giggled again. He pictured dangerous men in alleys with wide-brimmed fedoras pulled low over their eyes, concealing wedges of cheese beneath their long, black coats. A busboy began to scrape the food into takeout containers.

"That's right," announced Norbert to all within earshot. "There's a Great Cheese Conspiracy to insinuate cheese into every American meal. Every . . . single . . . meal! It extends to the highest levels!"

Wilberforce hooked an arm inside Norbert's elbow and began to lead him through the restaurant. With a sweep of his hand, Norbert scooped up the white, Styrofoam box of spaghetti from the table. "Big Dairy," Norbert warned the alarmed patrons, many of whom had set aside their cutlery to observe the spectacle. "This goes all the way to the top!"

When Norbert, Wilberforce, and Sasha were out into the parking lot, the manager smiled. The waitress sidled up beside him and, noticing the wrinkles formed at the edge of his right eye, said, "What are you grinning at?"

He turned and looked down at her, for she was a full two heads shorter. "There's cheese in the marinara, too."

En route to Des Moines, Wilberforce drove, Sasha sat on the passenger side, and Norbert stretched out snoring in the backseat. In his dream, Norbert sees a football spiraling downward from the bright white roof of the Carrier Dome. He catches it and begins to run. Dodging diving tacklers, he looks to his sideline. His coaches and teammates leap in slow-motion joy and anticipation. He spots the clock as time expires. Just one more stride, thinks Norbert; one more stride to the end line and certain victory. Norbert is snagged from behind, by his left foot. He falls short. He scrambles to his feet. He wants to see the face of the player who caught him. The tackler turns away, swallowed by the leaping, grabbing deluge of his ecstatic teammates. Norbert runs up to the wall of opposing players, tugs at jerseys, fights to worm his way into the melee. But the tackler is gone, vanished inside the nucleus of chaos and confusion.

Norbert woke. He stroked his belly, once flat and hard, now soft and doughy. He had just the other day sliced the buttonhole of his favorite jeans with his jackknife to gain a new half-inch of play. It was a sad state of affairs. Norbert had to shake his head at the thought of it.

Looking into the rearview mirror, Wilberforce noticed Norbert was awake. "Welcome back," he said.

Norbert grunted.

"Sasha and I have been discussing a name for our vehicle."

"A name?"

"Something heroic," said Wilberforce. "Or at the very least, poetic. Don Quixote had his Rocinante. Steinbeck, too, in *Travels with Charlie.* The Lone Ranger had Silver. Che Guevera called his motorcycle The Mighty One for his trek through South America."

Norbert was still waking up. He stretched his wingspan until the joints cracked.

"Rooster Cogburn called his stud Bo," Wilberforce continued.

"I get the picture," said Norbert. "What have you come up with so far?"

"The Pink Missile," said Sasha.

"*Gong*," said Norbert. "What else?"

"The Cherry Ferry," said Wilberforce.

"Jesus," said Norbert. "How long you two been working on this?"

"About an hour," said Wilberforce. "I'm afraid they're all like that. We were trying to make ourselves laugh."

"Let me think," said Norbert. He closed his eyes and leaned back into the smooth leather interior. "How about 'Fuck Osama'?"

Wilberforce cleared his throat.

"I like it," said Sasha.

"I saw it written across the nose of a Daisy Cutter in Afghanistan," said Norbert. "It's got a nice ring to it."

"Daisy Cutter?" asked Wilberforce.

"It's a 15,000-pound, BLU-82 high powered explosive device. A bomb."

"I see."

"They drop it from a C-130 by parachute. It's got a trigger that extends from the nose. When the trigger hits the ground, it deploys its payoff, obliterating everything above ground for hundreds of yards. A real motherfucker."

"I see," said Wilberforce.

"I like it," said Sasha.

"I don't see what it has to do with this trip," said Wilberforce.

"Are you kidding?" said Norbert. "Fuck Osama has got everything to do with everything."

"It would be better to select a name Sasha can say," said Wilberforce. "And besides, bin Laden has already been eliminated, his remains discarded at sea."

"True," Norbert agreed. "But the *idea* of Osama lives

on. He was always more powerful as a concept than as an actual person. How old are you Sasha?"

"Eight."

"You've lost your dad to the ocean. Your birth mother and family live a world away. You were pawned off on a relative you never met, then again to an orphanage. Then your adoptive mother was killed in a freak car accident and you were returned to that same orphanage. Is that correct?"

"Yes," said Sasha.

Norbert slapped his hand on Wilberforce's right shoulder, squeezed.

"The kid can say Fuck Osama. He's earned it."

In Des Moines, Iowa, Norbert, Wilberforce, and Sasha checked into one room together at a Travelodge. While completing their paperwork, the clerk noticed from Norbert's credit card and ID that he was a "Jr." The clerk told Norbert that he was a junior himself and that he was proud to be so named because his father was a fine man: successful in business and in life. He waxed on about how his father, bless his departed soul, was always there for him, supporting his decisions, taking him hunting and fishing. The clerk said he was honored to be named for his father.

Norbert stood staring at the clerk for an uncomfortable length of time.

"Everything okay, sir?"

"I don't feel that way at all about my old man," said Norbert. "Nope. Not at all. In fact, from this moment forward, I am no longer Norbert Sherbert Jr. I hereby renounce my juniorism."

Norbert leaned forward and scribbled over the "Jr." on his room slip. The clerk didn't know what to say to that. He looked away, unwilling to witness such a crude act of disrespect.

Waiting for the elevator, they watched a very small woman approaching up the length of the hall. She was not a dwarf or a midget, only a very small person of normal proportions. She approached slowly, stepping heavily, deliberately with each footfall. As she neared, it became apparent that she was wearing a harness-type apparatus with ballast strapped to either side of her torso. The elevator doors opened. Wilberforce and Sasha entered, but Norbert was determined to get to the bottom of this situation. He held his finger on the button until the woman was upon him.

"What is that?" said Norbert. "What do you have strapped to you?"

"What's it look like?" said the lady. "Twenty pounds of sand bags."

"What for?"

"Because I weigh less than 100 pounds, that's what for. Doctor says I got to strengthen my bones."

"Okay sand lady," said Norbert, walking onto the elevator. "You take it easy."

"Don't call me sand lady," she said as the doors slid closed.

In the room, Norbert used Wilberforce's Micronesian ritual knife to scrape the "Jr." off his credit card and driver's license. When he was finished, he asked Wilberforce for a ruling.

"As your spiritual adviser," said Wilberforce, "I have determined that there is no greater dishonor to one's parents than to reject the name they chose for you."

"Success!" said Norbert. "Scratch off number five."

"I was getting worried," said Wilberforce.

"Worried about what?" asked Sasha.

"Never mind," said Wilberforce.

"What's number five?" asked Sasha.

"Never mind," said Norbert. "Watch television."

17

In Las Vegas, Andy with the Red Boots unpacked his suitcase inside his high roller's suite. His laptop was open on the desk, connected to the hotel's wireless signal. He looked up a name on his cell phone and dialed.

"Hey, it's me. Who do I contact to get a gun in Vegas?"

Andy jotted some notes on hotel stationery. He hung up.

Andy's laptop made a *bing* sound. He opened a new window to see that Norbert had checked into a Travelodge in Des Moines, Iowa. Andy smiled. It hurt to smile. He touched his broken nose, ever so slightly.

Andy studied his reflection in the mirror above the laptop. He narrowed his eyes—ow . . . ow . . . It hurt to narrow his eyes.

"Come to papa, f-f-fucking N-N-Norbert."

18

Back in St. Agnes's Children's Mission outside South Bend, Indiana, the nuns were going nuts. They had finally conceded, after an exhaustive search of the building, that Sasha was missing.

"He must have somehow stowed away with Father Wendell and his skinny young friend," said Mother Superior. "But they would have certainly discovered him by now. Why haven't they phoned?"

"What should we do?" fretted Sister Isabelle.

"We can't afford a scandal," said Mother Superior. "The diocese is fishing for any reason to retract us. I wouldn't be surprised if the bishop was watching us right now from the bushes."

Sister Isabelle looked out the window. "The coast is clear," she said.

"This one can't get out," said Mother Superior. "That takes calling the police off the table."

"Sweet Mary," said Sister Isabelle. Confused, she searched the office nervously for a table upon which they might have placed a representative of law enforcement.

"Settle down, Sister," said Mother Superior.

"But what in heaven's name shall we do?"

"Let me think. Be quiet so I can think."

Sister Isabelle brought her fingertips to her lips, shushing herself.

Mother Superior leaned back in her creaky rolling chair behind her vast, oak desk, the wooden spindles fanned across her woolen back. As she thought, she made a church and steeple of her fingertips.

"We're going after them."

"Who?"

"Wilberforce and the other."

"But Mother, we're not even certain they have Sasha."

"They have him."

"But even if they do, we have no idea where they are, where they are going."

"I know exactly where they are going," said Mother Superior. "They're going to Denver, Colorado. Prepare the minivan."

19

Inside their room at the Travelodge in Des Moines, Iowa, Sasha chose the bed nearest the bathroom while Norbert and Wilberforce flipped two-out-of-three to see who would get the other bed. The coin determined that Norbert, since the motel was out of guest cots, would sleep sitting up in a chair. But before he turned in, Norbert told Wilberforce he needed a drink to fall asleep.

"Maybe I want a drink, too," said Wilberforce.

"Maybe you do," said Norbert. "But you should have thought of that before you invited along our young companion."

Junior at the front desk directed Norbert to a bar called Red Rocks, just a few hundred yards away along the wide highway. Norbert drove the Caddy.

At the door, the young bouncer carded Norbert and pitched him the evening's drink special: "All you can drink domestic drafts," said the bouncer, "Only seven bucks. Great deal."

"All right," said Norbert. He handed over the cash and the bouncer affixed a fluorescent band around Norbert's wrist made of strong, fibrous paper. Norbert found a stool, looked at the taps, and told the bartender—a zaftig Midwestern girl in her mid-twenties—to pour him a Sam Adams. She slid the drink to Norbert.

"Five dollars."

Norbert dangled his wrist before her eyes so she could see he'd opted into the evening's drink special.

"That's for domestic beers only," she said.

"This is a Sam Adams," said Norbert.

"Yeah," she said, "the special's for domestic only."

"Since when did Boston join the European Union?" said Norbert.

"I don't know anything about that," said the bartender.

Behind the bar was a 60-gallon, illuminated freshwater aquarium containing an ugly, round barnacled fish and an assortment of bottom feeders. Clearly the ugly fish was in charge. Whichever side he chose, his tank mates scrambled to the other.

"What kind of fish is that?" asked Norbert.

"That's Rufus," said the bartender. "He's a vegetarian piranha."

"How's that work?"

The bartender plucked a green olive from a plastic tray on the bar and tossed it into the water. Rufus instantly swam to it, seizing it in his mouth. For leverage, Rufus held the olive against the glass as he chewed. Halfway through his meal, the pimento ejected from the olive and floated gently to the bottom of the tank. As the pimento descended, Norbert could swear he saw Rufus watching it intensely. As proof of this observation, upon devouring the olive, Rufus dived straight at the pimento that no placo dare molest.

Norbert turned to survey the establishment and its patrons. He immediately noticed the high ratio of inter-racial couples mingling inside Red Rocks. He also took notice of his taking notice. How odd, he thought, that I'm from New York and I've never seen so many interracial couples in one place before—right here in the middle of corn country! He noticed some commotion, people gathering near the DJ booth—Holy Christ! thought Norbert, horrified . . .

Karaoke.

He pounded his exotic beer and ran for the door.

In the morning they ate breakfast at a 1950's-style diner adjacent to the motel. To annoy Norbert, Wilberforce and

Sasha specifically requested straws for their orange juices. While Wilberforce went on and on about the quality of the local pork sausage, Norbert jerked to attention, certain he had heard a voice call out his name.

"What is it?" said Wilberforce.

"Did you hear that?" said Norbert. "Someone just said my name."

They looked over the booths, all around the restaurant. There were only a few breakfast patrons and no one was seated nearby.

"Did you hear someone say my name?" Norbert asked Sasha.

Sasha shook his head.

A few hours west, near Lincoln, Nebraska, they stopped at a Kum & Go for fuel, snacks, and bathroom breaks. Norbert and Wilberforce perused the convenience grocery while Sasha made morning mud on the thundermug. Wilberforce boxed a dozen assorted Tasty-Crème doughnuts from a glass display case opposite the register. He made his selections judiciously, rejecting no less than three glazed for what Norbert could only assume was *staleness to the touch*.

Norbert selected six premade salami sandwiches and three Coca-Colas from the cooler. The cashier was an older man than he should have been, causing Norbert to fill in the blanks of his hard-luck story. Divorced? Multiple jobs to keep pace with court-mandated child and alimony payments? Picking up shifts in a dusty highway filling station to put three kids through private universities? The American dream. What was it that Lula from Cleveland said we all wanted? Oh, yes: A better life for our children.

"You want straws with them Cokes?" asked the enigmatic cashier.

"Not necessary," said Norbert.

"Get one for Sasha," said Wilberforce, plopping down his box of premium doughnuts beside Norbert's purchases.

With a twirl of his index finger, he told the cashier, "These are all together."

"He doesn't need a straw," said Norbert. "No one does."

"Straws are fun," said Wilberforce.

Norbert thought of Arlene. Driving home from church Sunday morning, she had told Norbert he did not know how to have fun. Maybe she was right. He had never once considered miniature plastic tubes an avenue to merriment.

"You make any sandwiches without cheese on them?" Norbert asked the cashier.

"All we got is what's there," said the cashier. "Those got cheese on them?"

"Yes."

"That's all we got."

"Mm," said Norbert.

"You allergic?"

Norbert walked over to the rack of baked goods and grabbed a box of mass-produced, crème-filled, chocolate-covered chocolate cakes.

"Ring up these ring-a-dings, too," he said.

In the parking lot, Sasha sucked his Coke through a straw while Norbert disappeared inside the restroom. Wilberforce lounged inside the Caddy with the passenger-side door open, savoring each sweet, glazed-dipped cake. Sasha drew "Fuck Osama" into the dust on the Caddy's trunk then twirled on his tiptoes, kicking stones while slurping his carbonated beverage.

A thin, panting golden retriever appeared from behind the Kum & Go. Sasha lured the dog closer with the uneaten half of his Ring Ding. The dog approached warily, but sat smartly before Sasha, tilting her head, as if to inquire whether the boy was willing to offer up his delicious treat, so scandalously taboo for canine stomachs.

"You can't feed a dog chocolate," warned Wilberforce, watching events unfold from the vehicle. "They'll get worms.

Here, give him this."

Wilberforce frisbeed a glazed Tasty Crème doughnut to Sasha, who caught it in his chest. The dog sat alert for Sasha, scooting her buttocks closer to him along the macadam by tiny increments. Sasha held the treat high. He made the dog shake with each front paw and kiss him on the cheek before rewarding her. Sasha planted a generous smooch on the dog's wet nose. He nuzzled her, clenching fistfuls of her soft, blonde hair.

"Hey! Get over here!"

A man, about forty and notably scrawnier than the dog, was standing at the corner of the Kum & Go. The man wore a sleeveless undershirt decorated with a faded American flag featuring the slogan "The One and Only!" His grease-smeared sweat shorts advertised a collegiate sports program from the Big Sky Conference. In his hand was a twisted paper bag over which peered the brown neck of a beer bottle.

"I said get the fuck over here. Now!"

He was yelling at the dog.

The dog's ears, once stiff as antennae, curled like dried flowers as her tail disappeared between her bony legs. The whole of her body seemed to lose several inches in height as she spun and crept, sniper style, toward the man in the unfortunate casual wear.

"Pain in the ass," the man mumbled. "Good for nothin' . . . " His thoughts trailed off, unfinished.

Norbert emerged from the entrance to the Kum & Go. He smiled at Sasha, noticed the distraught contortion of his little face, then turned just in time to watch the scrawny man deliver a swift, violent kick into the yellow dog's defenseless belly. The dog expelled a sickening cry. Sasha, involuntarily, cried out with her.

The man snatched the dog by the right ear. It yelped.

"What'd I tell you about scavenging? Huh? Huh?! You little shit."

Norbert crossed quickly to the man and his dog, a notice-able hitch in his gait.

"Hey!" Norbert hollered, halfway there. "Hey! What's the matter with you?!"

The man looked up at Norbert, genuinely astonished that his actions were being called into question.

"Let go of that dog." Norbert now stood before the man.

The man released the dog's ear. He was lean, rangy and muscular in the style common to the unemployed and feloni-ous. When he stood erect, he was equal to Norbert's height. He met Norbert eye-to-eye.

"Why don't you mind your own business?"

"I see you beat a dog, that is my business," said Norbert. Not wanting trouble, Norbert tried softening the tension. "Now, if it'd been a cat, that'd be another story."

The man was not interested in diffusing the situation, his manhood having been challenged by this stranger piloting a pink automobile with New York dealer plates.

"Climb the fuck back into your fagmobile," said the man. "And don't look back, if you know what's good for you."

Norbert nodded slowly, deliberately, like his head was on a thick spring. "What are you going to do to that dog once I'm gone?"

"None of your fucking business."

In a grand display, the man summoned a large volume of mucous and expectorated onto the pavement at Nor-bert's feet.

"That's my dog. I'll do with it as I fucking please."

The man's face was a fraction from Norbert's. He had not brushed his teeth in a great, long while. In one short motion, Norbert jabbed his left fist into the man's nose, breaking it. The man's bag-draped bottle fell from his left hand, smashing.

Norbert turned to Sasha, "Put the dog in the car."

Sasha grabbed the golden retriever by the scruff, leading it into the backseat of the Caddy. Wilberforce slid across the seat behind the steering wheel, shaking his head, murmuring to himself.

The dog's owner staggered backward, hands clasped to his wet, red face, screaming unintelligible invectives through his cupped palms before retreating back behind the Kum & Go.

Norbert settled into the passenger seat, clicked his safety belt.

"You can't keep breaking people's noses," said Wilberforce. "It's an unsustainable method of conflict resolution."

Fuck Osama roared to life. Wilberforce lowered the rear window so the panting dog could enjoy what small breeze there was.

"Hit it," said Norbert.

From behind the Kum & Go, the man reemerged in a dead run wielding a long metal pipe with both hands above his head like a woodsman's axe or some piece of medieval weaponry. Before Wilberforce could depress the accelerator, the crazed man was upon them swatting off the passenger-side mirror. Wilberforce hit the gas. The tires smoked as Fuck Osama launched from the parking lot. The man followed, hurling the pipe into the air like a javelin. It bounced well short on the roadway.

The wounded veteran, the priapic ex-priest, the Russian orphan, and their new, disoriented dog sped away from the Kum & Go near Lincoln. Sped away from the dog's owner, his face streaked with fresh, oxygen-rich blood—his patriotic wifebeater soaked in that same life-giving fluid.

"Guy like that," said Norbert, turning to Wilberforce, "ain't worth the blood in his veins."

"The fifth commandment," said Wilberforce. "Thou shalt not steal."

"Three down," said Norbert, adjusting the rearview mirror.

20

After Big Springs, Interstate 80 split into Interstate 76, which Fuck Osama followed southwest over the Colorado border. Sasha stroked the dog's smooth hair, nuzzling his nose into her warm flank.

"We need to name her," he said.

"Doesn't she have a tag?" asked Norbert.

"She doesn't even have a collar," said Sasha.

"How about Lucky?" said Wilberforce. He was pleased with his offering, certain it would be greeted with swift ratification.

"No," said Sasha. "That's boring."

"How about Highway," said Norbert. "That's a good name for a dog. C'mere, Highway. Fetch, Highway. Don't piss on the rug, Highway."

"No," said Sasha. "You got to name the car. It's not fair."

"Yes," Wilberforce agreed. "Give someone else a turn. Go ahead, Sasha. It's up to you. This dog's self-esteem is entirely in your hands."

"Let's call her Kum & Go," said Sasha. "That's where we found her, and that's basically what dogs do anyhow."

Norbert and Wilberforce stole a glance at one another.

"I like it," said Norbert.

"Kum & Go it is," said Wilberforce.

Sasha scratched a section of Kum & Go's hindquarter until her left leg gyrated involuntarily.

"How's that Kum & Go?" said Sasha. "You like that, don't you?"

Kum & Go licked Sasha's right eyelid until the boy giggled.

Norbert tuned the radio—mostly static and country-western stations that he quickly skipped past before the tune could seep into Wilberforce's head. Norbert turned the dial past a classical station.

"Stop," said Sasha.

"Here?" said Norbert.

"I like this kind of music," said Sasha. "I can see it best."

"See it?"

"Yes, I can see the notes. Sort of like they're floating in front of my eyes."

"I don't understand. This happens just with classical music?" asked Wilberforce.

"I like seeing this music best, but I see all kinds of music."

"Like, what else?" asked Norbert. "What's one of your favorites?"

"The Beatles," said Sasha. "I like watching Paul's voice."

"You had a music player with headphones when I first saw you in the mission," said Wilberforce. "What do you listen to?"

"*The White Album*. That's probably my favorite album to watch."

Norbert and Wilberforce were captivated by this information but had no clue what to make of it. Conversation ceased for a long while. The car filled with the sound of Mozart as they loped up and down on the Caddy's shot front struts.

Wilberforce motioned for Sasha to lean in. He whispered in Sasha's ear.

"What?" said Sasha. "What?"

Wilberforce whispered it again.

"What is he saying?" asked Norbert.

Sasha asked Norbert, "Why does Philip Philo Phipps think you saved his life?"

In Denver, at a National 9 Inn on Colorado Boulevard, Norbert, Wilberforce, and Sasha parked around back of the motel so they could sneak Kum & Go into their room. They made Sasha wait in the car while they checked in.

While checking in, the night clerk—whom Norbert thought looked exactly like a turkey vulture—insisted on several security measures they had not previously been subjected to. The clerk studied Norbert's credit card and driver's license. He refused to accept them because they had been tampered with. The clerk asked Norbert if he had ever attended a private flight school. Norbert explained to the clerk that his credit card and ID "went through the dryer."

Wilberforce offered cash for the room. The clerk photo-copied both driver's licenses and entered the numbers into his computer. He then made Norbert and Wilberforce pose together for a digital photo.

"Together?" Norbert protested. "That seems rather unorthodox. It's just a night in a goddamn motel."

"It's policy," said the clerk.

"*Policy*," snorted Norbert. "That seems to cover everything these days, don't it? No matter how ridiculous. Strip down naked and sit on a carrot, folks. Sorry, *it's policy*. This insurance bullshit is out of hand. Them and all the lawyers run this friggin' country."

The clerk's sharp facial features and close-set eyes nestled atop their dark, swollen sockets annoyed Norbert. Each time the man looked up from his paperwork he appeared to be sneering. Norbert grumbled about "post-9/11 hysteria." The clerk did not feel obligated to explain his actions, the invo-cation of "policy" having thoroughly covered all his bases. Norbert walked away from the desk to peruse the display of brochures and catalogs advertising all the regional attractions. He removed a brochure on the Hoover Dam and asked the clerk, "How far south of Las Vegas is the Hoover Dam?"

"Forty-five minutes." The clerk cleared his throat. "Going to the Hoover Dam, huh?" He watched Norbert with his narrow, deep-set eyes.

"Thinking about it," said Norbert, dismissively.

"Where you going to stay?"

Norbert, his back square to the clerk, rolled his eyes to the ceiling. "Vegas."

"You don't say," said the clerk. "My brother-in-law is a big wheel down there in Vegas."

"How about that," said Norbert, still studying the display of attractions. He slid out a thick, glossy Vegas dining guide.

"He's a manager at that New York, New York. Bet he could get you guys a heck of a room rate."

Norbert spun around. "Really?"

"You have any interest in that?"

Norbert chewed his bottom lip. This night clerk is a weird, nosy little fucker, he thought, but the New York, New York—that's the real deal. Right on the strip. "What's the catch?" said Norbert

The clerk chuckled, pursing his lips, making him appear eerily more birdlike. "No catch. I have all your particulars right here, I'll just call him and make the arrangements. Do I put the reservation under Sherbert or Wendell?"

"Wendell," said Norbert, looking at Wilberforce—*Mr. Moneybags*. "Wendell will be fine."

Around back of the motel, as Norbert and Wilberforce unloaded Sasha, the dog, and their gear into the room, the night clerk carefully watched their every move. The clerk could not help but smile to himself. Norbert was incorrect. The photocopied licenses and digital photos had nothing whatsoever to do with mandatory security measures in a post-9/11 world. Nor did they have to do with insurance coverage. No, they were for a different purpose altogether.

21

Back in The Halo, a sound not unlike a large gospel choir rose to a glorious crescendo. Elton Berryhill had just received a new email from another loyal subscriber.

This one was blockbuster! It was from an industrious night clerk at a National 9 Inn in Denver. He had attached a digital photo of one of the meanies. The meanie was traveling with another man and a young boy.

That's not just any meanie, thought Elton as he stared at the photo on his monitor, that's the BIGGEST MEANIE OF THEM ALL! Praise Jesus! So many blessings on this day!

The clerk told Elton that he had booked the meanie into a room at the New York, New York Hotel & Casino in Las Vegas. The clerk praised Elton for his good deeds, in His name, and wished Elton Godspeed. Elton opened his GPS software and plotted his drive to Las Vegas.

He powered off his computer, walked over to his heavy training bag hanging from the ceiling, and beat it tirelessly with his wooden baseball bat.

Upstairs in Ma Berryhill's bedroom Elton, sweating profusely, still holding the bat, looked in on his dead mother. He tucked a corner of the bedspread between the mattress and box spring. She was beginning to ripen.

"The Lord doth giveth, and the Lord doth taketh away," said Elton. "It is all part of his glorious plan for each of us."

Exiting her room, Elton clicked off the bedroom light before closing tight the door.

Meanwhile, at a black jack table in the New York, New York Hotel & Casino in Las Vegas, Andy with the Red Boots hit on 17.

Bust.

He felt a vibration in his pocket and checked his cell phone. It was an alert that Norbert Sherbert and his fat pal, Wendell, had just checked into a National 9 Inn in Denver.

"Sorry, sir," said the dealer, "no cell phones at the table."

"This isn't just a cell phone," said Andy. "But what the fuck would you know, you're just a stupid black jack dealer."

"You got me there," said the dealer. "But with what I had showing, I reckon I don't need my Ph.D. in molecular biology to tell you it takes some kinda bush-league douche bag to hit on 17."

22

The next morning at the National 9 Inn, Wilberforce proposed that he drop Norbert and Sasha off for breakfast then take Kum & Go along for a short visit with an old friend. Norbert asked who the "old friend" was, and though not forthcoming at first, Wilberforce finally admitted it was Margaret, his former lover and church secretary. Her mother's house was nearby.

"I'll drop you both at breakfast and be back in two shakes," said Wilberforce.

"Two shakes of what?" said Sasha.

"A lamb's tail," said Wilberforce.

"I don't understand."

Wilberforce dropped Norbert and Sasha at a Denny's. Norbert and Sasha sat at the counter. Norbert ordered coffee, Sasha an orange juice. Norbert snapped open a copy of the *Rocky Mountain News* he purchased from a steel box in front of the restaurant.

On the counter to the right of Sasha were a few dollars and some change. The money was left as a tip by an older man wearing a flannel jacket and hunting cap. The man had a kind, weathered face. He offered a smile to Sasha as he sopped up the last bit of coagulating yellow yolk with a crust of rye bread. Sasha smiled back. He lifted one of the man's dollars from the counter to study it more closely.

"Put that down," said Norbert from behind his newspaper. "It's not yours."

"Oh, it's all right," said the man in a folksy drawl. "He's not doing any harm. He's just checking for counterfeits. Ain't that right?" The man threw Sasha a wink.

"Feels weird," said Sasha.

"That's 'cause it's made of cotton and linen, not paper," the man smiled. "With tiny red, white, and blue silk fibers scattered through it."

"Put it down," said Norbert.

Sasha laid the bill back on the counter.

"There's nothing greater in this world than the dollar," said the man.

"That's the first time I ever touched money," said Sasha.

"Huh," said the man. The man leaned back to get a better look at Norbert. As he sized him up, Norbert knew he was trying to write the boy's bizarre biography—having not touched money by the age of eight—so he decided to head him off before he started asking probing questions.

"Why do you contend there's nothing greater than the dollar?" asked Norbert, reluctantly folding his newspaper.

"Because I believe this world would be a better place, a safer place, if we would all put our faith in money, rather than fantastic stories and books handed down from sheep herders. You want world peace? There's only one solution: democratic, unregulated, international, free-market capitalism. Democracies do not make war with other democracies. It's bad for business."

"That's one opinion, I suppose," said Norbert. "I see wide holes in that theory. The first one being that I'm unfamiliar with any circumstance where war is bad for business."

"It's much more than my opinion," said the man. "It's my faith. My name is Anton Figgis, and I belong to the Church of the Almighty Dollar. I've made a lot of money in my life. I've owned an insurance company and a car dealership and a dry cleaning business and, of course, dealt in real estate and done some general contracting. I have plenty of money, but I always felt guilty and unfulfilled because of my Christian faith. Christ taught that it is the meek that shall inherit the earth and that I must always think of the weak and the poor. This annoyed me. I could never reconcile my faith with my material successes. Frankly, I didn't see the contradiction as clearly as Jesus did, and I didn't see why I should be so miserable every Sunday just because I worked hard and was filthy rich. Then I found the Church of the Almighty Dollar and became a devout Buckologist. Ever since then, I've been a pig in hot manure. I couldn't be happier. Now I celebrate my money. The dollar is my deity, not some character in the sky. My God is in my pocket, in my house, in my children's educations, in my cars and boats, and in the security I feel as I'm living out my golden years. These are the best days of my life. And it's all because I rejected Christ's pity party and embraced the Almighty Dollar."

"What did you say your name was?" said Norbert, leaning across to shake hands.

"Anton Figgis."

"Well, Mr. Figgs—"

"Figgis."

"That's just about the sanest thing I've heard in a long time," said Norbert. "My name is Norbert, and this little guy over here is Sasha. I like how you think, Figgs. I'd like to visit your church someday. That sounds like a brand of faith I could support."

"Well you're in luck, Norbert. Today's service is followed by Carving Night, our greatest festival of the year. Why don't you both come along as my guests?"

"I don't think so," Norbert chuckled. "Thank you, though, for the offer, but I don't have much of a portfolio. I don't think I could afford the entrance fee."

"Nonsense," said Anton Figgis. "The first time is always free. Then, if you like the service, we can arrange to sit down and view your credit history and assets statement."

Norbert slurped his coffee. "So you really don't believe in the God of the Bible?"

"No sir."

"And you have constructed a full belief system around that nonbelief?"

"Yes we have," said Anton Figgis. "Most beautiful church you've ever seen, too. When we congregate, we worship the power of the Almighty Dollar."

"Is it a good service?"

"Balls out."

The waitress came over to Norbert and Sasha. "You boys ready to order?"

"We'll have whatever Mr. Figgs was having," said Norbert.

"But I want pancakes," said Sasha.

"The name is Figgis," said the gentleman seated beside them. "Anton Figgis."

Meanwhile, in the Cherry Creek section of Denver, Wilberforce knocked on the front door of a modest home located away from busy streets. A woman with sharp, delicate angles and a China doll complexion opened the door.

"Hello, Margaret."

Margaret blinked behind the thick lenses of her oversized eyeglasses.

"Are you surprised to see me here?"

"I am very surprised to see you here," said Margaret.

Margaret lifted her winter coat off a hook by the door and stepped out onto the porch, quietly closing the door behind her.

"My mother is resting. Is that your car?"

Wilberforce looked over his shoulder at the dented, salt-covered pink 1975 Cadillac Eldorado.

"It's very complicated. And that's not really why I am here."

"The car is complicated?"

"No," said Wilberforce. "Why I have arrived in that car is complicated."

"I didn't think you could come this far on a Vespa."

"You have my car, Margaret."

"Not anymore."

"What did you do with it?"

"I don't remember."

"You don't remember?" said Wilberforce. "You don't remember what you did with my car?"

"Is that your dog?"

"No. Well, I don't know. Partly, perhaps. I can't say for certain. What did you do with my car, Margaret?"

Margaret blinked.

"Margaret? Have you been taking any medications?"

"Keep your voice low. Mother is resting. Is that a yellow Labrador?"

"Golden retriever."

Margaret walked to the edge of the porch. She squinted. "It looks hungry."

"It's malnourished. It's had a hard life. In Nebraska."

Margaret turned to face Wilberforce. They locked eyes and he sensed, for a fleeting moment, a glimmer of awareness. She pursed her lips and nodded. "It's cold today," she said, sliding her hands into her coat pockets.

"Margaret, I've come here to apologize to you. I'm here to say I'm sorry. For hurting you. For, I don't know, everything."

Margaret glanced back toward the Caddy. "You should let that dog out. Maybe he has to tinkle."

"She. The dog's a she."

Margaret turned back to face Wilberforce. She nodded.

"Margaret, did you hear what I just said to you? I said I'm sorry."

"Yes you are."

"How's your mother?"

"Resting."

"Okay. Y'know what, Margaret? I think I'm going to leave now. I'm starting to think that this was a mistake.

It's pretty clear you don't want me here."

"You're always such a Gloomy Gus."

"Do you need anything? Can I get you or your mother something at the store?"

"Dog food."

"You have a dog in there?"

"No," said Margaret, "you need to buy dog food. And obviously not the kind from Nebraska."

"I'm just going to go then. Okay? I don't know what I expected by coming here. I guess I did it for my own edification."

"Big word."

Wilberforce descended the stairs from the porch and started down the sidewalk.

"Will," said Margaret.

Wilberforce turned.

"You believe, in your soul, that you deserve bad things. Because of mistakes in your past. That's why you're incapable of loving anyone. That's why you're fucking everyone."

Arriving back at the Denny's to pick up Norbert and Sasha, Wilberforce was told by the young waitress that they had left with a regular named Anton Figgis to attend services at the Church of the Almighty Dollar a few miles east of the city. They left directions for Wilberforce to meet them there. Wilberforce was annoyed and confused by this development.

"Why would they leave with this person to attend a church service?" Wilberforce asked the waitress.

"Beats me. Your friend and him just got on like they were lost cousins or something."

She smiled at Wilberforce.

Wilberforce turned to leave, then turned back to face the waitress. He reciprocated with a wide, toothy grin of his own.

In the parking lot behind Denny's, in broad daylight, the young waitress gave Wilberforce a vigorous blow job. The Caddy rocked on its bad struts, the St. Christopher medallion dangling from its rearview mirror, rhythmically tapping the windshield.

23

The Church of the Almighty Dollar was a colossus. A modern, multimedia smart church with plasma screen displays, state-of-the-art surround sound and dozens of other amenities. Everything was white—even the baby grand piano at the front of the church. The only other color in the room was the banknote green of the plush cushions atop the long pews.

Along the walls were magnificent stained glass windows, each in honor of a different Prophet of Profit. They were: Sheikh Zayed Bin Sultan Al Nahyan, Paul Allen, Warren Buffet, King Fahd Bin Abdul Aziz Alsaud, Larry Ellison, Bill Gates, John Jacob Astor, Cornelius Vanderbilt, Andrew Carnegie and, of course, John D. Rockefeller.

Seated directly in front of Sasha was a pretty girl his age with blonde curls. When she turned to look over her shoulder at Sasha, his faced flushed.

Wilberforce entered the church, having left Kum & Go in the car. He tried to talk to Norbert but the services were beginning. The lights dimmed. From the surround-sound speakers, a burst of thunderous music filled the church. It was the instrumental introduction to Pink Floyd's "Money."

The preacher appeared through a door at the right of the stage dressed in an open, shimmering green robe of billowing silk. At the center of his white vestment, partially obscured by his cordless microphone, was a golden dollar sign. Behind him followed the choir, also dressed in shimmering green silk. At the center of a white bar of fabric extending from their collars to the hem of their garments: a golden dollar sign. And around their necks, a white sash adorned with embroidered dollar signs.

The music receded.

"Welcome," said the white-haired, well-groomed preacher.

"Welcome," his flock responded.

"I bring good news," said the preacher, pausing as he steadily scanned his eyes back and forth across the room. He raised his hands above his head.

"The dollar is strong!"

The congregation rose to its feet, each thrusting his or her balled fist above their heads, bringing them down in the horn-blowing motion of a train engineer or interstate trucker. The room erupted in one voice:

"Cha-ching!"

"You may be seated," said the preacher. "I see some new faces tonight. Perhaps because tonight is . . . Carving Night!"

All five plasma televisions flashed the words: CARVING NIGHT! Alternating between black on white and white on black text. A boisterous cheer rose up from the congregation followed by a rumble of applause, followed by a lone "Woooo!"

The preacher adjusted his wireless microphone, "Let us begin with a reading." He nodded in the direction of where Norbert, Wilberforce, and Sasha were seated. Wilberforce began to rise reflexively. But it was the girl with the curls that the preacher was acknowledging. She rose, smoothed her skirt, shuffled past her parents into the aisle and walked briskly to the lectern. Stepping up onto a white, carpeted platform that the preacher moved into place with his foot, she paused, glanced right, then left, inhaled and said, "A reading from *Business @ the Speed of Thought.*"

After a few paragraphs, she closed the book, drew a dollar sign in the air before her, and said, "The word of Gates."

The congregation solemnly replied, "Cha-ching."

The girl made her way back to her seat. She smiled at Sasha before twirling and depositing herself onto the gleaming pew.

"Now," said the preacher. "Who will testify?"

A gentleman in front raised his hand.

"Yes, Tom," said the preacher. "Go ahead."

The man rose and said, "Two weeks ago, Nancy and I closed on our re-fi. We took $25,000 from the equity line and put it into a medium- to high-risk small-cap growth fund that focuses on the Nasdaq. I just checked my smart phone and we have already realized a thirteen percent growth."

The church exploded with a resounding, "Cha-ching!"

"Any questions for Tom?" said the preacher.

A voice from the back of the church called out, "Are those small-caps domestic or international?"

"International," said Tom. "Pacific Rim."

"Thank you, Tom," said the preacher. "Who will go next?"

An artificially tanned, strikingly beautiful woman in her forties rose. She was wearing a zebra-print dress, her body adorned with many golden baubles and bangles. So much so, she clanked as she stood. "We just closed on our condo in Big Sky. We bought it on spec three years ago for eight twenty-five, sold it for one-point-seven-five."

"Cha-ching!"

"Questions for Annabeth?" said the preacher. "All right, who else?"

Norbert raised his hand. Caught completely off-guard, Wilberforce tried to stop him but it was too late.

"Yes," said the preacher. "You back there. I don't believe I know your name."

Norbert stood. "My name is Norbert. I'm here as a guest of Mr. Figgs."

"Figgis," whispered Anton Figgis.

"We met in Denny's this morning. I'm here with my associates Sasha and Mr. Wilberforce Wendell."

A groan of wood and the ruffle of expensive fabrics filled the church as everyone turned to get a look at the trio Brother Figgis had brought in.

"Yes, Norbert," said the preacher. "Will you testify?"

"Well, the first thing I want to say is that I think this place is great. Really great. By far the most space-aged church I've ever been in. It looks like a set from *Star Wars* or something. I'm like, where's Darth Vader and the Millennium Falcon? You know what I'm saying?"

There was a low murmur in the congregation. Wilberforce snatched at Norbert's arm. Norbert ignored him.

"The other thing I want to say is that I think you folks are really on to something here. You've got the right idea. I think, in its own way, this system you've got going is very spiritual on account of the fact it's so pure. It puts the worshipper in direct contact with his God. In this case: money. If you ask me, I'm of the mind we need to get rid of organized religion altogether so people can start believing in God again. What I mean is, the more likely candidate for God.

"A friend of mine—well, truth is, she's this pretty girl named Lula I met just a few days ago in Cleveland—she told me she believes in a God that is a kind of energy: a singular consciousness that connects us all in a web of knowledge and compassion and love and understanding. I think that's kinda beautiful, and closer to the truth than some cartoon God from the children's storybooks. Some big, muscular dude who looks like a Bowflex Santa Claus. I also have a real hard time believing in a vengeful, jealous God who imposes all these rules and prejudices that, in my mind, were cooked up by regular human beings to maintain power and order in less-educated, less-enlightened societies. I mean, seriously, how to keep and sell a slave is actually in the Bible. How to beat your wife. That doesn't sound like the infallible words of a perfect being that sees forever into the past and future. That sounds pretty shortsighted to me. That sounds human. All too human.

"At least when you folks worship the buck you know what you're getting. The dollar is dispassionate. No one personifies it, giving it human attributes like jealousy or pride. It doesn't have opinions or a chosen people. It's just a buck. It is what it is, and people can use it for good or evil. The object itself has no say in the matter. It does not manipulate people; people manipulate it. Sorta like the Bible.

"So in summation, I guess what I'm trying to say, not so eloquently, is that I stand with you tonight and throw my support—er, *worship*. I choose to worship the Almighty Dollar, and reject the God as outlined in the Bible, because I believe your style of thinking, though deeply flawed, is nevertheless a step in the right direction. Thank you and good evening."

After Norbert lowered himself back onto his pew, the congregation collectively fell into a bewildered repose.

"Well," said the preacher, finally. "Uh, thank you, Norbert. Any questions?"

"Where are you from?" called a male voice.

Norbert quickly stood again. "Upstate New York. The Adirondack Mountains. We're driving across the country to deliver a Cadillac Eldorado to a friend of mine in California."

"What kind of deal did your friend get on the Caddy?" asked a different male voice.

"Not sure," said Norbert. "But it was purchased from a police auction in the state of Florida."

"Police auction," said a third man, "that averages 15 percent below Blue Book."

"Cha-ching!" roared the congregation.

Norbert sat back down. He winked at Wilberforce. Wilberforce nodded as he removed Norbert's list from his pocket. He crossed off the first commandment: "Thou shalt have no other gods before me."

Four down. Six to go.

Several more parishioners testified. They spoke mostly of real estate transactions, stock trades, estate planning—one gentleman had a positive experience with a class-action lawsuit, meaning that the lawsuit had failed and his company was found not liable for damages. When the testimony had concluded, the preacher introduced a tall, handsome man in his early thirties named Geoff Wannamaker.

Mr. Wannamaker strode to the baby grand piano and played a selection of the most rapturous classical arrangements Norbert and Wilberforce had ever heard. Some he played with vocal accompaniment from the choir; others he played solo. It mattered not which, for whatever music emanated from that gleaming white instrument, it held the congregation rapt in tuneful ecstasy. Then, during the fourth and final piece, Sasha turned to Wilberforce and said, "I can see all of that. Isn't it beautiful?"

"See what?" said Wilberforce, eyes closed, swaying to the music.

"All that music. I see the notes."

"I still don't understand, Sasha. Where do you see them?"

"In my brain. Floating in front of my eyes. It's hard to describe."

When Geoff Wannamaker concluded his final piece of music, he rose and bowed to a thunderous standing ovation from the congregation. There was already an electricity in the air surrounding Carving Night. Wanamaker's performance served to fuel it even more. In the dead space after the applause died, in the time it took for the preacher to rise from his seat and reposition himself at center stage, the room was abuzz with giddy anticipation.

"I know we're all excited about Carving Night," said the preacher. "But before we conclude, are there any final testimonies?"

This time it was Wilberforce's turn to raise his hand.

"Yes," said the preacher. "There, in the back."

An audible clamor of discontentment pervaded the room. Everyone was done with testimonies and Q&A. *It's Carving Night, goddamnit!*

"I have a question for Mr. Wannamaker," said Wilberforce. "My young friend here tells me that he can see the actual musical notes in his head as he listens to those lovely arrangements. And he has no musical training whatsoever. Have you ever heard of such a thing?"

Mr. Wannamaker sprang to his feet. "You say this boy sees the music?"

"That's what he says."

"Please," said Mr. Wanamaker, "bring him here."

A hush fell over the congregation as Wilberforce led Sasha to the front. Mr. Wannamaker sat the boy beside him on the bench in front of the piano. He talked with Sasha a bit, too low for anyone to hear, then placed the boy's fingers in a starting position on the keys. What happened next, what happened for the succeeding thirty minutes, was simply one of those miraculous moments in life that defy explanation, defy reason, defy faith or logic.

Sasha played Mr. Wanamaker's third piece, and played it better—with more grace and ease and with certain quirks and tones and choices that could only be characterized as genius. For the entire song, no one moved or made a sound above a shallow breath. They were transfixed at the sight and sound of the boy maestro pounding and stroking the keys with his short, slender fingers, scooting back and forth across the bench, his legs swinging freely. With each progressing moment of raw, inventive brilliance, the crowd began to further warm and loosen, growing more viscerally engaged in the music, becoming more invested in the phenomenon they were witnessing.

When Sasha concluded the piece, there was a standing eruption of applause, full of hoots and whistles and calls that lasted several minutes. Sasha, astonished, glowed with an innocent radiance.

Then, just as it appeared the congregation of the Church of the Almighty Dollar could stand no more, Sasha banged the keys and launched into a rendition of The Beatles' "Why Don't We Do It in the Road?" He belted out the first lyrics, to which the choir quickly caught the melody and began to sing along.

The congregation of Realtors and insurance providers, bankers and traders, physicians, lawyers, pharmaceutical executives, cyber-tycoons, import/exporters and all other incarnations of American wealth rose and danced, lustily clapping their hands, lost in the music. Norbert removed his harmonica from the inside pocket of his leather jacket and accompanied Sasha in the key of *C*, walking to the front of the church as he played. The people shook the church from its floor joists to it rafters. When the fever had reached its zenith, the preacher hollered for everyone to hurry outside for Carving Night!

The congregation poured into the rear property of the church. Sasha ran to the Caddy and let Kum & Go out so she could run free in the snow. A huge bonfire at the center of the area was set ablaze with flaming torches. There were long tables upon which church members piled high a festive display of covered dishes, hot drinks, wine, and cold beer. Surrounding the now roaring fire were dozens of six-foot-high, four-foot-wide blocks of ice. On the ground before each block of ice was a gas-powered chainsaw. For the next few hours, as the Buckologists laughed and ate and drank, they each tried their hand at carving six-foot dollar symbols into the ice. With abundant good humor, everyone took a turn plunging the chain-saw into the ice, trying to coax forth the iconic symbol of American capitalism.

When all the blocks of ice had been shaped as best

they could—some far better than others—the congregants of the Church of the Almighty Dollar partook heavily of the wine and beer and danced wildly around the bonfire, chanting and singing and laughing, bowing in worship to the frozen symbols of free enterprise they had created; pledging their allegiance to, and their love and faith in, the power of the Almighty Dollar.

Wilberforce and Sasha spent a long time speaking privately with Mr. and Mrs. Wannamaker. Mr. Wannamaker was passionately imparting the urgency of Sasha's study. Sasha, he said, was a prodigy.

Norbert knew that with his participation in the pagan spectacle called Carving Night he had broken the second commandment: "Thou shalt not make unto thee any graven image, or any likeness of *any thing* that *is* in heaven above, or that *is* in the earth beneath, or that *is* in the water under the earth: Thou shalt not bow down thyself to them, nor serve them: for I the LORD thy God *am* a jealous God, visiting the iniquity of the fathers upon the children unto the third and fourth *generation* of them that hate Me; and showing mercy unto thousands of them that love Me, and keep My commandments."

Five down, five to go, thought Norbert. I'm halfway home. I wonder if He is watching?

Just when Norbert, Wilberforce, and Sasha were starting to think they could not possibly have more fun, Wilberforce looked up and locked eyes with Mother Superior and Sister Isabelle standing in the snow.

Wilberforce excused himself from the Wannamakers and crossed to where the nuns were standing. Sasha meanwhile, as he watched the scene unfold, tried to make himself invisible.

"How did you find us?" said Wilberforce.

"That's what you have to say to me?" said Mother Superior. "After making me drive here from Indiana?" She folded her arms. "We stopped for coffee in town. At Denny's. A certain waitress there was very helpful."

Wilberforce nodded.

"This is a big deal, Wendell. Criminal. An episode like this could cost us the mission itself. I told you, we are hanging by a thread."

"A very big deal," said Sister Isabelle.

"That's enough, Sister," said Mother Superior. "I'll handle this."

Wilberforce shrugged. "What can I say? The boy has been through so much. He deserved an adventure."

"Adventure? This is simply unacceptable. We have been in a full panic. What happened? Did he hide away in your vehicle?"

"It's not important how it happened," said Wilberforce. "I take full responsibility."

"I beg to differ. It is crucial for me to learn how it happened."

"Then I don't recall."

"You leave me speechless," said Mother Superior. "I thought you would have a lot more to say for yourself. Do I not deserve an explanation for your actions? Despite your past transgressions, do you harbor that much disdain for the church? For me?"

"On the contrary, you deserve much more . . . In fact . . . " Wilberforce looked over his shoulder at the Wanna-makers. Sasha maneuvered to keep them between himself and Mother Superior's line of sight.

"He thinks I can't see him," said Mother Superior.

"Francine," said Wilberforce, "do you believe that the highest activity a human being can attain is learning for understanding because to understand is to be free?"

"Don't give me your Spinozan bullshit, Wendell. And *don't* call me Francine."

Sister Isabelle cleared her throat and took a little walk.

Wilberforce smiled. "I'd like to offer a solution that I think will make everyone happy."

Inside the church, Wilberforce, Sasha, Mother Superior, and the Wannmakers sat down to talk in the preacher's office. It was agreed that Sasha would stay with the Wannamakers to advance his musical study and realize the full potential of his gift. In exchange the Wannamakers would make an anonymous donation covering the full cost of the repair for the roof over St. Agnes's Mission. They also agreed to file paperwork to formally adopt the gifted young Russian. But Kum & Go could not be part of the arrangement, on account of Mrs. Wannamaker's severe pet allergy.

At the rear passenger door of the Caddy, Sasha hugged Kum & Go, wiping his wet cheeks against her cold, damp coat. Norbert opened the door and the dog jumped in.

"I never had a dog before," said Sasha. "This is a good dog."

"She's all right," said Norbert.

"You'll take care of her?"

"Scout's honor." Norbert lit a cigarette with a click and scrape of his Zippo against his thigh. He heard Sister Isabelle, standing a few yards away alongside Wilberforce, Mother Superior, and the Wannamakers, say, "Is he smoking near the child?"

"I've gotta hand it to you, little man," said Norbert. "That was pretty ballsy stowing away in our car like that. But look how it worked out. Fortune favors the bold. The world loves a man of action."

"Like Spider-Man," said Sasha.

"Exactly," said Norbert. "You're just like Spider-Man. Without the pantyhose."

Sasha giggled. He wiped his nose with his sleeve. Norbert placed his hands on Sasha's shoulders and crouched down.

"Good luck, Sasha. You were a good co-pilot."

"So now you're going to drive Fuck Osama to California?" asked Sasha.

"What did he say?" said Sister Isabelle.

"Wait in the car," said Mother Superior.

"Yeah," said Norbert. "All the way to California."

California, thought Sasha. *Colorado*. He was happy to be going to live with the Wannamakers in Colorado, but the word did not exude the same poetry, did not conjure the same element of mystery and excitement and warmth as California.

"I'll send you a postcard when I get there," said Norbert.

"Do you know my new address?" said Sasha. He was excited.

Norbert knew he did not. He was going to lie, then— "Padre! Make sure we get Sasha's new address . . . so we can keep him apprised of the whereabouts and general disposition of his canine companion."

Wilberforce nodded.

"I'll send you back an email," said Sasha. "I'm going to have the Internet again."

"Okay," said Norbert. "Sounds like a plan."

In the distance, on the other side of the waning bonfire, a parishioner helped Sister Isabelle try her hand at plunging a chainsaw into a block of ice.

24

At a rest area on Route 70 West, near Fremont Junction, Utah, Elton Berryhill purchased several eight-ounce cartons of whole milk. Returning to his burnt sienna Cutlass Supreme, he encountered a pregnant woman and informed her that he was "pleased she had chosen life over those who elect to murder their helpless, innocent children in the womb."

The woman told Elton to, "Fuck off, freak." She said she believed a woman's body is her own and it's nobody's business what she chooses to do with it. "It's ironic," she said, "that it's always some homely dork like you telling a woman what she can and can't do with her own body. You wouldn't know what to do with a woman's body if it was naked right in front of you."

Elton revised his earlier compliment by calling her a "harlot" and a "painted Jezebel." He said her unborn child was "doomed" and assured her she would "be consumed in the black fires of hell." He bid her good day.

In his car, Elton clicked through some of the digital photos he had taken thus far. He had traveled west along Route I-70 from Topeka, selecting a less expedient route so he could detour south on U.S. 56 to pay homage to the statue near Lyons, Kansas honoring Father Padilla who, as a member of Coronado's expedition in 1541, is considered the first Christian to conduct a holy Mass on the North American continent. Elton had snapped several angles of the monument with his digital camera. There were no other passersby who could photograph Elton smiling beside the memorial, but that was fine by him. Elton would never allow a stranger to fondle his expensive technology. The world was rife with thieves.

Back on the road again, Elton sang along at the top of his voice to the various mix tapes he had compiled of inspirational Christian folk music while remaining intensely focused on the divine righteousness of his crusade once he reached his final destination.

Elton raised the volume on the AM/FM stereo cassette deck as loud as it could go. He sang and sang in His Glory until he was so worked into a fever that tears streaked his cheeks and he had to pause for deep milk burps. The Spirit of Christ was very much alive inside him, and he was thrilled and humbled to be doing the Lord's work. So many blessings on this day!

25

One mile north of Hoover Dam, officers from the Bureau of Reclamation inspected each vehicle at a checkpoint. The officers studied Norbert and Wilberforce's driver's licenses and inquired as to their purpose for crossing the dam. Norbert said the dam was their destination and that their purpose was purely educational.

"You know this license has been tampered with?" said the officer to Norbert, pointing to the spot where he had scratched the "Jr." from his name.

"Yes." said Norbert. "That was a defect."

"Defect?"

"A misprint. I corrected it."

The officer made Norbert kill the engine so he and his team could investigate the contents of the pink trunk. The lead officer returned to the driver's door holding the long tribal knife in its simple, leather sheath.

"Can you explain to me why you are traveling with this weapon concealed in your luggage?" asked the officer.

Norbert was dumbstruck. After a moment, he recognized it as the knife Wilberforce had brandished back inside his room at the Robin Hood Motor Court, the one he had used to "correct" his personal identification. Wilberforce leaned in toward the window so he could see the officer's mirrored sunglasses above the roofline of the vehicle.

"That's mine, officer," said Wilberforce. "It was a gift from the Yapese chief during my missionary days on the islands of Micronesia. It's ceremonial."

"Are you clergy?"

"Former clergy," said Wilberforce.

"Why are you traveling with this knife?"

"It has been imbued with certain protective spiritual powers. Sometimes I use it to slice vegetables."

The officer stared at Wilberforce for a long, uncertain moment. He shifted his mirrored gaze to the rear seat. "There are no dogs allowed at the dam."

"We didn't know that," said Norbert.

"He'll have to remain inside the vehicle."

"It's a she," said Norbert.

"What?"

"The dog. It's a she."

"The penalties are severe," said the officer. "Keep the animal secured in the vehicle. With proper ventilation."

The officer turned the tribal knife in his hands. He considered with gravity the power assigned to him, authorizing him to confiscate objects of great personal value with caprice or good reason—in the final analysis, it mattered not which. The thought did not escape the officer that his brother-in-law enjoyed displaying weapons of similar styling behind the bar in his converted basement.

"I'm going to have to confiscate this weapon. It's a security risk."

"Officer," said Norbert, "are you familiar with an agent by the name of Philip Philo Phipps?"

"What about him?"

"We were in the shit together," said Norbert as he leaned to his right side, lifted his left pant leg, and exposed his prosthetic to the officer. "Over there."

The officer leaned forward and looked inside the vehicle. He adjusted his sunglasses, leaned back. "Keep this weapon secured in the trunk."

"Yes sir," said Norbert.

The officer handed the knife to a subordinate who returned it to the trunk, thumping it shut. The officer waved the Caddy forward and Norbert turned the key. Fuck Osama was back on its way.

In the parking garage above the dam, Kum & Go whined inconsolably in the backseat. She had to piddle. "No Dogs Allowed" signs were posted everywhere. Letting her pee in the garage was not an ideal situation, but what choice did they have? Kum & Go would not settle down, and her desperate whines unnerved Norbert and Wilberforce.

While the dog squatted to urinate near the Caddy, another dog barked wildly from inside a filthy RV parked nearby.

The barking grew more frenzied, ferocious. The unsettling sounds were emanating from a set of snarling white teeth behind a bent screen in one of the RV's windows. The teeth appeared flush against the screen, barking viciously, then retreated into the shadows of the vehicle's interior.

Clearly bored with this maneuver, the dog appeared, then disappeared into darkness one final time before leaping through the flimsy screen that separated him from his object of obsession. The dog, its black eyes as insensible as a shark's, was a frothing pit bull with only one thought on its tiny mind: disemboweling the scrawny golden retriever in its field of vision.

"Look out!" hollered Norbert, falling backward onto the hood of the Caddy, denting it. Wilberforce scrambled around the trunk to the far side of the vehicle. Kum & Go darted toward the stairs descending out of the parking complex, her pursuer twenty yards behind. Kum & Go nearly tumbled down the steps, crazed by the terror closing in on her.

"C'mon," shouted Norbert, sliding off the hood, "we have to stop it!"

"Stop it?!"

"Catch it! Something! We can't do nothing!"

Norbert and Wilberforce took off after the running dogs. Norbert knew he would never be able to catch up to them before they were intercepted by security, or some tourist intervened, or worse.

"You have to run ahead!" yelled Norbert from the top of

the stairs, carefully descending to the main concourse. "Run! Fast as you can! I'll catch up!"

"And do what?"

"Just go! That crazy fucking dog could kill a kid."

Wilberforce reached the bottom of the steps. He looked back at Norbert. Norbert was annoyed—

"Go!"

Reluctantly, Wilberforce jogged off toward the dogs, fists pumping. He was in absolutely no condition for such a sudden level of physical exertion. This is insane, he thought. What will I do if I catch up to them? I'll die of exhaustion at their feet and they'll feast on my flabby corpse. He pumped his fists quicker and higher. Every muscle sang out for him to cease. He had no breath in reserve—the stairs alone had winded him. Still, he ran.

The dogs raced along the concourse, past tourists young and old, and armed security. The dogs dashed across the roadway, past the power plant, and onto the walkway running along the crest of the dam. The pit bull was fast closing the gap between them. Behind the dogs, three security officers followed, guns drawn. Behind them, Wilberforce (fists pumping). Far behind Wilberforce, Norbert steadily advanced toward the action.

Midway along the crest, the pit bull caught Kum & Go—leaping in stride and locking his vice-like jaws around the retriever's neck. The two dogs tumbled forward, Kum & Go flailing and clawing at her attacker. But it was no use. The pit bull had her in its terrible grip. The security officers stopped short of the battling dogs and pointed their weapons at the rolling, snarling, twisting, yelping fracas of violence and death spasms. Wilberforce skid to a stop alongside the officers.

"Stay back!" yelled one of them. "Vacate the area!"

"Do something!" panted Wilberforce. The yellow dog's childlike cries of agony sickened him. "Shoot it!"

"Stay back!"

Wilberforce gripped his pant legs above his kneecaps, heaving hard, trying to reestablish some sanity to the rhythm of his respiration.

"Oh, fuck it all," said Wilberforce and lunged forward, seizing the pit bull's mouth at the top and bottom. He pulled and pried, working to loosen the dog's grip on the bloody, broken Kum & Go. Wilberforce succeeded, only to have the pit bull release its grip on Kum & Go's neck and chomp down on his left forearm. Wilberforce screamed in agony, his voice high-pitched and feminine. "Shoot it!" he screeched, pleading with the officers. "Shoot it now!"

Norbert arrived. He pushed past the officers, hooking his left arm around the pit bull's neck, punching it as hard as he could in the eye and nose and ribs. It was like punching the trunk of a pine tree—there was no give, no vulnerability. The dog refused to unset its jaw from Wilberforce's arm. Wilberforce screamed as the three of them spun atop the concrete—howled as his arm twisted in each new direction Norbert yanked the dog's head, punching it furiously with his scraped, bleeding knuckles.

"Shoot the fucking thing!" Norbert screamed at the officers dancing a semicircle a few feet clear of the commotion.

"Get off," said a second officer. "I can't get a clear shot."

Norbert kicked out his leg, exposing his prosthetic.

"What the fuck is this?" said the first security officer. "What the fuck is going on?"

Norbert reached back behind his belt and removed Wilberforce's Micronesian ritual knife. He had doubled back to the Caddy to get it. He plunged the knife to the hilt into the pit bull's side. Frightened he might miss if he pulled it out to stab a second time, Norbert twisted the knife into the dog. The pit bull uncorked a horrific cry of agony, releasing Wilberforce's red, shattered arm.

With great effort, Norbert rose. He looked down at Wilberforce—writhing, clutching his arm in his shirttale to stem the flow of blood. He looked at Kum & Go's lifeless body sprawled atop the cement. He looked at the dead pit bull, the knife standing straight up from its side like so many rifles he'd seen plunged into the sand.

"Don't even think about it, pal," said the first security officer. "Just step away. It's all over."

Norbert crouched down and, with tremendous difficulty, wrapped his arms around the carcass of the pit bull. He hugged it tightly to his chest and slowly stood erect, staggering backward.

The first security officer holstered his weapon as he approached Norbert, his hand extended as a calming force.

"Don't even *think* about it—"

Norbert turned and heaved the pit bull over the edge of the crest of the dam. He did not bother to step forward to watch it plummet the 724 feet onto the concrete platform above the shallow, standing waters of Lake Mead.

"Thou shalt not kill," murmured Norbert, half-smiling, as the officers descended upon him, taking him into custody.

"Number six," panted Wilberforce, sprawled flat on his back. Alarms sounded all around them as the rumble of many footfalls fast approached. "Nice work. Four more to go."

Two hours later, in a bright, Spartan box of a room deep within the bowels of the Hoover Dam, Norbert waited. He had removed his prosthetic to check and clear it of debris. His wounded limb had been aggravated by the activity and trauma of the afternoon. He tended to it as best he could under the circumstances before reattaching his leg.

Philip Philo Phipps—gangly, ginger son of Yuma, Arizona—entered the room.

"You got yourself eyeballs deep in shit, Sugar Bear."

"How bad is it?" asked Norbert.

"Bad."

"Am I going to jail?"

Phipps laughed.

"Jail? Do you think I'd let them cart you off to jail? The man who saved my motherfucking life?"

Phipps said that the pit bull's remains had been recovered from the base of the dam and that he had personally spoken to the owners: an angry, unwashed family from Forth Smith, Arkansas, with plenty of legal troubles of their own. In the course of his conversation with them they made it known to Phipps that their cousin's wife was a paralegal and that they would soon have him, and everyone else employed or stationed at the Hoover Dam, fired and, in addition, would rain fiscal ruin upon the treasury of the United States government itself.

Phipps tried offering them complimentary passes to several other area attractions, which they declined most vociferously. They made it clear that they could not be purchased with such a meager compensation for their loss and that Agent Phipps's government bribe would be so noted in their formal legal action. The family asked for the body of their beloved pet, to inter in the family plot, but Phipps told them the dog was evidence and now classified as official government property.

The truth, Phipps told Norbert, was that he did not want to release the body of the pit bull to its already enraged owners because it was missing its head. Since the dog had no vaccination tags, its head had been removed, double-bagged in plastic, and was now resting on ice.

Phipps told Norbert that the dog's head would be quietly transferred to the trunk of his pink Cadillac so that, when they arrived in Las Vegas, it could be tested for rabies upon Wilberforce's arrival at Desert Springs Hospital.

Wilberforce had a broken left arm with deep lacerations, possibly requiring surgery. Phipps had already called ahead to the emergency room, warning them to be ready for a pit bull head.

As for the government's charges, they were extensive. Phipps said he was forced to call in a one-time favor from their old unit commander, now a big wheel with the Department of the Interior. As a result, Norbert and Wilberforce were now free to go.

"Just like that?" asked Norbert.

"Not exactly," said Phipps. "But, yes, just like that."

Phipps did all of this, and did it gladly, because he believed that Norbert had saved his life in Iraq. But what people choose to believe, and what is the truth, is rarely the same thing.

"What about the dog?" said Norbert. "Our dog. What about its remains?"

"Your dog's alive," said Phipps. "He's been transferred to a veterinary hospital in Las Vegas. They think he might make it."

"She."

"What?"

"The dog's a she."

"Anyway," said Phipps. "You can deal with *her* there. It's been great seeing you, Sugar Bear. You sure know how to make an entrance. I'd offer for you stay a few nights, get drunk, but I actually need you to get your ass outta here ten minutes ago. Disappear and stay the fuck off the radar for a while. Copy that?"

"Phipps, I don't know what to say."

"There's nothing to say. I owed you."

"Phipps," said Norbert, "I didn't save your life."

"I know that's what you think—"

"No, really, I didn't save your life. I think we need to settle that right now. It was just a stupid coincidence."

"Soldiers don't believe in coincidences, you know that. We either execute or fail to execute. You executed the mission of saving my life. It doesn't matter what you *believe* happened. All that matters is what *did* happen. If it helps, think of it as fate. You intervened. God intervened. Whatever. In the final analysis, if it wasn't for you, I wouldn't be here today."

"Sully would."

Phipps didn't want to talk about Sully.

"That's got nothing to do with me, brother. I can only play the hand I've been dealt. You should think about doing the same. If I hadn't been late getting back from that covert beer run you convinced me to go on, I would have been there to get in that Bradley fighting vehicle. And if I was in that Bradley, I would have been hit by that RPG—just like the rest of them. I would have burned to death, just like the rest of them."

"And if I hadn't been late getting back from that beer run," said Norbert, "I would have arrived at my post in time to relieve Sully. Sully would still be alive and I'd be dead instead. As I should be."

"I feel bad about Sully. I feel bad about Ortiz and Miller and Schiff and all those guys in that Bradley. But I wouldn't change what happened. It's war, man. It ain't the real world."

"Yeah," said Norbert.

"Guilt will eat you hollow. You left your leg over there. Don't you think that's enough?"

Agent Philip Philo Phipps escorted Norbert and Wilberforce to their vehicle. He gave Wilberforce back his knife wrapped in a towel and secured the ice-packed pit bull's head inside an Igloo cooler in the trunk.

"Now go," said Phipps. "Quickly. I need to begin the painful process of forgetting you guys were ever here."

26

Inside the wound care unit at Desert Springs Hospital in Las Vegas, Wilberforce was having his arm set. He had received twenty-seven internal and thirty-five external stitches for the deep tissue lacerations he suffered in the attack, as well as several punctures from long needles injecting powerful antibiotics. Luckily, there was no surgery required, but there was much somber shaking of the head and a dubious "time will tell" from the attending physician when Wilberforce asked if he would suffer any loss of function or mobility in his arm.

With his arm set and a cast and sling applied, Wilberforce sat on the examining table alone in a small room swinging his legs and kicking the base of the table like a child. With his free hand he inflated a rubber glove, but when he tried to tie it into a balloon he lost his grip and it rocketed away. The glove slapped the wall beside the door as the nurse entered. She was returning to the room to complete Wilberforce's outtake interview and to ask if he had any questions about his physical therapy or prescribed medications.

"Bored?" asked the nurse.

Wilberforce blushed.

"You'll be out of here in a minute. You have your pain prescriptions and your physical therapy reference. Do you have any questions?"

"Where can I fill these? I'm from out of town."

"I can give you a list of local pharmacies before you leave. I recommend you also contact your primary-care physician and schedule an appointment as soon as possible."

"Okay," said Wilberforce.

The nurse smiled.

"And avoid wrestling pit bulls."

Wilberforce laughed. "Where were you earlier? I could have used that advice."

"So, you were trying to save the life of another dog?"

"A golden retriever."

"I think that's pretty terrific."

"Do you?"

Wilberforce looked directly into the nurse's green eyes. She held his gaze. She can't be more than a few years younger than myself, he thought. He studied her bright, plump face, its milky whiteness. He followed the matronly curve of her thick hips beneath her scrubs. Her sensible rubber-soled footwear.

"And pretty brave," she said.

"What's your name, sweet seraph?"

"Nurse Helen."

"Oooh, I love proper titles. Well, thank you, *Nurse Helen*. My name is Wilberforce Wendell."

"I know. I don't see a ring, Wilberforce. Are you married?"

"Not anymore."

"Me, either," said Nurse Helen.

"Do you drink coffee?"

"Not if I can avoid it. I prefer the taste of something harder."

"So do I," said Nurse Helen, her eyes flashing like a lioness edging closer to her wounded prey. "Harder the better."

In the waiting room, Norbert read an issue of *Time* magazine. Headline: "The God Part of the Brain." Wilberforce entered with Nurse Helen. He told Norbert that she was just getting off her shift and that he had invited her to dinner.

"So, Norbert," said Wilberforce, "I have good news and bad news. Since I am in no condition to drive, the bad news is, you will have to give Nurse Helen a ride back to her house after dinner."

Norbert looked at Nurse Helen. "Don't you have your own vehicle?"

"I take the bus," she replied.

"I see," said Norbert, annoyed. He was in no mood for new travel companions. "What's the *good* news?"

Wilberforce smiled. "I don't have rabies."

Norbert drove the Caddy while Wilberforce and Nurse Helen made time with one another in the backseat like they were being driven to their junior prom. Norbert found this chauffer-client arrangement most unsatisfactory. He didn't know why, but he was compelled to run interference between the two instant lovebirds.

"Don't forget to tip the valet at the hotel," said Norbert. "I don't have any cash on me."

"You never have cash on you," said Wilberforce. "Did you only bring one credit card on this trip?"

"Just tip the guy, that's all. Never mind my finances."

Wilberforce whispered something to Nurse Helen, she giggled. This rankled Norbert.

"What do you do for work, Norbert?" asked Nurse Helen.

"I'm on dis—," Norbert paused. "I'm between gigs. I was in community college before I went overseas."

"For school?"

"For war."

"Oh," said Nurse Helen. "I don't agree with the war at all. But I support the troops. Bring them home! That's what I say."

"Huh," said Norbert. "That's a unique philosophy."

"I mean I don't agree with our foreign policy is all."

"Well, Nurse Helen, agree or disagree, we're over there. Asshole-deep in ragheads."

Wilberforce looked into Norbert's eyes in the rearview mirror. "What do you think about the war, Norbert? I mean, what's your personal, private opinion?"

"Funny you ask, Padre, because I have a strong opinion. But I'm saving it for someone special. As you know."

"Yes," said Wilberforce, "by my count, four to go."

"Four to go," Norbert agreed.

"Padre?" said Nurse Helen. "Why did he just call you Padre?"

"I used to be a Catholic priest."

Nurse Helen sat up. "Are you serious? Why did you leave the church?"

"For the love of a woman."

"What happened to the woman?"

"It wasn't meant to be."

Nurse Helen looked deeply into Wilberforce's eyes. She grasped his hands in hers. "You are remarkable. And to think, I almost had someone cover my shift tonight. An angel must have whispered in my ear, 'Go to work tonight, Helen. *Go to work.*'"

Norbert watched this whole spectacle unfold in the rear-view mirror. He shook his head.

"So, Norbert," asked Nurse Helen, "you're waiting to share your innermost thoughts about the war with a certain, special person?"

"I am," said Norbert, watching the traffic.

"I wish you luck," she said. "I really do. Everyone should find their special person." She touched Wilberforce on the nose, ever so slightly. Wilberforce smiled. They smooched.

"Here we are," said Norbert, pulling up to the valet at the New York, New York. "Don't forget to tip."

Near the entrance to the New York, New York, obscured behind a pillar of concrete, Elton Berryhill watched Norbert, Wilberforce, and Nurse Helen exit the pink Cadillac. The loyal subscriber at the National 9 Inn in Denver had led him right to the meanie. Praise Jesus! Elton grinned as the three entered through the glass doors of the hotel. He tilted back his head and emptied the carton of thick, sweet milk down his throat. Thin, white rivulets cascaded down his chin from the corners of his mouth. He wiped them away with his shirtsleeve. Elton strolled out to the street and walked north along the sidewalk. He tossed the empty milk carton into a public trash receptacle.

Beside the trash bin, propped against the wall, was a homeless man holding a hand-lettered sign on corrugated cardboard. It read: "Ninjas killed my family. Need $ for kung-fu lessons to seek revenge."

Elton was approached by a man of Hispanic descent. The man, a full foot shorter than Elton, extended from his hand a glossy, full-color palm card depicting a naked woman in pornographic congress with a second woman dressed in, what Elton could only guess, was some sort of medieval torture costume. There was a phone number across the bottom of the card. The man was offering Elton the card by flicking it with his outstretched fingers, producing a clicking sound. Elton slapped the card away.

"Get that filth away from me," said Elton. "Burn in hell, heathen."

The man angrily responded in a foreign tongue that Elton assumed was Spanish. "Learn the language," said Elton. "On the other hand, don't bother, my diminutive Latino idolater. When the Rapture comes, you will be attempting to distribute your pornography to my pile of empty clothes while jibber-jabbering your gibberish because you will surely still be standing here on this vile corner in this pit of sin."

The man responded again in Spanish then turned away. There were plenty of willing customers. Elton turned to walk away, bumping roughly into a man walking in the opposite direction.

"Out of my way," said Elton. "I am on a righteous crusade for the innocent."

"Good luck with that," said the man.

Inside the New York, New York, Norbert, Wilberforce, and Nurse Helen walked through the casino toward the check-in counter. On the other side of a row of slot machines, headed in the opposite direction, walked Andy with the Red Boots.

Andy—with blackened eyes and still sporting his nose splint—led a phalanx of bridesmaids in a bachelorette party he had commandeered with his billfold. He wore a dark sport coat over a red T-shirt that said, "I'm a Legend in Japan." Several of the bachelorettes could not keep their paws off him. He stuffed a $100 bill into one young lady's ample cleavage, upsetting some of the others. But there was plenty for everyone, as Andy proved by tossing several bills into the air. A delirious scrum ensued. Elbows were thrown.

At the check-in desk there was a poster board resting on an easel welcoming guests to GODCON. Norbert and Wilberforce were informed by the clerk—whose nametag read: CHUCK, SOUTH DAKOTA—that, sure enough, they had a complimentary room booked at the hotel under Mr. Wilberforce Wendell.

Who woulda thunk, thought Norbert, that that creepy night clerk at the National 9 Inn in Denver would turn out to be such a swell fella?

Inside their room on the twenty-second floor, Nurse Helen cinched the clear plastic garbage bag from the trash bin over Wilberforce's cast so he could shower. Norbert started pouring miniature liquor bottles from the hospitality refrigerator into a single glass.

"Those little bottles are, like, ten bucks apiece," said Nurse Helen.

"Cha-ching," said Norbert. He laughed. The joke escaped Nurse Helen.

Wilberforce emerged from the bathroom, his hair wet and neat, threading his belt through the loops of his slacks with his good arm. He smelled like saddle leather. The bold, musky fragrance produced an abrupt, sharp pang behind Norbert's heart. An image of his purloined notebook flashed through his frontal cortex. The painful memory of its loss was so real, so stark, the image so vivid of the dark words and illustrations scribbled across the white pages, he squeezed closed his eyes and pressed his index fingers to his temples. He breathed in deeply, resting his elbows on the arms of the desk chair.

"You all right, boyo?" said Wilberforce.

Norbert opened his eyes. "Fine," he said. He rose, went to the refrigerator, gathered several more bottles in his hands and returned to the chair to fix himself another drink.

"Easy, Norbert," said Wilberforce. "You're our ride tonight."

"Take a cab. I'm not in the mood to drive you and Miss Daisy. Tonight I'm gonna get drunk, then head down to the bar and get more drunk."

Wilberforce fastened his wristwatch with his teeth before Nurse Helen could assist him, though she wanted to. He sorted his pocket things then looked at his reflection in the mirror above the dresser. Slapping his double chin several times softly with the backs of his fingers he said, "'Verily, everyman at his best state is altogether vanity.'"

"What's that?" asked Nurse Helen.

"Spinoza probably," said Norbert, emptying an eclectic variety of alcoholic beverages into his glass.

"Psalm 39," said Wilberforce.

No wonder you don't wear a hat," said Nurse Helen. "You're brain's too big."

"Where to for dinner?" Wilberforce asked Nurse Helen.

"No place fancy. I'm still in my scrubs. Tell you what, I know just the place."

"Want to come along?" Wilberforce asked Norbert, insincerely.

"You two have a blast. There's a barstool downstairs with my name on it."

Nurse Helen was relieved. She didn't care for Wilberforce's brooding young friend. "Are we ready?" she sang.

The door was nearly shut when it opened back into the room. Wilberforce peeked around it, wagging his finger at Norbert who was slouched in the chair by the window. "Watch yourself," he said. "That's my *professional* recommendation, as your spiritual adviser. Take a night off from the mission. We'll start fresh in the morning. Tomorrow is a new day."

"You think He's watching yet, Padre?"

"He's always watching."

Norbert nodded. Wilberforce closed the door.

Norbert pounded back what was left in his glass.

Downstairs in Nine Fine Irishmen, the pub on the ground floor of the New York, New York, Norbert stood at the bar. The stools had been dragged to the opposite wall to make room for more customers. Norbert ordered a Jameson. He recognized the young bartender from somewhere but couldn't place him. The bartender admitted that he had once been a contestant on a reality television show. "Oh yeah," said Norbert. "You were that guy. The one who was with that girl who had the thing."

"That was me."

Norbert sipped his drink. There was a live Irish band playing, reminding him of the Irish tunes Sully used to hum and sing the lyrics to, his favorite being: "They gave me a tin hat, they gave me a gun, and they sent me off to the war."

Inside the bar and milling about the casino was a large wedding party including a dozen or so marines in their dress blues. Women were hanging off of them, men seized their hands, shaking them vigorously, slapping their backs, buying them rounds. Norbert turned back toward the bar.

He thought, there is a self-consciousness to drinking alone—particularly if one is not a drunk. There's a pantomime to it. Men standing side-by-side on separate islands, pretending they are waiting for someone, routinely checking their watches, glancing toward the door, feigning interest in the sports broadcast flickering before them. Men desperate for conversation, aching to tell their story at the slightest provocation, yet terrified that the guy beside him might turn and address him directly. Behind that wall of machismo hides a chatterbox. This is the dance of loneliness, thought Norbert. The essence of masculinity.

Eavesdropping on the conversations in his proximity, Norbert found it hard to believe he was in Las Vegas. Everyone was talking about his Lord and Savior Jesus Christ! Flanked by holy rollers! Each with a GODCON convention tag draped around his or her neck. Norbert turned back toward the crowd and soon fell into conversation with a GODCON conventioneer and her husband from Houston. The woman told Norbert she was an engineer for NASA.

She said, "You wouldn't believe how many people mail their loved one's ashes to us to be shot into outer space."

"How many?" asked Norbert.

"At least one, maybe two per month," said the woman, who was quite intoxicated. "The letters that accompany the remains are quite compelling."

"What do you do with them?"

"Send them back."

"But what if there is no return address? What if they believe you will just shoot them into space if you don't know where to return them?"

"Then they go into a vault on the premises."

"Then what?" asked Norbert.

"Every seven years the vault is purged."

She told Norbert about "The Overview Effect," a term used by astronauts and cosmonauts to describe the phenomenon of looking at the Earth from orbit, coming face-to-face with the significance (or, insignificance) of one's own existence, then returning to Earth either thrilled or crippled by the experience.

"It must be incomprehensible for them to return from that and make any sense whatsoever of why we fight each other," said Norbert. "Of why we hate each other so passionately."

"Yeah," said the NASA engineer.

"It's madness. People who've been in orbit must think we're all crazy."

"Yeah," she agreed, "Horrible. Just a horrible experience. Like being forced to use the ladies' room in Penn Station."

"It's a miracle they don't all go crazy themselves. Returning from the tranquility and separateness of space to this asylum of a planet."

"Who?"

"The astronauts."

"Miracle," she said. "Hey, I like your haircut. Are you with these marines? Are you military? You look military to me."

Norbert glanced over at the group of laughing marines. "No," he said. "I just wear it high and tight."

Norbert needed a change of scenery. He exited into the casino and circled the slots and tables. Scanning the bustling throng of gamers he thought that, despite its clever advertising, the vast majority of pilgrims to Las Vegas were the sort of Americans who referred to brown paper bags with twine handles as "luggage." Norbert stopped at The Bar at Times Square, a boisterous establishment with a loathsome cover charge and dueling pianos. It looked like the patrons were having fun though, so Norbert slipped in without paying while the bouncer was otherwise engaged. At the bar he ordered another Jameson. The bartender was about Norbert's age. Over the music, Norbert said, "Where you from?"

"Huh?"

"Where you from?"

"Here," said the bartender. "Las Vegas."

Incredible, thought Norbert. A rare native sighting. "I met a fella from Las Vegas when I was in South Bend, Indiana."

"Uh-huh," said the bartender. It was not clear if he could hear what Norbert was saying over the music.

"He was a Michigan fan."

"Huh."

"I'll ask you the same question I asked him: What do they call people from Las Vegas?"

The bartender did not have a ready answer. The question seemed to stop him cold as he considered it.

"I have no idea," he said.

"And you're from here?"

"I was born here."

"Las Vegans?" Norbert guessed.

The bartender shrugged. "I really don't know."

Norbert decided Las Vegans sounded like people wandering around searching for misplaced salads. The bartender drifted away.

"I don't know either and I'm from here, too," said a petite blonde standing at the bar beside Norbert. "I've never even thought about it."

The little blonde, as it turned out, wasn't just a native, she was also a stripper at Déjà Vu. Her name—her real name, she swore—was Bambi. She was a single mom with a daughter named Destini. She said her father had served in the air force and that they lived in Germany when she was a kid, but he left when she was five. Norbert did not bother to ask where Destini was while her mother drank margaritas alone after midnight on the Vegas Strip. Bambi noticed Norbert looking at her drink.

"It's made with Corazon," she said. "I get paid by these guerilla marketing guys to say that to people."

"How much?"

"A hundred bucks a week."

"How can they possibly know whether or not you're telling people? Do they check up on you?"

"They say they do."

"It must be strange being from here and dancing at a gentleman's club," said Norbert. "You ever have an old classmate sit down in front of you and say, 'You turned me down when I asked you to the prom. Here's a dollar. Stick your pussy in my face?'"

"Yeah," said Bambi. "That's happened."

Suddenly, even over the ear-splitting performances of the screeching piano crooners, Norbert startled at the sound of a woman's voice—an *unmistakable* voice—standing directly behind him.

The woman said, "This singing is driving me f'n crazy."

That voice could belong to only one woman: Norbert's former soon-to-be fiancée, Arlene. Norbert turned to face Arlene and Pastor Zack.

"Norbert!" croaked a stunned Arlene. "Oh my God! Are you stalking me? Zack, he's stalking me."

"We don't want any trouble, Norbert," said Pastor Zack.

"You followed me all the way out here?" said Arlene. "You really have lost your mind! Should I fear for my life? Zack? I think I should fear for my life."

"You have nothing to be afraid of," said Pastor Zack. "I'm here."

"Oh, please," said Arlene. She was more than a little drunk and seemed to be carelessly alluding to a level of masculinity on the part of Pastor Zack that had fallen far short of her expectations. "Don't make me laugh." Arlene took a drink of her white zinfandel.

"Explain yourself, Norbert," said Pastor Zack, a bit wounded by Arlene's affront. "Why have you followed us here? How did you obtain our itinerary? This is extremely absurd behavior, bordering on mental illness."

"What are you talking about?" said Norbert. "I had no idea you two would be in Las Vegas."

"Oh please," said Arlene. "Admit it! You're obsessed with me. And now you've followed me across the country to profess your undying love. All right. Go ahead."

"Arlene, please," said Pastor Zack. "You're hurting my feelings."

"Boo-fucking-hoo, Zack," said Arlene. "Suck it up." She looked at Norbert. "Well . . . I'm waiting."

"I didn't follow you here," said Norbert, a little drunk himself. In that moment, he made a snap decision to dive into the vacuum he sensed between the two lovers. Clearly the beast of travel had reared its head on their first sojourn together, dumping its heavy shit bucket upon a fragile romance struggling to blossom. "But now that I see you," said Norbert, "in that sparkly tube top of yours that I love so much. And that leather skirt. And those heels."

"All right," said Pastor Zack. "This stops here."

Arlene ignored him.

"Zack hates this outfit. He told me to change. I said, 'I'm in Vegas, baby! What do you want me to wear, an f'n gunnysacks dress?'"

"I think Zack looks like fifty pounds of shit in a ten-pound bag."

"Ha, ha, Norbert," said Pastor Zack. "It's a religious conference. Her attire is inappropriate."

"What religious conference?" said Norbert.

"We've been planning this for weeks," said Pastor Zack.

"This is GODCON, the largest fellowship convention in North America."

"In Vegas?" said Norbert.

"Where else?" said Pastor Zack. "This is the center of the hard work that needs to be done."

"Oh, put a cork in it," said Arlene. "What a bunch of kooks."

"Arlene," said Pastor Zack. "Please. I think you've had enough. Let's go back to the room."

Pastor Zack hooked his arm around Arlene's. She recoiled from it.

"I'm not going anywhere with you," said Arlene. "I'm staying right here." She slid onto a stool and waved her empty wine glass at the bartender. "Another white zinfandel."

"Arlene, please," pleaded Pastor Zack. "Don't make a scene. Let's go back to the room and talk."

"I'm sick of talking," said Arlene. "I thought I wanted to talk. That's why I left you, Norbert. It is. I wanted to talk and you didn't. And then, when I forced you to talk, you told me all sorts of stuff I didn't want to hear. Well I'm sorry, Norbert. I'm sorry. I was wrong. I'm realizing that sometimes there's great beauty in silence—long stretches of comfortable silence. Maybe that's what they call love. Maybe love isn't in the things you say, but in the silence. I don't know. All I know is this windbag doesn't know when to shut his yapper. He talks till I want to douse myself in gasoline and dive into a goddamn furnace."

Norbert finished off his Jameson. "So why don't you send Pastor Zack to bed, and we'll spend the rest of tonight not talking to each other?"

"Hold on," said Pastor Zack.

Arlene turned to Pastor Zack. "You heard him," she slurred. "Hit the bricks."

"I don't think you know what you're saying," said Pastor Zack. "I blame myself for not better monitoring your alcohol intake. I think you're going to have a lot of regrets in the morning."

"I'll tell it to my confessor," said Arlene.

The three of them stood staring back and forth at one another for a long, awkward moment.

"Well?" said Arlene.

"Well what?" said Pastor Zack.

"Hit the bricks."

"You can't be serious."

"I think she's serious," said Norbert. "Are you serious, Arlene?"

"Hell—" she hiccupped. "Hell yeah I'm serious. Beat it, Zack-o."

Pastor Zack glared at Arlene. He said, "This is the man who 'tortured your soul.'"

"Yep," said Arlene.

He shook his head. "Patently absurd." Pastor Zack scooped his cash from the bar and tucked it into his wallet. He looked at Arlene again, tugged out a twenty, and handed it to her.

"Here's cab fare for when you've played out your little drama this evening," he said. "I'll be waiting up."

"She doesn't need your money," said Norbert.

Arlene snatched the bill and tucked it between her sparkly breasts.

Pastor Zack began to say something then stopped himself. He looked at Norbert, then looked at the door and started to walk away. Norbert turned toward the bar, caught the bartender's attention, and ordered another Jameson.

Zack looked over his shoulder at Arlene. He winked.

Arlene winked back.

Norbert turned and watched Pastor Zack exit briskly through the casino. When he was out of sight, Norbert swirled his drink with its thin red straw, depositing the straw on the bar when he was finished. He looked directly into Arlene's green eyes for the first time since they fought inside the Ford on Sunday after church.

"So," she said.

"So."

"You want to take a walk?" asked Arlene.

"That would be splendiferous," said Norbert.

28

At the Grand Lux Café on Las Vegas Boulevard, Wilberforce and Nurse Helen were finishing their dinners, sipping Turkish coffees, chatting. Nurse Helen told Wilberforce she could not drink because she was on call that night in the emergency room.

Wilberforce told her the story of Sasha.

As he spoke, Nurse Helen thought, Is there no limit to this man's charity? "It's late," said Nurse Helen, "and you've been through the wringer. You must be tired?"

"Not really. I'm like the old waiter in Hemingway's 'A Clean, Well-Lighted Place.' One of those who like to stay late at the café. Who doesn't like to go to bed. Who needs a light for the night. I enjoy listening to your voice. It's a good tonic."

Nurse Helen talked excitedly about a trip she took to Amsterdam the previous summer with a recently divorced co-worker. It was clearly her first, and only, overseas excursion. She explained that Amsterdam was the capital of Holland, which in turn was a province of the Netherlands.

"That clears that mess up," said Wilberforce.

"The old pubs in Amsterdam are called brown cafés. Can you guess why?"

Wilberforce shook his head.

"It's because the walls have turned brown from all the years of tobacco smoke."

"Did you walk the Red Light district?"

"I wanted to, but my friend was too embarrassed."

"Smoke dope?"

Nurse Helen blushed, "No."

Pity, thought Wilberforce. What a lame trip to Amsterdam. An attractive, young waitress returned to the table

and asked if they wanted refills. They did. The buxom waitress leaned over the table, filling their cups with the hot,
steamy beverage. Wilberforce paid the waitress no mind.

"I want to tell you something," said Nurse Helen.
"Something personal."

"All right."

"Do you know the stock footage they show on the national
news every time they do a report about the obesity epidemic
in America? You know, with the people walking around
on the street, the man with his gut hanging out and the
woman with the wide rear end wearing black stretch pants?"

"Okay," said Wilberforce.

"That's me," said Nurse Helen. "The woman they always
show in the stretch pants. That was me, 260 pounds and
seven years ago."

"Okay," said Wilberforce.

"I've had three surgeries to remove excess skin."

"You look lovely. I would never have guessed had you
not told me."

"I've run five marathons. And I'm registered for my sixth
in the spring."

"You don't need to prove anything to me," said Wilberforce.

"I just like to be up front with people. Okay?"

"Okay."

"Good," said Nurse Helen. "I'm glad that's out of the way."

Her cell phone rang. She was called into the emergency
room. Out front, they stood wrapped in each other's arms.

"Let's go to the zoo tomorrow," said Nurse Helen.

"Seriously?"

"I don't know why I said that. It just popped into my head.
Isn't that strange? That is so strange. I just want to make
plans to do something together. Anything."

"Is there a zoo in Las Vegas?"

"I don't even know," said Nurse Helen. "Probably. This
whole place is a zoo."

Wilberforce roared like a lion. Nurse Helen tamed him with her imaginary whip.

"Do you know why lion tamers use a stool?" asked Wilberforce.

"Why?"

"Because the lion tries to focus on all four legs at the same time, thus paralyzing it."

Nurse Helen smiled. "You're neat."

Elsewhere on the Vegas Strip, in the backseat of a taxicab stopped in traffic, Norbert massaged Arlene's left breast through the thin fabric of her sparkly tube top. He licked her neck. The cab driver observed all this peripherally in the rearview mirror.

"I knew you couldn't leave me," said Norbert. "I knew you'd want to get back together. We just had to be away from that town, that life, for a little while."

"Will you love me?" said Arlene.

"Yes," said Norbert.

"Honor and cherish me?"

"I will."

"Why?"

"Because I'm so hot I'm going to explode," said Norbert.

Arlene placed her hand on Norbert's cheek.

"No. Really, Norbert. It's important that you tell me why?"

"Why what?"

"Why do you want to be with me, forever?"

"Because I'm hammered," said Norbert.

He tried to kiss her. She pulled away.

"I'm serious, Norbert. Right now, tell me why."

Norbert disengaged, sliding against the opposite door.

"This was a mistake," said Arlene. "It's my fault. I'm a foolish girl. My faith has blinded me, made me too trusting."

"This is why we always fight," said Norbert. "I don't know what the hell you want. I don't know that I ever have. First you don't believe in God, then you're a church nut. First you love me, then you don't, then you do. Now you don't again. Which is it?"

"I just need to know *why*, Norbert. Why do you love me so much? Why should we be together instead of apart? Tell me in your own words. We've been a couple for so long. Since we were kids. Be straight with me for once in your life."

"Tell you why I love you."

"Yes," said Arlene. "Tell me why."

Norbert rubbed his eyes with his knuckles, scratched his fingertips through his hair. He looked in the rearview mirror at the eyes of the cab driver but couldn't tell if he was paying attention.

"Because I need love," said Norbert, "Without it, I feel like I'm heading straight into the abyss. That's why. I'm driving straight into the void. I'm on this collision course with God and California, and I don't think it's gonna end well. It can't end well. There's this space inside of me, Arlene, that's empty and I need to fill it up. I *want* to fill it up. I want to *feel* again, like I used to before—

"I get angry. I cry sometimes. But I don't *feel*. I'm numb. I hurt, but it's a physical pain. My gut hurts, or my eye throbs, or my leg. Sometimes I cry so hard I'm just exhausted after. My muscles are wiped out. My head pounds. But there's no feeling behind the tears. It's just . . . I don't know. I can't explain it. I don't understand it, so how do I explain it? Did you know I lost my notebook?"

"Oh, Norbert!"

"Of course not. How could you know?"

"I'm so sorry. I know how much it meant to you."

"I left it in a motel room in Cleveland."

"Maybe someone will return it."

"Don't tell me that, Arlene. Okay? Don't tell me that. It's gone."

"I'm sorry."

Norbert sighed. "No, I'm sorry. You're right, maybe someone will return it. The point is I should hope for the best to happen. That's why I need you, Arlene, because you remind me that it's okay to hope for the best. I'm afraid that without someone like you in my life, that empty space inside me will keep expanding until I'm all hollowed out. Empty. You're my conscience. You give me perspective. When you told me you were leaving me, I guess I went a little nuts. I got it into my head that I needed to do these things, these bad things, to make something happen that's never going to happen. Not everything in life gets resolved.

"Things have been tough for me these past two years. And I have guilt. A lot of guilt about what happened over there. I think I'm even dangerous without you, Arlene. Aimless. You've always been my anchor. You've stuck by me through so much already. I want you to stay with me the rest of the way. I don't need to go to California. I don't need to finish this thing I've started. It's probably best that I don't. All I need is you."

Norbert scooted over to Arlene. He rested his head on her bosom.

"All I need is you saying you'll love me. I think if I have that, I can get through this. I can come out on the other side. Have a life. That's why, Arlene: because I believe we can have a life together. We can have a few brats. Be normal. And I promise, I'll do whatever it takes from this point on to make you happy."

Arlene stroked Norbert's hair.

"Okay," she said.

"Okay?"

"Yes, Norbert. That's all I wanted to hear."

Norbert smiled. From the inside pocket of his leather jacket he pulled out the box containing the diamond engagement ring with the white gold band. He opened it. Arlene was taken aback.

"I was waiting to give you this. Then, when you left, I decided to return it to Mr. Klein, but his store was closed on Sunday. Then, I don't know, I just decided to hold on to it. Try it on."

Arlene slipped on the ring. "It's gorgeous." She looked at Norbert and said, "You look about sixteen years old right now." She tried flattening a cowlick on Norbert's head, but it would not cooperate. "Like you just came from your last class and are headed out to the practice field."

Norbert buried his head in Arlene's bosoms. Her GODCON tag crinkled.

Arlene raked her painted nails through his hair. A tear somersaulted down her cheek. She caught the cab driver watching her in the mirror. She looked away, disgusted with herself.

29

Wilberforce strolled between buildings, whistling "Why Don't We Do It in the Road?" as he headed back toward the New York, New York. He loosed a burp that echoed down the alley.

"'They return at evening,'" said a voice from the black space behind a dumpster. "'They make a noise like a dog, and go 'round about the city.'"

The dark figure of a man stepped forward from the shadows, his right hand wrapped tightly around the handle of a wooden baseball bat, his left cupped around the barrel. "'Behold! They belch out with their mouth.' Psalm 59."

"Excuse me?" said Wilberforce. "Are you speaking to me?"

"'There is nothing covered that shall not be revealed and hid that shall not be known. No more mockery of justice. No more favoring the wicked.' Matthew 10:26. 'Let the weak and the orphan have justice.' Psalm 82."

Wilberforce, paralyzed with fear, stared into the face of the stranger. He thought his eyes were playing a horrible trick on him.

"Elton?"

"It's been a long time, Father Wendell."

"Sweet Jesus," said Wilberforce, trembling. "It's really you."

"You've moved around quite a lot over the years, haven't you? This parish then the next. Popping up here and there then dropping off the radar. But I see you now. I found you. There is no place you can hide. Remember, 'the Lord watches over the way of the righteous, but the way of the wicked is doomed.' Psalm 1, verse 6."

"What are you doing here, Elton?"

"It's simple, Father. You were hiding and now you are found. Praise Jesus! So many blessings on this day!"

"It's not simple, Elton. There's nothing simple about this at all."

"You're wrong. All is clear if you put your faith in God. I shouldn't need to tell you that. Your ignorance of scripture only proves how far you have fallen, ye of little faith. My faith has never been shaken. Never for one moment. How else can I reconcile what the meanies have done to me unless it was all meant to be? This is my path. There is no other. It is all part of God's beautiful plan for me."

"I heard what happened to you, Elton. I learned many years after the fact, but I heard all about it. I was so sad to learn what Father Kavan admitted to doing to you after you left St. Agnes's. I had such hope for you when you left to live with that nice family in Kansas. What was their name?"

"Berryhill."

"Yes. The Berryhills of Topeka."

"Father Kavan," said Elton, "'he deviseth mischief upon his bed; he setteth himself in a way that is not good; he abhorreth not evil.' Psalm 36."

"But Father Kavan has been dead for many years, Elton. He took his own life. He has faced his judgment at the feet of his Maker."

"*My* father is dead."

"I'm sorry to hear that. How long since he passed?"

"Don't try to be friends with me. I'm not a little boy anymore."

"No," said Wilberforce. "Of course you're not."

Wilberforce looked quickly down the short end of the alley. It was too far to run, too risky to yell. His darting eyes did not escape Elton's attention. Elton quickly sidestepped between Wilberforce and the street.

"What's your hurry?"

"I heard about the settlement you received from the diocese," said Wilberforce. "It was quite a lot of money—enough to live comfortably. Do you look after your mother?"

"She's not my mother! Do you think I care about money?!"

"No," said Wilberforce. "No, I don't."

"That money happened to me. You hear? It happened to me and I'll spend it as I please."

"As you should," said Wilberforce.

"I'm not going to waste it on the *cable bill*, when she can't even remember to take her pill."

Elton took a step toward Wilberforce. Wilberforce backed away.

"I tithe the church and I maintain my website. I pay for travel and technology. That's how I choose to spend it. The rest stays locked away from beggars and thieves."

"It's your money, Elton. Spend it as you please."

Elton regrouped. He was angry with himself for veering so far off course from his intended purpose. He narrowed his eyes at Wilberforce, refocusing.

"I see you're up to your old tricks," said Elton. "Now you've taken your show on the road, traveling with a young boy. Sleeping with him in Denver. And you've enlisted an accomplice in your sick, twisted schemes against the innocent."

"That's not true, Elton. Not true at all. You've got it all wrong."

"Have I?" said Elton. "Have I got it *all wrong*? Where on earth would I get such wild ideas?"

"This was all so long ago, Elton. This *you and me*. I was fresh out of seminary. Confused about so many things. I was just a kid."

"No!" shouted Elton. He advanced another step toward Wilberforce. Wilberforce backed against the brick. "You don't get to say that. You were my teacher, my priest, my hero. You were the *man*. *I* was the kid. A little kid. Sister Kate trusted you. I trusted you. You broke the covenant."

Wilberforce shook his head slowly. "That was the only time, Elton. The one and only time. I've changed my ways.

I have atoned. What happened that afternoon between us was a mistake, my mistake. So many years have passed. We have both paid dearly for it in our own ways. But I'm a changed man, Elton. A different person completely. That was so long ago. A lifetime. I'm not even a priest anymore. I left the church for a woman. A *woman*, Elton. And now . . . now . . . I've just met someone new. A nurse—someone who heals—and I think I may be falling in love."

"I know you left the church," said Elton. "Do you think that makes a difference? I'm glad it was a lifetime ago for you, but for me it was yesterday. You took my innocence, my childhood. You meanies took all our childhoods. My website keeps track of all of you. I have devoted my life to it. Some of you may leave the cloth, or change parishes, but there is no place you can hide. My loyal subscribers are everywhere. How do you think I found you here? Until you leave this mortal coil I will shout from the mountains what you have done, hunt you down and photograph you and post your whereabouts for all the world to see."

"And hurt us?"

Elton patted the bat into his open palm. "No, Father. This is just for you. Only for you. I have been waiting, preparing for this moment, for so many years. I have so much anger inside me. 'Lord, give me strength to spare not the rod.'"

"What about forgiveness, Elton? Can you see past the weakness of my flesh? See Christ in me? I just told you I'm falling in love. What about love, Elton? Can you find it in your heart to forgive?"

Elton's eyes began to well and burn with tears. Snot bubbled beneath his nose. "You always tried to be friends," said Elton. "That was your way. You didn't force the issue—always friends. Until it finally happened. So sneaky. So clever. That's what makes you the biggest meanie of them all."

"Oh, Elton. I'm so sorry. Not a day goes by when I don't wish I could seize that version of myself, shake him and slap him and stop him from causing so much pain. Make him choose a different path. I curse my foolishness, Elton. My immaturity."

"What happened to your arm?" asked Elton.

"I injured it trying to stop a pit bull from killing another dog."

"You see," said Elton. "You can't help yourself. It's always a story with you. You may think you're different, but men like you can never change. That's why you must be punished."

For the first time, Wilberforce studied the bat Elton was twisting in his hands. "Is that the Tony Gwynn signature I gave you?"

Elton wiped his nose on his sleeve. "It is."

"That was our joke, remember? He played for the Padres . . . I played for the Padres. Always be sure to shift your weight from your back foot to your front, remember?"

Elton did not respond. Wilberforce swallowed hard.

"Elton? What is this all about? What are you here to do? Have you come all this way from Kansas to hit me with that bat?"

"I have."

"And you believe that beating me will ease your pain somehow? That vengeance will afford your soul some measure of peace?"

"An eye for an eye. Don't you see? It is all part of God's beautiful plan for me. For you. Stop bargaining and accept this as God's will."

Wilberforce dropped his gaze to the dark concrete between them. He inhaled deeply, lifting his shoulders in a sort of boyish shrug, then exhaled long and low. He slid his good hand into his pocket and stared into the slick whites of Elton's tortured eyes.

Wilberforce thought about how he believed he deserved bad things, he thought about Margaret, and the waitresses, he thought about Spinoza and how he believed that all things happen as they should. He thought about that rock suspended in midair and how we are all headed in one, inevitable direction. He thought about Nurse Helen. And he thought about God and the sign he had hoped for so long to receive from Him.

"Well, Elton," said Wilberforce, "get on with it, then. Show me what you can do with that bat of yours. Because I believe that you should."

30

In a dark club throbbing with house music, Andy with the Red Boots was sweaty, hammered, and merrily grinding with his fervent band of horny bachelorettes. One girl kissed him hard on the neck, coming away with some flesh pinched between her teeth. She tried to move over to his lips but he cautioned her to, "W-Watch the nose."

Andy felt a vibration in his pocket. He stepped back and removed his cell phone. He had just been alerted that Norbert Sherbert had used his credit card to check into a room at The Venetian.

Andy walked away from the dancing girls without so much as a word of goodbye. Stunned, they watched him exit the club, then looked around at one another and silently resolved to party on.

In The Venetian, Norbert met Arlene outside the ladies' room. As they walked to the elevators, she tapped a message into her cell phone.

"Everything cool?" asked Norbert.

"Yep," said Arlene, smiling as she pocketed the device.

She moved in to kiss Norbert on the lips as the elevator doors opened. Inside, Norbert and Arlene giggled and kissed, stumbling out onto their floor and down the corridor, neither one having much luck supporting the other, which made them laugh all the more. Arlene fumbled for the key card and opened the door, letting Norbert back into the room while he groped at her breasts. Arlene slipped inside, quickly shutting the door behind her.

"Now, Norbert," said Arlene, "just give me a chance to explain all this before you completely freak out."

"Explain what?"

The lights were already on. Norbert wheeled around to discover that the room was filled with people, seven in all—not counting him and Arlene. The furniture had been pushed against the walls and all the people—including Pastor Zack, standing center stage, acoustic guitar draped around his neck—were completely nude.

"Welcome, Norbert," said Pastor Zack. He strummed a G chord.

"Welcome," echoed the naked semicircle.

Norbert closed his eyes and reopened them. The same image still appeared. He recognized them all as parishioners from The Church of Abundant Waters and the Splendiferous Blood of Christ vis-à-vis the former Orange Julius in Ticonderoga, NY.

Norbert turned back to face Arlene, still standing flat against the door. Norbert was certain this was nothing more than a drunken hallucination. Arlene raised her hands to calm him.

"Before you freak, just hear me out."

"Norbert," Pastor Zack interrupted, "We are overjoyed to welcome you into our healing circle."

Norbert, his eyes still fixed on Arlene, said, "I'm hearing a voice behind me, but it's not really there, right?"

"I'm sorry Norbert," said Arlene. "I feel terrible for having tricked you this way. But I want this so badly for you. You need this, Norbert. I was finally convinced of it tonight in the taxi. Just listen to Pastor Zack. Please, Norbert, give this a chance. It will change your life."

"This is really happening?"

"Give yourself permission to trust me, Norbert," said Arlene. "Release your inhibitions and your cynicism. Reject what you think you know to be the truth. Agree to take the waters so you may begin your preparation for the Rapture. Please, just trust me."

"Trust you? Trust you?! You're sick, Arlene. Have you. . . have you been playing me since the Irish pub? I can't . . . I don't . . . This is fucking crazy. Trust you? Give me one good reason why."

Arlene shrugged, "He works in mysterious ways?"

"The bathtub has been prepared, Norbert," said Pastor Zack. "If you'll just disrobe. The sooner we perform your baptism, the sooner we can all commence the sanctifying orgy, in His name."

Norbert faced Pastor Zack. Pastor Zack crossed to Norbert, member swinging. "And I just want you to know," said Pastor Zack in a low voice, "everyone here is aware of your deformity and we're all totally cool with that."

"You're all a bunch of Fencepost Fuckers. That's what you are. Every last one of you."

"I'm sorry," said Pastor Zack, "I don't understand what you just said."

And with that, after showing great restraint under previous circumstances, Norbert finally popped Pastor Zack as hard as he could in his nose, breaking it. It was the broken-nose hat trick on the trip.

"Norbert!" screeched Arlene. "What have you done?!"

She rushed to Pastor Zack, who staggered backward into the sweaty embrace of his flock. His guitar made a hollow, tuneless reverberation as they genuflected to halt his downward progress, his nose purpled and bleeding.

"You're an animal," hissed Arlene. "This is how you address all your challenges—with violence. I should have known this is how you would react. I'm a foolish girl. Foolish for trying. You simply can't be saved, Norbert. You're a lost cause. You have to spoil everything."

Norbert twisted off the cheap wedding band they had purchased at the chapel and threw it at Arlene. He went to leave, but before the door closed he reentered the room, crossed to Arlene and twisted the diamond ring with the white gold band off her finger. He stuffed it into the front pocket of his blue jeans.

"You're a child!" she screamed.

Several minutes after the door slammed shut, the flock continued tending to Pastor Zack. Despite the preceding drama, things were getting hot. Norbert be damned, they would have their sanctifying orgy. As Arlene disrobed, there was a knock at the door.

"He's come back," said Pastor Zack. "Forgiveness," he cautioned Arlene. Arlene, nude, swung open the door.

At the door stood Andy with the Red Boots.

"Who the f-f-fuck are you?" said Andy.

"I was just going to ask you the same question," replied Arlene.

Downstairs in the lobby, Norbert stopped to speak with hotel security. He described to them a deviant sex ring, fueled by illicit substances, going on right under their noses— in their very hotel! He told security how he was kidnapped, at gunpoint, brought to The Venetian and nearly devoured by his captors' insatiable sexual hungers. He said he even watched them beat up an innocent tourist on the street, stealing his wallet, so they could charge the room to his credit card. Norbert gave them the room number. They asked Norbert his name and contact information. He told them he was, "Anton Figgs from Denver, Colorado." As security headed to the elevators, Norbert slinked out of The Venetian.

Upstairs, security pounded on the room door. Arlene answered, nude. Security entered to discover the lewd scene Norbert had so accurately detailed. Andy with the Red Boots was among them, also nude and well ensconced in the orgiastic festivities.

Security also discovered an automatic pistol in Andy's jacket, tying up Norbert's story with a big red bow—though Norbert would never know it. Everyone was taken into custody.

"Absurd!" screamed Pastor Zack, kicking out his legs, bicycle-style, as his bleeding face was elbowed into the bedspread while being cuffed from behind.

The ninth commandment: "Thou shalt not bear false witness against thy neighbor."

Three to go.

Norbert entered the room at the New York, New York to discover that Wilberforce had not yet returned from his dinner with Nurse Helen. It was three o'clock in the morning. Norbert collapsed into bed and fell immediately to sleep.

In his dream, Norbert watches the spinning football descend from the white roof of the Carrier Dome into the basket he forms with his arms. He darts along the sideline, dodging one tackler then another, fists upper-cutting the air, knees thrusting forward, propelling him toward the opposite end line.

Norbert looks over at his sideline. Everyone is naked: his high school coach, his teammates, Arlene and Pastor Zack, all the other congregants from the Church of Abundant Waters and the Splendiferous Blood of Christ—even Wilberforce and Sasha. And Lula: the slender, clever waitress from Cleveland with the sharp tongue. They are all naked, jumping up and down, screaming, encouraging him ahead, their parts bouncing, agitated in the most unflattering of ways—all but Lula's, her pert, palm-sized breasts maintaining their perfect firmness. Norbert cannot take his eyes from her gorgeous breasts, her slim, natural form. He smiles a goofy, love-struck smile.

Pow! Norbert is leveled onto his back by a tackler.

He opens his eyes under the white canopy of the dome. Closes them. Opens them again under the orange-black sky in Iraq. Impenetrable black smoke billows from a white Nissan truck. Dozens of voices scream unintelligibly. Norbert rolls in the sand onto his belly. His leg is gone. Below his knee are only red shredded tentacles of bone and muscle and tissue. He claws his fingers into the sand, that fucking sand, and drags himself toward—*what?* He has no idea. "Sully!" he screams. "Sully!"

Morning. Norbert woke inside his hotel room. For a long moment, he did not recognize where he was. Dull, dust-filled daylight brought the room's features slowly into focus. Norbert looked over at the other bed—no Wilberforce.

The phone was ringing. Norbert rubbed his eyes. He fumbled for the receiver.

"Hello?"

"Is this Norbert?"

"Who is this?"

"Norbert, this is Helen."

"Who?"

"Nurse Helen. From the hospital."

"Oh, right," said Norbert.

"Norbert, you need to come down here."

"Down where?"

"To Desert Springs Hospital."

Norbert sat up in the bed. "Why? What's happened?"

"It's Wilberforce. He's been attacked."

"Attacked? Is he all right?"

"You need to come down here."

"How bad is it?"

"It's not good," said Helen, her voice failing a bit at the end. "It's not good."

31

Norbert met Nurse Helen outside Wilberforce's room in the intensive care unit at Desert Springs Hospital in Las Vegas. She explained that Wilberforce had undergone surgery during the early morning hours to stop internal bleeding.

"He's scheduled for more surgery today for a detached retina. The attending ordered a full battery of tests."

"Can he speak?" asked Norbert.

"He came out of sedation about thirty minutes ago," said Nurse Helen. "He's speaking with the police right now."

"What happened?"

"He was attacked in an alley across from your hotel."

"Mugged?"

"Not mugged. He has all his money and identification. He was found by some passersby who called the ambulance. They said he asked to be brought to 'Helen at Desert Springs Hospital.' That was about three o'clock this morning."

"Do they have any idea who could have done this?"

"It could be anyone," said Nurse Helen. "Drunks. Kids. There are a lot of sickos in this city. This world."

Norbert and Nurse Helen entered the room. When Norbert rounded the white curtain, he was horrified by how gruesome Wilberforce's injuries were. His head was wrapped in a bandage that wound around a gauze patch over his right eye. He had a cast on his left leg and a fresh cast on his already broken arm. There was an oxygen tube stuffed into his nostrils and an IV pinned into his good arm.

"Jesus Christ, Padre," said Norbert. "You look like shit."

There were two police detectives on the far side of Wilberforce's hospital bed. One was about thirty-five, white, doughy, with a pockmarked face, close-cropped hair and a thin, sandy mustache. He held a reporter's notepad in his hand and introduced himself as Detective O'Grady. The other detective, who O'Grady called "Holman," was in his fifties, black, shaved bald, also with a mustache and an ample belly that protruded from his open suit jacket, spilling over his belt. He was drinking coffee from a paper cup.

"What's your name?" said Detective O'Grady.

"Norbert."

"Norbert what?"

"Sherbert."

"Spell that," said O'Grady, scribbling in his notepad.

Norbert spelled it.

Where is your permanent address?"

"Ten Elk Road. Ticonderoga, New York."

"Phone number?"

Norbert gave the detective the number that would cause the princess wall phone to ring in his kitchen.

"You have a cell number?"

"Not currently."

"What's your involvement here?" asked Detective O'Grady.

"Friend," said Norbert. "I'm his friend. We're traveling across the country together."

"Uh-huh." O'Grady kept his pen moving. "And where were you last night?"

"Out. Then I went back to the room and slept."

"That's the room at the New York, New York?"

"Yes," said Norbert.

"Can anyone verify that?"

"Yes. I mean, no. I don't know."

"You don't know?" said O'Grady.

Norbert looked at Wilberforce. Wilberforce told Norbert with his one, watery eye: *Keep it simple!*

"What I mean is," said Norbert, "we just got here yesterday. Plenty of people can verify where I was. I just don't know any of them."

Detective O'Grady waited a moment to let Norbert decide if he wanted to add anything to that statement. "Have you encountered anyone since you arrived that might have wanted to bring physical harm to Mr. Wendell?"

"No," said Norbert. "No one."

"Have you been gambling? Been involved in any transactions concerning the purchase of drugs or sexual favors?"

"No," said Norbert. "None of that. The only person we've met since we've been here is her."

"What's that supposed to mean?" said Nurse Helen.

"It's not supposed to mean anything," said Norbert. "I'm just answering the question."

Nurse Helen was angry. She folded her arms. "I'm certainly not involved in any of that monkey business."

"What make and model of vehicle are you driving across the country?" asked O'Grady.

"Is that really pertinent to the investigation?"

"Right now, everything is pertinent to the investigation. Why, is there a problem with telling me the make and model of your vehicle?"

"No," said Norbert.

"Then what is it?"

"A 1975 Cadillac Eldorado convertible."

"That's a nice car," said Holman. "What's it got under the hood?"

"A hundred and ninety horse," said Norbert. "Five hundred cubic inches."

"Turbo hydra-matic?"

"Yep."

"Power steering?"

"Power everything."

"Nice."

"What color is it?" asked O'Grady, his pen poised over his notepad.

"Pink," said Norbert.

"Pink?" said O'Grady.

"That's a damn shame," said Detective Holman. "That's a fool color to paint that car. I should arrest you just for that."

Norbert wanted to tell the detectives it was not his car, that he was simply delivering it from Duncan "Cakey" Hines in Utica, New York to Pete Hines in Monterey, California. But that would only complicate matters further, add more names to Detective O'Grady's notepad. Keep it simple, thought Norbert. *Keep it simple.*

"What can I tell you?" said Norbert. "I'm a big fan."

The detectives shared a look. Detective O'Grady presented his card to both Norbert and Nurse Helen, assuring them he would be in touch soon. Until then, he suggested they make a list of all the people they thought could be responsible for the attack. When they were gone, Norbert slid a chair beside Wilberforce's bed.

"Helen," said Wilberforce, "Could you please give Norbert and me a few minutes alone together?"

"Certainly," said Nurse Helen, noticeably miffed but ever eager to assume the role of good sport. "I'll go to the snack machine and buy some cheese and crackers. Do you want a cheese and crackers, Norbert?"

"No thanks. There's a Great Cheese Conspiracy, and I refuse to be a party to it."

"Well," said Nurse Helen, "that doesn't make any sense at all. Not one bit of sense." She exited the recovery room.

"I'll tell you what doesn't make any sense," said Norbert. "This whole goddamn thing doesn't make sense. Someone attacked you but didn't rob you? They beat you half dead for no reason?"

"Listen," said Wilberforce, "I already told you I deserve bad things. I've resigned myself to a certain *amor fati*. A love of fate. But this is a new chapter, boyo. Get my wallet, will you? In my pants over there."

Norbert grabbed the wallet.

"Open it."

It was packed tight with $100 bills.

"Where did you get all this money?" said Norbert. "I thought you took a vow of poverty."

"My parents died in a commercial airline accident when I was a boy. It's not important. Count out one thousand dollars."

Norbert did as he was told.

"That's for you. Gas money."

"Don't be ridiculous," Norbert protested.

"'How many things there are in this world I do not want.'"

"Jesus?"

"Close," said Wilberforce. "Socrates."

Norbert argued some more with Wilberforce about the money but finally, reluctantly, accepted it. "Listen," said Norbert, "I can wait for you."

"No. I'm staying here, with Helen. She wants to love me and I'm going to let her. In fact, I'm finally ready to love someone back. I'm done moving around, Norbert. Done with waitresses and all my other juvenility. Done with being a Gloomy Gus. Freud said that 'no one believes in his own death.' Well, now I'm a big believer. Remember how I told you I was waiting for divine intervention? I got it. In a big way."

"You can't be serious. You can't believe that being beaten like this is a sign from God."

"It's more than a sign, Norbert. It's a revelation. I was delivered from evil in that alley last night. I received my absolution. Redemption for past sins. I was purged of the sinful blood that coursed my veins for far too long. I was literally reborn."

"You've been hit very hard on your head."

"No, I'm thinking clear as a bell. Besides, 'through life's school of war, whatever does not kill me makes me stronger.'"

"Is that one Jesus?"

"No."

"Spinoza?"

"Nietzsche."

Norbert nodded.

"This is the end of our road together, Norbert."

"What about the police?"

"What about them? There's nothing to investigate. I was jumped. No one saw it happen. I can't identify the assailant. Case closed."

"What about the dog, Kum & Go? We still need to pick her up."

"Leave that to me and Helen."

"*Helen* doesn't even own a car."

"I'm going to remedy that. We're going to make a life here, Norbert."

"I think I should wait. You're delusional."

"I'm not delusional. And you can't wait, you only have two more days and four commandments to go."

"Three. I broke number nine last night."

"Bearing false witness? What happened?"

"A story for another time."

"Ah," said Wilberforce. "Like your friend, Mr. Phipps."

"Exactly."

"Take your list with you," said Wilberforce.

Norbert removed the list from Wilberforce's wallet and put it in his pocket.

"Here, this is yours," said Norbert.

Norbert laid the St. Christopher medal that swung from the rearview mirror onto Wilberforce's chest.

"He's a kindred spirit you know," said Wilberforce. "The church kicked him out, too. No, you keep this, Norbert.

Let him watch over you all the way to the ocean. Look at him and think of me."

Norbert pictured the image of the ocean from the photo on Pete's postcard: the purple sky, the white caps, the foaming surf crashing against the unforgiving cliffs of Big Sur.

"I guess I should give you some final advice," said Wilberforce, "as your spiritual adviser. I'll leave you with this: Look into your heart. Focus your mind."

"Thanks, Obi-Wan."

"Seriously. If you wish it, Norbert, it will happen. Focus your mind on your goal and the world will bend to your reality. Jung said, 'When you have done everything that could possibly be done, the only thing that remains is what you could still do if you only knew it.' If you want to speak with God badly enough, it will happen. But then, don't forget, you promised me you would seek absolution. Regardless of what you choose to do, in the end only you can decide for yourself what is right and what is wrong. True absolution comes from feeling genuinely sorry for the bad things you've done in your life—not from avoiding them in the first place."

"Strange how it works that way."

Wilberforce's eyes began to droop. "'In the end,' said Diogenes, 'I would rather have a drop of luck than a barrel of brains.' I'm sorry Norbert, I'm fading into la-la land. They've got me all doped up. I feel so tired."

"I'll leave your bag with Nurse Helen. I put your dissertation inside it."

"The Beast."

Norbert stood. "Finish your book, Padre. Get all that clutter out of your brain and onto the page. You never know who might appreciate it some day. We used to have a saying back at Walter Reed: 'Inch by inch it's a cinch. Yard by yard is hard.' Finish your book. Don't let Nurse Helen, or anything else, distract you from it."

Wilberforce smiled beneath his cocoon of bandages. His smile slid into an expression between fear and a wistful sadness. "I wish I had more to share with you, Norbert. But I suppose, in the end, we all must find our own way. I'll pray for you."

"Don't bother," said Norbert. "Friends are my prayer, and you're a good one." Norbert folded the cash and slid it into his pocket. He returned Wilberforce's wallet to his slacks. "You rest now."

"Take good care, Norbert," said Wilberforce. "I will tell you something: you move around better than a man with three good legs."

Norbert took Wilberforce's good hand in his and shook it.

"Say hello to God for me," said Wilberforce, drowsily. "Tell him I'm still trying my best."

"I will," said Norbert. "He knows."

CALIFORNIA

"War makes strange giant creatures out of little
routine men who inhabit the earth."
–Ernie Pyle, WWII GI and journalist

32

Norbert, on his own for the first time since Wilberforce skidded beneath his front bumper, had it in his mind that he was going to drive straight through to Monterey to wake up his buddy Pete for breakfast. It was eight and a half hours and more than 500 miles from Vegas, most of which was the black, monotonous drive across the Mohave Desert.

The radio reception in the desert was abysmal, and when the signal was strong, it was usually country-western music. Fine for Wilberforce, but a form of aural torture for Norbert. He made good time, pinning the speedometer in the straightaways, passing Edwards Air Force Base and the Salt Flats. He made it as far as Bakersfield, California, before turning into a Wal-Mart parking lot. It was cold in the Caddy. Norbert wrapped himself in the blue wool blanket and slept for three hours.

In his dream, Norbert is running with the football tucked tightly beneath his arm. The field is white and the yardage lines are black. Suddenly the lines begin to move. They bend and curl and loop until Norbert can plainly see they are forming themselves into letters, words, sentences. Norbert looks down at himself from above. He is running across the pages of his leather notebook.

Now Norbert is holding the notebook in his hands. He closes it, runs his fingers along its smooth brown covers. He brings it to his nose, inhales its sensuous fragrance. It's so much more than a book, thinks Norbert.

He is hit across the back with a wooden baseball bat, falling to his knees. He is hit again, on his left leg—his full, left leg. The pain is excruciating—yet, perversely intoxicating. He looks at his attacker: a Christian priest.

The priest hits Norbert again with the bat.

"It's so much more than a book," says the priest. Norbert looks at the book in his hands. It is a Holy Bible.

Norbert looks up again. Now standing before him is the Saudi grad student with the dead eyes. "It's so much more than a book," he says. Norbert looks in his hands. It is a Koran. The young man clutches at his belly.

"No!" screams Norbert. "Stop! It's only a book! It's only a fucking book!"

He woke at daybreak. The engine was stubborn starting, so Norbert ran several disaster scenarios and contingencies through his head before, finally, the starter engaged the carburetor.

He drove west on Route 46, north to Salinas, then a short jog south on California 1 into Monterey. He lowered the automatic convertible roof to absorb the warm wind and salt air through his weary pores. He slid on a pair of dark Elvis glasses he purchased from a spinning display rack in the newsstand at New York, New York. At last, the selection of rock 'n' roll stations on the radio was decent. Norbert cranked the dial on the AM/FM 8-track stereo as loud as it would go.

Pete lived in a two-floor condominium a couple of blocks above Cannery Row. Norbert parked in a small, paved lot to the left of the building. He walked to the front door with his grip in one hand and a bottle of Southern Comfort, Pete's favorite, in a brown bag swinging from the other. He dropped his grip at the top of the stoop and knocked. The door swung open.

Norbert was greeted by the gleaming white smile of a petite, firm, tanned, blonde teenage girl with sparkling blue eyes. She wore an orange bikini that barely concealed her alert, comely breasts and exposed nearly every mole and crevice of her sunbathed youth. She was a radiant vision, a consummate cultivation of that unique California hybrid of inquisitive, energetic vitality and beach-weaned indifference.

"Hi," she said. "You must be Sugar Bear. Welcome to California."

Pete came to the door wearing a tank top, cargo shorts and flip-flops. He was a beautiful, tall, muscular black man. Pete's face and demeanor always gave Norbert the impression that he had just come from laughing very hard in another room. Pete shook Norbert's left hand, as was his way, since his right forearm, from above the elbow, was a prosthetic.

"Sugar Bear!"

"Pete."

Pete pulled their handshake into a rough, manly embrace.

"Come in, come in. Pismo, get my boy a beer."

"Your name is Pismo?" said Norbert.

"That's just what he calls me. My name is Kelly."

"Go on," said Pete. "Chop-fuckety-chop."

Norbert and Pete sat down in the living room—Norbert at the end of the couch, Pete in his big comfy chair. Norbert handed Pete the bottle of booze. Pete smiled broadly.

"Look at you, Sugar Bear. You look good." Pete leaned forward and knocked on Norbert's prosthetic leg. "How's the hardware?"

"It's holding up," said Norbert. "Yours?"

"The same, the same."

Pismo entered the room with three bottles of beer. "Sorry about your leg," she said, handing a bottle to Norbert. "That's a bummer."

"Sure is," said Norbert. "So, I'm assuming Pete calls you Pismo because that's where you're from?"

"I'm actually from Santa Monica. Pismo Beach is where we met. I was in a surfing tournament. Pete has a nickname for everybody."

"You can't keep this bitch out the water," said Pete as Pismo handed him his beer. "Like a fucking dolphin."

"Why does Pete call you Sugar Bear?" she asked.

"It rhymes with my last name," said Norbert.

"Oh," said Pismo. "When I saw Pete write it out, I thought it was pronounced Sherbert, like the ice cream."

"That's actually pronounced Sherbet," said Norbert. "There's no *r* in it."

"No," said Pismo. "It's definitely pronounced Sherbert."

"Why don't you go Google the motherfucker," said Pete. "I want to visit with my friend. Nobody wants to talk about fucking ice cream."

"Fine," said Pismo. "I'll just go down to the beach. Leave you boys alone to tell your war stories." She went to the refrigerator to grab a snack. "Sugar Bear, you want some string cheese?"

"He don't eat no cheese," said Pete. "He hates it."

"No," laughed Pismo, certain Pete was having fun with her. "Nobody hates cheese."

"He does," said Pete. "Says that the government's trying to make us get all fat and lazy by putting cheese in all our food, or some shit like that. Right?"

"Not exactly," said Norbert. "The Great Cheese Conspiracy is a bit more complex. But it does extend to the highest levels."

Pete roared with laughter. "I know you serious, too. You crazy. You crack me the fuck up."

"All right," said Pismo. "I'm leaving. What are you guys doing today?"

"We're going to get drunk," said Pete.

"Actually," said Norbert. "I really wanted to get to Sully's grave today. Maybe even make it to his parents' before dinner. I'm sorta on a schedule."

"A schedule?" Realizing Norbert wasn't kidding, Pete shrugged. "Suit yourself. That's all up in Santa Cruz. I can give you directions, but I know one thing: I'm not going back up there. Once was enough for me. That was the saddest fucking funeral I've ever been to. I thought black people could grieve . . . let me tell you, it was heart wrenching. Fucking heart wrenching. I always heard the Irish had fun funerals—got drunk, did a little leprechaun dance. It wasn't nothing like that, I'll tell you what." Pete took a long swallow of his beer.

"Of course, it was mostly on account of his girlfriend."

"What about her?" said Norbert.

"She was pregnant."

Norbert's heart started throwing itself against his rib cage, blood pounding in his eardrums. The sharp pain returned behind his right eye with blinding fierceness.

"I . . . I didn't know that," said Norbert.

"Yeah," said Pete. "Neither did Sully."

Norbert opened the bottle of Southern Comfort. He took a swig from it.

Pete chuckled, "Indian giver." But he could see that he had upset Norbert, so he let him drink.

"Nobody ever told me that," said Norbert. "Why didn't anybody tell me that? Did she have the baby?"

"Hell, I don't know. Shit, man, that was two years ago."

Norbert took another swallow of booze. He leaned back into the couch, resting the bottle between his legs, his stare fixed on something six thousand miles away and two years in the past. Pete snapped his fingers. "Hey? Can we change the subject?"

Norbert jerked out of his trance. "Yeah. Sure."

Pete scooted forward in his chair. "How was she?"

"How was who?"

"My ride. Was she sweet or what? How'd she handle? I'll bet you had to beat the pussy back with the tire iron. Huh? Where'd you park it?"

"In the lot on the side of the building."

"I hope you were super-careful how you parked," said Pete. "Not too close to anyone. I don't want nobody opening their door into it. Let's go take her for a spin." Pete stood. He slapped his hand hard against his prosthetic and did a rhythmic side step followed by a full twirl. "Yow! I can't wait to see it. I'm gonna be the motherfucking Marquis de Monterey! Let's go."

"Um," said Norbert, "about the car."

"What?"

"There were a few hiccups along the way."

"No," said Pete. "No, no, no, no, no . . ."

"It's not that bad. Nothing that can't be buffed."

"Buffed?"

"Or painted."

"Painted?"

"Or replaced."

"I'm gonna be sick. I'm gonna throw up on your ugly motherfucking shoes. You fucked up my Caddy, didn't you? I knew it. I fucking knew it. I should have listened to that voice in my head. That voice kept my ass alive in that motherfucking sandbox. It told me not to trust you and I ignored it. Shit!"

Pete stormed out of the condo, down the steps toward the parking lot with Norbert on his heels. He rounded the corner and was stopped cold by the condition of his Eldorado. Slowly, Pete approached the vehicle as though following a casket through the French Quarter.

"Noooooo," he wailed.

"It's not that bad," said Norbert. "You're overreacting."

"The trunk is smashed."

"That was some crazy guy in Cleveland."

"There's a dent in the hood."

"That's from my ass. I was diving away from a pit bull. Hoover Dam."

"The mirror is missing."

"I can explain that."

"Look at the finish," moaned Pete. "There's scratches all over it."

"That's where you'd do the buffing." Norbert drew tight circles in the air with his hand.

"You promised, Sugar Bear. You promised."

"I'm sorry."

"You swore to God you'd be super-careful with my ride. Remember? You swore to God."

"That's right," said Norbert. "I *did* swear to God."

"You broke your promise to me, and to God," said Pete. "That's some ballsy shit."

"Yes," said Norbert. "I suppose you could say I took His name in vain."

33

After much coaxing—even stooping so low as to invoke the Soldier's Code, tapping into Pete's pride in unit and helping out his fellow soldier—Norbert convinced Pete to let him borrow Pismo's Kawasaki motorcycle to drive up to Santa Cruz. Pete adamantly refused to give Norbert any further opportunity to damage the Caddy, and letting him anywhere near his brand new convertible Audi was simply out of the question.

The drive to Santa Cruz was only 45 minutes north, straight up California 1. Pete printed out the directions to the cemetery and to the Sullivan house from the Internet. Pete did not remember where exactly in the cemetery Sully's grave was located but that, if you were standing right in front of it, there was a "big-ass" flagpole close behind, slightly to the right. Pete gave Norbert his cell number and told him if he so much as scratched the motorcycle, not to bother coming back. He would strangle him to death.

Norbert sped along the coastline with the ocean to his left. He pictured the dirty, crusty February snow still piled high back in the Adirondacks. He let the rush of Pacific air fill his lungs. This is not a bad place to live, thought Norbert, if living is a priority.

At a drug store in Rio Del Mar, Norbert purchased a postcard from a spinning wire rack near the door. He asked the lady cashier for a stamp and she told him they didn't sell them, but he coaxed a stamp from her purse that she kept below the counter. Norbert tried to pay her, for the stamp, but she wouldn't take it. She could tell from his haircut that he was military.

On the front of the postcard was a picture of the Santa Cruz Beach Boardwalk. Outside, Norbert leaned over a blue, steel mailbox and addressed the postcard from a slip of paper. He wrote:

```
Dear Sasha,
    Just wanted to drop you a line as promised.
Hope you have already dived into your musical
studies. Kum & Go is swimming in the ocean and
she barked for me to say "Hi." Hope you are
enjoying the World Wide Web.

See you around. Your pal,

Norbert
```

He opened the spring-activated door and dropped the card into the mailbox.

It was almost 2 p.m. when Norbert pulled into Evergreen Cemetery. There was a tall, lone flagpole incorporated into a veteran's memorial at the center of the park. Norbert wound the motorcycle slowly through the narrow roadway to a spot just across from the memorial, then killed the engine. He retrieved a brown paper bag from the small cargo compartment underneath the seat and started walking. He worked his way backward from the flagpole, row by row, until he came upon a granite monument standing roughly four feet high, flanked by miniature American flags pressed into the thick green grass, fresh flowers laid at the base. There was an etching transposed into the stone of Sully's lean young face from the official military photo they had all been made to sit for after graduating boot camp. "Timothy Patrick Sullivan Jr.," the stone read. "Beloved son and grandson. Friend. Soldier." Sully was barely nineteen when he was blown to pieces that day under the hot desert sun.

"There you are," said Norbert. "Right here where they planted you."

Norbert reached into the bag and pulled out a bottle of Jameson and two long, fat cigars wrapped in clear cellophane. He placed one of the cigars atop the grave marker then unwrapped and lit the other. He cracked the seal on the whiskey, unscrewed the cap and took a long swallow. He poured a few shots' worth of the booze onto the grass in front of Sully's grave. "Irish whiskey and a cigar," said Norbert. "Those are the first things you said you wanted when you got home. Where did you get a taste for whiskey and cigars at nineteen years old? Probably saw it in some movie. Everything we said over there was from a movie: all our mannerisms, all our punch lines—straight from the movies. We even thought the fighting itself would be just like in the movies. And for a while there, it was. How fucking cool was that? Firing rockets, shooting ragheads, blowing shit up. Then Ramirez got killed. Then Tank. Sergeant Williams got shot in the face. Pete lost his arm. Then Lieutenant Tuttle, and Ortiz, Miller, Schiff, and the others got burned up in the Bradley. Then you. You and me. Not so fun anymore. Nothing like the movies."

Norbert inhaled deeply on the cigar, took another drink of whiskey, poured some more onto the ground.

"Look at me. Look what I'm doing. This even looks straight from the movies. The line is so blurred between what's real—*authentic*— and what's bullshit. All the time I'll do things or say things because I think I really mean them, because I think I really *feel* them, and then I see some character doing the same shit on TV, or hear some voiceover using the same words, my words, to advertise a mutual fund or boner pills or whatever. But here I am, talking to your tombstone, pouring booze onto your grave, just like in the fucking movies.

"Anyway.

"I'm here to say I'm sorry. I going to say the same thing to your parents, but I wanted to tell you first. I'm sorry,

Sully. It wasn't your day to die; it was mine. That was my detail, my position you were holding when that truck came through the checkpoint. But I was off fucking around, as usual, making angels in the sand. Always working the crowd, trying to get a laugh. I was coming to relieve you when it happened. I knew it was gonna happen, too. When I called your name, that fucker turned and looked right at me with his dead eyes. Looked right through me. I don't know why he didn't wait until I reached the vehicle. Maybe he was scared. Maybe he knew I knew. At the very least I should be dead, too. But more importantly, you should be alive—you *would* be alive—if it weren't for my fuck-up. You'd be playing with your kid. And I'd be dead.

"Yeah, I should be dead."

Norbert took a long gulp of whiskey and poured the rest out onto Sully's grave. He capped the empty bottle and placed it on the stone. He stubbed out the cigar and laid it beside the other.

"I've come to California to rectify that situation. And now that we've talked, now that we're straight, the sooner the better."

Norbert reached into the pocket of his leather jacket and removed his Purple Heart and Bronze Star. He placed them alongside the bottle and the cigars. Norbert stepped back and brought his fingertips sharply to his brow in a salute.

"Just like in the movies," said Norbert. "They've turned us soldiers into stock clichés. Straight out of central casting. Anyway. You know what it means. You know it's real."

34

Twenty minutes later, Norbert crept Pismo's motorcycle along the Sullivans' street searching for number 801. Their house was a bungalow style covered in yellow stucco. There were an American-made sport utility and sedan parked in the driveway in front of the attached, one-car garage.

Norbert opened the metal screen door and knocked on the maroon, paneled front door. A red-faced, white-haired older gentleman with bushy white eyebrows answered the door.

"Yes?"

"Mr. Sullivan?"

"Yes?"

"Tim's dad?"

"Yes."

"I'm Corporal Norbert Sherbert. I was good friends with your son."

Norbert sipped a cold Harp beer from the bottle. He was seated in a leather club chair facing Mr. and Mrs. Sullivan inside their dark, Arts and Crafts-style living room. Mr. Sullivan also drank a Harp. Mrs. Sullivan was a plump older woman, comparable in age to her husband, with black, up-styled hair and dark eyebrows she drew on with a crayon pencil. She was drinking whiskey from a rocks glass filled with crushed ice. It did not appear to Norbert to be her first serving of the afternoon. Mr. Sullivan was a soft-spoken man. He explained that Timothy was a change-of-life baby. That they had tried for years and finally given up then—boom! Mrs. Sullivan got pregnant.

"He was such a blessing," said Mr. Sullivan. "He was our night and day. I'm so glad you knew him, Norbert. I'm so happy to know you. I thank God we hadn't left yet."

"Where were you going?"

"I was taking Mary out to dinner," said Mr. Sullivan. "It's Valentine's Day."

Norbert shook his head, took a swig of beer. He had no idea. This was to be the day he proposed to Arlene with the diamond ring with the white gold band. As it turned out, he had already married her from the backseat of a taxi at a drive-through chapel in Vegas.

Norbert told the Sullivans some amusing anecdotes from his and Sully's time in boot camp at Fort Benning. He told them Sully was a good man, a man everyone knew they could count on, that he was a good soldier—the highest compliment he could pay. He said that Sully liked to hum and whistle and sometimes sing Irish music. This seemed to please Mr. Sullivan. It was clearly something he had proudly imparted on his son.

Mrs. Sullivan was distracted. She rarely looked at Norbert. At one point she went into the kitchen to fix herself another drink. She did not ask while she was up if either of the men were ready for another beer. She sighed audibly a few times while Norbert spun his tales. Mr. Sullivan appeared quite embarrassed by this, but said nothing. After almost thirty minutes, Norbert decided it was time to say what he had come to say.

"There is actually a very specific reason why I've come here today, Mr. and Mrs. Sullivan. It's difficult. It may be hard to hear. But I hope you'll listen while I tell you what I need to say."

"Please, Norbert," said Mr. Sullivan. "Tell us anything you feel you must."

Mrs. Sullivan took a sudden, haunting interest. With half a smirk, she looked Norbert straight in the face. Her expression seemed to say that she wanted to hear something macabre, something gruesome. She wanted the straight dope. *Hit me with your worst. My son is dead, my only son. What can you possibly say to me, you little turd?*

A chill blew through Norbert. Right away, he felt clammy, foreign, uncomfortable. He wanted to grope with his hand for an ejection lever. Am I doing this for them or me, he thought? *Am I really this much of a selfish prick?* Fuck it! Be done with it already! You've come all this way. Get it over with so you can get far away from this place, forever, and get on with finishing this thing that you've begun.

"It's my fault Sully is dead. I'm to blame."

Mrs. Sullivan laughed—a shrill, disturbed laugh. She slugged down what was left in her glass and placed it loudly on the end table. "So," she said, "that's what you came to say?"

"Yes," said Norbert. "That, and I'm sorry."

"Why would you say such a thing, Norbert?" said Mr. Sullivan. "It's no one's fault but the war's. Timothy was a soldier. You can't blame yourself for what happened over there."

"But Mr. Sullivan, he was standing where I should have been standing. It was my detail. My fault. I should be dead, not Sully."

"No, son," said Mr. Sullivan. "I don't accept that. I won't have you believing that. Timothy died overseas defending our freedom. He died a soldier in the field of battle. It's no one's fault but the war's. That's how I feel about it."

"You feel better now?" said Mrs. Sullivan to Norbert. "Has a terrible weight been lifted from your shoulders? Do you feel at peace now with your tortured conscience?"

"Mary, please!" said Mr. Sullivan, raising his voice.

"Was your guilt just tearing you apart inside? So much so, you finally had to come all this way, all the way to California, to unburden yourself? Lighten your load. The guilt and the pain were just too goddamn much to bear?"

"Mary! Shut up!"

"Well bear it, bucko!" said Mrs. Sullivan, "Bear it! Live with it. Wake up every morning with it and go to bed every night with it right here." Mrs. Sullivan poked the center of her forehead several times with her index finger so hard it left a mark. "Don't come in here and try to transfer your shit onto me. Deal with your own shit. I'm dealing with mine."

"Mary that's enough. I'm sorry, Norbert. This has been exceptionally difficult for us. Timothy was everything to us. Mary has just—It's been very hard."

"Or keep it all inside," said Mrs. Sullivan. "Jam it right down and don't talk about it like the merry Mick over here. Be charming and stoic like the fucking Irish. Well I'm Italian and I say fuck you, mister. Fuck you for coming here trying to find closure or whatever other new-agey, keeping-it-real bullshit your pussy, bullshit generation is crying about this week. Fuck you. Get outta here! I can't look at you. Get out of my house. Get out!"

Norbert was shaking. He got up from the leather chair and walked unsteadily toward the front door. Mr. Sullivan rose with him. Mrs. Sullivan laughed a mocking, menacing laugh.

"He's a soldier after all," she said. "Does exactly as he's ordered."

In the front yard, Mr. Sullivan wrapped his left hand gently around Norbert's bicep.

"I don't know what to say, Norbert. It's the drink. It's got her in its demon grip. That's not Timothy's mother in there who said those things to you. I apologize for her."

"No, Mr. Sullivan. She got it right. That's what I needed to hear."

"You're wrong, Norbert. And it makes me sick to think about the guilt you've been carrying around. Don't you do it any longer. Look at me, son. *Don't you do it.*"

As Norbert climbed onto Pismo's motorcycle, Mr. Sullivan saw a flash of steel between his cuff and boot.

"Were you injured over there?"

Norbert situated himself atop the bike. "No," he said. "I was one of the lucky ones."

"Come back tomorrow, Norbert," said Mr. Sullivan. "I'll keep Mary away from the drink. She's a different person then. Come tomorrow and you can meet the twins."

"The twins?"

"Timothy's twin girls. Identical. They'll be two come April. I'll have Britney over here. She'll be thrilled to speak with you. And Timothy's friends from school. Maybe not here. I'll leave Mary here and we can meet at the pub. Say you'll come tomorrow."

"I really—"

"Let me fetch a pen," said Mr. Sullivan. "I'll give you my cell phone number. You won't have to speak with Mary. We'll all meet down at the pub. Wait right here while I fetch a pen and paper."

Mr. Sullivan hustled back into the house. The screen door slammed behind him.

The motorcycle roared to life.

Mr. Sullivan leaned over his kitchen table jotting his cell phone number onto a yellow sticky note. He got down the area code and the first three digits when he heard the fading whine of the motorcycle's engine. He stopped writing and set the pen aside.

35

When Norbert arrived back at Pete's condo it was almost five o'clock. Pete was gone. Pismo told Norbert that Pete had to race off to help a client who was having a crisis with his "vendor website or whatever." It was a big client, she said, and a big problem, and Pete had no idea when he'd be back. He left instructions with Pismo that, despite his indiscretions with the Caddy, she should "show Norbert a good time."

Pismo told Norbert that she had surfed all afternoon. Norbert knew nothing about surfing and so he had precious little surfer trivia stored in his brain, thus limiting his friendly banter. When he asked how the waves were, Pismo answered, "Gnarly." Pismo asked Norbert what he felt like doing. He said he'd like to draw a nice warm bath and drown himself in it. When she asked what else he felt like doing, he said he'd like to go to the beach and watch the ocean. Pismo looked at Norbert like he was an unthawed Australopithecus when he said that his flesh had never touched the waters of the Pacific Ocean. That was all Pismo needed to hear. She grabbed the bottle of Southern Comfort from the coffee table and led Norbert from the apartment down to the beach. "We'll be just in time for sunset," she said.

"Oh, goodie."

There it is, thought Norbert, the ocean from Pete's postcard. Sitting in the sand at the edge of the beach, watching the red sun plunge into the western horizon, Norbert and Pismo passed the bottle back and forth in a secluded space shadowed in a grove of palm trees. Norbert couldn't help but steal carnal sidelong glances at Pismo in her bikini top, board shorts, and pink flip-flops. Her salt- and sun-scorched hair was so blonde it was practically white. Her deep bronze skin accentuated the constellation of dark freckles spread across her nose. She was all at once adorable and sensual, innocent and erotic. Norbert wanted to bite the flesh that slightly bubbled just above her bikini bottoms. He knew he had just two commandments left to break. Two more "sins" and his unholy undertaking would be complete.

"How old are you?" said Norbert.

"Nineteen."

"Bullshit. How old are you really?"

Pismo turned to Norbert and smiled. "Nineteen."

"Sixteen."

Pismo smiled.

"Lower?"

She took a swig of the sicky-sweet booze. "I'll never tell."

"Where are your parents?"

"Where are *your* parents?"

"Pismo passed the bottle back to Norbert. She tucked her knees against her chest and hugged her arms around them.

"How long have you and Pete been hanging out?" said Norbert, removing his leather jacket and wrapping it around her shoulders.

"About a month. He's pretty cool. He doesn't treat me that great, though. When he's around other people he's always joking, always laughing but I think, for real, he's pretty sad inside. He gets really mad sometimes over stupid stuff."

Pismo looked at Norbert's prosthetic leg. "I can't imagine losing my leg. I'd die if I couldn't surf."

"I get around okay," said Norbert. "It just takes getting used to, same as anything else. It's about balance—like surfing, I guess."

"Can I see it?"

Norbert lifted his pant leg as far as he could, exposing the steel tube.

"I'd take it off, but I don't want to get sand in it."

"Can I touch it?"

"Sure."

Pismo ran her purple-painted fingertips along its smooth, cool surface. "Wow. That's whacked, but pretty gnarly."

Norbert gently pinched an errant strand of Pismo's hair and tucked it behind her ear. His hand lingered. She looked at him, her eyes so blue in the evening afterglow, Norbert thought he was looking through her at the ocean. Or was the ocean looking through her at him? Norbert pulled her face to his. They kissed.

Pismo sat up on her knees. She placed both hands flat on Norbert's cheeks and kissed him long and deep. She leaned her weight against him as he eased backward onto his elbows, reclining into the soft sand. Pismo rubbed Little Norbert, its vessels stiff with surging blood beneath his faded blue jeans.

Pismo unhooked Norbert's belt. She undid his jackknifed buttonhole and lowered his zipper, kissing his pale, fleshy stomach in the place where, once upon a time, six square muscles resided just below the skin. Norbert placed his hand on her cheek and made her look him in the eyes.

"We can't do this." He sat up. Zipped his fly. "We won't do this."

"Pete won't know," said Pismo. "Don't bail now."

"You're a sweet girl, but you're a kid. You shouldn't be with me. You definitely shouldn't be with Pete. No, this is wrong. I can't believe I'm saying this but it's *immoral*. I want you, believe me I want you. You're so beautiful and pure. I see in you a vision of a life I wish I had again. I wish there was a way for me to wind back my own clock, start over again from where you are right now. I wish I could be just like you again: carefree, willing. I want to have what you have.

I covet everything about you: your health, your innocence, your optimism. I had those once. Then I saw too much. I'm a lot older than I look." With effort, and help from Pismo, Norbert stood. He asked for the bottle of booze, still half-full. Pismo brushed the sand from it and handed it to him.

"Listen, Kelly. Go back up to that condo, pack your things and leave. Go home. See your parents, your family, your friends. Reconnect with your world. Quit this half-assed bad girl routine, playing house in Monterey with a big, injured vet. Get far away from here and don't look back."

"I do kinda miss my sister. I don't see her much anymore. She's going to graduate this summer. I even sorta miss my mom—even though she's crazy."

"Here," said Norbert, handing her the $1,000 Wilberforce gave him. "Take this. Trust me, I know Pete and I love him, but he's not the guy for you. Chalk this up as an experience and move on."

"Why are you telling me all this? Why are you giving me this money? Why do you even care?"

"Just tying up loose ends."

Pismo took the cash. She tried to hand Norbert back his leather jacket.

"Keep it," he said. "Take this, too."

Norbert removed the St. Christopher medal from around his neck and draped it over Pismo's head. "He's the patron saint of travelers. Rub it between your fingers as a reminder to keep moving ever forward. *Umquam porro*. New places, new adventures."

Pismo's eyes were wet and red, "I can't remember the last present someone gave to me. Thank you."

"Thank me by leaving."

Pismo kissed Norbert gently on the lips.

She walked along the beach to the public jogging path, turning back once, then twice, before disappearing around the corner of a building.

There was a strange car parked in front of Pete's condo—a rental. As Pismo approached the stoop, she saw
a woman cupping her hands around her eyes, peering
through the window beside the door. The woman was
tall and thin, short blonde hair tied back with a scrunchie
into a ponytail. She had a large, flower-print canvas bag
slung over her shoulder.

"Can I help you?" said Pismo.

"I'm sorry," said the woman, jumping backward. She
was embarrassed, flustered at having been caught. "Is this
where Pete Hines lives?"

"Who are you?"

"My name is Lula. I'm looking for Norbert Sherbert. Is
he here?"

"It's pronounced Sher-*bear*," said Pismo. "Like his nickname: Sugar Bear. Not Sher-*burt*, like the ice cream."

"Oh," said Lula. "I should know that. I feel really stupid
for not knowing that."

"It's okay. I didn't know, either."

"Wait," said Lula, "isn't the ice cream pronounced
sher-*bet*?"

"Whatever."

"Is Norbert here?"

"I just left him. He's down on the beach. Are you a friend
of his?"

"Sort of," said Lula. "Not exactly. This is so weird. I don't
know what to say. This is like the most crazy, impulsive
thing I've ever done. Oh my god! You're not his girlfriend,
are you? If you are I'll just kill myself."

Pismo laughed. "No. I just met him today. He's right
down on the beach. You want me to walk you down there?"

"Not yet," said Lula, chewing her thumbnail. "I don't
know what I'll say."

"Say about what?"

"You look too young for me to be asking you this, but do you have any alcohol in there? I could really use a drink."

Pismo retrieved the key from under the rubber mat and unlocked the door. She let Lula into the condo and offered her a seat on the couch. "How about vodka tonic?"

"That sounds perfect. Just hold the tonic. And the ice."

"So how do you know Sugar Bear? I take it he's not expecting you."

"I don't know where to start," said Lula. "Anything I say is going to sound ridiculous. You're going to think I'm insane."

Pismo came in with the vodka and two glasses and poured. Lula drank hers down in one gulp. Pismo laughed and filled the glass again.

"We hardly know each other at all," said Lula. "We met Tuesday in Cleveland at this restaurant where I work. He was with his friend, Wilberforce."

"Who's that?"

"His spiritual adviser. He's not with him anymore?"

"No," said Pismo. "He showed up here alone."

"There's a lot I don't know, I guess. Christ! I can't believe I'm here. I was going to call first, then I convinced myself that if I called I would never come to California. I mean, I sorta have the excuse that this is where I want to be anyway, but still—so, I decided to just fly out here. Stupid, right?"

"No," said Pismo, "romantic. Norbert's really sweet. You must be in love."

"That's just it, we hardly know each other. We only spent part of one night together, dancing and talking and . . . kissing. But it was nice; it was special. It felt like we were already connected somehow, like old friends who just happened to run into one another and start talking again. Then out of nowhere this psycho named Andy, who I dated, like, two times attacked Norbert and he beat him up."

"He beat Norbert up?"

"No, Norbert beat the creepy guy up."

"Gnarly."

Lula finished off her second vodka and poured the third herself.

"Anyway, that's only half the story. That night I found this in the nightstand in Norbert's room." Lula lifted Norbert's leather notebook from her canvas bag. "It's his notebook. I opened it and read the first few pages, but when I realized what it was I closed it and refused to read it. I thought it was wrong to read it. Don't you think so?"

Pismo smiled. "So what did it say?"

"Well, I kept it for two days just staring at it lying there on my dresser. Finally, I couldn't stand it any longer. I opened it up and began to read. He started writing it when he was still in high school. It goes all the way through his time in Afghanistan and Iraq. It talks about his injury—did you know he was wounded?"

Pismo nodded.

"He wrote all about that: how it happened, what he remembers from it, the tremendous guilt he feels. He talks about the surgeries and the recovery and the physical therapy. It's full of all these clippings and gorgeous drawings. See?"

Lula held the book open to a line drawing of Norbert supporting himself on a pair of parallel bars, surrounded by other trauma victims in a physical therapy ward.

"He writes about his family and his regrets about college, and it's all so beautiful and sad and angry but also kind of hopeful. And he writes about his dreams. He writes about these dreams he has where he's playing football and he gets tackled before he scores a touchdown to win the game. He gets tackled by his leg. The leg he lost."

Lula took another sip of vodka.

"And so I guess why I'm here . . . I mean, I guess what I'm saying is that yes. Yes! I *do* love this man. I've fallen madly in love with this man I barely know. Isn't that crazy? I'm out of my fucking mind. But see, I'm sort of a writer myself and I've never done anything impulsive. I just dream up characters that do impulsive things and . . . So, anyway. I just can't stop thinking about him. I absolutely had to see him again. I had to be with him. He's so wounded. So wounded. I want to hold him. Comfort him. Tell him everything will be okay."

"How did you find him? How did you know he'd be here?"

"The address is right here," said Lula, pointing in the notebook. "He writes about how his girlfriend Arlene dumped him for some cheesy preacher. She just up and moved out on him Sunday."

"What a bitch."

"I know," said Lula.

"I guess I shouldn't say that," said Pismo. "I'm dumping my boyfriend, too. I'm taking off tonight."

"Oh, I'm sorry. I didn't—"

"No biggie," said Pismo. "It's all good. Keep going."

"So then he writes how his Guard buddy, Pete, wants him to drive cross-country with his 'sweet ride.' When I had finished reading it all, sick with love for this man, I was determined to find him. I called the motel to see if Norbert was looking for his journal, and this address in the journal is the exact address that he gave the motel should anyone find it."

"This is great," said Pismo. "This is perfect. You have to go down to the beach right now and find him."

"I haven't decided what to say. I think I'm going to be sick."

"Tell him you love him."

"That will totally freak him out. He'll think I'm some desperate, psycho-stalker crazy woman. Yeah, I'm definitely going to be sick. This was way too impulsive."

"Maybe," said Pismo. "But maybe not. Either way, you've traveled this far."

"You're right," said Lula, downing another vodka. "God help me, I'm going right now."

36

As soon as Pismo had rounded the building out of view, Norbert headed along the beach in the opposite direction, toward the pier. The footing was uncertain and it was slow going, but he was determined. Beneath the pier, the sand was wet and rocky. Norbert almost lost his balance, but steadied himself on one of the thick vertical support posts. He walked out to the edge of where the water met the sand. In the dusky twilight he watched the surf roll in, then recede. It was all at once soothing and frightening to Norbert. All I have to do is keep walking, he thought. Just keep walking straight out till I can't walk anymore. Then swim. Swim and don't turn back. Simple as that. Norbert finished off the bottle of Southern Comfort and tossed it, Frisbee-style, splashing into the dark water.

Norbert stared at the water. The water stared back.

Someone began clapping behind Norbert. Norbert turned. Behind him stood a young man, maybe eighteen. He was slender and athletic, wearing long shorts and an oversized T-shirt with no shoes.

"Bravo," he said as he applauded. "Bravo, my friend."

"Who the hell are you?"

"Oh, let's not do this, Norbert. Okay? Let's not do this 'Who are you? I don't know, who are you?' bullshit. Cool? You wanted to talk so badly. Fine, talk."

Norbert looked around for other signs of life. He looked in both directions down the length of the beach—nothing. No one. Even the sounds of the gulls and the rhythm of the surf had ceased.

"There's no one else, Norbert. Just you and me. This is your conversation. Lay it on me, bro."

"You're God?"

"Whatever. *God*. Sure, you can call me that if that's your thing."

"You're a kid."

"I'm your vision, dude. You should recognize me."

"I don't. I've never seen you before."

"How about now?" The young man pulled a football helmet over his head. "Recognize me now?"

"Are you . . . Are you the player who tackled me in my high school championship game?"

"Grabbed you by your leg, remember? Your stupid left leg. You cursed your leg that day. I'm sure the irony hasn't been lost on you." He removed the helmet and tossed it in the sand.

"Why are you here as this person? It doesn't make any sense."

"It's got nothing to do with me, bro. It was your choice. Ask yourself that question. Anyway, it's not important. Let's not get bogged down in the details. You earned your conversation with the Big Guy. So, talk."

"But I didn't break all Ten Commandments."

"I know. That was kinda sweet back there with the little blonde chickie. You could have finished but you stopped, because it was wrong. You know, if you think about it, Norbert, each time you broke a commandment, you did it for the right reason. In each situation, it was the moral thing to do."

"I didn't realize that."

"Break it down," said God. "Commandments one and two you broke back-to-back at the Church of the Almighty Dollar. Greedy and screwball as that place is, you were following your heart for the right reasons. You're searching for faith and spirituality outside the dogma and mythologies of organized religions. You want peace on earth, but you know through your own understanding, and through your own firsthand experiences, that there can be no peace in the world so long as people love their stories more than they love each other. It is a terrible thing to always be certain you are right. Too many people twist religion, dude. Twist it into something perverse to serve their agendas rather than to serve their fellow human beings.

"And so you went to the Church of the Almighty Dollar and worshipped the God of Money and carved a false idol because you are searching for a purer form of faith. I can dig that. You want to cut out the middleman, so to speak—the middleman being organized religion with all its doctrines.

"Since this whole trip of yours has been based on the tenants of the Christian faith, let me hit you with some Matthew 6:6, where Jesus says, 'When you pray, enter into your inner chamber, and having shut your door, pray to your Father who is in secret, and your Father who sees in secret will reward you openly.' I dig where you're coming from, Norbert. You want to reject organized religion so you can embrace a true spirituality. I don't think you'll find it with the Buckologists, but you went to their service, and broke those commandments, in an honest search for meaning.

"Breaking the third commandment was really just an accident. You didn't even realize you had broken it until your friend Pete reminded you that you had 'swore to God' to be super-careful with his ride. There was no malice, no sinful intent behind delivering his car damaged. And anyway, the worst of the damages occurred while you were in the act of helping others. No sweat. Material things have no spiritual value and can always be repaired or replaced.

"When you worked on the Sabbath, it was an act of charity. You lent a hand to a woman who had just scorned and rejected you. You also lightened the load of the other movers and you did not accept payment for your toil. It was sarcastic, sure, but in the end your actions served the greater good.

"You choked the first time you tried to dishonor your parents. You wanted to tell them what you thought they needed to hear: that they held you back so many times in your life because of their own petty jealousies and fears. Your father makes you feel like a failure for not fulfilling his vision of himself. Your mother, too timid to contradict him, never offered you the encouragement or the tiny bit of assistance you craved so desperately to chase down your dreams of college and after. You live a different life because of their decisions. You even blame them, in part, for the loss of your leg.

"But when it came down to it, you couldn't break their hearts by dishonoring them to their faces. You quietly dropped the junior from your name. That shows charity, dude. Parents do the best they can. Besides, dishonor doesn't come in the opinions of your parents, it's in the eyes of Me.

"You killed that pit bull to save Wilberforce's life. It doesn't get more cut and dried than that. That crazy dog tried to kill Kum & Go. He had a taste for blood that day. There are times when killing is justified. That was one.

"And you stole Kum & Go in the first place from a man who mistreated her. You rescued her and for the first time in her life exposed her to the unconditional love of a child. By breaking the eighth commandment, you delivered an innocent creature from evil and filled its heart with joy. And now she will live happily with Wilberforce and Nurse Helen, digging holes in their new backyard.

"At the Venetian in Vegas, you broke the ninth commandment by exposing a bunch of phony baloney holy rollers. Preachers like Pastor Zack prey on the weak-willed and simpleminded—people so eager to follow any crackpot who offers them a quick path to faith and meaning. And Pastor Zack was a shitty guitar player. You did everyone a favor by bearing false witness against him and the rest of that crew.

"You broke the tenth commandment by bearing your soul to young Pismo, or Kelly, or whatever you want to call her. You were honest about your jealousy of her youth and innocence. You covet all the opportunities that lay ahead of, not behind her. Opportunities you feel you squandered. You gave her cash to head home, rather than stay here, playing out a silly girl's fantasy—all the while wasting her youth. That was brave and unexpected. I was impressed."

"But I rejected her," said Norbert. "And by rejecting her I failed to complete the mission."

"Ah yes," said God. "Adultery. The seventh commandment. Yes, it was the only commandment you think you didn't break—could have, but didn't. Again, your actions were motivated by morality. Again, you did what you did for the right reason. If you had made love to her, you would have committed your first immoral act of this adventure: she was underage and in a relationship with your friend. And don't forget, technically, you're married. Those Vegas weddings are for real, dude. I'd get that annulled. You see, Norbert, morality is its own reward. Blindly following the Ten Commandments is meaningless when each individual act is lifted from its context. The Commandments are only words, Norbert. Just words. Actions are what matter.

"But if you want to get technical about it, since your whole mission is based on the Bible, you did indeed commit adultery. With Pismo and with Lula. In Matthew 5:27-28, Jesus says, 'Ye have heard that it was said by them of old time, Thou shalt not commit adultery: But I say unto you, That whosoever looketh on a woman to lust after her hath committed adultery with her already in his heart.'

"So there you have it, dude. Ten for ten. Congrats. You achieved what you set out to do. And now I'm standing here beneath this pier with you in the golden state of California. So, I'm all ears. What do you want to say?"

Norbert was quiet for a long moment.

"You took Sully," said Norbert. "You took Ortiz, Miller, and the others. You took Pete's arm, my leg. Why must so many innocent people, good people, die and suffer in this world? Why is there war when we all want to live? Why do we fight when we're the same?"

"First, a correction: *You* took your leg."

"What're you talking about? That's crazy. That doesn't even make any sense."

"Trust me, it's not crazy. I'm God, remember? The fact is it doesn't have to make sense to you. Never mind. You know what? Forget it. Let's not get into it. Otherwise, this could go on all night. Time is infinite in both directions for me, not so much for you."

"How did *I* take my leg? I don't understand what you mean by that."

"It doesn't matter. Forget what I said."

"But I want to know."

"You won't understand the answer."

"Try me."

"It's a waste of time."

"Say it anyway."

"The reason I say you took your own leg. That indeed, you also took Sully's life and were responsible for the rest of the guys who died or were injured in your unit, in the war . . . Let me back up. Norbert, first you need to understand that you are responsible for all the death and suffering in this world, but also for all the joy and compassion. The reason is because I'm you."

"But you're God."

"Correct."

"I'm God?"

"Yes. You're God. I'm God. Wilberforce, Sasha, Sully, Kum & Go, all the little fishes in the sea. All souls past and present. All pieces of The One. All God. All you. Billions of versions of you."

"I don't understand."

"I told you you wouldn't understand. It doesn't matter. It doesn't matter that you don't understand. It can't be understood. Accept it as Your will."

"Then what am I supposed to believe?"

"Believe whatever you want, or nothing, it doesn't matter. Belief is extraneous. There is only what *is*."

"But it has to matter. It has to. Something needs to be the truth."

"Something *is* the truth, but you will never know it."

"Why can't I know it?"

"See, I thought we'd be able to avoid the heavy stuff. The brainteasers. I was so sure you were just going to rant and rave about your pain and sadness and anger and guilt over your time in the desert, your bum luck with your leg and all that kind of stuff. I didn't think we'd get into this. I was just going to listen, dude."

"Well, we're into it," said Norbert. "Tell me why I can't know the truth."

God sighed.

"The short answer is because truth is covered by belief. The long answer is infinitely more complicated and ultimately unknowable—despite the fact that Truth, capital *T*, is simplicity in a perfect state of flawlessness. There is no physical world, Norbert. Everything is viewed, touched, discovered, experienced—you name it—everything is a product of your consciousness. We're all in your mind, Norbert. And your mind is our mind. It's all the same. Even this novel. Even this novel you are reading right now is a product of your consciousness. It's the way it must be because it is the way it is. There is no other way. That's the Truth."

"That's fucked up."

"Yes."

"So that's the truth?"

"It's close. I'm doing the best I can. English is extremely limited and clunky. Language is a terrific barrier to pure understanding. There are better ways to convey this. The words are just not available. I think it was Wittgenstein who said, 'The limits of my language mean the limits of my world.' But you would know about that better than I would."

"But we're the same."

"Exactly."

"So now I *kind of* know the truth?" said Norbert.

"Yes."

"About the universe."

"About everything, really. But you always knew it. Right now, you're essentially conversing with yourself. It's energy. This novel in front of you doesn't really exist—I mean, in the physical sense of existing. This is frustrating for me. Again, the words just aren't there. I have to approximate."

"I don't know what to think about that."

"The worst part is that now that you know, it's no big deal. And since all knowledge is eternal, you pretty much knew it already anyway and are now just sort of reminding yourself—over and over again, the cycle continues. Our conversation doesn't change anything. You still have to live your life like any other normal person. Sorry to say, knowing the truth doesn't make life any easier. It probably makes it harder, lonelier. Whitman called it 'the noiseless operation of one's isolated self.' Strange how you can be everything and everyone and still feel so alone."

"This is so fucked up."

"Yeah, but like I said. No big deal. Are you still going to kill yourself?"

"I'm not sure. I mean, I don't know. I have to process all this. I think it changes things. I'm just not sure how."

For a moment, Norbert retreated into his thoughts. He slid his hands into his pockets. With his right thumb and forefinger he stroked the smooth curve and sharp angles of the diamond engagement ring with the white gold band. He rearranged some sand with his boot. He thought of the inscription Grandpa Sherbert had scrawled inside the cover of his notebook: *A man's life, if he's living it right, has many beginnings.*

Norbert said, "So Lula is up there in the condo right now talking with Pismo. She flew here from Cleveland because she read my notebook."

"Yep. Turns out this was a love story the whole time. She's on her way down here as we speak."

"I know."

"I know you know. What will you do when she gets here?"

Before Norbert could answer, the world roared back to life. The surf washed in with alarming force, up to Norbert and God's knees. Instantly, the tide ripped back to sea, sweeping Norbert and God out with it. As the water overtook them, Norbert hollered to God, "Why am I doing this?"

God shrugged.

Norbert was carried into the ocean, away and away. He flailed below the surface—frantic, wild, clawing for air. He was too deep in the whirling, unrelenting blackness. Too deep! But he never quit fighting, never stopped reaching for air.

I want to live!

Norbert ceased struggling. Calmed himself. Closed his eyes and thrust his arms above his head.

The sea began to boil. Great swirls of current churned into foamy whiteness.

The dark, ferocious water roiled as the sea began to part. Norbert sank to the ocean floor.

Two walls of water formed. When he reached the bottom, Norbert stood dwarfed by the towering halves of the Pacific Ocean, higher than a dozen skyscrapers placed one atop the other.

He started walking back to shore.

As he neared the beach, he spotted the figure of a woman in the distance. She was searching for someone. Norbert picked up the pace, double-time. The sharp edge of the diamond ring digging into his one, good leg.

Acknowledgements

There are so many people to thank when undertaking something as irrational as writing a novel. It's insane, really, to even try. But I am indebted to many terrific people who have generously shared their time, talents, and alcohol with me. It would be a shame to let all that good karma go uncredited.

First, it's with tremendous gratitude that I thank the extraordinary talents of The Vermont Press: my irradiant lead editor Nancy McCurry, my literary, convivial co-editors Shawn Kerivan and Lloyd Noonan, my brilliant copyeditor, Greg Melvin, and my talented designer and graphic artist, Hillary Hersh.

Thank you to Brian Kaufman and the staff at Anvil Press, Vancouver BC for publishing *Small Apartments* back in 2001, starting me down a professional road I had never anticipated.

Thanks to my inspirational creative friends Matt Lucas, Jonas and B Akerlund, and to all the incredible actors, actresses, support staff, and tireless crew that taught me so much throughout the filmmaking process. Thanks to Rob and John Schneider and their families, Phyllis and Mike Paseornek and Lionsgate Films, Mark Piznarski, Mimi Kaupe, Goran Dukic, Noj, Cool Steve, and my community of friends and colleagues in Los Angeles. In Texas, thanks to my friends at Throttle Films in Dallas, and the wonderful community of Austin and SXSW.

Thank you to Ian Kleinert and the team at Objective Entertainment, my patient, supportive entertainment attorney, Les Abell, Todd Hagopian, Steve Katz, Chris Marker, Sam Cipolla, Paul Ziter, Peter Barton, Kevin Brophy and family, and to all the producers and collaborators that have supported me and put their faith in my work.

At Goddard College in Vermont, I was incredibly fortunate to study under Neil Landau and Richard Panek. Paul Selig has assembled a serious program of study and I appreciate all the effort and love the faculty and administration put into sending thoughtful, disciplined writers into the world. Thanks to everyone in Buffalo, especially to my extraordinary Dean of Undergraduate Students at Buffalo State, my mentor and friend, the late Dr. Phil Santa Maria.

I owe a debt of gratitude to all the colleges, seminars, groups, and associations that have invited me to speak, to Nathalie Thill at the Adirondack Center for Writing, the staff at Blue Mountain Center, Adirondack Life Magazine, Stowe Story Lab, Chip Devenger and the YMCA Silver Bay Association on Lake George, and to all the students and attendees that have shared their talent, drive, curiosity, and work with me.

Much love and thanks to my hilarious, accomplished, lifelong pals Scott Sheldon, Dan Allen, Adam Valente, and John Sullivan. To Colleen, Brett, Alicia, and my family, friends, teachers, and community in Saratoga Springs, NY (the Veitches, Clarks, Sisks, Munters... all too numerous to name)—not least of all, John McPherson, who taught me early on that I could forge my own, independent path as a creative artist. And to Mandy Dennis, who has enthusiastically provided her photographic talents since the first day I needed a brooding, black-turtlenecked promo pic.

Love and thanks to Scott and KI LaClair and family for their sincere friendship, support, and for providing a critical hot tub in Lake Placid in which I do my best writing. And thank you to our terrific network of friends in the Adirondacks and North Country.

Thanks to Sarah and Jeff Lerro (and Kate) for their love and support and the use of their camp and booze on Lake Ontario, gifts of space, privacy, and libation so critical to the creative process.

Love to my moms and dads: Tracy and Debbie Millis and Jack and Linda Van Iseghem. To Gram and Gail. And to the incalculable influence of all my grandparents, who have each returned to the stardust from which they formed.

How does a creative person's brain develop? Beats me. The more random the influence the better, I think. For those who wonder about such things, here are some of the creative minds that significantly impacted me over the years: Charles Portis (my literary guru), Mark Twain, Roald Dahl, John Gardner, Kurt Vonnegut, Haruki Murakami, Spike Jonze, Charlie Kaufman, Joel and Ethan Coen, Alexander Payne, Jim Abrahams and David & Jerry Zucker, *The Beatles*, Mark Oliver Everett and *Eels*, John McCrea and *Cake*, Liz Phair, Don Martin, Pat Oliphant, Berkeley Breathed, Bill Watterson, Gary Larson, Ralph Steadmann, Carl Jung, Bertrand Russell, Dr. James Hollis, Howard Zinn, Lao Tzu, Joseph Campbell, Dr. Edgar Mitchell, and even the late, great storyteller, Blake Snyder.

All my love and gratitude lives each day in Lisa, Harrison, and Jack. And thank you to the late Jameson the Dog who, while still with us, provided levity and warmth—especially when she slept on my feet while I was writing.

Finally, thanks to the fact that there's more than one way to serve your country.

Doheny Library
University of Southern California
April 2014

Afterword

After 9/11, I was really pissed.

It was a common reaction.

That day jolted me into an existential angst. Two days after the attacks, I turned twenty-nine years old, haunted by the questions: "What is my unique contribution to this nation; to this universe?" In a year I'd be thirty. I mean, when was I gonna grow up?

Newly married and struggling to make a career as a freelance artist I had a narrow view of the world, my goals, and my responsibilities. In the aftermath of that day in September our leaders persisted in urging us to "get back to normal." I didn't want to be normal anymore. Our normality bred the beliefs and politics that created 9/11. If that was normal, then I wanted to be completely fucking different.

The thing is, every male has this *warrior window* in his life. As the years unfold, that window slowly shuts on any experience in military service. My grandfathers and father served. It's by no means a family tradition, but there's no denying that, in our society, military service continues to represent a singular passage into manhood.

But boys don't come back from combat as men, and girls don't come back from war as women. And believing that they do is one of the great failings of our culture. Responsibilities are clearly defined in combat; decisions delivered with sharp clarity, right or wrong. In everyday civilian life, things get much murkier. Necessarily so.

In WWII, my Grandfather Millis was a nineteen-year-old P-51 fighter pilot in the European Theater. A real flyboy-hotshot. In his fading days, disappearing into the shadows of Alzheimer's, he suffered *Sundowning*—a form of increased confusion and dementia. But one day towards the end, while visiting with him in his living room, in a moment of wet-eyed clarity my grandfather described his heroic military service in the exploding skies over Nazi Germany with these three words:

"Little boy lost."

So, rather than leap through my own, fast-closing warrior window, I let it shut tight—with the caveat that, if my contribution after 9/11 was not military service, than it needed to be expressed in another form. It just couldn't be nothing.

That's when I decided to go to graduate school in Vermont to earn my MFA in Creative Writing. As motivation, I went off to the program with the talisman of my grandfather's first lieutenant bar pinned to my wallet, often rubbing its patina with my thumb thinking, "If not this—if not military service—then something else."

Remember, I was *really pissed*. I wanted to write a novel that was ambitious, dark, sprawling, existential, weird, funny, sad—a novel in which to channel all that rawness, anger, and exasperation swirling in my mind and belly. I was determined for it to be a project that assured I'd do anything but "get back to normal."

I also hoped that the process of writing it might help me grow up.

The result of that nine-year effort is *God & California*.